*Dreams of Love
and Modest Glory*

By the same author

NOVELS

After Colette
The Women's House
Reasonable Doubts
Sisters by Rite
The Second Flowering of Emily Mountjoy
Greenyards
The Lord on Our Side
A Sort of Freedom
The Headmaster
The Tide Comes In
The Prevailing Wind
Liam's Daughter

CHILDREN'S BOOKS

Lizzie's Leaving
Night Fires
Hands Off Our School!
Between Two Worlds
Tug of War
Glad Rags
Rags and Riches
The Guilty Party
The Freedom Machine
The Winter Visitor
Strangers in the House
The Gooseberry
The File on Fraulein Berg
Snake Among the Sunflowers
The Clearance
The Resettling
The Pilgrimage
The Reunion
The Twelfth Day of July
Across the Barricades
Into Exile
A Proper Place
Hostages to Fortune

Dreams of Love and Modest Glory

Joan Lingard

SINCLAIR-STEVENSON

Acknowledgments

I should like to thank Meg Luckins, Co-ordinator of the Scottish branch of the British–Russia Centre, for her invaluable help and advice. J. L.

The author and publisher are grateful to Farrar, Straus & Giroux for permission to quote from the Alan Myers translation of Pushkin's work.

First published in Great Britain in 1995
by Sinclair-Stevenson
an imprint of Reed Books Ltd
Michelin House, 81 Fulham Road, London SW3 6RB
and Auckland, Melbourne, Singapore and Toronto

A CIP catalogue record for this book
is available at the British Library
ISBN 1 85619 745 X

Typeset by Falcon Oast Graphic Art, Wallington, Surrey
Printed and bound in Great Britain
by Mackays of Chatham plc, Chatham

For the family

Our dreams of love and modest glory,
Delusive hopes now quickly sped,
Our pranks and games, our youth's brief story,
Like sleep or morning mist are fled;
And yet, within, desires still quicken,
Our souls impatient for the hour,
While yoked beneath a fateful power
Our country calls to us, heart-stricken.

Pushkin

Crossing to Leith

April 1913

On the boat, they discussed love and glory. The subject was raised, of course, by Sergei. As the ship rose and dipped with the grey-green swell of the North Sea, he quoted Pushkin.

> *Our dreams of love and modest glory,*
> *Delusive hopes now quickly sped,*
> *Our pranks and games, our youth's brief story,*
> *Like sleep or morning mist are fled.*

Tomas listened patiently. Russians were forever quoting Pushkin and talking about love. Or the soul. When Sergei had subsided, Tomas asked, 'Are love and glory bound up together for you? Do you anticipate your love leading to glory, or will there be glory in your love?' They enjoyed teasing each other.

They were aboard a cargo boat bringing timber from Riga to the port of Leith in Scotland. From there they would travel by train up to the grey granite city of Aberdeen. Sergei had come down from St Petersburg to join Tomas in Riga so that they could embark together. He'd arrived with valises and boxes and expensive presents for his bride-to-be, and his mother-in-law, and sisters-in-law, one of whom was to be Tomas's bride. (Tomas had brought presents, too, but they

1

were less ostentatious and took up less room, being pieces of amber jewellery, in the form of bracelets, necklaces and earrings, and cuff links for Lily's father and brother.) Sergei loved to buy presents for women, could linger for hours in shops such as Fabergé and Treumann's, choosing knick-knacks and scent. He was also fond of the English shop on the Nevsky, and had recently purchased there a navy-blue barathea blazer and a straw boater. He liked to wear them around the town, deluding himself that he could pass for an Englishman.

While Sergei debated, and shop assistants ran hither and thither, opening up boxes and pushing back whispering layers of soft tissue paper, Tomas would grow restless and wander over to the door to watch the crowds passing on the Prospekt. Shopping bored him, but then he did not have as much money to spend as his friend, though he was unsure how much Sergei actually had. Sergei seldom paid cash. 'Send me the account! To the Burnov Palace, on the English Embankment.'

It was Sergei who'd wanted to travel by cargo. He'd thought it a suitable way to arrive for a wedding. Especially one's own.

'One could have a glorious career, I suppose,' said Tomas. 'If one was lucky. Though not many architects achieve that. Unless they're Palladio or Michelangelo!'

'*You* might, Tom! Well, maybe not quite on such an elevated level. But you're talented. And don't mind hard work. I'm too lazy. A glorious life would do for me. The only word I don't like in that bit of Pushkin is "modest".' Sergei laughed and the boat bucked and a slap of water came up, half soaking them and sending them into retreat.

When the sea had calmed, and they were approaching the thin line of the Scottish shore, lightly veiled by a pale grey haar, and the crowd of following gulls had thickened, Sergei said, 'That verse about love and glory, and hopes having sped—'

'Oh yes?'

2

'Do you know how it goes on?'

'No doubt you're going to tell me.'

'"And yet, within, desires still quicken,"' Sergei quoted softly. '"Our souls impatient for the hour . . ."'

Riga

July 1993

The taxi swerved to avoid a pothole and they were thrown forward against the blue furry back of the seat in front. There were no straps to hold on to; no seat belts, either. The driver went on smoking his long American cigarette.

'I can't think what I'm doing here,' said Lydia, which was ridiculous, because, of course, she could. The smell of the cigarette and of the car itself – cheap petrol, hot oil, human sweat – was making her feel as if she might throw up at any moment. The flight had been bumpy and they had landed in a thunderstorm on the weedy runway. Most of thc travellers had cheered. Touching native soil. Re-touching it. Exiles. Probably hadn't seen the weeds or felt the bumps. Unlike her. She'd noticed her cousin's colour had mounted. She groped now for the window winder in an effort to get air, but the winders were missing in the back; they'd have been wrenched off years ago, probably when the car was new, if it ever had been. Sold on the black market, more than likely. Along with the front passenger's headrest. Two spikes marked its former place of rest. Two dangerous spikes, in a crash. Lydia put her hands over her cheeks to protect them.

' "'Tis time, dear friend, 'tis time!"' she quoted.

'I suppose that's Pushkin!' said Katrina. 'I really can't understand his appeal. Not his poetry, anyway. So cloying, somehow.'

'He doesn't translate well into English. And perhaps,' said Lydia lightly, 'to appreciate it fully one needs a Russian soul.'

'*That*!' said Katrina.

They swerved again, mounting the pavement briefly.

'It was a manhole,' said Katrina, looking back. 'The cover was standing up. You wouldn't have wanted us to drive into it, would you?'

'Certainly not.'

'There must be just as many potholes in St Petersburg. There *are*.'

'I didn't say there weren't. I don't suppose you could ask the driver to put out his cigarette?'

'You ask him.'

'*I* don't speak Latvian.'

'*I* don't speak Russian.'

'*Is* he Russian, do you think?'

They regarded the breadth of his neck. Thick, dark hair gushed over the collar of his tan mock-leather jacket. He was giving no sign of understanding English. Lydia coughed two or three times and cleared her throat. The cigarette smouldered on, bunched between the second and third fingers of the hairy right hand spread across the steering wheel. The fingers were yellowed to well below the second knuckle. It was unlikely that any amount of coughing or choking would have any effect.

'Take your mind off yourself,' suggested Katrina. 'Look out of the window. It's a beautiful city.'

'I *know*. You've told me. God, what it is to travel with an architect! Fine mediaeval buildings. Hanseatic. I can see that from the funny bulging gables.'

'It's a spectacular city! Such colour! Fabulous. My grandfather must have found Aberdeen very grey coming from Riga. They often put the most surprising of colours together, and they get away with it. Look there, at those three sweet little old houses in a row! Lemon yellow, lime green, dusty pink. They love decoration too.'

5

Since her teens Katrina had been enthusiastic about the Arts Nouveau and Deco, though she had moved on from that in her own design. Lydia preferred classical forms. 'Less fuss', was how she put it.

'It's wonderful to see the street names written *just* in Latvian.' Katrina smiled. 'Do you see – the Russian versions have been blanked out?'

They had left the narrow, twisting streets of the old town behind and were now running alongside a park.

'Look there!' cried Katrina. 'You see that Art Nouveau building? That's one of my grandfather's.'

Lydia had not been able to see enough of it to comment and, anyway, they were barrelling round a corner, and Katrina was being flung against her.

When they'd righted themselves Lydia frowned, and said, 'It looks like we're heading for the docks.' Cranes and gantries stood etched against the steel-grey sky. 'Could our hotel be at the *docks*?'

The driver had in front of him an open stretch of road. Oh hallelujah! He stamped on the accelerator and they had no opportunity to make any further comments. He swung from side to side, in an effort to avoid not only the potholes but the crazy tramcar tracks also, and they swayed and swung with him, with no breath left for idle comment. When they came to a halt they saw that they'd stopped outside a modern block some dozen or so storeys high. The driver rested immobile now, impassive, as if he had done all that he intended to do and was waiting for them to react.

Katrina leant forward. 'How much?' she asked. In Latvian.

He grunted, keeping the back of his head turned to them.

She tried to peer over his shoulder but saw that the gear lever, shrouded in furry blue material to match the seats, and looking as if it were trying to masquerade as a poodle, was conveniently obscuring the meter box. Conveniently for the driver, that was. Katrina asked again.

He held up two handfuls of thick fingers, presenting the backs to them. He had one hand on either side of his shoulders, which made him look as if were surrendering to someone or something out there in front, but certainly not to them.

'Lats?' she queried, trying hastily to work out the conversion rate.

'Pound,' he said in English.

'Sterling?'

'Sterling.'

'That's ridiculous! They're *supposed* to be dealing in lats these days. I'm sure it's illegal.'

Lydia laughed and said, 'Don't give it to him!'

'Why don't you speak to him?' suggested Katrina. 'He's obviously Russian.' Lydia was usually the forward one. Bossy, Katrina called it. Her cousin liked to feel in control of a situation and was irritable that here she could not be.

'Oh God, give him something and let's get out of this smelly car!'

Katrina gave him five pounds. The driver showed no gratitude and they did not offer a gratuity. He tossed their suitcases out of the oily boot and left them to struggle up the steps to the glass wall in which was secreted the front door of the hotel.

'Do you think it was necessary to bring *quite* so much stuff?' asked Lydia. 'I mean, all that coffee and tea and *two* ghetto blasters, as big as submarines! Look like submarines, too. Nuclear ones.'

Katrina nudged open the door with her elbow and led the way into the foyer. A policeman dressed in khaki, hand inert over a holstered gun, was sprawled untidily in a corner, watching television. His eyes jerked away from the screen momentarily to note their presence. Two women were on duty behind the counter, one sitting, one standing. The sitter was knitting ferociously. They could see only the top of her head and her elbows as they moved in and out. They looked as if they were working a squeeze-box. The woman on her feet was leaning against the counter and engaged in yawning, letting the world see into the deep recesses of her throat.

7

She closed her mouth with a snap and greeted the new arrivals. She did not smile.

'We have a room booked,' said Katrina.

The woman responded in poor English so that Katrina knew at once she was Russian. Irritated by the woman's inability or refusal to speak Latvian, Katrina persisted in the language, while Lydia stood beside her, smiling faintly and running her fingers along the counter top, making no attempt to participate in any tongue. A key was plopped down in front of them and then, perfunctorily, an information sheet telling of the hotel's facilities.

'Does it have any?' murmured Lydia.

'The receptionist *should* be able to speak Latvian,' said Katrina, when they had managed to get their suitcases into the lift. 'They're obliged to, by law, nowadays, if they're in the communications business.'

'Maybe she hasn't had time to learn it.'

'Time? The Russians have been here for hundreds of years, for God's sake!'

The lift stopped, and the doors slid open to reveal a narrow grey corridor. They bumped their cases along to number 27.

The room was all right, they couldn't complain about that. It did lack curtains, which might be a problem on these long northern summer nights, but the place was clean, had two beds with red, yellow and black woven covers, and a small but perfectly adequate bathroom, with a shower that worked and gave forth *hot* water. There were towels, too, and some low-grade toilet paper, greyish, what you'd expect, and even a tiny bar of soap.

'Things are looking up,' said Katrina. 'Compared with when I was last here.'

'That's the market economy for you.'

'Tourist economy! Probably haven't got hot water in their houses.'

A television set was mounted high up on the bedroom wall, as is common in hotel rooms, so that it could be viewed – with a cricked neck – from the beds. Katrina punched the button and a woman sprang to life reading the news. In Russian.

'Bloody Russians!'

'Don't you think we've had enough of that?'

Katrina grinned. 'Sorry! Let's go and find something to drink. I'm dying of thirst.'

They consulted the information sheet; there appeared to be café bars on three different floors. However, they knew it was safer to maintain a wary scepticism in these matters, for there would be no guarantee that the bars actually existed. They took the lift to level seven and found the bar. 'Ha!' cried Katrina. 'Can we be so lucky?' They were not. No amount of rapping on the frosted glass or twisting of the locked door handle produced any result. They proceeded up to level ten, where lights shone behind the glass and the clink of glasses was audible, as too was a hubbub of voices, though their owners' nationalities were not discernible. The handle turned, and they entered a small, smoky room with a bar at one end and half a dozen tables set around the edges. At one table sat two dockside women, recognisable by their symbols: net stockings, skimpy, shiny skirts, tortured hair, glazed eyes. Across the way two seamen sucked beer from brown bottles and half-heartedly eyed the prostitutes.

The blonde-braided woman at the bar was Latvian. And she was smiling at them.

'Hurrah!' said Katrina. 'What shall we have?'

'Will there be a choice?' said Lydia.

It was either beer or wine. They took a bottle of Georgian champagne and some *pirogi* to a table in the corner from where they could watch the other parties in the room.

'*Prosit*!' They raised their glasses, relaxing now that they were here. Travel wasn't easy; they were agreed on that. '*Slainte*!'

They were halfway through the bottle when the door opened and another Western couple came in. Both of them, man and wife, were wearing cream polyester slacks, short-sleeved, cream acrylic shirts, trainers tied in double bows, and rimless glasses. They blinked for a moment in the sudden rush of light, then turned to the bar. Having purchased two cups of coffee, into which they gazed for several moments, they glanced uncertainly around the room.

When they sighted the two women from the West they came forward, with smiles of recognition, as if they'd already met.

'Hi. Would you mind if we joined you? We've just arrived, you see, and we're kind of feeling our way . . .'

'Please do!' Lydia indicated the two spare seats.

The couple introduced themselves. 'Janis and Mara Smilgis, from Philadelphia. Born in Riga. Left in '44. First time back. We're here for the Song Festival.'

'Katrina Zale,' said Katrina, using her maiden name. 'From Aberdeen, Scotland. Born in Riga. Left in '44 also.'

'You can't have been very old?'

'I was five.'

They looked at Lydia.

'Lydia Burnova,' she said. 'Also from Aberdeen. Born in St Petersburg. Left in '53.'

The Smilgises were uncertain what to make of that information. The husband said, 'You ladies here for the festival too?'

'Mainly to visit relatives,' said Katrina. 'And our fathers' graves.'

'We've all got graves to visit!'

'We're going to spend a few days at my family's house in the country. It was designed by my grandfather. My uncle has just managed to get it back.'

'The Soviets requisitioned it, I guess?'

'Yes, in '44.'

'So, what made your folks choose Scotland to go to?'

'Our grandmothers came from Aberdeen,' said Katrina. 'They were sisters. Twins, in fact.'

'They married two friends,' said Lydia. 'One from Riga, and the other from St Petersburg.'

Aberdeen

April 1913

Mr & Mrs Alexander McKenzie request the pleasure of your company at the marriage of their daughters, Garnet Henrietta, to Count Sergei Burnov, son of Count Nikolai Burnov & Countess Sophia Burnova, of St Petersburg, and Lily Jemima, to Mr Tomas Zale, son of Mr & Mrs Markus Zale, of Riga, in Queen's Cross Church of Scotland, Aberdeen, at 2.30 p.m. on 8 April 1913.

The twin girls had been born on the first day of January 1892, a raw day, with a snell wind bellying off the North Sea and the windows of the house in Queen's Road shuddering in their frames. Their mother, Jemima McKenzie, had not expected twins; she had thought her size might be due to the presence of a well-built son in her womb. She had not been particularly concerned whether she gave birth to a boy or a girl, except that her husband, in this respect, was rather traditional, and vaguely thought that boys were better born before girls, so that brothers could be older than sisters, and thus protect them. He should not have worried on that score, for Andrew, their only son, to be born two years after the twins, would struggle manfully to help his sisters in the coming years.

In other ways Alexander was not so traditional; he saw no

reason, for example, why women should not have the vote as well as men (he knew his wife was well capable of casting a vote) and, in his profession, which was that of architecture, he was progressive, though not outlandishly so. He had seen and found exciting the work of Charles Rennie Mackintosh in Glasgow, and was aware of the American Frank Lloyd Wright from reading the Wasmuth publications, sent to him by friends in Berlin. He could not be charged, therefore, with being insular, unlike some of his fellow Aberdonian architects. He himself was an enthusiastic follower of the Arts and Crafts movement, and an admirer of William Morris. His own house of Rubislaw granite and red sandstone facings, which he had designed and built, reflected these influences, with its overhanging eaves, banded casement windows, ogee-arched portico, and wide front door. On Queen's Road it was considered to be forward-looking, compared with many of its severe, imposing Victorian neighbours lording it further down the street. It faced open country – though that, alas, would not last, for the city would encroach throughout the 1920s and 1930s, spreading its rash of *bijou* bungalows.

Garnet pushed her way first into the world, which no one believed to be an accident. Garnet would always want to be first; it was likely that she had elbowed Lily out of the way in her effort to reach the tunnel and the light beyond, for the second baby surfaced with a bruised face and a lopsided nose, both of which had righted themselves after a month. Garnet emerged perfect. Her parents were admiring the beautiful shape of the baby's head and her flawless tiny pearl fingernails when Jemima felt another searing wave of pain course through her abdomen. She cried out. It would be the afterbirth, said the midwife, wrapping the baby in a white cloth and passing it to Nessie the maid. She laid her hand on the still-distended stomach, Jemima caught her breath, and a second child slithered between her legs.

'Help my kilt!' cried Nessie, almost dropping the firstborn.

'Another lassie,' said the midwife sorrowfully, and reached for the child's ankles.

12

Garnet, then, was always to lead the way; she had a tendency to be impatient, would get bored waiting for Lily, who was inclined to be a dreamer and seldom noticed the time. They were identical, with dark curly hair and dark eyes handed down through Orcadian ancestry on their mother's side.

The family could easily tell them apart. Garnet's face was thinner, and her nose a little longer, but not too long, and she was generally regarded to be the prettier. She was a restless girl, liked to be on the move, to walk fast even when out for a stroll along the seashore. She tossed her head when displeased, but she could be generous, if not particularly thoughtful. About Lily there was a quality of stillness, which concealed much of what she was thinking.

The girls were devoted to each other: everyone was agreed upon that, and wondered how they would survive separation through marriage. They had never spent a day apart, and would not do so until after their joint honeymoon in Venice, when they would each go their separate ways, to St Petersburg and Riga.

'So you've got two Russian sons-in-law,' said Mrs Sibbald, a guest at the wedding.

'Oh no,' said Jemima. 'Only Sergei. Seryozha, as we call him. Tom is Latvian, which is quite a different thing, and he wouldn't thank you for calling him Russian! He is from Riga, the capital of the province of Livonia. The Russian Empire is made up of many different peoples and provinces.'

'As ours is, I suppose,' said Mrs Sibbald vaguely, even though she had visited various parts of it on her husband's postings. 'How did the young men come to be in Aberdeen?' She had been abroad, had missed out on all the gossip.

'They were in Scotland on an architectural tour of the British Isles last summer and came up to Deeside to see the castles. They were over the moon about Crathes and Craigievar.'

'That pink stone is rather pretty, I must admit. But last

summer! A whirlwind romance, then? Two whirlwinds! They do everything together, those two. But aren't you worried about them? I know I would be if it were my Rose. Going somewhere like Russia? Is it all that civilised?'

And with two foreigners: Jemima McKenzie knew that was what Mrs Sibbald meant. She was not worried on that score herself, though she knew the girls would have much adapting to do. But then, all women had to adapt on marriage. She was a little worried about their physical safety, for Europe was not in a particularly happy state. Was it ever? There was the trouble in the Balkans, where the Allies were trying to bring the appalling slaughter to an end and get the combatants – Greeks, Bulgarians, Serbs, Montenegrins, and their foe, the Turks – round the negotiating table. What a mess!

But the Balkans were rather far away. Nearer at hand existed a more threatening power. Her husband was convinced that Germany was redding itself up to go to war. People in the south of England had even been discussing what they would do in the event of invasion. But crises kept passing, and Jemima was hopeful that sanity would prevail. And, if the worst did happen, the girls could always come home. She fully understood the pull of the new. In her family the women were strongly independent and had minds of their own; and, being accustomed to the long seafaring tradition of the men, they found nothing exceptional in the idea of crossing the water. Her own unmarried sister had travelled in all manner of unlikely places for a woman alone: the Caucusus, Siberia, China; at present she was in Argentina, riding across the pampas.

'Both Riga and St Petersburg are very civilised, from what I hear,' said Jemima. 'And exceedingly cultured.'

'But isn't there talk of revolution and unrest?' persisted Mrs Sibbald, who would always root around until she found a tender spot. 'I thought I read something in the *Press and Journal*.'

'They had a revolution in 1905.'

'I'm talking about *since* then! Mr Sibbald says their unrest has never gone away.'

'Nor has ours. We've got our share here too. We can't be complacent.'

'I was not suggesting—'

'Do you think our unskilled workers are content with their miserable wages and terrible living conditions?' Jemima knew it was too easy to attack Mrs Sibbald, but she allowed herself one more burst. 'Do you think they're happy that the incidence of tuberculosis, ringworm and eye defects is intolerably high amongst their children?'

'Well, no, of course, not,' Mrs Sibbald hastily agreed. She hated political talk and deplored it in drawing rooms. And surely at weddings it was quite out of place. The McKenzies were known for their socialist leanings. (How, then, did that match with their daughter marrying a count?) In his student days Alexander McKenzie had been an enthusiastic follower of Keir Hardie and had helped organise meetings.

'I have every confidence that the girls are able to look after themselves,' said their mother, closing the subject.

As Jemima looked across at her daughters, who were both standing beside their new husbands, she intercepted a quick glance being exchanged between Lily and Sergei. Their eyes had engaged, and then Lily had immediately cast hers down. A flare of pink showed high on her cheekbones. At the wedding ceremony, when making her responses, she had hesitated before saying 'I do'. So Jemima had thought. And had held her breath. For Lily could be impulsive and wayward, whereas Garnet, once she'd made up her mind, stuck to a decision. Earlier, dressing for the wedding, Lily had looked pale, compared with Garnet, who'd been flushed and laughing. But Jemima had not been particularly worried about Lily then, for marriage *was*, after all, a big step, usually the biggest a woman would ever take, and everyone coped with pre-wedding nerves in a different way. However, this glance between Lily and Garnet's groom that she'd just seen did puzzle and disturb her, and it made her think again about the evening before.

Lily had come in quite late from the garden. She'd looked feverish and somewhat dishevelled, but she'd parried her mother's questions, saying she'd had a headache and gone out for some air and now she was fine, really she was, and there was nothing whatsoever to fuss about, and she was going to bed or she'd never get up in the morning. And she'd gone.

Jemima had stayed downstairs in the morning room, going through her wedding list for the final time. Ten minutes later, she'd heard the side door click open again and gone to see who was coming in.

'I was in need of fresh air, Mrs McKenzie.' Sergei was smiling. 'So I went for a walk. It is a very lovely Aberdeen evening.'

Jemima had to put these niggles to the back of her mind, for guests were thronging all around, wanting to talk, to claim her attention, to compliment her on the buffet. And she was not one for dwelling on matters she could do nothing about. Her motto was to hope for the best and cope with each thing as it arose.

'Mrs Sibbald, meet Seryozha's father, Count Burnov.' Jemima laid a hand on the arm of each, restraining the count from moving away to talk to another, younger female guest. 'Count Burnov, my neighbour Mrs Sibbald.'

The count bowed over Mrs Sibbald's hand and grazed it with his lips. Above his head Mrs Sibbald's eyes dilated and sought Jemima's, but her hostess had turned away and was conversing in sign language with the Latvian in-laws, who seemed not to speak much English. The count, whilst being fluent in French – and Russian, well, naturally he would be, wouldn't he? – was proficient enough in English to be charming to women. He was very obviously that kind of man. They had them in Aberdeen too – oh yes, indeed! Their Scottish versions tended to be more muted and they didn't go in so much for the kissing of ladies' hands. The count had come on his own to the wedding. The countess found travel difficult on the stomach and had sent apologies and a trunk-load of gifts. Mrs Sibbald murmured commiserations. Stomachs could be such a hindrance to the furtherance of plans. She gazed at the Russian's countenance. He looked like an older version of his son. One could see that he might at one time have been handsome, but the years – and his manner of living? – had most certainly left their mark. His colouring was hectic. Pouches of slack flesh underhung his eyes. Surely he looked *dissipated*?

(Jemima herself was well aware that he did, but had not drawn it to the attention of her husband, who did not indulge in the reading of faces. Buildings took up most of his attention.)

'How are you enjoying our country, Count?' asked Mrs Sibbald.

'Very much. It is delightful.'

'And what is the state of affairs in Russia these days?'

'People like to say we are backward—'

'I'm sure not!'

'But we have much for the world to admire, and envy. You know about our Maryinsky Theatre? Our Ballets russes? You know the work of Fokine, and Diaghilev? You have seen the wonderful Pavlova dance? And Karsavina?'

'Well, no, I can't say I've ever been to Russia.'

'*They* have been to England. They took London by storm!'

'This is not England. Here we are not so easily conquered!' Mrs Sibbald gave a little laugh and covered her mouth with her hand.

'You have not experienced ballet if you have not seen the Ballets russes. You have seen only pretty prancing about the stage.'

'I have never seen dance on the stage, in actual fact. Nor do I wish to. It is not quite my cup of tea.'

'You should see it! It would heat your blood.'

Really! What was Garnet McKenzie getting herself into? It was all very well for her mother to say she wasn't worried, but had she actually thought about it, and all its implications?

The whole dance business seemed to be getting out of hand, even here. Mrs Sibbald's own daughter, Rose, had called along at the McKenzies a couple of evenings ago and had found the young people engaged in dancing the tango and the turkey-trot.

Jemima McKenzie, catching Mrs Sibbald's eye signals at last, came back to release her, and in the next instant Andrew appeared alongside them saying, 'Excuse me, Mother. You've to come. They want to take the photographs now.'

The two brides, in matching dresses of ivory satin (pure white tended to make them look sallow), were placed in the centre of the photograph, holding their mixed bouquets, flanked by their grooms, Sergei at six foot three topping the rest of the party with his flamboyant red-gold head. His handsome looks and winning smile, combined with his easy relaxed manner, were sending a few flutters through female breasts. And he was a count! Nothing could take away from the magic of that, even though Garnet maintained that counts – and princes – were two a penny in St Petersburg. (Did she expect them to believe her?) And now Garnet, after saying 'I do' in Queen's Cross church, was a countess!

'It's like a fairy tale,' said Rose Sibbald.

'Quite a catch,' said her mother, and added, 'I suppose.'

The women, then – most of them, at least – could well understand Garnet being so enamoured of Sergei, as she obviously was. Her eyes flickered after him every time he moved. Not like Garnet at all. She'd flirted her way through a number of the young local men, and each time it was she not they who had called the tune.

'It was love at first sight,' Effie, the twin's eighteen-year-old sister, was telling a group of the younger guests who were clustered around her, avid to hear the details. 'She saw him, she wanted him, and she snapped him up!' Effie snapped her fingers in the air and laughed. 'Lily didn't get a look-in. That's if she'd have wanted one. But Tom seems to be really very nice. He's quieter than Seryozha, and more serious-minded.

He can't pass a building without stopping. He must get a crick in his neck from looking up! Seryozha's an architect too. Though I don't think he needs to work for a living. They've got pots of money. They must have, mustn't they? I mean to say, they live in a *palace*. His mother's a distant relative of the Tsar, some kind of second cousin twice removed. Look at Seryozha! He loves to lark about.'

Sergei was cracking jokes and making his bride laugh, and acting rather differently from most Scottish grooms, who tended to stand soberly in their dress kilts, frilled shirts and brogue shoes, awed by the seriousness of the occasion and the commitment they were making.

'The grooms seem to speak quite good English,' commented Rose.

'Seryozha had an English governess when he was a child. And Tom has been taking English lessons all winter.' Effie had her eyes on the brides' bouquets, though her mother said she was too young to think of marrying, she should wait until she'd matured a little and knew more about the world.

'Effie!' Andrew had come to collect his sister for the photograph.

'Andrew seems a very attentive young man,' observed Mrs Sibbald, as she watched him lead Effie away. 'Very dutiful to his family. It is always nice to see that.'

'So it is,' agreed Rose.

The families of the brides and grooms were grouped on the front steps of the house and the photograph was taken that would grace three different walls in three different northern cities. Only the one in Aberdeen would be allowed to hang in peace.

Venice

April 1913

Venice, as a place, was to suit Lily's temperament more than Garnet's – their father was of the opinion that reaction to environment was in the main temperamental. Rome would have agreed with Garnet better, he wrote in response to her Venetian postcard; it was more tangible. (Also, it had a harder edge, but he did not pen that thought to his daughter, lest she misconstrue it.) For Lily, Venice was a city for dreams and reflection rather than movement, where every few steps she was tempted to stop and marvel. She crammed a card to her father with tiny writing extolling the vast, shimmering panorama of sea and sky meeting and melting the one into the other, the pink and gold palaces appearing like mirages across the lagoon, the narrow canals filled with dense green water, the splashes of colour made by the hanging baskets of flowers, the humpbacked bridges, the black barges filled with glowing fruit – oh she could have gone on for ever! She also mentioned the radiance of the light.

'Look at the light!' she kept saying. 'It's so luminous.' Her eyes were dazzled. She was captivated from the moment they began to cross the long causeway over the lagoon, when the train seemed to float and the rest of the world dropped away. And then there was the gondola waiting to waft them from the station to their hotel.

'The houses must be damp,' said Garnet, as they bobbed past ancient, steep-sided buildings with water lapping at their steps. She put up the collar of her coat and leant in closer to Sergei. The air was cooling rapidly as dusk moved in along the canals. A grey, pearly dusk: as Lily saw it. Lanterns sent streaks of wavering light across their watery path. The canals seemed astonishingly quiet after the wearisome rattling of the train that had borne them on their long journey across the continent.

The gondola bumped against the landing stage of the Hotel Luna, and a jumble of servants issued from the door. Suddenly all was noise and bustle.

Garnet was first to jump ashore after the gondolier, leaving the boat rocking. Lily lay back, letting herself go with the motion, then she blinked and noticed that Tomas was holding out a hand to her.

'I think you need to go to bed early,' he murmured as he helped her up.

Since their wedding they had not passed a night in a bed. They had been tossed about in narrow berths on heaving seas and in swaying trains. The sea-crossing had made Lily feel sick and the clickety-clack of the train wheels had given her a headache. It had not been the most romantic way to start a honeymoon. Attempts to consummate the marriage had tended towards the farcical, but their mother had warned her daughters not to expect too much from the physical side in the beginning. It took time to adjust. 'Patience, girls!' she had said. Pleasure would come later.

The night passed pleasurably enough in both bridal rooms, more especially for the grooms than the brides, which perhaps was inevitable. Tom was tender and loving towards Lily and anxious not to give her pain; he was surprised that, indeed, he did not seem to hurt her on their first full fusion. He had not expected it to go so smoothly. He said nothing; they spoke little during the act, other than to murmur into each other's hair, and in the morning it was not referred to.

21

There was a shyness between them. Sergei's lovemaking, on the other hand, was confident and exuberant and, as Garnet could not but realise, wrought from much experience. That he was well-practised she did not resent, for she knew that a man such as her husband, with his huge appetite for life, would have kept the company of other women before his marriage. As long as he did not so afterwards. *That* she would not be able to tolerate! She felt sure, however, that she could hold him; she could respond to his sexual drives, and would deny him nothing.

They rose to find the city submerged in a quiet mist.

'It's like the North Sea haar,' said Garnet, pouting.

It would disperse by mid-morning, promised Sergei.

The two couples breakfasted together in the hotel dining room. Tomas brought his Baedeker to the table. He cleared some of the silver to one side so that he could lay it open on the snowy-white cloth.

'There's so much to see.' He had been reading to Lily about the Piazza and the Basilica of San Marco while she'd been dressing. She had stood as close to the window as modesty would allow so that she could watch the prows of the gondolas come gliding like phantoms out of the mist. They were in high spirits. Lily, elected to play 'mother', poured the tea. She passed a cup to Sergei, who accepted it with a bow.

'Your little finger, Seryozha!' she said. 'What's wrong with your pinkie? I've never noticed it before.'

He turned his left hand over so that she could see the way the little finger curled inward. 'I can't straighten it. It runs in the family. Just one of our oddities!'

'How many do you have?' asked his wife.

'You shall find out!'

'I certainly shall.' Garnet leant over to lay a kiss on his cheek.

They decided to begin with San Marco, since it was virtually on their doorstep. And then, said Tomas, if either of the girls were to grow tired they could return in only a few steps to the hotel.

'Tired?' said Garnet. 'Lily and I don't *tire*.'

When they went out they saw, as Sergei had predicted, that the sun was beginning to break through the mist.

'I think,' said Lily, 'that Venice must change every single minute of the day.'

'Like you!'

'Like me?'

'Yes, you puzzle me at times. I can't keep pace with your shifts of mood. But don't worry about it, Lily my love, for I like your sensitivity, and in time I shall come to know you properly.'

Lily was not sure that she wanted to be *properly* known. She wondered if she might not like to be anonymous, not Tom's wife, not Garnet's twin, just an unknown woman free to wander. She'd confided her desire to Garnet, who'd been slightly impatient. 'You mean you want to traipse about the pampas and such places like Aunt Hetty? I suppose it's she who's put the notion into your head. It has its drawbacks, you know, that kind of life. Physical discomfort, horrible food, loneliness. Don't you think you'd be lonely? You've never been alone.'

Perhaps that was part of it, thought Lily: never having been on her own. Although she and Garnet were very close she had often longed to be a single person, to have a birthday to herself, a history, thoughts. For they often shared the same thoughts, she and Garnet; they would turn to say the same thing at the same moment, in the manner of twins. But now that they were about to be separated, to stand alone, begin new histories, Lily felt highly nervous.

Garnet wrote up her journal:

What a lot of things we have seen. What a lot of churches! Lily seems to have taken to the images of the Roman Catholic church. She hangs about in front of the altars and stained-glass windows until we have to drag her away. She won't find all those gilded virgins in Riga.

23

The church there is Lutheran and won't go in for all that ornate stuff. It'll be much more like the C. of S., I imagine. Seryozha says I shall see plenty of pomp and gold paint in Petersburg. Plenty of water, too. It's often called the Venice of the North.

I am dying to get there! To be settled in my very own house with Seryozha, and start our new life together. This is like an interim period, between home and married life. I dare say that is what a honeymoon is for, to make a bridge between the old and the new, as well as to get to know one another. And I do like what I know of Seryozha!

Venice is mournful at dusk when the mist creeps in and it becomes almost eerily quiet along the canals. As for the canals! Some of them stink to high heaven! And then there's all the rotting fruit and vegetables floating about, not to mention the carcass of a rat which our gondola nudged aside this morning and a mangy dead cat that I saw lying on the steps of a house waiting for the water to take it. So many of the houses and the *palazzi* are in a dreadful state of repair, with their stones crumbling and window frames rotting. Seryozha says parts of Petersburg are dirty and scruffy too, not to expect a pristine clean city. I wouldn't expect any city to be that, I told him. Aberdeen also has its slums.

On the afternoon of their last day in Venice, Tomas, who had been scrambling up a wall to get a better look at the back of a *palazzo*, slipped and made an awkward landing. He'd twisted his ankle – not seriously, but badly enough to need to rest it. After they'd helped him back to the hotel and Lily had soaked bandages in vinegar and water and bound his ankle, he insisted that they should not waste the rest of daylight. He knew Lily wanted to have a last walk around the city and to go back and take another look at Santa Maria dei Miracoli. He was fine, he protested, he would read, there was nothing more they could do for him, and if he needed anything he could ring for it.

24

Garnet decided not to go. She'd had enough of naves and transepts and Tintoretto and Titian and Veronese and powder-blue virgins and golden haloes and smelly canals and wanted to get on with her packing.

'You go with Lily, Seryozha,' she said.

'I can go alone,' said Lily quickly. 'Really, it's not necessary.'

But Sergei was already on his feet, ready to escort her.

The mist had made its appearance by the time they came out of the Miracoli. Lights flaring in alleyways made flickering shadows on the walls.

'I love this time of day,' said Lily.

'I, too,' said Sergei.

'I thought you liked the evening best?'

'That's true, I do. Whereas Tom likes the clear light of day! But this time of day for me signals what is to come.'

They walked a little apart, with Lily keeping the distance between them.

They came to a humpbacked bridge and Lily paused to rest against the parapet and look into the heart of a narrow, dark canal. Washing hung like ghostly shrouds between the buildings. Sergei put a hand on her shoulder. Her head arched back and her spine went rigid.

'Lily,' he said softly.

'No!' she cried.

Turning away from him she fled along the winding network of paths that edged the canals. Her footsteps echoed between high walls. She heard the sound of her breath labouring, and of her heart thudding, and of his voice calling, from somewhere behind her. She spurred herself on. She crossed bridges, turned this way and that. She slipped on uneven stones, clutched at greasy walls for support. She passed women carrying bundles, men lounging, men smoking, children playing, children staring. She saw them all in a whirl like a kaleidoscope shaken.

And then she stopped. She had to stop. She was gasping

for breath and a stitch was gripping her side. For a moment she was bent over double, until the constriction eased and her heart slowed, and she lifted her head to see that she was lost.

She was in a part of the city that she had never seen before. It was not a place where tourists would venture. The houses were very tall, eight, nine, maybe ten, storeys high, like the tenements back home; grimy with dirt, they looked set to crumble into the scum of the canal at their feet, and they were separated by such a narrow stretch of water that the darkness between them was almost complete, except for the swatches of yellow light cast by the occasional lantern. Most of the windows had no glass, and those that retained a pane or two were crazed with cracks. The others had been papered over.

She saw, then, that she was being watched. Two men were standing only a few yards away, their bodies angled towards her. Their eyes seemed to burn like coals in their pale faces. She felt panic rise from the pit of her stomach up into her throat. She thought she might vomit. Something touched the back of her neck, and she screamed.

A third man stood behind her. He was wearing dark clothes and a bright scarf knotted at his neck. She smelt his breath on her face, hot and fetid. She tried to scream again, but her throat had closed.

'*Signorina,*' said the man, stretching forth his hand.

He swivelled sharply at the sound of someone approaching. Someone running. And calling, calling Lily's name.

Her throat cleared, and she shouted, 'Seryozha! Here, Seryozha!'

The man in dark clothes cursed and slipped into the shadows. Lily fell, weeping, into Sergei's arms.

Garnet, in the middle of packing, looks up, disturbed. Nothing has changed in the room. No one has entered. She gets to her feet, smooths down her cream shantung dress, goes over to the window and gazes out at the grey water. It seems very quiet, both without and within. A restlessness has entered into her like a breeze that has sprung up from nowhere. She feels there is something wrong with Lily. But what could have happened to her? She is being silly! Seryozha is with Lily: he will look after her.

She takes her key and goes along the corridor to Tom's room. She knocks and when he answers she says, 'I feel like some tea. Shall we go downstairs and wait for Lily and Seryozha?'

'What a fool I was,' said Lily. 'To run like that. What an absolute idiot!'

'Hush now,' said Sergei, tightening his arm around her waist. 'Don't distress yourself. You're safe – it's all over.'

They had left behind the dark, ill-lit canals and alleyways and were walking once more in the safer part of the city, where the mingling of respectable Venetians and tourists created a mood of safety in the streets.

'Take me back to the hotel, please, Seryozha.' She was quivering.

'We could run away.'

'*Now*?'

'Yes!'

Even in the midst of her anguish Lily could not help but think that only a Russian would make such a proposal. Only a Russian could suggest anything so *extreme*.

'Don't be ridiculous! Think of all the people we would hurt! Think of Tom! Think of *Garnet*!'

'You should have listened to me that night in the garden. Before it was too late.' Sergei was holding on to her arm, and she would travel to Riga with a maroon and yellow bruise flowering. He bent his head and kissed her and for a moment her head went into a spin; then she pushed him away.

'I want to go back to the hotel!'

'Very well!'

Lily was still agitated when they reached the Luna. Tom and Garnet were drinking tea in the salon.

27

Garnet put down her cup.

'What's happened?' Tom leapt up in alarm, forgetting his injury, and winced.

'Oh, just some men,' said Lily. 'It was nothing, truly it was not.'

'*Men*? My God! How did you let this happen, Seryozha?'

'She ran—' Sergei stopped.

Little more was said. Tomas took Lily upstairs, where he insisted she loosen her corset and lie down even though she did not wish to. Garnet was left in the salon with Sergei.

'Tea?' she asked, the pot in her hand.

'What? Oh yes. Please.'

She wanted to ask him what Lily had been running from, but dared not. The look on his face seemed to exclude her; and he had gone, for him, strangely quiet.

The parting between the sisters in the morning brought its own release.

Riga

July 1993

On the way into town, Katrina pointed out the late-nine-teenth-century block of apartments where Tomas Zale had brought Lily as a bride. 'They had a four-roomed flat on the ground floor, facing the park.'

They had to duck their heads to see, which was difficult through the press of bodies. The tram was packed, and they were standing. The windows were firmly shut. They were glad when they reached the centre. They got off on the corner of Theatre Boulevard and Brivibas Street.

'*Brivibas* means freedom,' said Katrina. 'This street says it all! When I was last here it was called Lenin – his statue was down there; gone now, of course. It was Freedom Street before the war and, prior to that, Alexander Street, after the Tsar. It would have been Alexander when Lily arrived.'

They made their way down towards the Freedom Monument, stopping when they came across a pavement flower seller so that Katrina could buy a bunch of red and white carnations.

'The colours of the country – red blood on white snow!'

On a warm summer's day, with shreds of white trailing across a bright sky, and the trees thick with greenery, it was difficult to imagine the country in winter, under deep snow. People milled bare-armed in the streets and relaxed at pavement cafés under coloured umbrellas flaunting the names of Martini and Coca-Cola. Katrina was astonished at every turn. So much had changed so quickly.

A small crowd had collected in front of the monument, a soaring pink and grey granite plinth supporting a statue wrought in copper of a woman with her arms stretched upwards. Between her hands she held three gold stars, one for each of the former territorial districts of Latvia – Kurzeme, Vidzeme and Latgale. The Zale family house was in Vidzeme.

'So that's where our fathers' graves will be,' said Lydia. Nikolai Burnov, son of Sergei and Garnet, lay in the Zale family plot beside Luke, son of Lily and Tomas. 'You know, it still seems strange to me that a Russian soldier was buried in a Latvian cemetery at that particular time. After all, they were at *war*.'

Katrina shrugged. When she'd asked her uncle about it he'd turned her question aside, saying that soldiers in time of war must often be buried near where they fell. What a massive job it would be to return all the bodies to their origins. They'd fallen silent at the thought.

'Our fathers *were* cousins,' said Katrina.

'I'm going to try to get to the bottom of it,' said Lydia.

Katrina laid her flowers beside the others at the base of the monument. Lydia always looked for complications, could seldom accept that anything was straightforward, and people were not being devious. Katrina attributed it to Lydia's early life under Stalin. She'd been nurtured in an atmosphere of suspicion and mistrust. We must make allowances, their great-grandmother Jemima used to say. We are all fashioned by our backgrounds. Katrina felt she'd been making allowances for Lydia all her life, ever since the day her cousin had arrived in Queen's Road and she'd had to give up half her bedroom to her. It was only charitable; Lydia was homeless, a refugee, as she'd once been herself, but at fourteen she'd had her own life and friends in Aberdeen, and was used to her own space, which Lydia, accustomed to communal living, did not appreciate. She would throw her schoolbag on

Katrina's bed, and borrow her clothes without asking, and her friends. Fourteen was undoubtedly a very selfish age; their own children had brought that home to them. She hoped Lydia wasn't going to be too tiresome on the subject of her father's grave when they went to Cesis. There were some old wounds the Zales would prefer to have left alone, and why should they not? They'd suffered enough, damn it! Most people here had. But Lydia, when she got something into her head, could be tenacious, whereas she herself, whilst not advocating sweeping everything emotional under the carpet, thought there was a limit to how much one should invade other people's feelings. Their great-grandmother had been on her side there. Once the limit was overstepped, Jemima had said, problems could just become exacerbated and relationships impaired. Better to 'haud your wheest' at times, had been her advice. Lydia was not good at taking advice. Her emotional outbursts had always been put down to her Russianness by the household.

'There's a purity about her,' said Lydia, gazing up at the woman on her plinth. 'She's very moving.'

Katrina felt immediately contrite – that Lydia should praise *her* freedom monument – and suggested they go and fortify themselves in the Hotel de Rome, before starting on the old town. Their sightseeing had to be staggered, or Lydia would complain too much. Katrina had agreed to make a tour of hospitals and clinics for Lydia's benefit. That was the trade-off. Lydia didn't mind looking at buildings, she said – she liked it – but got restless when Katrina spent half an hour looking at one window detail.

'Let's have a little high life!' said Katrina, and took her cousin's arm.

The hotel had been recently rebuilt (with German money) for foreign tourists. It now looked and smelt like any other international hotel.

'To stay here for a night would cost our cousin Helga three months' salary,' said Katrina, as they went up in the lift.

'Of such statistics revolutions are made,' said Lydia.

31

Most of the customers in the café appeared to be German, and resident in the hotel. One elderly man was clearly an expatriate Latvian who had made good in the United States. The woman with him was Latvian also, but local, a little younger than he, and dressed in a cheap coat and shoes, with a cracked imitation-leather handbag that she was keeping out of sight on her knee. Every now and then her hand strayed nervously to it. He had money; they saw the roll of bills when he pulled out his wallet and rifled through it with heavy, yellowed fingers. He called for champagne in a loud voice. He raised his glass to the woman. 'For old times' sake.' She looked shy. He looked rough at the edges, like a retired steelworker from Pittsburgh, suggested Lydia. Would he take her back with him? wondered Katrina. Lydia shook her head. The only other Latvians in evidence were those serving.

The cakes were expensive, but good, and the coffee fragrant and quite unlike that served in their dockside hotel.

'I'm glad the café is internal,' said Katrina, 'so that we can't be seen by the outside world.'

'Guzzling, you mean?'

'Trouble is, one feels guilty half the time at having so much money and being able to eat what one wants. Yet what is one to do?'

'Eat. It doesn't make sense not to. We're putting money into the economy.'

'Of some fat German pockets!'

Katrina finished her chocolate cake and, having enjoyed it, sat back, replete, one hand resting on the table.

Lydia smiled and spread out her own hand alongside Katrina's.

'Our shared inheritance – our crooked pinkies! Look at the two of them! Identical. That's always puzzled me, too, you know. I thought mine came from the Russian side, from Sergei.'

Riga

May 1913

'So there, Lily, is Riga!' Tomas kept his arm firmly around her waist. She felt the pressure of it, and the heat in his fingers where they rested against her lower ribs. Did he fear she might plunge overboard and start swimming back to Scotland? Or on up through the Baltic Sea into the Gulf of Finland and St Petersburg? But no, he would not suspect *that*!

They were edging steadily closer to the shore; the deck-rail was lined. Hooters blared. Gulls swooped low over the water. They had sailed in clear spring sunshine from the port of Danzig up through the Baltic into the warmer waters of the Bay of Riga, which was fringed with white sand and one-storeyed, summer wooden houses set amongst pine trees. The sea voyage in the cool air, with the familiar smell of salt spray in her nostrils, had helped to clear Lily's head, which in the past few weeks had seemed at times close to delirium; and it had served to mark as a division between her old life lived with Garnet and the new one with her husband.

At the moment of separation, the twins had stepped back and looked at one another and thought that this could not be happening to *them*. How had they *let* it happen? They had always guarded their union so closely, been careful not to let outsiders infiltrate. They re-closed the gap and held on tightly. Through a blur of tears Lily saw Tom's wavering face, troubled and anxious, and she wept afresh, knowing her sorrow was tinged by the confusion of guilt and shame that was raging deep inside her.

'Lily love,' called Tomas, 'we'd better get aboard. The guard's about to blow his whistle.'

'You'll have to go.' It was Garnet who made the break. 'Are you all right, dear? You're trembling.'

'Lily,' said Tom desperately, coming closer, venturing to touch her arm.

Sergei, who had been standing motionless on the edge of the platform, his long arms dangling, looking like a man who might suddenly cast himself upon the rails, moved now, and came to embrace Lily. He kissed her solemnly on both cheeks.

'Goodbye, Lily,' he said.

Lily liked the look of Riga straight away, with its mediaeval church spires dominating the skyline and colourful buildings lining the waterfront. Tomas's younger sister, Veronika, was waiting for them with a bunch of pink and white carnations. The quay had the appearance of a great flower-stall; everyone meeting the ship seemed to be carrying a bouquet.

'It's a Latvian custom.' Tomas was smiling and waving at his sister. 'We bring flowers for every occasion.'

Veronika was a tall, blonde girl and she wore her hair braided round her head.

'She looks nice,' said Lily nervously.

'She's my favourite sister,' said Tomas, and Lily suddenly saw how lopsided their lives were going to be: Tom would be rooted in his own place, flanked by his own people, while she would stand alone, far from her centre, and her people. Letters would be her only link.

My very dearest Garnet,
    I have been here two weeks now – can that be *all*? It seems more like two months, two years, a lifetime! I am

still finding it odd to be living with a man after twenty-one years of sharing a room with you. I can't get used to the sight of his brushes lying on the dresser and his shoes beside the bed! And sometimes I waken thinking of something I simply must say to you and am startled to find Tom's fair head lying on the pillow beside mine.

Then I am occupied with all the cares and concerns of housekeeping. Not that they are too severe, for our flat consists of only four rooms and they are simply furnished with bentwood furniture that Tom had made to Thonet designs. He cannot stand heavy lumps of mahogany and overstuffed sofas any more than our father can, though he does love decoration. And flowers in the house! We have masses of flowers always.

I have a young girl, Mara, to help me. She does the laundry and cleaning and goes shopping with me. Latvian is the language of the markets, whereas the official language is *German*, which has taken me by surprise – I mean, Livonia is a part of the Russian Empire. And so I have to learn *three* languages.

Lily had been surprised to find shops displaying signs in Russian and German, but not Latvian. Street names also were written in those two languages. 'We live in Elisabetes *Strasse*? Why not Iela?' She'd learnt the Latvian name for street, and station, and garden. She felt cheated. 'Not as cheated as we feel,' said her sister-in-law Veronika. 'Our own language is seen as subservient!'

She had become friends with her sister-in-law. Veronika taught English at a local high school and would often drop in on her way home from work. Sometimes they'd go out walking together, would cut through the park and along by the canal into the old town. Lily had fallen in love with the narrow streets and their mediaeval buildings. She liked their soft colours, found them easier on the eye than grey granite, though how often did she long for the sight of that!

The old town is encircled by boulevards, Elisabeth Street being one of them. So we are just into the St Petersburg suburb. I have a link to you there! Our flat is on the ground floor of a brick-and-stone late 19th c. building. 'A Neo-Classical concoction', Tom calls it! He himself prefers a newer style which we at home know as Art Nouveau – do you remember Father talking to us about that Glasgow man Mackintosh? The French call this architecture *style moderne*, and the Germans, *Jugendstils*, so my brother-in-law Herman informed me. He is the type of man who likes to inform. Tom is not as fond of his elder sister, Agita, as he is of the younger, Veronika, and he dislikes her husband, Herman, who is a Balt. (Balts are Germans who've been settled here for a long time.) Herman is a baron, and a big landowner. They invited us to dinner in their grand house here in Riga. It was all very formal.

Herman went on about *Jugendstils*, saying it was too fussy and had a decadent air to it. He likes straight lines. 'Purity,' he said, looking at me sternly: 'that is what one should aim for.' My husband sat and glowered at him, and then said, finally, 'You can't like much of Riga, can you, Herman, for we Rigans like to decorate our buildings, and have done long before *Jugendstils*?' It was Herman's turn to glower. He regards himself as a Rigan *and* a German. He was born here. His father settled in Latvia in the 1860s. I don't look forward to returning their hospitality. I shall have to get out Mother's *Book*!

I am doing some cooking. Yesterday I made pastry you could have soled your shoes with! Tom is long-suffering and doesn't mind as long as he has his cucumbers and sour cream – sour cream with everything! – and pickled herrings and caraway cheese for breakfast. I am trying to get used to the sweet-and-sour rye bread, though find it a bit on the dry side, and would give anything at times for a good Scots soft white floury roll!

Tom has just got a big commission, tell Seryozha, and is very busy.

The doorbell scattered Lily's thoughts and she laid aside her pen. She'd been thinking anyway that she wished she could say what was really in her mind: that she was missing Garnet desperately, that she was often lonely, even though she was trying to use her time wisely by reading and studying Latvian (which she was finding difficult), that she was missing Aberdeen and her mother and the sound of Scottish voices, that she spent most of her day with Mara, with whom she could communicate only in bare words, like *ludzu* (please) and *paldies* (thank you), that Tom worked excessively long hours and after eating his supper would be ready for bed and sleep.

The visitor was Veronika. Lily sprang up, delighted. She asked Mara to bring coffee and shortbread. And some plum wine.

Veronika was looking at the wedding photograph on the back wall.

'I should like to meet your sister Garnet. I always wondered what kind of woman Seryozha would marry.'

'You know him, then?'

'Oh yes! And this photograph – is it your home in Aberdeen?'

Lily nodded. 'It was designed by my father.'

Veronika thought she would like the house; she found its mien *sympathique*. 'It looks inviting.' She admired also a painting of an interior by a Scot called Cadell. A woman in a pale-lilac dress and black hat was leaning against a mantelpiece, with a mirror behind.

'The reflections are interesting.'

'It's as if she's got a twin!' Lily smiled. 'My father gave it to me as a wedding present. My sister Garnet has a similar painting, but her woman is wearing red.'

She poured the plum wine from the Edinburgh crystal

decanter into the little matching glasses. Another wedding present. From the Sibbalds. Everything she handled was so new. She felt as if she were playing at houses the way she and Garnet used to do as children.

'A glass of wine is most agreeable after a hard day of work,' said Veronika.

'I wish I had some work to do, other than housekeeping.'

Veronika said she might be able to find Lily some pupils to teach English to.

'Do you think I could do it?'

'Of course! You can do anything you want to do.'

She sounds a little like Garnet, thought Lily. And Mother.

She offered the shortbread diffidently. 'Freshly made this morning. Yes, by me! First time ever. I got the recipe from a book my mother gave me. *The Woman's Book*. It contains everything a woman ought to know! About cooking and laundering and conducting oneself properly and dressing becomingly so as to please everyone in the household!'

'It must be an amazing book.' Veronika bit into the shortbread and pronounced it good. 'It is a Scottish thing this, isn't it? Scotland is quite different from England? So Tom has been at pains to impress upon me! But yet you seem to be a part of England.'

'We're not a *part* exactly. I think it's just the way the outside world perceives us. We belong to the United Kingdom, as equal partners with England, Wales and Ireland.' Lily rattled it off as she might have done sitting at a desk at Aberdeen High School for Girls, which was where she had learned it, an excellent educational establishment, operated by women who believed in instructing their pupils not only in the more obvious subjects for girls such as English Literature, French, Drawing and Painting, but also in Latin and Greek, Physics, Chemistry and Biology.

'But Ireland doesn't wish to stay a part, so I have read,' persisted Veronika.

'There's been some trouble there, that's true, over Home Rule.'

'We have had our trouble here too. We tried in 1905 to get rid of both our Russian and German masters. A tall order. Tall – is that correct? We had an uprising.' Veronika got up to close the door, which was slightly ajar. 'One can't be careful enough, though I am sure Mara is a good girl with the right heart. We know her family.'

'She doesn't understand English,' said Lily, who was not quite following her sister-in-law's train of thought.

'It was a great pity our uprising did not succeed. They had one at the same time in Petersburg when two hundred thousand workers and their families marched to the Winter Palace with petitions. They only wanted better working and living conditions. That wasn't too much to ask, was it?'

'No, not at all. Our workers back home want better living conditions too. Our father gets very angry about it.'

'The soldiers opened fire on the crowd. Hundreds were killed and thousands wounded. It is a day that must stand in the history of the world. It was called Bloody Sunday. You must have heard of that?'

'I have *heard* of it. I'm sorry I know so little . . .'

'Our little revolution here in Riga was squashed too, with much spilt blood. The German barons hold on to this city now with clenched iron fists.' Veronika clenched hers and colour raced into her cheeks. 'They control most of our trade and finance. They are the élite! My brother-in-law, Herman, has twenty thousand acres, and he is by no means the biggest of the landlords. The average peasant has about a hundred. Do you think that is fair?'

'No, no,' cried Lily, 'most certainly not!'

'This domination of us by the Balts must some day come to an end. And when it does we shall have our country for ourselves. Long live Latvia!'

Lily felt herself reeling. 'You think it's possible?'

'It has got to be! If we are resolute enough.'

'You would be in favour of another revolution?'

'If that is the only way, yes.' Veronika dropped her voice. 'Don't speak of these subjects to other people, though, Lily.'

'I don't have many people to speak to.'

'Not to Agita and Herman. Definitely not to them! Speak only if you are very sure they are one of us.'

One of us. The words thrilled Lily, who was not so ignorant she was unaware that any talk of revolution must carry with it a hint of danger.

Tomas was even later than usual returning home that evening. Lily had drunk several small glasses of wine with Veronika and by the time her sister-in-law had left was feeling intoxicated, both by the alcohol and the political talk. She'd heard plenty of the latter at home. Her parents were always discussing the Social Problem and what to do about it and she and Garnet had accompanied their mother regularly on her soup rounds to some of the worst slums in Aberdeen. They'd seen eight and nine children living in two miserable rooms, with cracked window panes and cockroaches scuttling round the skirting boards, pieces of paper on the floor serving as lavatories. The children had looked stunted and their teeth had been rotting in their poor lousy heads. As well as soup they'd taken sweets. Black and white balls, clove balls, bull's-eyes, jelly babies. Lily remembered the sticky feel of them, and their sharp smells of clove and peppermint. Perhaps they hadn't been ideal gifts for children with decayed teeth, but they'd loved them. The dirty little fingers had scrabbled in the bags and crammed the hard round balls and rubbery babies into their mouths and snot had run from their noses. She and Garnet had been quite put off eating sweets. They'd never talked about these children, hadn't wanted to think about them, she supposed. They had hated the slum-visiting, though had never objected; they'd known it was their duty to go. Often when their parents had talked politics they'd shut it out. But she was pretty sure there'd never been any mention of revolution!

She'd felt so ignorant listening to Veronika, who had a questioning, ferreting, mind. Her own head was full of information; she could quote dates of battles and recite the reigns of kings and queens (British), but not much of what she had been taught, she realised, had she tried to relate to her own life. But now, here she was, plunged into a country – a vast empire – where history didn't mean Agincourt and Culloden but revolutions that had taken place a mere eight years ago and might be rumbling yet!

The flat was quiet. Mara had gone to bed in her little box-room. She slept the untroubled sleep of a young child, being early to bed, and early to rise; and as she went about her work she sang softly to herself, Latvian folk songs that celebrated nature or told of maidens dancing with their true loves in the meadow. Lily went to the front door and gazed up the street into the blue shadows. These May evenings were lengthening; there was little sign yet of night in the sky other than the pale tracery of a half-moon. She watched as a pair of lovers crossed into the park and vanished behind a clump of bushes. She thought of the garden at Queen's Road, remembering the density of the darkness in the shrubbery, and the smell of phlox and warm grass, then she pulled herself up. She couldn't allow herself such memories. That night in the garden with Seryozha had been a spell of madness. She believed she had truly lost her sanity; she had been transported into another realm where she had forgotten who she was. She turned and went back inside.

She picked up *Madame Bovary*, but found it difficult to settle. An unfortunate book to have brought with her all the way from Aberdeen. It made her feel even more feverish. Not that *she* could ever be compared to Emma Bovary, God forbid! She had not deliberately set out to deceive. She also had amongst her books *Anna Karenina*. An obvious choice, perhaps. But why *two* books about adultery? She was much more sympathetic towards Anna than Emma, and when she would reach the part where Anna begins to decline and Vronsky is less attentive she would find it almost unbearable. She took up instead a volume of Chekhov short stories (all of the books were in English translation, though she could have, if she were to have persevered, read the Flaubert in the original),

41

and opened it at *The Lady with the Lap Dog*. A safer topic. The book lay on her lap. She looked at the clock on the mantelpiece. It had a painted face and long thin hands. A wedding present. From somebody. The hands seemed to be frozen.

She rose, forgetting the book, and it tumbled to the floor. She stood in front of the clock. She tapped the glass case sharply and just then the long spidery minute hand shuddered and leapt and she, keeping time with it, shuddered and leapt also. A minute had passed. One whole minute. Sixty seconds. She began to count. Each number she spoke vanished into the room like a little puff of smoke. How slowly the next minute was taking to pass. An age. The hand jumped again, and resettled itself. Sixty minutes in an hour. Three thousand six hundred seconds. She faltered at the thought of so much counting. How many seconds, minutes, hours, till Tom would come back? If it were not for the state of his eyes in the evenings, and the soreness in his shoulders from hunching over his drawing board, she might have begun to wonder if he were visiting another woman. She had consulted *The Book* but found nothing there on How to Deal with Late-Returning Husbands. Say nothing, she presumed. Greet him with a kiss. Ask if he is tired. Fetch his slippers, kneel to put them on, lead him to his armchair, massage his shoulders, let him tell you what a hard day he has had. Don't rail at him, don't tell him you are going out of your mind, night after night, sitting here waiting for him, and that it's all right for him, but *you* cannot go out and walk the streets after dark or sit in the lounge of the Hotel de Rome on Theatre Boulevard and drink vermouth. Certainly do not do that!

The clock had pinged eleven times before Tomas appeared. Lily, in another shift of mood, had by now run in her mind through a variety of accidents, had envisaged her husband under the wheels of a carriage or a tramcar (he tended to be absent-minded, was often thinking more of his precious buildings than of traffic), robbed and knocked unconscious by a thief who had waited for him in the shadows of one of the numerous narrow, twisting streets or alleyways of the old town. She had seen herself a widow, veiled, garbed in black from head to foot, leaning on the rail of a ship, steaming westward, and the gulls mewing piteously.

Tomas came into the room with a smile ready to break.

'Do you know what time it is?' she demanded, even though she had planned to greet him affectionately, and thus make him feel guilty.

He held out his hands, palms upward. 'I'm sorry, Lily love. I've been working.'

'That is not enough. Just to say *sorry sorry sorry*! Anyone can say *sorry sorry sorry*!'

'You look flushed. Are you running a temperature?' He came towards her; she backed away.

'No, I am not running a temperature. I am perfectly cool.'

'Lily, I had to finish a drawing. I have a deadline for morning, it's a most important project—'

'Your supper is finished! Stuck to the pot. Dried up. *Its* deadline has passed.'

'Lily, I have work to do. Can't you understand? I am not drinking in night clubs and cafés or playing cards, as my good friend Seryozha might be doing right this very minute in Petersburg. It is my living. It is *our* living.'

'Do you call this *living* – for me – sitting here in this box . . . ?'

Their row was not original but it was none the less distressing for that.

When it had run its course Lily went into the bedroom and slammed the door. She paced the room. She thought of Seryozha. Well, why should she not? It was her soul that had attracted him, he'd said (apart from her beauty); it was that which marked her out from Garnet. Ah, how difficult those words had been to resist! Perhaps Seryozha was right, and they should have admitted that they'd made a mistake. It might have been terrible for a year or two, and then the stour would have settled, and the families would have accepted them. She did not permit herself to think of Garnet's rage if they had done it.

There was no sound from the living room. She put her ear

against the door. What was he doing? He was stubborn, she knew that already, and slow to admit being in the wrong. As he clearly was tonight. She turned and went to the wardrobe.

The door opened quietly behind her.

'What are you doing?'

'Taking my clothes out of the wardrobe. Are you blind? Do I have to spell it out for you? I'm packing.'

'If that is what you want to do, then that is what you must do. I shan't hold you here by force.'

'In the morning I shall go down to the harbour and ask about sailings to Leith and Dundee.' At the mention of the Scottish ports, Lily burst into tears.

Tom came to comfort her. He said he was sorry, he knew it was not easy for her having had to leave her country and her relatives, and he would try to come home earlier in future. He must not let himself be a slave to his work. It was a habit of architects, he ruefully confessed. They found it difficult to leave their drawing boards and they were always under pressure of deadlines. She said she was sorry, she would try to be more sympathetic and understanding; and she would stay.

'I'm glad,' he said.

She closed the wardrobe door and they went to bed.

'You must be starving, you've had no supper,' she said, and he took the opportunity to compliment her.

'That was a nice thing to say,' she murmured.

'Russians are not the only ones who can say nice things to women.'

What did he mean by that? she wondered, as she opened her arms to him.

Afterwards, lying entwined, they talked for a little while as they liked to do after making love, and Lily brought up her conversation with Veronika.

'Are you in sympathy with the idea of revolution, Tom? Would you like an independent Latvia?'

'Of course! What true Latvian wouldn't? Who wants to be ruled by others?'

44

'I've never heard you speak this way before.'

'How could I, with Seryozha around? He's a dear friend, but he's a supporter of the Tsar and the Russian Empire and cannot – will not – see beyond that. He thinks we benefit from being part of it. He thinks we are privileged. That we would be too small to survive on our own.'

St Petersburg

May 1913

Garnet was trying to write to Lily. Every time she picked up her pen someone would knock at the door, usually perfunctorily, and it would fly open, before she had time to say 'Come in!' and the intruder would demand to know why she was hiding herself away. Was she sick? It was difficult to be private in this house. The front door banged from morning till night, voices clamoured, vying for attention. They all seemed to shout at one another. And laugh at the tops of their voices. Seryozha's two older sisters, Natalya and Elena, vivacious and fashionable young women, both married to officers in the Hussars, called every day, bringing offspring, nursemaids, and lapdogs. Other women, related in some way to the family, though Garnet had never been able to work out in exactly which, appeared at less regular intervals; and the priest, Father Paul, sat snoozing in corners. Seryozha's cousin Leo also spent much of the day here. There was always a great deal of gaiety in the salon and around the dining room table – you never knew who or how many would be seated – and the wine flowed, as did the talk, which covered subjects ranging from the Arts to politics.

'Doesn't Leo have any work to do?' she'd asked Seryozha, who said Leo was an intellectual and a poet. She'd never seen any evidence of Leo's poetry, though he could recite the work of others, and he had given her a poem about 'The Russian God' to pin up above her desk.

'It might help you to understand what Russia is about,' he'd said.

She looked up at it now and read the first verse again.

> *God of snowstorms, God of potholes,*
> *Every wretched road you've trod,*
> *Coach inns, cockroach haunts, and ratholes –*
> *that's him, that's your Russian God.*

It was not a Russia she had yet seen, though she did not doubt its existence. Every country must have its potholes and ratholes. She lifted her pen once more.

Dearest Lily-of-the valley,

How are you? Where are you? What are you thinking about? Last night I had a dream. It was misty and quite dark and we were together on a narrow path. Was it Venice? I was peering, trying to find out, and then it slid away, in the irritating way dreams do.

I scarcely know where to begin! There is so much to tell and I can't possibly go over it all. I only wish you were here beside me so that I could tell you in person – show you – my new world. I am sitting at my desk in front of the window looking out over the Neva. I love the view already: I can see the Academy of Arts opposite and, on its right, the buildings of the university. There's always something happening on the river – lighters going by, sailing ships, even rowing boats, and steamships, fresh in from the sea, their deck-rails lined with people.

A little black tug was puffing past at that moment, dragging behind it a long barge so loaded with wood that Garnet wondered if it might not sink. The bargee was waving to someone in the street below her. She stood up to get a better view. It was Dolly, one of the maids, who was down there on the pavement waving back, blowing a kiss with both hands, and now the bargee was miming leaping off the boat to come to her. He looked very Russian to Garnet, with his wide beard and smock and big felt boots. She sat down again.

The English Embankment is an interesting place. Diaghilev used to live a couple of doors along. Our house is a smallish *palazzo*, not overly grand, as *palazzi* go, so don't get carried away thinking we live in something like Holyrood Palace! It's quite French in aspect, with long sash windows that let in lots of light, and black, wrought-iron balconies, and a raised pediment; and it's ochre-coloured, a popular colour in P. It's the Burnov family house, in actual fact. Seryozha's parents live here too, which you might find odd – I know we wouldn't do that back home. But people look at things differently here – they love to be *together*. Seryozha and I have our own apartments and so we can be private when we want to be.

Garnet chewed the end of her pen. That was not *exactly* true: Seryozha and she were seldom alone, except in bed. It was the only place the family didn't follow them. And she wouldn't even put it past them to do that! She didn't want Lily to think that her living arrangements were not of her own choice. She had been rather taken aback when Seryozha had announced they were going to live with his parents. As a married woman she'd expected to have a place of her own. 'It would be much too quiet if we were to live by ourselves,' Seryozha had said, sounding almost shocked by the idea. 'And more costly.'

A cousin of Seryozha's is teaching me Russian and showing me the city. Seryozha is busy designing a dacha for a friend on his estate at Rozhdestveno, a pretty area, favoured by the intelligentsia, on the road to Pskov. He's had to stay overnight once or twice. Distances are so vast

48

here. Even the sky seems vast – the Russian sky! (They're always talking about the Russian this, and the Russian that!) I don't think we'll be spending much time in the country. The Burnov estates are far away, on the edge of the Urals. It sounds as if one would be permanently knee-deep in mud and have to be jolted in horse buggies over unmade roads, and the hours would yawn past, like in those plays of Chekhov we read at school. Remember? (I keep wanting to say 'Remember?' and have to tell myself that that will not do!) Leo, the cousin, is charming. He's small and dark, and quite intense. Here a man considered to be charming is looked upon as having an asset. Whereas at home we'd probably think of him as 'a smooth talker', and therefore to be regarded as suspect, isn't that so? Here, too, men will talk about their hearts and their souls, and of being in love.

Garnet paused again. Leo had confessed to being a little in love with her. She had told Sergei, who had been amused. 'He's a romantic, and harmless.' 'You're not worried I might be tempted?' She was teasing, of course. 'You're taking it for granted that I wouldn't be unfaithful to you?' 'I am! You wouldn't be, would you, my lovely dark Garnet? Leo likes to flirt, and to be in love. What safer woman to pay court to than one married to his cousin? He's a man who is careful not to compromise himself. He is a favourite of my mother's. He amuses her. And pays her compliments.'

Garnet decided not to tell Lily any of this. She had been a little hurt that Seryozha had not minded Leo flirting with her, just as she had disliked the idea of sharing a house. But Garnet was a pragmatist and would try always to adapt. She also knew that she would not be tempted by Leo. She was too much in love with her husband.

How is your Latvian progressing? My Russian improves slowly, but since everyone speaks French and English I don't really need it except for the servants, of whom we have some two dozen (I've never actually counted them all). We've got housemaids and kitchen maids and porters and little men called *moujiks* who wear brightly coloured shirts and high boots and clean the windows, wash dishes, sweep the carpets and slide about the floors on cloths to polish them. Seryozha says it gives people employment, and I suppose he's right. So I have no housework or cooking to do – I am a lady of leisure! I don't think I'll have too much need of Mother's *Book*. How to Make Orange Cake, Starch Bed Linen, Work a Mangle and Wringer!

Garnet felt vaguely guilty about that, but only vaguely. The indolence of the female members of the family was seeping into her; it was impossible not to be affected by it. And what woman if she were honest actually *wanted* to work a mangle and wringer? She got up in the morning wondering what pleasures the day would hold, thinking about soirées and what she would wear and whether she would have tea at the Hotel Europe or the Astoria. She had quickly become accustomed to the idea of eating out in restaurants and to the sophisticated French food and fine French wines. (In Aberdeen they'd eaten out but seldom, usually as birthday treats and the like, in rather formal, stuffy places, such as strait-laced hotel dining rooms, where people conversed in murmurs and a dropped knife made a clatter and po-faced waitresses crackled up and down in black-and-white uniforms with little starched white caps set primly on their heads. In Petersburg there was nearly always music on the balalaika and harmonica and someone singing and dancing and the diners would get up and dance too and there would be much hilarity and noise.) As for the other information in *The Book*, about being a hostess and entertaining, well, she wasn't the hostess in the house. That role fell to her mother-in-law, who complied with none of the rules set out therein. She didn't stand at the head of the staircase to receive her guests; she lay on her sofa. She didn't notice if the curtains were clean and bright or whether the flowers had been daintily arranged in their vases, and she didn't take care not to crumble her bread at table, or to fidget with the cutlery. And Garnet was rather pleased that she didn't, for all of that was a bore, surely it was, and she remembered some of the women in Queen's Road, such as that awful Mrs Sibbald (Rose's mother), who had afternoon-tea parties at which the women kept their hats skewered to their heads with fearsome hat-pins and held their backs straight and raised their pinkies when they lifted their cups to their lips. She and Lily had sworn never, ever, to live like that.

Mother wouldn't be at all pleased to hear me describing myself as idle! Seryozha's mother speaks English, after a fashion, with some French words scattered about here and there. She had an English governess when she was a child, a Miss Talbot, who was a frightful frump – the countess thought her mother engaged the woman so that her father's eye wouldn't be diverted. To tell the truth, life doesn't seem to have changed much since the days of *Anna Karenina* (which I am rereading when I can get a moment's peace).

Garnet had reached the place where Levin returns home to the country to contemplate his life and dreams of having a wife who would be the counterpart of that 'ideally charming and adorable woman, his mother'. She had snapped the book shut on that, forgetting to put in the gold-embossed leather marker that Leo had bought for her in Treumann's during a promenade on the Nevsky. Surely Seryozha wouldn't regard his mother as ideal? He *appeared* to admire her. But did he not *see* her?

On the Friday after we arrived, we got married again! In the Church of the Resurrection, an amazing Byzantine-looking affair with wildly decorated domes. We had to have the blessing of the Orthodox Church, otherwise we

51

would be considered to be 'living in sin'. Seryozha wasn't allowed to stay in the apartment with me until after the ceremony. Never mind that we'd already honeymooned in Venice! Only close family was present, since this was not quite a 'real wedding' with a virginal bride, as my mother-in-law charmingly put it. We stood side by side in front of the priest, who held lighted candles draped in orange blossom, and we exchanged rings, and then the priest led us around the lectern with our two best men (one was Leo) trailing behind us holding crowns above our heads. A bit different from the C. of S. ceremony in Queen's Cross.

In the evening, there was a ball in our honour, and what a splendid affair that was! A veritable army of hired servants arrived in the morning carrying their own pots and pans with which to prepare the banquet. The food was sumptuous. We started with *zakuski* (hors-d'oeuvres): several kinds of caviare, smoked salmon, little salted cucumbers, ham, tiny sausages, creamed mushrooms, stuffed eggs, all served with ice-cold glasses of vodka, so cold it was almost viscous. (I am developing a taste for it!) We had such an array of dishes to follow that I couldn't possibly list them all, except to say that they included partridges and pheasants cooked in wine and chicken breasts in smooth sauces and *saumon en gelée* and sturgeon (of course). Champagne flowed as if it were coming out of a pipeline from the Neva. Seryozha looked very fine in a tail coat, and I wore my garnet-coloured dress (Russians fortunately love red, as you know I do), with the diamond and ruby earrings and necklace that Seryozha gave me for our wedding, and I had my hair swept up Empress-style, with a few ringlets left dangling at the sides.

I have never seen so many jewels in one room. They dazzled the eye. As did the medals of the men, and their vivid uniforms, in scarlet, blue, and white, with gold trim. Goulesko's gypsy orchestra played with great verve and we danced until dawn. Waltzes and quadrilles and mazurkas and – this will surprise you! – the Dashing White Sergeant! The Tsar's children have an English tutor, a Mr Gibbes. Apparently his first task when teaching them English was to remove their *Scottish* accents, which they'd picked up from a previous teacher! No one has made any comment on my accent (my mother-in-law doesn't have a discerning enough ear to know how I speak), except for Leo, who says he finds the soft burr attractive.

So, anyway, we did the Dashing White Sergeant, and the Master of Ceremonies called, '*Avancez*! *Reculez*!' Seryozha's mother didn't join in for that. '*Trop fatigante, trop agité, pas élégante,*' she said. She did get up to waltz.

As to my mother-in-law, the countess—

Garnet broke off as there came a knock at the door and Dolly poked her kerchiefed head into the room. The countess was bored and would like Garnet to come and take tea with her.

The countess's samovar steamed gently on a side table. She drank tea all day, and ate: Turkish delight, which left soft dust on her cushioned fingers, smooth-centred chocolates that slid on the tongue, Black Forest gâteau oozing cherries, wafer-thin honey-and-almond cakes, delicate French pâtisserie, sustaining coffee-and-walnut cake, meringues that melted instantly under the teeth, profiteroles in profusion, tarts of all types. If she saw nothing on the table that took her fancy she would dispatch Kiril, the oldest retainer in the house, to Eliseivs for fresh supplies. He was in attendance much of the day, rearranging her satin pillows, pressing pastries into her hand. She was immensely fat. Garnet had been about to write in her letter, 'She is a fat old woman, with ghastly rouged cheeks and kohl-rimmed eyes and lashes so thick with blacking they look like the bristles from one of the witches' brooms in *Macbeth*, and I detest her. On the dance floor she looked like a moving sea of blancmange.' That wasn't quite true, for the countess, like many heavy women, had shown herself to be light on her feet and Sergei had spun her around the room on his arm with seeming effortlessness. And seeming enjoyment. The count had not danced; he had spent the evening in another room, smoking and drinking and playing cards. A number of the men had ended the evening drunk and had had to be helped into their carriages.

'Come sit by me, Garnet Alexandrovna!' The countess patted the gold brocade sofa with her soft white hand. She always gave Garnet the two names. 'We Russians do not forget our patronymics,' she had told her foreign daughter-in-law. 'It is good that your father has a Russian Christian name, and a great and noble one!' Garnet was expected to address her mother-in-law by her patronymic, Sophia Mikhailovna. Usually she refrained from calling her anything at all.

Garnet picked her way among the myriad of small tables, pouffes and footstools – and Kiril, who was hovering – to reach the countess. The room was excessively cluttered (Garnet's father would have a fit, he who believed in space and air!): ikons of various sizes covered those areas of wall that were not taken up by pictures, family photographs, gilt-edged mirrors, lace-edged fans, fancy French clocks, on whose faces time varied; china shepherds and shepherdesses languished on ledges; heavy, dark green plants leaned against the windows, sucking in light and keeping it from those who sat within. The atmosphere also was heavy. The room seemed seldom to be aired, unlike back home in Aberdeen, where the maids flung open the windows wide in the mornings and one went about shivering for the half-hour that they remained so.

Garnet stooped to kiss the countess on both of her powdery cheeks before moving to the other end of the sofa. Her mother-in-law stank of scent. Many Russian women did, she'd discovered. They discussed perfumes, talked of their favourites. There were shops that sold nothing else.

'Kiril will bring you tea. And *une tranche de gâteau*. You should eat more. You are *un peu maigre* for the Russian taste.'

Garnet took the tea, but declined the cake. She had set herself to control her temper in the company of her mother-in-law, but she was determined not to be bullied by her. The countess had made it plain that she and her husband had not been overjoyed at this match of their only son. To a Scotch nobody, with no aristocratic blood and no dowry! Garnet could well imagine how strongly they must have campaigned to persuade Seryozha to give her up. She *knew*, for his sister Natalya had done more than hint at it. Russians seemed to have no reticence about private affairs or secrets, which in Scotland they would close ranks to protect. 'Mother threw a box of Turkish delight at the wall! Father made threats. The place was in an uproar. But in the end they had to shrug and accept. And once it was done, it was done.' The knowledge that Seryozha loved her enough to resist his family's opposition strengthened Garnet and helped her to suffer his mother with some measure of patience. She could imagine Lily's astonishment at the idea of her being patient. But marriage did bring about changes in a person, there was no question of that.

'You are liking our house, I think, dear?'

'It is very grand.'

'It must seem very *agréable* after your Scotch one. The count told me that in Scotland there are many big grey houses with twirled bits on top – how do you say?'

'Turrets.'

'Not real turrets, I think.'

Garnet presumed she meant imitation, or as a visiting American relative had slangily referred to them, 'phoney', but she was not going to supply any help there.

'*Très laide*, the count said, 'as in much Victorian England.'

'It's Scotland. And Victoria is no longer on the throne. It's George. The Fifth. And our house doesn't have turrets. It's in the Arts and Crafts style.'

'You are a lively girl. May I offer you some advice? Do have a piece of Turkish delight. The sweetness will be good for you. You will not try to restrict my son too much?'

'Restrict him?' Garnet's spine stiffened.

'Stop him playing cards, meeting his friends. It does not come *au naturel* to him to spend his evenings in the parlour.'

'I could go with him.'

'I think not, Garnet Alexandrovna. Not to some of the places that men frequent.'

'What places are these? I know about the baths!' Garnet wished to lighten the conversation. 'I would hardly expect to go with him there!' Sergei went regularly to Yegorov's baths with his friends. To her they sounded incredible. The disrobing room was designed like a Moorish tent, apparently, and the pool was decorated with ornamental tiles and statues and trailing greenery, and had a fancy little bridge across the middle. The men lay on slabs in steamy heat, quite naked, talked business and exchanged the news of the day, and were beaten by attendants with birch boughs. It was good for men, according to Sergei. 'It makes us strong and the blood run free.' Sergei was never in any hurry to cover his body and did not seem to mind even when a servant (male or female) saw him naked. (Only that morning Dolly had come in and stared at him quite openly and it was Garnet who'd turned away in embarrassment.) There were women's baths, too, which Natalya and Elena planned to take Garnet to. So far she was using a rather uncomfortable hip bath in her dressing room.

'I was not thinking of baths,' said the countess.

'Do you mean drinking dens?' asked Garnet boldly.

The countess was not going to specify. She nibbled the end off a piece of pink Turkish delight. 'You are not used to Russian ways.'

'I realise that.' Careful now, Garnet told herself; do not rise. She could feel her pulse racing.

'You must not be hard on him if he should stray a little.'

'*Stray*? But we have just got married. He loves me!'

The door opened, and in bobbed Dolly again, to announce

a visitor.

Leo came straight to the sofa and kissed first the hand of the countess and then of Garnet. He looked enquiringly at Garnet, sensing her irritation.

'I was wondering if Garnet might like to come and take a little air along the quays? It's a beautiful soft May day.'

'Ah, Leo Konstantinovich, I was hoping you had come to entertain me! To play a game of cards perhaps.'

'Later, Countess, if I may?'

'I do not know why you want to go *walking*, Garnet Alexandrovna. Our young women do not walk.'

'I like fresh air.'

'Take the carriage.'

'I like to walk. In Aberdeen we are used to walking.'

'Petersburg is not Aberdeen.'

'I cannot change *all* my habits.'

They strolled along the Embankment in the sunshine. The spires and domes of the city glinted gold against the blue sky.

'She's harmless,' said Leo.

'To you maybe, but not to me.'

'No woman is ever good enough for another woman's son.'

'But he *listens* to her. And he tells her things.'

'I like it when your colour is high and you are annoyed! Your eyes spark! And now you've started to walk rather fast. Do you think we might go a little slower? I like to take my time. I don't like to miss seeing people. One comes out to see what is happening. Or perhaps we might just stop for a moment and lean on the parapet and look at the river? Do you mind?'

'Sorry,' said Garnet. She always forgot Leo was slightly lame. One of his legs was longer than the other; he'd had infantile paralysis as a child.

'No, it's not that. I can keep up! But it's a pleasant day to stand and stare.'

'You are right!' Garnet let her shoulders slump, and her

eyes rest on the river. It was true that the sight of water was soothing. She sighed.

'It will all settle,' said Leo. 'The days are early yet. But you're developing a love for our city, I think? Is it getting under your skin? You know what Pushkin said of Petersburg? Ancient Moscow has paled, like a purple-clad widow, before a new empress.'

'The city *is* like an empress. Very fine. Very serene.'

'Not so *very* serene!'

She had seen the poor and the beggars. Who could miss them? The beggars in their withered clothes, their hands cupped in supplication, when they still had hands, or sitting in a heap, legless, on the cold pavement, some missing even noses and ears. Perhaps she shouldn't have used the word 'serene'. She felt a little ashamed that she had.

'All is never quite as it seems,' said Leo, intriguing her a little, though she was finding that Russians liked to be mysterious. They were not nearly as straightforward as the Scots. 'Do you feel like walking along to the Nevsky?' asked Leo. 'We might take some tea in the Writers' Café, or would you prefer the Europe?' He put a hand under her elbow to guide her across the road. They cut round the back of the Admiralty to reach the foot of the boulevard.

The broad avenue was busy on such a fine, sunny afternoon. It was always busy – and noisy! – with the clangour of tram bells, rumble of horse-drawn carriages, blare of automobile horns, used like toys, it seemed, and then there were the raised voices. Russian voices. Indecipherable to Garnet's ears, for the most part. How they loved to shout! How they loved to make a drama! The beggars were out, and the drunks. Strollers were thick on the pavements. Leo bowed to a number of people but did not stop. 'No one it would amuse you to know.'

They passed the Singer Sewing Machine shop, which had a crowd gathered in front of its window. Garnet liked passing the shop; it made her think of her mother pedalling away on her machine at home, crisp cotton flowing between her strong fingers to emerge as a pretty blouse or a dress. Jemima McKenzie was an excellent needlewoman. Garnet enjoyed the shops on the Nevsky, liked the way their façades were decorated to show what was on sale inside. It helped when one's Russian was inadequate!

'I think the city *is* beginning to get under my skin,' she said with a smile.

They swerved to avoid a drunk lying half on the pavement, half in the gutter. There seemed to be much more drunkenness in Petersburg than in Aberdeen, she commented. People did drink in Aberdeen too, but one didn't see them lying around in the gutters in daytime. Drunkenness was a big problem, admitted Leo. Everywhere in the country. People drowned their sorrows in vodka and *kvas*.

'God of brandy, pickle vendors,' he quoted.

'I suppose that's another form of your Russian God? How many does he have?'

'Unlimited.'

Garnet was concerned about the man. Would he be left to lie there? Leo said the police would take him away later. 'To a cell, where he'll be kept for twenty-four hours to sober up. In the cold and dark.' Garnet shivered, and Leo said, 'Yes, it's not very humane.'

On the next corner a group of students were talking and arguing vociferously. Garnet and Leo had to veer into the road to get past.

'They seem agitated?' Garnet looked back, then turned at the sound of hoofbeats.

Six policemen on horseback were coming at a clipping trot down the Prospekt. The traffic was giving way. A tram braked, pitching its outside occupants forward, threatening to tip them into the road; two horse-drawn carriages swerved and looked set to collide; an automobile pulled in to the side and almost bounced up on to the kerb, scattering pedestrians, who were voluble in their response.

And then it went strangely quiet. All eyes were fixed on the police. The six mounted men rose in their saddles, dug in their heels against the beasts' glossy chestnut flanks, and came charging straight at the students, with arms upraised, long batons clenched in their gloved hands, their faces impassive beneath their helmets. The onlookers held their hands to their mouths. The students fled. One went down under the flying hoofs. A scream of terror flew out of his mouth.

'Let's go back.' Leo took Garnet's arm. 'I'm sorry you had to see that.'

They turned off the Prospekt, down the side of the Moika Canal. It was less busy there, between the grand palaces lining the banks.

'What was it all about, Leo?'

'There's a lot of unrest amongst the students. And members of the intelligentsia. There's bound to be when you have virtually autocratic rule! The police have been breaking up meetings and making arrests. I'm telling you this since I think it is best that you know, and Seryozha doesn't take it all seriously enough. He thinks it will blow over! He's always been an incurable optimist. If there's trouble, Garnet – and there might well be at some point – stay back from it.' Leo spoke urgently. 'You, as a foreigner, should be all right.'

Cesis

June 1913

On the train to Cesis, Lily read snippets aloud from Garnet's letter. It had arrived that morning.

'St Petersburg sounds absolutely amazing. You must have loved being a student there?'

'Oh, I did,' said Tomas. 'I was only there for a year, after I'd finished my training at the Polytechnic in Riga. It was very stimulating. But I was pleased to come home.'

'You're a real homelover! The Burnovs' house must be very splendid?' Lily had been about to say that Garnet always fell on her feet, but had repressed the words, if not the thought.

'I'm sorry I can't offer you anything comparable, Lily.'

'I don't mind, Tom, really I don't. I like our flat.'

And she did, really very well, for the rooms, after all, were spacious, and high-ceilinged; she could not complain of lack of light or air, especially on these long, luminous evenings.

Her life within their apartment walls was simple, a little too simple perhaps, not peopled, like Garnet's. Veronika had found her one pupil so far, a German woman whose husband, a diplomat, was being posted to London. Frau Hensler was not fond of the Russians; this she had announced when Lily had told her that her sister was married to one and living in St Petersburg. 'They are no friend of Germany!' Not according to Herr Hensler, whose opinions his wife quoted liberally during the lesson. Herr Hensler said the current customs policy of Russia was harming German trade. 'He thinks something will have to be done about it. I hope we will have no war.' 'War?' said Lily, who could not imagine such a thing, even though there had been talk of it at home for some months before her marriage. 'Herr Hensler says if it is necessary, it is necessary,' said Frau Hensler. 'Some things cannot be up put with. That is correct?' 'Put up with,' said Lily. She did not find her pupil's visits cheered her.

Lily sat close to the window. How she loved journeys! The train was passing through Sigulda and Tomas was telling her about the prehistoric hill forts in the area. He added with a certain wistfulness that the Gauja river, which flowed through it, was captivating. Lily looked at him. He had spoken of the river as a man might his lover. It was very un-Scottish, this. She could not imagine her father speaking of the River Dee in such a way, although she supposed he was fond of it. He fished it on fine Saturdays. It was very peaceful, he said; a retreat from care. Perhaps he meant the same thing as Tomas. She was finding some of the qualities in her husband that were present in her father: a quietness at the centre, and a solidity, combined with a certain amount of stubbornness, which at times could be infuriating. It was said that girls often married men similar to their fathers. But then Garnet had married Seryozha.

'Are you dreaming?' asked Tomas.

She started. 'No.'

'I was saying that I expect you'd like to visit Petersburg?'

She nodded. Not yet, though; she was not ready for that. Her emotions surrounding Seryozha – and therefore Garnet – were still muddy and confused. There were moments when her whole body burned at the memory she carried deep inside her. She would look in the glass and see that the blood was suffusing her face right up to the roots of her hair, and she would turn on the cold tap and bend over the basin and rinse and rinse until her skin began to pale. She had resolved never to give way to the temptation of confession. She could not expect Tomas to forgive her when she could not forgive herself.

'I should like to go to Petersburg,' she said, and added, 'sometime.' Tomas seemed pleased that she was not pressing him on the matter.

'It is a seductive city,' he conceded. 'It's one that enters the imagination, and inhabits it. But politically it's like a steaming kettle with the lid rattling. There's a lot of unrest. Garnet makes no mention of it in her letter, but perhaps she's not aware of it, sitting in the Burnov house looking over the Neva.'

There was no sign of unrest in Cesis. It looked a tranquil, pleasant little town, especially with the sun shining on its round, whitewashed castle and yellow and white houses. Tomas's father met them at the station with a pony and trap. Soon they had left the town behind and were trotting along a country road past a trudging line of women shouldering bundles, carrying chickens by the legs, trailing children by the hand. The women wore homespun dresses and white kerchiefs on their heads. It was market day. Some would walk miles to come, said Tomas. He himself walked a great deal when he was in the country; it was not just the peasants who went by foot.

'We Latvians are great walkers.'

'Today we ride!' said his father. He did not crack his whip, but let it lie loosely against his leg. The pony, Lily judged, as it ambled along, was no longer young or nimble. Markus Zale had been a very successful timber merchant, but now that he was retired he had no desire to go anywhere near the city. 'You like to walk, Lily?' he asked.

She did, she said. Yes, exercise was good. 'At home we walk in the hills.' As yet she could have only limited conversations with her parents-in-law, owing to her scanty knowledge of Latvian and their lack of English. They were still having to make do with much smiling and nodding.

Tomas chatted to his father about his latest commission, and Lily let her mind drift.

So what is she thinking as she jolts along, the sound of the men's voices mingling with the rumbling of the cart wheels? First, she is hoping that the jolting will not be bad for her, that it will not disturb the small seed growing inside her. She is thinking that it is only five weeks since she landed on these Baltic shores, seven since her marriage in the grey granite Aberdeen church. Can it be true, *only* seven? Surely it's not possible! In that time all her senses have been assaulted, have had to absorb a multitude of sensations. They have been bombarded by the architecture of Riga, so new to her, so lovingly expounded by Tomas, conducting her round the streets, saying, 'Look here, Lily, this is a fine example of National Romanticism, this is Art Nouveau [she will keep confusing the two], look there, Lily, that is Neo-Classicism, and that Eclecticism'; by the babel of strange tongues spoken around her; by the talk of uprisings and political unrest; by the physical desires of her body, and the proximity of another lying close to her throughout the night, exuding heat, breathing in a way that is unfamiliar, moving in its sleep suddenly to throw a heavy male arm across her chest. And now here is the countryside, different again from that of her homeland; a low-keyed landscape, with no mountains to be sighted, even in the hazy blue distance (something she half expects to see when she lifts her eyes), a gently rolling terrain, patchwork of green farmland, spliced by forests of dark pine and fresh green birch, its farmhouses built of wood and thatch, instead of stone and slate. They have just passed one made of round logs, caulked with mud, and now here is another, planked this time, roughly hewn, with a cluster of timber barns and outhouses at its back forming three sides of a square.

The wild flowers, though, are familiar, and that is a relief. They are bursting out of the hedgerows, splashing colour across the fields. Scarlet poppies, deep blue cornflowers and harebells, nodding white heads of tall daisies (taller than

Scottish daisies), purple foxgloves and purple vetches, deep pink rosebay willowherb, yellow buttercups and yellow vetches, and fat pink clover, its sweet scent lying on the soft air. They are going so slowly Lily has time to lean over and let her hands trail through the grasses. She knows how much Latvians love wild flowers and that the women weave garlands for their hair on John's Eve. Her head is packed with newly acquired information.

'Are you all right?' asked Tomas, turning to her.

'The flowers are just like at home,' she said, which made him smile. He was anxious always that she was going to like what she saw.

They turned off on to a road bottomed with large stones. The pony picked its way gingerly and the trap rocked from side to side. Tomas said they often made up the country roads by dropping barrowloads of stones into the ruts, and then the traffic would come along and grind them down. 'That, at least, is the theory. Trouble is, there's not a great deal of traffic! And I don't think Milda will make much impact.' Milda was the wide-rumped pony.

The next road had not been made up at all, and was full of potholes. Lily wondered if she should get out and walk. But what excuse would she give? She didn't want to tell Tomas here, right now, with his father present. She had been biding her time, awaiting the right moment. She would be all right, she decided; she would hang on to the side of the cart, and she would not let herself be alarmed. Tomas's father suggested she put her scarf over her mouth to protect her throat from the dust. A pale film was settling on her lilac shot-silk dress. She was silly to have worn such a dress on an outing into the country.

'Soon be there,' said Tomas.

His father brought the trap to an abrupt halt, and sent them rocking. He pointed his whip at the top of a tall thin birch. 'Look, Lily!'

A stork was perched, one-legged, on top of the tree, his

sharp head uplifted. Lily was excited, and half rose out of her seat. 'Shh,' said Tomas, putting a finger to his lips. 'He's listening.'

'Watching over his babies,' said her father-in-law.

The house stood on a slight rise, sheltered by tall birch trees. It was two-storeyed, stuccoed, washed a pale almond-green, with a balcony on the upper floor, and casement windows, which today were flung wide to allow the sun and air to enter. The design was Art Nouveau, though its ornamentation was influenced by National Romanticism, as Tomas explained to Lily. The balcony rail, wrought of metal, was in a floriated design, as were the wooden window bars, and in the door was set a panel depicting the Sun King's daughter with her hair radiating out from her head like the rays of the sun. That was a very Latvian motif, said Tomas.

'I think all of it is,' said Lily. 'Very Latvian. Sun, flowers, ornament.'

'You like it?'

'Very much.'

It would be theirs some day; his father had willed it to them.

She liked the garden, too, with its apple trees and fruit bushes and wealth of flowers. She admired it, which pleased her mother-in-law, whose passion it was. Gertrude Zale was a farmer's daughter and preferred being outdoors. Her cheeks had the pink hue of a ripening apple. She grew vegetables as well as flowers. Every Latvian worth his salt grew his own vegetables, said Tomas, and Lily already knew how important salt was in the culture. When visiting people in a new home one would take bread and salt; these were the necessities of life, along with water, which could be obtained from the as yet clear, unpolluted streams and rivers.

The house had been built on the site of an old farmhouse and Tomas had designed it so that most of the trees had been retained.

They sat on a bench under the shade of an elm and drank

plum wine with flaky little almond cakes. Lily felt relaxed after their buffeting ride. The sun was touching her cheek and the wind fidgeting quietly in the tops of the branches.

'You're not tired after your journey?' asked her mother-in-law.

'I think Lily might like a little rest,' said Tomas, and jumped up to help her to her feet.

They went up to their room, and Tomas closed the window on his parents' voices below.

'Well?' he demanded. 'Do you have something to tell me?'

Tsarskoye Selo

June 1913

Garnet was not in her own home, either, when she told Sergei her news. They were on their way back from Tsarskoye Selo.

Sergei is driving his newly acquired Bugatti, and she is sitting beside him, comfortable in the leather passenger seat, admiring the skilful way her husband is handling the machine. He has a natural flair for driving. Very sure, very smooth. His hands know exactly what they want to do. It is the way he makes love also. The top of the car is open, and their hair is ruffled by a pleasant breeze. She feels she is floating in the clear air above and can see the long-bodied blue car on the road, the heads of the man and the woman close together, one dark, one reddish-gold, catching sparks of sunlight. The woman sits slightly turned, her arm lying along the back of her seat, her fingers extended, their tips resting on the shoulder of the man – her husband. He glances sideways to smile at her. And now he laughs, exuberantly. Anyone can see how happy they are, how they belong together. The world, and the day, are theirs. Little other traffic is on the road. They have been at the Summer Palace to take tea with the Tsar and his family.

Garnet was excited when the invitation came.

'Of course, the Tsarina has a special fondness for Seryozha,' said his mother.

'And Grigori Rasputin,' murmured Leo.

'What is that you're saying, Leo Konstantinovich?'

'Very little, Countess.'

'I hope you are not repeating the tattle-tittle about the Tsarina?' said the countess, who loved gossip and was a regular purveyor of it. 'She is a very spiritual woman, in spite of being German. Perhaps that is why she is not strong in the body? *Très religieuse*, forever upon her knees. Though to my eyes she does not look weak.'

'You think her energy goes to her spirit instead of her body?'

The countess cast Leo a suspicious look and reached into the tartan tin for a stick of the soft Edinburgh rock that her daughter-in-law's family had sent from Scotland. 'One thing I cannot understand is the Tsarina's penchant for such *un homme*. Rasputin! I have always found him arrogant, peasant that he is! Semi-literate. How did a peasant get so close to the throne? This rock is *très bon*, Garnet Alexandrovna. I shall try another. I did not think I was going to like it when first I saw it. It had a dusty look. He is not the kind of man you expect the Tsarina to admire. He looks filthy half of the time.'

He cannot have paid much attention to the countess, thought Garnet.

'They believe he saved the Tsarevich's life,' said Leo. 'They think he has special powers.'

'*Moi-même*, I do not see him as a *starets*. That is a man of God, Garnet Alexandrovna. He is a man of the flesh too, from what one hears. He drinks heavily and he has affairs with women.'

'Isn't that what you expect of men?' suggested Leo, teasingly.

'Not men of God. This one is an impersonator, Garnet Alexandrovna, you take the word from me. Do not look at his eyes, if he is there. They are the eyes of hypnotism.' The countess made a vague sign of the cross somewhere over her bosom.

Tsarskoye Selo lay fifteen miles to the south of St Petersburg. Sergei was pleased to have such a good stretch of open road on which to try out his new toy (as Garnet called it). They passed wooden dachas set in amongst trees where families sat on verandas with samovars and turned but slowly to watch the blue bullet hurtle past leaving dusty clouds in its wake.

Garnet reflected aloud that it might be rather nice to have a dacha. 'Near town, I mean.'

'Oh, I don't know.' Sergei did not sound very interested. 'What would we do out here? Apart from make love and drive cars!' He laughed and the wind whipped his hair back and Garnet thought yet again how handsome he looked and how favoured she was to have such an attractive husband.

Her excitement built as they drew close to the Imperial Park. Forming the guard were Cossacks in brilliant blue. Sergei produced his pass, and they were admitted.

Two palaces stood within the park. Garnet found the turquoise, white and gold façade of the Catherine Palace too gaudy. Very *Russian*. She was tempted to call it 'vulgar' but their father had cautioned them against easy use of the word. She was glad to hear they would be seeing the Tsar in the smaller, ochre-coloured Alexander Palace. This was where the imperial family lived.

The gardens were spectacular also, with their terraces and triumphal arches and statues and smooth, verdant lawns. The lilac trees were in bloom. Garnet drew in her breath. She would have much to tell Lily. Lily had been in her mind a great deal that day, was every day. She'd been talking to her in her head.

Can you imagine what is happening to me, Lily? What about you, perhaps you too . . . ?

The Tsar and his family are posing on the terrace for a photograph. They are keen photographers and employ a technician full time to develop their work. He brings the pictures to them each evening for inspection and the girls enjoy pasting them into albums.

Tatiana, the second eldest, at seventeen (said to be a little bossy, fond of organising), is arranging the group: the mother and father in the centre, the boy of the family, the heir, Alexei (aged nine, pale, auburn-haired), next to his father, fifteen-year-old Marie (said to be lazy but cheerful) beside him; next to the mother is Olga, the eldest, at eighteen (said to be shy and to resemble her father), with Anastasia, the youngest daughter, at thirteen (said to be self-possessed and lively), alongside her. When everything is set out to her liking Tatiana will take her place on the other side of Marie, and Mr Gibbes, the English tutor, a tall Yorkshireman, with a high forehead and light brown hair, will step forward to take the photograph, as instructed. (Charles Gibbes will later become an Orthodox priest and take the name of Father Nicholas, after the Tsar, and spend the latter part of his life in Oxford.)

The father is of middling height, with a brown beard and gentle eyes; there is nothing in either his appearance or his expression that is intimidating. The mother is dignified, and some find her beautiful. The women's dresses, summery in shades of pastel and white, sweep the ground. Their hair is worn up, except for Anastasia's, and topped by straw boaters. They might be any family of the period, except that the father is an emperor and sits on the throne of all the Russias, and the destiny that awaits them is one that no family would choose.

Mr Gibbes stepped forward to perform his task. The members of the group held their poses, keeping their eyes fixed on the black rectangular box, ready to be frozen in time. A man with a black beard and compelling grey-blue eyes, dark hair parted in the middle, gold cross lying against his black chest, watched from the side, discreetly, below the terrace. The shutter clicked. Now the family could move, separate out, laugh and talk again.

71

Tatiana noticed the visitors waiting.

'Sergei Nikolaevich!' she cried. 'And this must be your Scottish wife, Garnet Alexandrovna! We have been looking forward to your coming. You must come and have your photographs taken too!'

And so Sergei and Garnet were photographed with the four daughters of the Tsar.

Since the boy Alexei was tired, he was taken away by Mr Gibbes. His mother's gaze as it followed her son was anxious, until it met that of the bare-headed man with the black beard. Then it seemed to soften, to find some relief, and she managed a smile. Garnet remembered her mother-in-law's advice and kept her eyes averted when the man addressed her. He made her feel peculiar inside. There was no doubt that the man emitted *something*, some strange power, which she could not define, as she told Leo the following day when he quizzed her. Rasputin did not join their tea party, and of that she felt partly glad, partly deprived. She would have liked to observe more of the unsettling monk so that she would have had some further anecdotes to relate to Leo. 'Watch him,' Leo had urged her. 'Listen to him. Try to form an impression of his relationship with each member of the family.'

They took tea with the Empress and her daughters. The Tsar, having other business to attend to, left them. They did not see the Tsarevich or his tutor again that day. But as they drove away, Garnet looked back and saw, watching from an upper window, a face with a black beard.

'Shall we call the baby Alexei, if it's a boy? And if it's a girl, what about Anastasia? I did like Anastasia, didn't you?' Garnet had noticed that Seryozha had talked to Tatiana more than to anyone else, and she'd had to tell herself not to be jealous, that she was being silly to mind. She couldn't expect him to talk to *her* at a tea party at the Summer Palace! The Tsarina had not said much; she'd seemed rather far away. Thinking of the Tsarevich perhaps, or the strange monk? Or

God? Eventually she had excused herself, taken a fond farewell of Sergei, addressing him as Seryozha, and asked the girls to continue to entertain their guests. The party had become livelier after her departure.

'I'm not sure about calling our child after the Tsarevich,' said Sergei. 'It might bring bad luck.' Like all the other members of his family he was superstitious. He wouldn't shake hands with anyone over the threshold of a room and he wouldn't go back into the house if he forgot something. And he said if someone passed in front of you with an empty bucket it would bring bad luck!

'He's so sickly, poor boy,' Sergei went on. 'I'd like to think our son would have better health than that.'

'Of course, he will! We're both very healthy, aren't we? I suppose you hope it will be a boy? I know your mother will. Though she didn't have a boy first, did she? She had two girls, then you.' Thank goodness for that, thought Garnet.

'If it's a girl we can have some boys later. I expect we shall have many of each.'

'Not too many.'

'Why not? You can have all the wet nurses and nursemaids that you need. We might have sets of twins. That would be rather amusing. After all, twins run in your family. Which reminds me, how is Lily? Have you had a letter recently?'

'Not for a few days. But she seems to be well.'

'I should write to Tom. But you know me! And he's no better on that score. Men have other things to do than write letters.'

'Like play cards and drink vodka!' Garnet could not understand Sergei's passion for cards. He had tried to tell her: about the excitement he felt as he and his fellow gamblers gathered round the green baize table, how the light from the low-hanging lamp cast mysterious shadows on the men's faces, how their eyes burned with a kind of hunger. 'It's the hope of a win, a change of fortune. How can one resist the idea of changing one's fortune! When one turns over a card one holds one's breath.' He had numerous packs of cards in a drawer, bought in cities all over Europe. He attached great importance to which set he would play with on any particular occasion.

He squeezed his horn with vigour as a cart came swerving out of a side road.

'Garnet, my love, you're not going to start berating me about my habits on such a fine afternoon!'

She was not, and already regretted her rather tart interjection. She brought the conversation back to the subject of the baby. She'd calculated it would be due in January.

'Not the best of times – midwinter!'

'Oh, well, there are times when one just has to go the way cards fall,' said Sergei cheerfully.

The twins' mother was not surprised when news of her daughters' pregnancies reached her simultaneously in Aberdeen. It was no coincidence, she felt, that their children were due on the same day.

'They married on the same day, didn't they?' she said, as she read aloud the girls' letters to their father and sister over lunch. 'They went on their honeymoons at the same time.' The twins had begun to menstruate within an hour of each other on the eve of their thirteenth birthday too, though that she did not bring up at the dining table.

Effie let her heavy silver spoon lie in its puddle of broth, not caring if her mother were to remonstrate with her and tell her that the poor were starving. She had often wished she had a twin, another half, to combine with to make a shield against the world, someone to share with, to whisper to at night, when the heavy curtains were drawn and the light extinguished. She felt she might be more complete if she had one. When she was little she'd asked her mother, 'What happened to my twin?' She invented in her head another half, whom she had called Evie, but had got tired of talking to someone in her head who didn't answer back or, if she did, sounded strangely like herself. Their conversations went round and round obsessively, like a fish trying to swallow its

74

tail. In the end Effie would growl, 'Oh, go away, Evie!'

She looked over at her parents, who knew none of these things about her. She'd always felt the odd one out in the family, hovering on the rim, excluded from the whisperings, the secrets, the closeness which was thick and impenetrable. Andrew was also a single child, but, being a boy, and the only one, had seemed different. Was different. He'd not wanted to share secrets with her, either; he'd been out and about from early on, involved, in life. He still was: a student at the university, playing rugby, learning to fence, moving around the city at night in a pack, a male pack, with its own secrets, and code of conduct, his head – when he was not engaged in these activities – filled with thoughts of modern history and careers and travel. He did not spend his time thinking about Rose Sibbald in the way that Rose did about him.

When Jemima McKenzie went down to Union Street that afternoon she bought a silver frame for the photograph that Garnet had enclosed with her letter and hung it on the wall of the drawing room with the other family pictures. On the back Garnet had written who was who and so Effie was able to rattle off the names and ages of the Russian royal princesses to visitors such as Mrs Sibbald and Rose, and thus impress them. But even as she was doing so (and she could not resist it), she was longing to be able to make an impression in her own right.

Riga

July 1993

They dined at the Ridzene, a modern, state-owned hotel staffed and run by Latvians, where prices were lower than their international rivals'. Before independence it had been the haunt of top Communist party officials and high-ranking military.

'We used to hurry past with our eyes averted!' said Helga, first cousin to Katrina, second to Lydia. They had met up with her in front of the Freedom Monument. She'd arrived carrying a bunch of anemones which she'd pressed into the hand of Lydia, whom she was meeting for the first time, and said, 'Welcome to Latvia!'

Helga Zale was the daughter of Alex, son of Lily and Tomas. She was dark, and resembled Lily – and Katrina – except that her eyes were grey rather than brown. She fixed them unblinkingly on the other two women while they were talking, listening intently to everything they had to say. She spoke very good English herself; with the hint of a Scottish burr, they were amused to hear. Lily's legacy.

Helga told them that during the struggle for independence running battles had been fought between the hotel and party headquarters further along the street. 'Tanks stood out there in Freedom Street – only two years ago! It's amazing to think of that now.' She forbore from saying that the tanks had been

Russian. She showed them two holes in the glass balustrade of the open, interior staircase. She touched the jagged edges gently. The glass was frazzled round about like splintered ice. 'Bullet holes.' They had been left in commemoration. 'Lest we forget. As if we could!'

Katrina touched the holes, then followed the others up the stairs to the dining room, where some of the people eating still looked like Party officials. But perhaps it was only the suits that had been left over.

They had a pleasant, simple meal of cauliflower soup and chicken in a whitish sauce, with a bottle of Bulgarian wine. The price was modest, only the equivalent of five pounds sterling per head, and the visitors from the West had to bite back the urge to comment on its cheapness, though on her previous visit Katrina had remembered eating for only two pounds. Helga ate with relish, they called for another bottle of wine, and talk flowed about life in the East and West.

Helga spoke about her teaching at the university. Her students were Russian and Latvian; they had to be able to speak both languages as a requirement for entrance. Groups were mixed. They managed to coexist fairly well, in her experience.

'It is not a problem. Nor for the three of us, either, is it?' Helga grinned. 'We are mixed!'

It was after eleven when they rose to go. Helga said she had enjoyed the evening very much. She was not going in their direction; she lived on the other side of town from the docks, in a high-rise flat, which she shared with another woman who worked at the university. She caught a tram, resisting their offers to pay for a taxi for her.

'No, no, the tram is fine. Taxis are not necessary. Next time you come to me!'

They waited until the tram had swung round the corner, then they flagged down a cruising taxi for themselves.

'I know she wants to return our hospitality,' said Katrina, when they were settled in the smelly dark interior of the cab. 'Her flat is pretty frightful. It's so awkward trying to give her money, yet she needs it.'

'To give *is* more pleasant than to receive,' murmured Lydia, as she was thrown forward and back. She made no complaint. They were becoming more adept at coping with their taxi rides, even with the inevitable bartering that went on before setting foot in them.

'Look, there's Tom and Lily's flat again now!' Katrina glanced back. She liked to look every time they passed. There had been lights in all the ground-floor windows, something one didn't often see here, they were so energy-conscious. Perhaps someone was giving birth! She thought of Lily going into labour in the middle of a January snowstorm.

Riga

January 1914

The snow had started falling early in the day, and later the wind would rise and shriek like a banshee in the chimney behind the tall white porcelain stove in the corner. The stove, which was built into the corner and reached up to the ceiling, warmed the room much more effectively than their open coal fires back in Aberdeen. There, one's front was roasted and one's back frozen. And the maids had to keep the fires stoked throughout the day and evening and lug the coal in buckets up the basement stairs. Mara did not need to tend this stove nearly so often.

In the morning Mara had gone to market, alone, as she had been doing for the past six weeks. It had become too tiring for Lily to accompany her, especially over snow-packed pavements, when she tended to slip and slide, even with galoshes fitted over her ankle boots, and, like most pregnant women, she feared falling. The doctor had advised plenty of rest. She had grown quite large and at times had such a fearful amount of kicking going on inside her that she naturally wondered if she might be carrying twins; and, if it that was so, could they be trying to murder one another? Cain and Abel in the womb! Tom laughed at the idea. The doctor thought he could hear only one heartbeat. He was a doctor experienced in obstetrics. She told him twins ran in the family. He told her they usually skipped a generation.

The pains began to surface in the mid-afternoon, only a twinge every now and then, but enough to make her wonder. Mara, seeing her flinch, asked if she should fetch the midwife. No, not yet! Lily said it was much too early. There would be hours to go, and she wanted as little fuss as possible. She and Garnet had been reared to make light of their ills, to pick themselves off the floor and dust their knees when they fell, and not to moan unnecessarily. Mara retreated to the kitchen to make fish soup and cabbage rolls for dinner.

Standing at the window, Lily watches the snow, as it performs a soft, dreamy, white dance in the fading light. There is no wind at this moment; the air is perfectly still. The flakes hover like blown dandelion clocks before drifting on to the glass to glissade lightly down. They make her feel bemused.

People will keep asking how she is coping with the winter. She comes from a northern city herself, she tells them: the light fades early in the day there, too. Aberdeen and Riga are on the same latitude. The winters, though, are much fiercer here; the cold has a bite that penetrates the bone and the snow lies deeper and for longer. She knows it is because the dauntingly solid land mass of Russia lies behind them, making the climate more continental, whereas Scotland – the British Isles – is surrounded by water.

She is thinking about Scotland as she watches the snow, can see it as it is in her atlas, its mountainous areas coloured brown, its coastline serrated, its sea inlets long and blue, its islands lying to the west and north. Her mind pauses when it sweeps up round Cape Wrath and reaches Orkney. She can picture Stromness, the small port where her grandmother was born, with its fishing smacks in the harbour, the men unloading their catch, the women in striped aprons waiting on the quayside, their knives at the ready for the gutting. They spent many summers there as children, she and Garnet, Effie and Andrew, running free over the green island, swimming in the cool waters of the Pentland Firth, playing at Vikings. Garnet always had to be the captain standing in the prow giving orders. When they re-enacted the story of the Maid of Norway who came to marry Malcolm Canmore, King of Scotland, it was Garnet, predictably, who played the Maid, and Andrew, being the only boy, the king. Lily and Effie and Andrew stood on the cliff, facing out across the sea, towards Norway, watching for a sighting of the Maid's boat, and Lily had thought that one day she might like to go to that other northern land. She did not imagine she would go further, onto the shores of the Baltic Sea.

She moves on round the coast now and berths in Aberdeen. She can see the harbour, and the esplanade, and people walking with heads bent into the wind, and grey waves curling in to break with a white crust on the pale sand. She can see the spires of the university.

Andrew is a student there, reading history. He wants to be a foreign correspondent, so that he can travel the world. At nineteen (and being male), he is not thinking yet of marriage, though he does seem somewhat taken by pretty little Rose Sibbald. He seeks Rose's company on Sundays, says Effie, when she writes; that is the only day he has time to spare.

Effie has got engaged, which is what she has wanted ever since she put out her arms and trapped the bridal bouquets of both her elder sisters against her chest. Her young man, a solicitor, comes from a family the McKenzies have known all their lives. They are members of Queen's Cross church. His father is an elder of the church and manages the business affairs of Effie's father, with whom he plays golf once a week. Effie will stay in Aberdeen.

Lily hones in at last on Queen's Road, like a swallow swooping from high above, returning after wintering abroad, and settles into her home. She wishes she were there, in body as well as mind and spirit. Oh, how she wishes it! And if she cannot be there, then she wants her mother to be here, beside her. A pain seizes her, girdling her abdomen, making her gasp; and then it slackens, and she breathes evenly again. Garnet will be having the same thoughts, she knows, and their mother, who is a practical woman, would say, 'How can I be in two places at once?'

Last summer, their parents came in a cargo ship from Leith across the Baltic. They sailed first up the Gulf of Finland to Kronstadt, the port for St Petersburg. They spent two weeks with the Burnovs before coming back down through the Baltic Sea to Riga, bearing news and gifts from Garnet and Seryozha and the countess. The countess sent boxes of Turkish delight and tins of Beluga caviare and an enormous cake box tied with pink and gold ribbon and filled with rum babas that had grown soggy and sticky on their journey; Garnet sent leather slippers embroidered in silver and gold for Lily and an exquisite porcelain box made by Fabergé. For Tom from Seryozha there was a new book on contemporary Russian architecture, with a short note.

> You will see, Tom, that we are becoming a little more Russian – more 'homely', as some might put it, less formal, less elegant, less French, less Petersburg! Less everything, in my opinion. We are beginning to move away from Neo-Classicism, which will not surprise you who has moved already. There is a mood here towards nationalism, which is permeating the arts as well as politics. I fear it will lead to brashness. I can hear you telling me change is not only inevitable, but desirable. I have heard you telling me in the past, haven't I, when we used to talk till late into the night? And I, as a romantic, want the world to stay for ever the same and for none of us to grow older. Don't upbraid me for my lack of realism! Leave me my dreams.
> *As I was ever, so I am today:*
> *carefree, susceptible . . .*
> Your loving friend, Seryozha

Tomas smiled. 'Pushkin,' he said, folding the letter.

He had a full programme planned for his father-in-law, an intensive architectural tour of Riga. Hardly a stone in the old town was to be left unexamined. This suited Lily, who wanted to be alone with her mother, to talk, and talk, and hear every tiny morsel of news from both St Petersburg and Aberdeen.

The McKenzies arrived at the approach of midsummer. They were enthusiastic about everything; they loved Riga, the countryside, the people, the customs of the country. Jemima took numerous photographs. It was a new hobby. The rest of the party resigned themselves to sitting on walls and canal banks and admiring the view, while she unpacked her tripod and plates and set up her camera. She planned to give a talk on her travels in the Russian Empire to the Woman's Guild at the church on her return.

Lily and Tomas took their visitors into the country to celebrate John's Eve.

Veronika went with them on the train to Cesis.

'A nice lassie, seems sensible,' was Jemima's McKenzie's verdict of her. 'Good fresh complexion.' Lily was glad they were not to be joined by Agita, who, like Herman, had no time for 'peasant' celebrations.

Lily spent the afternoon picking wild flowers – cornflowers and daisies, buttercups and clover – and weaving them, with the help of Veronika, into garlands for herself and her mother. They sat under an apple tree, the skirts of their muslin dresses spread over the grass, their voices mingling with the drone of bees that buzzed the flowers. Veronika thought she might have fallen in love. She was not sure. How could one know for sure? Was it a blinding conviction, a pure moment of knowing, like Saul on the road to Damascus? She looked at Lily. 'I don't know,' said Lily, not liking to admit it, and keeping her eyes on the floral plait taking shape between her hands. She had been giving some thought to this business of falling in love and come to the conclusion that she had not fallen in love with either Tom or Seryozha, but with the idea of romance, and of marriage, of being spirited away to something new. She didn't think she could be blamed; for years she and Garnet had talked – sometimes with their friends too – about love and men as the means of bringing about these concepts. How could you really love someone you did not *know*?

Veronika sighed, but softly, and without distress. She talked of the young man, a lecturer at her university, a chemist. 'I would have preferred him to be involved in art or literature.' Lily loved this idle talk, these lazy summer afternoons, the knowledge that the light of the day would extend until almost midnight. And there, dozing on the hammock under the elm tree, was her mother, who had even consented, on account of the heat, to remove her stays and lisle stockings, and somewhere within her house were her father and her husband engaged in talk. There was only one more thing that Lily could have wished for, and that would be to hear the creak of the gate, to turn her head, and see Garnet coming into the garden.

'There!' The garlands were finished and Lily set one on top of her mother's greying hair.

Jemima was perfectly prepared to wear the headdress, and even to indulge in another local custom, a session in the sauna. It was set up in a wooden hut at the bottom of the garden, behind the vegetable patch and the glasshouse.

'Your mother's game for anything,' said Lily's father. 'She likes to enter into the spirit.'

'Mercy me!' said Jemima, blenching at the blast of heat and penetrating smell of hot timber. 'Can this be good for a body?' She questioned whether it would be good for Lily, but Tomas's mother said it would do neither Lily nor the child any harm, as long as she stayed only a little while and on a lower shelf.

The four women had come together. In the little anteroom the others stripped naked, even Gertrude, who was seemingly unconcerned to be showing her ageing body. Jemima kept on her shift and her knickers. There were some parts of one's upbringing that were difficult to put aside, she said to her daughter, who was taking off her clothes, though feeling a little shy about it. 'After a certain age, at any rate,' added her mother, taking care not to look directly at Gertrude, whose breasts were bobbing freely. 'One gets stuck in one's ways. You can't teach an old dog too many new tricks.'

Lily was amazed enough to see her mother reduced to a shift. Jemima, though, declined the birch-twig treatment. She emerged from the hut with a bright red face and the damp shift clinging to the generous contours of her body. Lily helped wrap her in a towel, so that she could go 'decent' up to the house. She felt like a cloutie pudding, she declared, drying her forehead with the towel end; however, she conceded that she did feel cleaner, and she would not deny that the impurities must have been well steamed out of her. But, all in all, she thought she preferred a good old Scottish tub to lie in.

In the late evening they drove in two traps to their neighbour's farm. It was light yet; the features on their faces were easily discernible, though the spaces between the trees they trotted past were clotted with darkness. The western sky was rosy as if lit by fire. The smell of burning, the unmistakable tang of wood smoke, was in the air. Fires were springing up all around, like beacons spread about the countryside signalling to one another.

As they approached the farm they heard singing. The drivers slackened their reins. Rounding a corner they saw, spread across the road in front of them, a group of girls, some half-dozen, dressed in folk costume, their heads decked with flowers, their arms linked. The Zale party allowed the singers to lead them into the farmyard.

There, a huge bonfire blazed. Faces glowed in its light. Most of the women were dressed in folk costume, as was Veronika, who had her hair dressed in a single braid down her back. She wore a white embroidered blouse and a full reddish-brown skirt, decorated with braid around the waist and hem. Everyone but the Scottish visitors was singing. But before long Lily heard her mother's powerful voice rise and join in, using humming as a substitute for words. Jemima McKenzie sang in the church choir at home.

A smaller bonfire had been lit for the children to jump over.

'I'm not sure about letting bairns loup a fire,' said Jemima. 'It might be a tradition but I can't believe a few haven't got bits of them roasted before now. Tender bits, at that. I don't think I'd let your bairn do it, Lily, if I were you.'

The celebrations went on throughout the night. As they cantered home the sun was shooting streaks of pink and turquoise into the eastern sky and the birds were starting up their chatter.

'Well, I fair enjoyed myself,' declared Jemima, whose garland had slipped over one ear. 'What do you say, Alexander?'

But Alexander was asleep in the back of the trap, his starched collar splayed open and the top stud lost and gone for ever. As his wife observed, he had drunk a fair bit of John's Day beer.

They had to leave next morning to return to Riga, as the McKenzies were to set sail for Scotland the day after that.

'You must come back next summer,' said Gertrude, as she and Lily's mother embraced. Jemima by now was well used to all this hugging and kissing.

'We will! We wouldn't miss it for words, would we, Alex?'

It was the summer of 1913.

On the journey back to Riga, Tomas and his father-in-law sat separately from the women, in a smoking carriage, so that they could puff their cigars and carry on their architectural dialogue. Veronika took her book and found a seat a few rows away, to give Lily and her mother the chance to talk on their own.

'Filthy things, cigars,' said Jemima. 'They make a right fug in the place, though I have to admit I quite like the smell. I wouldn't admit it to your father, mind. And I wasn't too pleased to see Garnet had taken up the habit, either. Oh, yes! She was smoking those black Russian cigarettes. Her sisters-in-law were too. Even the countess had the odd one, though all she did was splutter and choke. What pleasure she could get from that I can't imagine. They even smoked at the table, between courses!

'To tell the truth, Lily, I think you have the better life. No, I really mean it. A life is often the better for being simpler. Garnet's has got too much of everything. Too much rich food. Too many servants. They just make a body idle. Too much socialising, out here, there and everywhere, gadding about. She's too restless. And then there's that cousin of Seryozha's, Leo. Couldn't make much of him. He was very "charming", kept bowing over your hand and all that nonsense. Well, I find it does get a bit much. He was hanging about the house half the day. A lot of folk were. The priest was never away, especially at mealtimes. Round as a roly-poly, he was. But Leo didn't seem to have a job to go to, or anything better to do. An essayist, they said. And a poet. I mean to say! That's not what you'd call a profession, is it? After all, Burns was a ploughman first and foremost; wrote his verses in his free time. I hope Garnet'll change her tune once she's got her bairn. I wouldn't like to see it brought up by nursemaids, tossed from one pair of none-too-clean hands to another. It's all right having a bit help, but a bairn needs to know its mother before anyone else.'

Lily is ready to know her bairn. The pain is increasing and the wind is rising, turning the white flakes into whirling, skirling dervishes. She can no longer see the outline of the trees in the park. The room behind is dark; it is time to light the lamps. The jingle of the front doorbell breaks her trance, and she turns back into the room. Her sister-in-law comes in asking why she is standing there in the dark. Is she all right? Has her time come? Should word be sent to Tomas?

A midwife and doctor were both in attendance for the birth. The labour was long and protracted and both Tomas and Veronika in the other room were anxious. Tomas smoked thin cigars, stubbing them out halfway down. He paced the floor, to and fro, up and down, between the door and the window, as fathers in waiting were expected to do. Veronika drank several cups of tea and told her brother that Lily was a healthy young woman. Mara huddled by the stove in the kitchen with her kettles whistling and steaming, listening to the maniacal cry of the wind. She hated high wind; it made her nervous, made her want to cower under the bed. She jumped when the midwife came in demanding more hot water.

Tomas, having heard the bedroom door open, intercepted the midwife in the hallway.

'Any news yet?'

'It's on its way down. Should be here any minute now.'

Tomas left their door ajar. After what seemed like an age they heard the cry of a baby.

'There you are!' said Veronika.

'Thank God! But it sounded feeble, didn't you think?'

'It's coming through the bedroom door, silly!'

They stood in the corridor. They could hear Lily moaning and the doctor speaking to her in a calm, low voice, encouraging her. Now she cried aloud, quite sorely.

'What's going on?' said Tomas.

'It'll be the afterbirth,' said Veronika.

A shout arose behind the bedroom door.

'That sounded like the doctor,' said Tomas.

'Listen!' said Veronika.

A baby was crying. Was it a different one?

The midwife came whisking out of the room again, calling to Mara for more hot water.

'Is she all right?' Tomas seized her arm.

'Perfectly all right. And so are *they*. You've got two fine boys.'

*

Tomas and Veronika were allowed to enter once Lily had been cleaned up. She was resting against a bank of pillows, holding the babies one on either arm. She looked pale but she was smiling. Tomas went to the bed and put his arms around all three.

'She did well,' said the doctor, who was washing his hands in the china basin on the dresser. He was an old family friend. 'The smaller one came out first. I was foxed to begin with, I must say, because I could see straight away that he was a good month premature. Yet I knew that Lily couldn't be before her time.'

'How can you tell he's premature?' asked Veronika.

'By his finger- and toe-nails, and his skin is wrinkled. Look for yourselves.'

They looked at the smaller of the two babies, the dark-haired one.

'And the other is not premature?' asked Tomas.

They looked now at the bigger one, who had a shock of downy blond hair and whose skin was smooth and pink.

'That's right.' The doctor took the towel from the midwife and dried his hands. 'They've been conceived about a month apart. Oh yes, it's perfectly possible. I've had a case before. Twins that are not identical are fertilised from different eggs, after all.'

'Well!' said Tomas.

'So which, then, is the elder?' asked Veronika.

That, said the doctor, was a debatable point; it depended on which way you looked at it. Was it the one who emerged first? Or the one who was the elder in terms of conception? The point would remain debatable, and the two boys, who were to be named Lukas (the bigger of the two) and Alexander (the smaller), would often scrap, claiming, 'Me first, I'm the elder.'

'One blond and one dark,' said Veronika. 'So there is one to take after each of you.'

Lily, who had been saying nothing, was the only one to

notice that there were definite tints of red in Lukas's golden hair. And later, after everyone had left to go to their own beds, when examining the babies' tiny, fragile fingers, to make sure that they were all intact, she saw that the little finger of Lukas's left hand – his pinkie, as they called it in Scotland – was turned inward. She tried to ease it out, but it did not seem to want to go.

St Petersburg

January 1914

The storm is even wilder in St Petersburg, and the temperature lower. When Garnet goes out, dressed in her long fur coat – her *shuba* – and her fur hat and fur muff, her feet encased in felt-lined boots, she gulps as her lungs suck in the raw air. She has been prevailed upon to rub goose grease into her cheeks and chin to ward off frostbite, although to begin with she resisted. But the thought of frostbite is more off-putting than goose lard. Some days have been shivery damp, and fog has hung from early morning like a grey skein over the river, with its snaking tendrils moving gradually in to invade the city's streets; others have been crisp and exhilarating, and the frost and snow have dazzled her eyes under the winter sun. On the bright days she has enjoyed being taken out, by Leo, and occasionally Seryozha, when he could make the time, in a troika or a *vozok*, a sledge with felt runners. Wrapped in furs, the horses skimming the white ground, the breath of the animals and humans rising in white clouds above them, sounds carrying on the diamond-clear air, it is pure delight. And then, out in the countryside, with the snow lying deep and purely white, the world is vast and quiet. Yes, Garnet will agree that winter brings its own pleasures, though she will be glad when spring comes and the ground is free of ice and snow and she no longer has to keep her eyes cast down. Walking on the pavements has often not been easy. Even on the Nevsky, which is traversed by so many people, heaped-up piles of dirtying snow have to be circumnavigated. Pregnancy has made her less sure, too, on her feet.

Her labour has started. For the last hour and a half she has been having contractions at a space of thirty minutes. She is standing at the window of her sitting room, though there is little to be seen but the mad careening of the snow. The river exists out there somewhere, behind the crazy flakes, with trams running over its frozen surface; but perhaps they won't be today, not in this blizzard. They lay the lines for the trams when the river freezes, and set up lamp standards. She watched, amazed, while they did so. What if it were to thaw? And the ice caved in? It wouldn't thaw, said Sergei; not before spring. No chance at all! And she'd know when it did; she'd hear the violent cracking and the steady drip of water.

Few will venture out on a day like this, not even here, where they are used to wild winds and temperatures dropping ten, twenty, thirty below freezing. The city will have come to a halt. Seryozha has been gone since morning, before the wind rose. He is too restless to stay at home and Garnet knows he would prefer to return to find the baby born and the blood and pain out of the way. There is time yet, though, for him to return; the baby is taking its time.

She knows the storm is there, but she is cocooned, safe, with her arms cradling her soon-to-be-born child; she cannot even hear the full rage of the tempest, as the windows are sealed in for the winter by another matching set fitted over them. They have been double-glazed, in fact. Garnet thinks this is a good idea and reminds herself to write and tell her father. There are always draughts in the house in Aberdeen.

There have been other winter compensations, apart from riding on sledges on sunny days. The Maryinsky Theatre, for one. The whole family went for the opening night of the season, to see Glinka's opera *A Life for the Tsar*. Garnet was not so taken by that – a patriotic piece, played annually for the opening – but it was a splendid occasion. The audience of two thousand filled the magnificent tiered blue and gold auditorium; the sky-blue velvet seats and the boxes were flanked by silver candelabra and a huge crystal chandelier glittered overhead like a million raindrops. And then there were the clothes and jewels of the spectators. Her mother thought Russians were inclined to be showy. Garnet, in their defence, said that was just part of their exuberance: they loved colour and decoration.

She knows her mother thinks her life is frivolous, but really it is not true! What is frivolous about going to the ballet? To the Hermitage Museum? Learning to appreciate great art? Hasn't her father always exhorted his children to do just that? 'Look!' he was always telling them. 'Open up your eyeballs!' Leo is very well informed and is instructing her on the Italian school of painting. And why should she not have a good time? She is young, even if she is about to become a mother, and people in this city know how to enjoy themselves. Her mother has nothing against art, she will say – said, when she was here – as long as it is kept in its place.

'What do you mean, its "place"?'

'That it shouldn't exist at the expense of the poor. That the poor should have a chance to enjoy it also.'

'Seryozha says equality is not possible,' said Garnet. Jemima looked at her daughter. She disliked women taking refuge in their husbands' opinions and Garnet, who was aware of that, added quickly, 'All right, I know it should be striven for.'

'Equity at least. I like theatre, too, dear, you know that. I only question the necessity of chandeliers and boxes done up in so much gold leaf.'

'You're far too puritanical, you Scots!'

'You Scots indeed! What do you think you are, madam?'

'I am living now in Russia. Father told me I should do as the natives do! Don't you remember him telling me.'

'Don't tell me all the natives live like this!'

That was the only time Garnet and her mother came close to quarrelling. She enjoyed her parents' visit, although at the end she did not shed as many tears as Lily had when waving them off at the quayside. Garnet has always had a more difficult relationship with her mother. They are both strong-willed, and more inclined to clash. It is not that Lily is weak-willed, for she can be stubborn; it is just that she has a habit of sliding away when confrontation looms. On this visit Garnet and her mother were taking care not to lock their horns in argument; and when they did, in unguarded moments, they were both ready to back off. They knew that they would not see each other for some months. And Jemima McKenzie did not want to upset her daughter when she was carrying a child. She was careful, too, not to be critical of her son-in-law's family. Of the countess she merely said, when invited to give her opinion by Garnet, 'She is not the kind of woman I am accustomed to.'

Dolly comes in. Garnet has told her to wait to be called to enter, but it has made no difference.

'You are in the dark, Madame,' scolds Dolly, and flits around the room, lighting the lamps. She is small and doll-like, with a high narrow forehead bound by a blue kerchief.

'There is always light from the snow,' says Garnet, and catches her breath. When the spasm passes she looks at the little gold watch pinned to her bodice that Seryozha gave her as a present for her birthday. (It was the first birthday she and Lily had ever spent apart.) Twenty minutes this time. 'Perhaps you'd better get someone to fetch the midwife.'

'She's here already, Madame. She's in the kitchen.'

She'll probably have been there for some hours, sitting by the stove, with her shawl wrapped around her shoulders and her feet steaming; she'll be eating and drinking, and trading stories of her more dramatic and hair-raising confinements for bits of gossip from the house. It is a noisy place, the kitchen. On the few occasions that Garnet has ventured in she wondered how anyone could find peace to cook, yet wonderful meals are produced every evening and brought up on silver platters to the long, chandelier-lit dining room, and the table is set with fine blue and gold china and the heavy family silver bearing the letter B.

Her mother enjoyed her food when she was here, except for the caviare, and she thought the sour cream overdone, as she would in Riga also. She found the quantities amazing, though she refused to let them overwhelm her. She hated to see good food go to waste, and was perturbed to observe that not everyone at the table felt the same way. The McKenzie children had always been exhorted to finish up what was on their plates before they were allowed to leave the table.

'At this rate I'll need to be loosening my stays,' said Jemima on the second day. 'It's a wonder you've not been putting on any more weight, Garnet, and you expecting as well. Of course, you're young. Wait till you're my age.'

Garnet was determined not to have her mother's shape, not at any age. She could not quite believe the photographs of her mother on her wedding day: poised, with tip-tilted chin, and a haughty air, she looked as slim as a reed.

They took her parents out to eat, at the Hotel Astoria and the Writers' Café and the famous Medved (Bear) Restaurant on the Nevsky where gypsies played and sang. And they took them to see the sights: to the Hermitage, of course, and other museums, and monasteries and churches, the Winter Palace and the Summer Palace out at Tsarskoye Selo. (This time they did not visit the royal family, though they saw Mr Gibbes, the English tutor, crossing the grass and he waved to them, and Garnet thought she glimpsed Rasputin at a window, and Sergei said it was extraordinary what an impression that charlatan made on women – they thought they saw him everywhere, even in their sleep.) They drove her parents along the embankments and out into the country. Jemima went everywhere armed with her camera.

Garnet was pleased that Seryozha took the time to show his father-in-law around.

'He works hard,' said Garnet to her mother.

'He looks as if he's thriving.'

Garnet thought her mother's tone a trifle tart. 'You do like Seryozha, don't you, Mother?'

'Oh, yes, indeed! He is very charming.'

'I expect you think Lily's Tom is more worthy?'

'I never make judgments between the two. Any more than I would between you and Lily.'

Dolly touches her arm, and she starts. 'Shall I tell the midwife to come up now?'

'Oh yes, yes, I suppose you'd better. I hope she's not been fed on too much *kvas* down there?'

'Oh no, Madame.'

Garnet is not worried. She feels sure the baby will slip out with no bother. If her mother is to be believed – is she? – giving birth is not something to make too much of a palaver over.

One day, when they were shopping on the Nevsky for gifts for Lily and Tom, she and her mother and Leo – Seryozha had taken her father off to see a building he was working on – Jemima stopped dead in the middle of the crowds and said: 'I want my talk to the Woman's Guild to be as comprehensive a picture of life in Russia today as possible. I don't want them to have a one-sided view. I've got dozens of snaps of fancy shops and grand palaces and churches – I've never set eyes on so much gold leaf in my life! And I've enjoyed it all too, don't think that I haven't. I'm not being ungrateful. But there must be parts of the city I've not seen, where the ordinary folk live. The poor.'

'Of course,' said Leo. 'We have our soup kitchens where the unemployed can get their bowls of *kasha* – a kind of porridge. They're grim places. The dosshouses are worse! The men are given shallow compartments to lie in, no wider than a shelf, and no blankets.'

'You've seen them?' asked Garnet in surprise. He'd spoken passionately.

96

'Well, yes. Though I don't think I could take you ladies in to see them.'

'Let's go and see the outsides at least,' said Jemima.

'Are you sure?'

'Mother is not known to say much that she does not mean,' said Garnet.

Leo hailed two *drozhky* waiting on a corner. Each could take only two passengers in comfort.

On leaving the fine streets behind, it was not long before they ran into what was quite evidently a poor quarter. As Jemima said, in any city the slums are instantly recognisable. The grime, the litter, the smells, the pinched faces. The general squalor. The atmosphere of hopelessness.

A wooden building was smouldering. Close by, watching with dull eyes, stood a ragged mass of people, men, women and children. Out in the street with them were their belongings: damaged dressers, lamps, wicker baskets, chairs with missing legs, scorched rugs, bundles of clothing.

'Do you think they all came out of there?' Jemima twisted in her seat to look back. 'I wonder what will happen to them?'

'God alone knows!' said Leo.

'The God of potholes,' said Garnet, and Leo nodded.

He asked the cabmen to slow down and come abreast. 'That's a *kvas*-seller over there, Mrs McKenzie. Our traditional beer, made from fermented rye bread.' They waited while she took a photograph. 'And that's a government vodka shop on the corner where they're queuing with empty bottles.' She snapped again.

'Looks busy.'

Leo quoted softly:

> *God of brandy, pickle vendors,*
> *those who pawn what serfs they've got,*
> *Of old women of both genders –*
> *that's him, that's your Russian God.*

Jemima bent her head to listen. She was becoming accustomed to Leo breaking into poetry at odd moments and had scribbled down some of the verses so that she could recite them to the ladies at Queen's Cross.

'Watch out!' he cried now.

Jemima ducked as an object came flying over her head. It dented her hat feather on its trajectory and came to rest on Garnet's lap. Garnet leapt up and sent the cab rocking.

'What is it?' she cried.

'Half a cabbage. Rotten, of course.' Jemima removed it with her gloved hands. 'Rather slimy.'

'It looks revolting.'

'You wouldn't expect them to throw a good one, would you?'

Garnet, who was eyeing the grinning faces watching from the sideline, could not help but think of Gorky's *The Lower Depths*, which Leo had recommended and she had bought in Wilkins English Bookshop on the Morskaya. One old man had suppurating sores round his eyes; another was leering, spittle hanging in a large globule from his open, toothless mouth.

'No harm done.' Jemima dropped the cabbage over the side of the *drozhky*.

Leo ordered the cabmen to drive on.

'That wasn't very pleasant,' said Garnet, knowing she could not put it any more strongly without being challenged.

'You could say we asked for it,' said her mother.

During the long hours of her labour Garnet wished many times that her mother could be there, for surely she would have known what to do. She would have laid her hand on her hot, steaming forehead, and said: *Now take it easy, breathe evenly and deeply, don't panic, having a baby is an everyday experience, it is not uncommon, and you are strong, everything will be all right, I shall see to it that it is all right.* Garnet's pains continued, and she struggled to tolerate them, bearing down when they told her to, again and again, but the baby would not come.

She could not understand what they were saying, these women with the sour breaths and the shadowy faces who were gathered around her bed, whose tongue she thought she should recognise but could not. When she called out she did so in her own language. After a while her sister-in-law Natalya came, and she spoke to Garnet in English, and then she understood.

'We can't get the doctor here, because of the blizzard. Everything is cut off.'

The women gave Garnet whiffs of chloroform, and her head moved in and out of terrifying dreams.

'It's a breech birth,' said Natalya, close to her ear. 'Garnet, do you hear me? Do you understand? The baby is lying the wrong way.'

'Turn it, turn it!' screamed Garnet. 'I am going to die.'

She saw one of the women turn to the ikon-stand in the corner. The sanctuary lamp was shedding a rosy glow over the three ikons placed there earlier by Sergei. Each depicted a serene-faced, gold-banded madonna with child. Garnet saw the woman make the sign of the cross.

In the end, the baby turned itself. Garnet, held down by unseen arms, gasped, thinking she must surely split asunder, and made a final push. The baby emerged, a boy, its head elongated and lopsided, its face a terrible purple. Someone seized him by the ankles and slapped his skinny buttocks. He did not cry.

Sergei arrived in the morning with the doctor, when the storm had abated.

'Garnet, my love,' said Sergei.

'Where *were* you?' she demanded.

'I couldn't get through—'

'I want to know where you were while *I* . . .' She could not go on.

'You must calm yourself, Countess,' said the doctor, taking her wrist and fumbling for her pulse.

'A sedative, Doctor,' said Sergei. 'Can't you give her a

sedative?'

'I don't want a *sedative*. I don't want to be *calm*. I want to know what you were doing!'

'Oh, all right, I was playing cards. And I lost! Our luck must have been out last night. When I was leaving the house Dolly passed me in the hall with an empty bucket.'

The midwife was sent back to her village. The under-cook who had fed her the vodka was fired. The other servants who had been in the kitchen that night were berated at length by Sergei, alternately ranting and weeping, for having allowed the under-cook to get the midwife drunk.

The doctor said there was no reason why Garnet should not go on to have several more children.

Aberdeen

April 1914

Lily and Tomas arrived first, with the three-month-old twins, and Mara, who was both excited and dismayed at the prospect of her new adventure. She had never been on the sea before. They travelled by boat from Riga to Hull, and then by train up to Aberdeen, changing at Newcastle and Edinburgh. It was a tiresome journey with two infants. Garnet and Sergei were coming by train across Europe, via Warsaw and Berlin, and stopping off in Paris for two weeks *en route*. Sergei was hoping the pleasures of the French capital would take Garnet's mind off her loss.

'It's going to be terrible for her,' said Lily, who was suckling the larger of the twins, Luke (born second). Mara had taken Alex for a walk up Queen's Road in the big black double per-ambulator that Jemima had hired for their visit. From the window Lily had watched them go, Mara glancing apprehensively about her, pushing into the wind, her arms at full stretch, her head full of instructions about which way to look for traffic when crossing the road. Lily had felt a little apprehensive about letting her go; she was particularly protective of Alex, on account of his being the smaller and weaker. But her mother had said, 'The lassie's not daft and she's got strong arms on her. And you don't need to know the language to walk up Queen's Road.'

'Poor Garnet,' sighed Lily.

'She's got to face it sometime.' Their mother was not being unsympathetic. 'She knows you've got the two bairns. You can't pretend you haven't. Or give one to her. It might have helped solve matters if you could have, but you can't! He's a hungry feeder, that one. Wants more than his fair share, if you ask me! Still, he's bonny. They both are. A fine pair of lads they'll make. And quite a contrast, too. Not like you and Garnet, whom nobody but ourselves could tell apart.'

Luke was gradually slowing down. He took a last gulp, breathed a deep sigh, in the manner of an old man, and his puckered mouth slid from the nipple and relaxed. Lily straightened him up, holding his back firmly with the splayed fingers of her left hand. He wanted to sleep now. He yawned, and his chin slumped into his chest. His pink cheeks bulged, reminding her of a hamster she'd kept as a child.

'That's a good boy!' she said, and dropped a kiss on top of the delicate baby head. She loved the way the babies looked when they'd just been fed. So pink and soft and warm. So satiated. So satisfied. She shoogled him a little, rubbed him, spoke gently, encouraging him, rousing him against his will, until the burp came. For the last three months she had felt she must reek of milk. Tom said she just smelled of babies. He was enjoying them, in the few hours of the week that he saw them. He had to go to work, of course. Men did. Her life consisted of feeding first one twin and then the other, burping and bathing and changing them and wheeling them out in the air.

She could see that her mother was aching to hold Luke. She passed him across, swaddled in his lacy Shetland shawl. She felt totally immersed in all things Scottish again: food, clothes, weather, talk, people, even the calendar. Here it was the month of May, but April still back in the Russian Empire, where they lagged thirteen days behind with their calendar. In the afternoons, the ladies in her mother's circle of friends called to inspect the babies, and were served Assam tea with milk and lump sugar, buttered scones, Scotch pancakes, shortbread and Dundee cake. Three kinds of jam were offered in cut-glass dishes. Raspberry, strawberry, black-currant. All homemade. Sitting among the women, listening to their talk of the parish and the town, of births and chris-tenings, afflicting illnesses and funerals, she felt as if she had never been away.

'He's got his wee fingers caught in the shawl.' Luke's grandmother tutted and carefully disentangled them. 'They're so fragile still, the bones. Look, he's taken hold of my finger! He's got a good strong grip. Not the pinkie, though.' She bent her head to examine it. 'What have you been doing to yourself, son?'

'It's crooked,' said Lily, rearranging her bodice, dabbing at a spot with the towel, then swiftly gathering up the baby equipment that was lying around, dusting powder, zinc oint-ment, gripe water. 'He was born with it.'

Their train was running along the side of the Dee. Garnet watched for a while as the river gurgled and sparkled over cool grey stones, so different from the broad, sluggish Neva in St Petersburg, then she shifted her eyes up to the hills, whose tops still held a touch of snow. She had missed the sight of mountains this past year.

'Won't be long now.' She stretched and turned back to Sergei. 'I feel as if I've been travelling for ever! I expect Father will meet us. And perhaps Tom. But I dare say Lily will be too busy with the babies.' She did her best to keep her voice level.

Sergei took her hand. Was she going to be all right?' 'You won't be too upset when you see them?'

'I can't avoid them for ever, can I? I'll be all right, Seryozha, really, I will.' She gave him a little smile. She had started to smile again since leaving St Petersburg and the winter behind.

The winter had seemed endless; the cold had persisted, and the freezing fog, and even when spring came creeping in the days were damp and the slush made the streets filthy and walking unpleasant. Garnet had felt cooped up in the big house on the embankment overlooking the Neva. The view from her window had no longer seemed entrancing but grey, nothing but grey, in varying shades. Her husband and Leo, and her sisters-in-law, Natalya and Elena, had done their best to divert her, but her sadness had tipped over into depression; she hadn't wanted to go shopping, or to museums, or to the ballet, no matter who was dancing, and Seryozha had called in an English doctor to attend her. She hadn't been able to rally herself even to go to the Ball of the Coloured Wigs, one of the biggest events of the social season, given by the Countess Betsy Shuvalova in her palace on the Fontanka Canal, though Sergei had done his best to persuade her. In the end he'd gone alone. Garnet had said she didn't mind if he went. She had not minded anything, then, had reached a state of total apathy in which she watched the days drift past as if they could not possibly contain anything that might interest her.

It had been a strange experience for Garnet, whose spirits before had always been of the liveliest and who had thought she had hold of life by the tail. It was the countess who had suggested Paris. 'Springtime along the Seine will bring love into her heart again, Seryozha, and chase away the sadness. What woman can resist Paris? You might see if you can buy me a painting by the Frenchman Matisse while you are there – I have a fancy for him. He is all the rage, I hear. And some *bonbons* from that shop on the rue de Rivoli.'

A contingent of four was at the station to greet them: Alexander McKenzie, Andrew, Effie, and Tomas. Garnet hugged each in turn, as did Sergei.

'Mother's waiting up at the house,' said Effie. 'And Lily's nursing— ' She broke off.

Garnet linked her arm through her sister's, and they followed behind the four male members of the family and the four porters. She and Sergei seemed to have brought masses of stuff, presents for everyone, immediate family and close friends, as well as their own clothes, and they had acquired more in Paris, including a couple of large paintings and several drawings bought at the *bouquinistes* along the Seine. Sergei had had to be restrained. He would have taken away half of Paris otherwise.

'You mustn't be embarrassed, Effie,' said Garnet. 'I don't expect the babies to be kept hidden. Now, tell me all about your plans. Is the date set for your wedding? Next spring! So soon? Oh yes, I know Lily and I married quite quickly after our engagements, but you are still young – our little sister! I can't get used to the idea of you becoming a married woman. So, April it's to be. We'll just have to come back over again then, won't we?'

It was unusual for Lily to have something that Garnet did not; and especially two of it. Everyone was conscious of this reversal of fate. There was Lily wheeling *two* babies in a pram, the tassels of the twin cream sunshades shivering in the spring breeze. And beside her walked Garnet, empty-handed.

They went out walking every day, in Hazelhead Park. The sun shone much of the time out of an untroubled sky. Squirrels scuttered up the trees. Birds sang lustily. What a relief to see blue overhead and smell fresh earth, said Lily and Garnet simultaneously, and they laughed. They had been used to having the same thoughts at the same moment. And the narcissi were out, in great rashes of white and yellow, with their sharp sweet scents tossed on the wind.

It was easy to understand why Lily would want to be out every day with the pram, but what about Garnet? Was it not just a constant reminder for her, like grit rubbed into a graze? But it seemed that Garnet was determined to face up to this divergence in their fortunes and make no attempt to sidestep. And she had her pride. She walked with her head up, and met everyone's gaze. They encountered many people they knew, for the family was long established in the area. Garnet did not want commiseration, and when it was offered she changed the subject. As a child, when she had taken a tumble

105

she had always been quick to spring back on to her feet and declare, though her knee might be gushing blood, that there was nothing wrong with her. She had never liked to be seen to fail. (Not that this was a case of failing, as her mother was trying to din into her, or if it was, then that damned midwife must be the one to hang her head.)

At times Garnet even rested a hand on the pram handle, alongside Lily's, and when they were going up and down a kerb or came to a steep part she would help give it an extra shove.

They were heard talking and laughing everywhere they went, just as they had in the days of their girlhood. Talk and laughter seemed to bubble out of them, like water that has been dammed by winter ice and is now released. When the conversation became intense, they would stop in the middle of the path and face one another, and for those few minutes the pram and its contents would be forgotten. Their lopsided status had apparently made no difference to their relationship.

'They seem as close as they ever were,' observed Mrs Sibbald as she poured tea for Jemima McKenzie in the upstairs bay window of her house, which afforded an excellent view of the street.

'So, Lily, are you happy with Tom?' asked Garnet.

'Oh, yes,' said Lily, startled, wondering where Garnet's questioning was going to lead, 'very happy.'

'Are you – well, how shall I put it? – *fulfilled*?'

'Fulfilled?'

'Physically, I mean.'

Lily was looking blank.

'In bed. Do you enjoy it?'

'Naturally,' said Lily primly, though she did not feel at all prim. She was beginning to feel hot and uncomfortable. This felt like dangerous ground that they might be embarking upon. She did not want to hear about Seryozha's lovemaking. She leant over the pram to straighten Alex's hat, which had slipped over one eye.

'I adore it!' said Garnet, without waiting to be asked. 'Seryozha is the most wonderful lover imaginable.'

'Have you imagined others?' This tack was safer.

'Well, yes. Haven't you? In the past. You remember how we used to talk? We would pick out a man at church or in the street and wonder what it would be like with *him*!'

It had been one of their secrets.

'We were girls then,' said Lily.

'Oh, I didn't mean that we should do it now that we're married women. That would be tantamount to adultery. Would it? What do you think? Can you commit adultery just by *thinking*? After all, sin starts in the mind, doesn't it? Here comes the minister! Should we ask him?'

As he approached them he tipped his black hat and slowed and said, 'Good afternoon, ladies! Taking the little ones out to enjoy the air? Nice day for a stroll.'

'Very nice,' they chorused, turning to watch him go.

'What *about* the minister?' said Garnet, and they both began to giggle.

Upstairs, ensconced in the Sibbalds' bay window, with a cup of tea in her hand, their mother was happy to see her married twin daughters laughing together.

'Marriage is all very well,' she said to Mrs Sibbald, 'but it does tend to cut off a girl's youth.'

Mrs Sibbald made no reply. Surely it was only *natural* for a girl to relinquish her youth on marriage? All the girls she had ever known had done so willingly. Think of the alternative! Jemima McKenzie did have some rather odd ideas. Rose had run into her in Union Street only last week carrying a placard advocating VOTES FOR WOMEN and she'd said something to the effect that eventually one had to stand up and be counted. But, really, how could she associate herself with those dreadful Suffragette women with their bombing and burning campaigns, and only last month one of them had slashed a Velasquez with a meat cleaver at the National

Gallery in London! Rose had said she couldn't imagine Mrs McKenzie wielding a meat cleaver or throwing bombs and maybe it wasn't such a bad idea that women should be allowed to vote. Her mother had been scandalised and regretted having given her blessing to this friendship with Andrew McKenzie. But it was too late now. Rose's affections were engaged. 'Leave politics to the men,' Mrs Sibbald had advised her daughter. 'And under no circumstances go out into the streets with a banner!'

Garnet noticed Luke's pinkie in the drawing room one Sunday afternoon. It being a Sunday, everyone in the family was there, including Effie's betrothed, Hamish Robertson, and Rose Sibbald, who had wanted to see the twins. Andrew said Rose was very fond of babies, and all children loved her. She taught Sunday school at Queen's Cross.

They had gone to church in the morning, the McKenzies, plus their attachments, leaving Mara with the babies, and, inevitably, the four who had been married there the previous year remembered the occasion and spoke of it, or at least Garnet and Sergei did.

'I can't believe it's only a *year*!' said Garnet.

'Nor can I,' said Sergei. 'Can you, Lily?'

'What?' said Lily, flustered, fussing with the buttoning of her gloves.

'When you think back,' said Sergei, 'it doesn't seem possible. More like yesterday.'

Lily hastened to catch up with her mother.

When they had returned from church they sat down to eat a heavy lunch of Scotch broth, roast beef and Yorkshire pudding with roast potatoes, parsnips and Brussel sprouts, followed by Eve's pudding with custard, and oatcakes with Stilton. They then went for a stroll round the park to try to walk some of it off, and Jemima complained to her elder daughters that her stays were near to strangling her. 'It's daft what we women put up with!' Throughout the walk her younger daughter drifted moonily along several yards behind the rest of the company, holding hands with her fiancé, her face upturned, listening to every word he had to say on the subject of real estate, as if he held the secret to a magic cave. Jemima considered him a bore, though she had not said so to Effie. And then there was Lily. Jemima had not quite been able to decide what was going on in Lily's head.

So now the family was assembled in the drawing room, drinking tea. The grandmother clock in the corner had just struck four. Only the young men had any stomach for the shortbread, Victoria sandwich and plum cake on the three-tiered, doilied, mahogany cake stand. Andrew, especially, could eat any amount. Lily and Garnet had seen a difference in him after their year away: he had shot up another couple of inches to stand well over six feet, almost as tall as Sergei, and his shoulders had broadened. He had an open countenance, was popular with young and old alike. The twins were very fond of their brother; they'd been two years old when he was born and had treated him like a doll. By the time Effie had come along, babies had lost their novelty.

Their father sat slumped in the high wing chair beside the hot fire, looking as if he might be about to slide into a long sleep. His eyelids kept alternately sinking and fluttering up with alarm, and then sinking again, and from time to time he emitted the odd grunt. Effie's Hamish was holding the floor, telling them how good his mother's plum cake was. The secret lay in flouring the cherries beforehand, to make sure they didn't sink. Glacé cherries tended to be moist and heavy. Was that so? said Jemima, and he had the grace to blush. He was not a bad young man, really.

The baby boy twins were also present. Alex was sitting on his grandmother's knee, trying to grab her pearls, but missing, for he was not yet of an age when he could co-ordinate his eye and hand movements. Luke was reclining on his Auntie Garnet's rose-silk knee, staring up at her face with total fascination. His gaze was amazingly steady. He did not blink even when she swung her earrings at him.

'He looks hypnotised!' said Andrew.

'Perhaps he's wondering if Garnet's his mother!' said Rose, and then coughed, and her cheeks grew hot, and she looked down into her disturbed cup of tea. Oh, how dreadful of her! How could she have been so thoughtless? Would Andrew ever forgive her? If she had looked up she would have met the withering eye of her potential mother-in-law.

'So what did you think of the sermon this morning, Tom?' asked Alexander, who had been roused by a none-too-gentle poke from his wife's toe after he'd emitted a couple of rumbustious snores. 'Were you able to follow it?'

'I confess my mind wandered rather far from thoughts of God,' said Tomas, and his father-in-law laughed. Tom would always tell the truth, thought Lily, and was pleased about that, on the whole.

Luke had had enough of staring. He reached for Garnet's ruby-and-diamond-encrusted locket, given to her at Christmastime by Sergei, and sent it swinging between her breasts. Then his eye hit on her breast, with a sense of recognition, and he made a grab for the soft, rounded mound, his mouth opening wide like that of a baby bird.

Garnet eased his head to the side with a laugh and took his hands in hers. 'You're a little monkey, aren't you? Your mother's going to have her hands full with you.' She was becoming fond of this baby, and had told Lily so, and Lily had said she was glad, for, after all, Garnet was his aunt. Garnet brought Luke's hands up in the air, so that the ten tiny fingers were displayed. And it was then that she noticed his funny little one.

'It's like yours, Seryozha!'

'So it is.' Sergei crossed the room to come and look. He crouched down in front of Garnet and took Luke's left hand in his.

'It's not uncommon,' said Jemima, whose instinct told her to say so, though she did not fully understand why. She had never known anyone but her Russian son-in-law to have a crooked pinkie. She glanced at Lily, who by now was up on her feet at the sideboard dispensing tea, her back to the room.

The moment at the wedding reception, when she had intercepted a shared look between Lily and Sergei, returned to
her.

Garnet seemed not to attach any importance to the matter
of the pinkie, other than being rather amused by it. Only two
people were left dwelling on the oddity: the baby's grandmother and Garnet's husband.

'Don't be silly, Seryozha,' said Lily. 'How could he be your
child? They're twins. And Alex is very like Tom, you can see
that for yourself, except that he has my dark hair, though
that may lighten.' She waited for a bus to pass, then bumped
the pram down the kerb and walked smartly to the other side
of the road, followed by Sergei. She had known he would try
to get her on her own, had watched him awaiting his chance,
and done her best to avoid him. But today Garnet had gone
to the dentist, Mara was having a day off, and the twins had
needed a walk, for they didn't want to settle and were making a racket, and their grandmother was having some ladies
to luncheon. Lily had thought Seryozha had gone downtown
with Tom.

'But they're not identical twins,' persisted Sergei.

'Whoever heard of—?' Lily broke off and tried to walk
faster, but that was difficult with the pram being so heavy,
and they were on a slight incline, going up, which was making her puff. *Whoever heard of two different men fathering one set
of twins?* she had been about to say. She was perspiring heavily, could feel the curls damp around her face. She took off
her hat and laid it on top of the pram cover.

'Let me help you with that,' said Sergei, and he took the
pram from her.

'Men don't push prams, not in Scotland!' said Lily, hasten-
ing to keep up. 'Or in Russia either, I wouldn't think.'

'Why not? My arms are stronger than yours. I am going to
lower these sunshades. I want to see their faces. It is nonsense to keep all sunshine from them. You must let its rays
bless them. It's not as if it were hot, like the south of Italy.

111

How could you burn in the spring sun of Aberdeen?'

Lily conceded that it was unlikely, and the twins did seem to like the light. They stopped their girning and looked about them. Sergei raised their blue satin pillows and propped them up.

'Now you can have a better view of the world, you two young men. You can look at all the people in the street who want to admire you and you can watch the birds and see the trees waving their branches to you.'

Alex was happy to look at the birds and the trees, but Luke wanted to stare only at Sergei. He was facing Sergei; Alex had his back to the handles.

'Luke is a great one for staring at people,' said Lily nervously. She felt exceedingly nervous, and vulnerable, with Seryozha in control of the pram. For with that he seemed to have gained control of her too. It would be impossible for her to wrench the pram away from him. A scene could result, in the middle of the street, with goodness knows which friend of her mother's or father's looking on. And Seryozha would not shy away from a scene. She was having almost to run to keep up with his long strides. The twins were enjoying the speedier transportation and the way their vehicle bounced on its springs.

'Let us go into the park,' said Sergei, turning in through the gate without waiting for an answer. 'All boys love parks, isn't that so?'

Luke smiled back at him, a seductive smile, as the smiles of all three-month-old babies are, and guaranteed to raise a tender response. Lily for once wished that Luke would open his mouth and bawl as if the pin of his napkin were piercing the most private of his parts. Now he was gurgling. Sergei leant forward, took the bib that was lying on the pram cover and gently wiped the dribble from his mouth.

'He knows me,' he said softly. 'He recognises me as his father!'

'Nonsense!' cried Lily. 'He smiles at *anyone* who smiles at him. He wouldn't stop grinning at the street scaffie yesterday.

Or the window cleaner this morning. His eyes followed the man everywhere.'

'That was because the man was making the glass shine. But I am only *looking* at him – my own son.'

'Seryozha, he is not your son!' Lily remembered Sergei's suggestion in Venice, on the path beside the shadow canal, that they run away together, there and then, just like that, without extra clothes, money, anywhere to go. She wondered if he were capable of another extreme thought. But he would not try to kidnap the baby, surely he would not! Or tell Garnet or Tom?

'I think we should turn back,' said Lily.

'Why don't we sit on this seat for a few minutes?' Sergei parked the pram in front of the bench and put on the brake. 'You see how easily I handle it. I could be a nursemaid!'

Lily sat down. Her legs felt as if they were filled with sand.

Sergei seated himself beside her, allowing his shoulder to touch hers. Then his hand travelled sideways, seeking her hand.

'No, Seryozha!'

The twins were not pleased either by this turn of events. They had enjoyed the rough ride; sitting still was not nearly so much fun. Alex was merely frowning but Luke was squalling and growing rapidly red in the face.

'I had better lift him up,' said Sergei, and without waiting for permission he leant forward and undid the harness that restrained the child. He swung the delighted baby high up in the air, holding him for a moment against the blue and white sky, before bringing him down to land on his lap. 'You liked that, didn't you? Yes, you did!' He jiggled the baby expertly on his knee, as if it came naturally, and he supported the back of the floppy head with his hand. He looked sideways at the child's mother. 'You know I still love you, Lily.'

'No, I don't. And you don't. And I don't want to hear it. You love Garnet, I know you do. I've seen you with her, you're very tender and affectionate with her.'

'A man should be tender with a woman. But yes, I do love

113

her, that is true. She is my wife. But that does not stop me loving you, too.'

Lily is confused. She has grown up to believe that a man or a woman can love only one person at a time, that love is exclusive, cutting out all others. How can Seryozha love both her and Garnet? If his sisters were here they would be able to tell her that Seryozha has a great capacity for falling in love, that he is a romantic, and even when indulging in an affair that some might consider sordid he has to believe himself in love. Or would they be undervaluing what he feels for Lily, for they cannot possibly know all the intricacies of their brother's feelings? And there is another factor in the picture now: man and woman on park bench, with child.

Lily is less confused about her own feelings. She loves Tom, she came to that conclusion some time ago, for he is a lovable man, and already she cannot imagine how it would be to live without him, but Seryozha still holds an attraction for her, and that is undeniable. It is a form of animal magnetism, she has decided, an allure to be firmly resisted. She cannot ever lose her head again as she did on the night before her wedding.

After a few minutes Luke wanted his mother. He was hungry and knew how to make his wants understood. He arched his back and thrashed his arms and legs.

'He feels like a killer whale,' said Sergei, helping him to reach his mother's lap. 'What have I fathered?'

Such talk disturbed Lily. She implored Sergei to desist. 'I keep telling you that you cannot *possibly* be his father.'

'You had better feed him,' advised Sergei. 'He might have a convulsion.'

'I can't, not out here, in the open! It's not done.'

'Well, do it.'

'People might see.'

'There's no one around. And I shall put myself in front of you and protect you.'

'But— ' She had not fed the children in front of any man

114

other than Tom, not even her own father, who would be embarrassed. Women withdrew to a private room to feed their children.

'Hurry up!' said Sergei. 'He's getting into such a rage.'

Luke was burrowing under Lily's short cape and trying to tear the buttons off her bodice. She had to comply. Luke grasped the nipple greedily and began to suck.

'No wonder he is hungry for that,' murmured Sergei, his head close to Lily's, his hand curled around the baby's face, the tips of his fingers resting on the globe of Lily's breast. She felt a shiver right down into the depths of her body.

'People will see,' she said again.

'I have my back to the world,' said Sergei, and did not move.

Jemima McKenzie was showing out the last of her luncheon guests when Effie arrived home. The girl was flushed – she seemed to have been running – and she was agitated.

'Whatever's the matter, child?'

'I was coming through the park with Bella—'

'Did you see something unpleasant?'

'Well, yes, Mother, I did!'

'A man? Was he doing something he should not? I've always told you not to walk too close to the bushes unless you have Hamish or Andrew with you. Come into the morning room and calm down.'

Effie subsided into a chair in the cool back room. Her mother closed the door.

'Now tell me everything that happened, Effie.'

'Well, nothing much *happened*. It was just that Bella and I were cutting through the park – Bella had to get home for her music lesson and Mr Phipps is always annoyed when she's late—'

'Yes, yes, we know Mr Phipps! But what then?'

'We saw the pram.'

'The pram?'

'Yes, the big black one. The twins' pram. It was parked

beside a bench. I recognised it at once because it was double.'

'And Lily? Where was Lily?'

'On the seat.'

'I'm sorry, Effie, but I can't quite follow you. What was so strange— ?'

'Seryozha was with her.'

'I see.' Jemima went to the window and tried to straighten the blind. It was hanging halfway down, and lopsidedly. She must speak to Fraser, their general handyman, about it. 'Well, there's nothing so extraordinary in that. Not enough to make you run all the way home and get yourself in a lather. Seryozha is Lily's brother-in-law.'

'But she was feeding one of the babies. *Outside*. In the *open*. They didn't see us. Seryozha was *watching*, Mother. I mean, *really* watching. He seemed *fascinated*.'

Jemima gave the blind a last irritable tug, upon which it unwound totally, obscuring the window and making the room dim. 'I can understand you thinking it all rather odd, Effie, but you must remember that Tom and Seryozha are foreigners, with foreign ways, which perhaps you and I cannot understand or would not want to adopt for ourselves. It is different for Lily and Garnet; they must adapt. You remember I told you how in Livonia four of us ladies went for a steam bath together, and the others – all but myself, that is – stripped themselves naked.'

'I'm glad I'm not marrying a foreigner,' said Effie.

'You see, men are different in Russia,' Effie told Bella. 'They have different ideas about the body. And children. Seryozha absolutely dotes on children – he's never out of the nursery. I dare say that's why the other day we saw, well, you know . . . what we saw. Mother says one should read nothing into it. Not many men here would spend hours in a nursery playing with babies, shaking rattles at them and talking to them in baby language. I mean, the child's father might spend some time, but not as much as *that*. And also, Mother said, Seryozha might be feeling the loss of his baby very much but hasn't been able to say so, because everyone has been so con-centrated on Garnet. Anyway, Seryozha and Tom leave the day after tomorrow. They're travelling from Leith to Helsinki together, and then they'll separate. They only came for a month, they've got to get back for their work. Lily and Garnet are to stay another month. Mother thinks it'll be good for them to have some time together on their own without their husbands around. I would hate to be parted from my husband for a month, wouldn't you? I should *pine* if Hamish and I were ever to be separated for even one night.' And Effie blushed at the thought of *spending* a night with Hamish.

Lily was on tenterhooks right until the moment the men were due to depart from Aberdeen on their journey home. She was exhausted from trying to avoid Sergei. He would wait for her round corners, jump out of doorways when she was coming along the corridor, sit beside her in a crowded room and whisper to her. He was so reckless! 'People will talk!' Telling him so made little difference. He had not tried to make love to her, not *fully*, but he wanted to talk to her and look at her and touch her. He touched most people, male or female, when he spoke to them, so no one had thought that unduly odd, not now that they were used to his ways. Unless her mother . . . ? Lily was not sure what her mother was thinking. It was often said that Jemima McKenzie had second sight. Jemima herself said it was mere common sense but-tressed by some keen observation and a knowledge of human nature.

Lily and Garnet went with their husbands to Union Street station. Lily had said maybe she should stay at home with the twins, but her mother had said, nonsense, she and Mara were more than capable of keeping those two laddies in check, and she, Lily, would not be seeing her husband again for a month. 'He needs a proper send-off!'

The train was already at the platform when they arrived. The men put their luggage on board.

'A month seems so long,' said Garnet, whose spirits had

drooped again on setting foot in the station. She wished she were going with Seryozha, yet on the other hand she wanted to stay, so that she could see more of her mother and father and old friends, and of Lily.

Lily was less troubled about the length of the separation, for she knew, since having the babies, that a month was no time at all, and would soon fly past. Perhaps too fast, and bring with it the next parting. Another home-leaving. She and Garnet were both agreed that this still felt like home, and when they contemplated Riga and St Petersburg those cities appeared as shimmering mirages set in water. They had reorientated themselves amazingly quickly in Aberdeen, confirming their mother's belief that human beings are infinitely adaptable.

'That's that, then!' said Sergei, leaping down from the carriage step.

The engine was puffing steam.

'Five minutes,' said Tomas, taking out his watch.

The guard went past with his green flag.

'Hadn't you better get on board?' said Lily.

Tom turned to say goodbye to Garnet first, and Sergei came to Lily. He bent his head and kissed her full on the mouth. She felt herself begin to shake.

'Take care of my son, Lily,' he said softly, keeping hold of her shoulders, and for a moment she thought he was not going to let her go. A whistle pierced the hustle and noise around them.

'Seryozha!' said Tomas.

He and Lily had time to exchange only a quick kiss; the whistle was going again and the guard was holding up his flag.

The men leapt up the steps and Sergei slammed the carriage door. He pushed down the window. The train was moving. Sergei blew kisses through the open window with both hands. Lily held her breath. She would not put it past Seryozha to leap down from the train even as it was gathering speed and was thankful that Tom would be with him to make sure he embarked at Leith and didn't turn tail and head back up north.

*

Garnet and Lily had a last walk in the park.

'I don't know that I could cope with twins,' said Garnet. 'In spite of being a twin myself!'

Lily glanced at her sister, but could see her face only in profile. She knew their mother would think it healthy that Garnet had spoken so openly. It was the first time that she had.

'It is a lot of work,' admitted Lily. 'It's the feeding.'

'I wouldn't have fed them if it had been me.'

'You'd have put them on bottles?'

'I'd have given them to wet nurses. Don't look so shocked! You reminded me of Mother there. It's the custom in Russia – no one thinks anything of it. You can see flocks of them out with the babies in Petersburg. They wear national costume, blue if their charge is a boy, pink if it's a girl, and a white mantle with silver tassels and a white cap shaped like a diadem decorated with imitation pearls and silver.'

'I couldn't imagine that catching on in Aberdeen,' said Lily, which made them laugh. 'But I'll have Morag when I get back.'

Her mother had decided she could be doing with another pair of hands. And what better than a Scottish pair? Also, it would be good for her to have someone to talk to in her own tongue while she was waiting for Tom to come back from work. Jemima had found a strong-looking girl from Stromness, the eldest of a fisher family of eight, reputed to be good with children, firm, but not unkind. Morag was to return to Riga with Lily and Tomas was to look for a larger apartment.

'Lily,' said Garnet, 'I think I may be pregnant again.'

'That's wonderful! Seryozha will be thrilled.'

'Yes, I rather think he will. I've never seen a man so fond of children. It was amazing how he took to your two.'

In the last few days Lily had also begun to suspect – fear – that she might be pregnant. She said nothing about that now, in the hope that she might be mistaken. It would be too soon to have another child. Or children? She refused to allow the

119

thought admission.

'One thing,' said Garnet: 'I'm going to come back to Scotland to have this next baby. No more drunken Russian midwives for me!'

'What a kerfuffle it was getting them away!' said Effie to Bella. 'They had so much luggage. Garnet had all the stuff she'd bought in Paris – frocks by the rack-load and shoes by the bagful – and people had been giving Lily presents for the babies. Father said they looked like refugees with their thousands of boxes and bundles. We thought they might not get it all into the guard's van. I suppose the ship's hold will be bigger. It was a good job they had Morag as well as Mara to help them. In the end they had to leave a picture behind. It's by a French painter. Called Matisse, something like that. It's sort of greenish, a room, with red curtains, and a woman sitting at a table. I'm not sure if I like it or not. It's different. I think I prefer Renoir. Father seems to like it, though. He said he'd hang it in his study in the meanwhile. Until they next come back.'

St Petersburg

August 1914

They began to gather at first light. By noon the sun beat fiercely down and the vast square was filled with people. The men carried banners and the women pictures of the Tsar.

'I don't know that I should have brought you,' said Leo.

'Why not?' said Garnet. 'I might be foreign, but I'm not *German*.' She felt excited. The mood of the crowd was touching her.

'Stay close, don't lose me.'

The men were punching the air with their fists and calling down curses on the heads of all Germans, everywhere. It was like an infection running through the square.

'God,' said Leo, 'such fervour! I've never seen it before, for anything.'

Something was happening up on the balcony of the Winter Palace. The crowd quietened.

'Here comes the Tsar!' said Leo.

At the appearance of the Emperor the people sank to their knees in their tens of thousands, going down in wave after wave as if a giant tidal bore were pushing them over. Garnet glanced uncertainly at Leo and then they, too, knelt. She knew it would go against Leo's inclination – he always said, mockingly, that he was a bystander in life – but in the midst of so many it would be impossible to stand out. Did he mind

121

playing the role of onlooker? Was he being serious when he claimed it for himself? She found it difficult to judge at times if he were being flippant. She did with all of them, even Seryozha. A lot of their talk appeared on the surface to be idle, but one sensed that underneath they actually meant what they were saying.

The crowd was gazing expectantly upward, at their sovereign, the Tsar of all the Russias. He looked small and lost raised high above them on the balcony of the vast building. Was the Little Father suddenly going to show himself to be strong and full of purpose? He had no option, murmured Leo. Poor man, said Garnet. And now here came the Empress with her hands shrouding her face. All eyes had swivelled to rest on her. What was *she* thinking about this turn of events? Were her shoulders shaking? Was she weeping behind her hands? What was Rasputin saying? Did he want to appease the Germans? The Empress was German by birth, don't forget that! Blood will out. The murmurs swelled to a soft crescendo.

Leo and Garnet returned home along the Embankment with the clamour of the crowd and the refrains of the National Anthem ringing in their ears.

> *God protect the Tsar!*
> *Powerful and sovereign . . .*
> *Reign to the terror of our enemies . . .*

'I doubt if your enemies will be so easily terrorised,' said Leo.

Dolly was loitering in the entrance hall. 'The countess has been waiting for you!'

The countess was desultorily playing patience. Her hair looked damp against her head. It was very hot in the room. She tossed aside her cards.

'You've been an age.'

'The crowds were huge,' said Garnet.

122

'You look *un peu échevelée.*'

'We're at war!' said Leo.

'May God be with us!' The countess made the sign of the cross over the sloping shelf of her bosom. 'I hope my Seryozha won't have to go and fight.' She mopped her brow. 'Was it a moving sight, out there on the square? How I wish I could have come with you but my poor legs would not take me.'

'The people actually want this war,' said Leo. 'More fools them! They think they're going to achieve glory.'

'Come, come, Leo Konstantinovich! What is wrong with glory? They want to defend our great country. Surely that is a noble aspiration? We Russians are good patriots. What about your country, Garnet Alexandrovna? What is it going to do?'

'Britain is expected to come in with us and France,' said Leo, 'though it's dragging its heels.'

'I'm glad to hear that. That it comes with us. I don't know about its heels. But it would be bad show if your country was to take the opposite end from ours, would it not, Garnet Alexandrovna?'

The door opened to admit the count. He was smiling.

'Good news eh? Have you heard?'

'You think it's good?' asked Leo.

'Absolutely! A short sharp knock is what those devils need. They've been annoying us for far too long. Taunting us. Trying to encroach on our industrial markets. It's a matter of honour, too.'

'No doubt the motives of all the governments involved are complex.'

'We must be bigger than them,' put in the countess.

'We've got nearly a million and a half men in our standing army,' said the count. 'Fully mobilised, we should be able to field five million. What other country could do that?'

'I always thought there were a lot of Chinese,' said the countess.

The count ignored that remark.

123

Having a lot of men was all very well, said Leo, but what were they to use for arms? 'We're desperately short of artillery and our transport system is pathetic, you've got to admit that, Count.'

'I admit nothing! Such talk is unpatriotic, Leo. Where do you get your information from? Your fellow poets? That Gorky chap has some pretty extreme views.' The Count laughed to show he bore neither Gorky nor Leo any illwill. 'No, we are well equipped. And our peasants are patient men; they will make good soldiers. They've proved before that they can endure.'

'I hope Seryozha won't have to go,' said the countess again.

'Highly unlikely. The reservists will be called first, if they're needed. It'll all be over before they get round to mobilising untrained men like Seryozha.'

Garnet was thankful for that. Seryozha, as a student and an only son, had been exempted from military service. It was easy, it seemed, for those who belonged to the upper eche-lons of society to gain exemption. Garnet recognised that as unfair, since her upbringing had taught her to, but she was still grateful that her husband wouldn't have to go and fight the Germans. It was only human nature to want to preserve one's own! (It was her mother she was talking to in her head.) Nor would Leo have to go, she presumed, on account of his lameness. But what about Andrew back home? He was a fit young man. And Effie's fiancé Hamish? Oh, this was ter-rible, all of this happening, when life was beginning to look more settled, and she had another baby on the way. Unless the war were to end very quickly she wouldn't be able to go over to Aberdeen for the birth.

'I think perhaps we need some tea to settle us,' said the countess. 'And perhaps a little gâteau would be *une bonne idée*. Will you ring, Leo?'

'It's champagne that we need,' said the count, 'not tea. We have something to celebrate. Kiril, fetch up a couple of bot-tles of Moët et Chandon. And watch you don't drop them!'

While waiting for the old retainer to bring the champagne the count said, in an aside to Leo, 'One good thing about a war is that it should put an end to all that revolution business. Most of them will be sent to the front with a bit of luck. There'll be other ways for them to work off their energy.'

It seemed that the count was right. Strikes and demonstrations against the government were abandoned. The people now had a common purpose, something to strive for. The defeat of the enemy. The glory of Russia. Even the literary establishment was gripped by patriotic frenzy, Leo reported. Optimism ran high. The Tsar appointed as Commander-in-Chief of the forces his uncle, Grand Duke Nikolai Nikolaevich, a man disliked by both Rasputin and the Empress, who thought he had designs on the throne. The Tsar and the sickly Tsarevich donned military uniform. The Empress and her two elder daughters, Olga and Tatiana, became Sisters of Mercy and went about with white wimples on their heads and red crosses on their chests. Women gathered to knit socks for soldiers and sewed nightshirts for them to wear when they would be wounded. Hospitals geared themselves up. Others were set up in *palazzi*. Soldiers drilled in the streets. Some of the Burnovs' servants were mobilised. Everyone had to be prepared to make sacrifices, said the count when his wife complained. Even Kiril deserted them. He died, of natural causes. His heart gave out. The state vodka shops were closed and the sale of alcohol prohibited in an effort to stamp out drunkenness. In spite of the prohibition, as is often the case, drinking continued unabated. Vodka gushed from illicit stills and *khanzka* was fermented from bread and commercial cleaning fluids. Hatred for Germany and everything German mounted, reaching peaks of hysteria. The Empress's German birth was not forgotten. Mobs attacked and pillaged German-owned city bakeries. Factories with German names were fired. The Tsar took the decision to take the 'burg' out of Petersburg and changed its name to Petrograd. It did not affect most of its citizens, who continued

125

to call it Peter, as they always had.

'Everything is changing,' lamented the countess from her sofa.

With the advent of war, Garnet found that invasions on her privacy lessened. People had other affairs to occupy them. Natalya and Elena came less often; they were organising the rolling of bandages for the Red Cross and helping out at the Anglo-Russian Hospital, where Garnet sometimes joined them. And twice a week women gathered at the Burnov Palace, in the dining room, to sew shirts for soldiers. The count had suggested it, said they should lead the way. The countess herself did not sew; this would not have been expected. She could not have seen sufficiently well, anyway, to thread a needle, and her fingers were too puffy to hold one. She reigned at the samovar, dispensed tea and sweet-meats, and tossed titbits of gossip into the group for them to nibble at. Garnet rather enjoyed these sewing bees, sitting in a circle with other women, their hands occupied, their tongues free to talk. They spoke of the war, it was impossible not to – the Russian army seemed to be making good progress on its advance into East Prussia, which cheered them, though they did not, in fact, feel despondent and were hopeful of an early, satisfactory resolution – but also of domestic and familial matters, such as children, servants, and the like.

Amongst the women Garnet made friends with an Irishwoman called Eithne, who was married to a banker, a Russian. Garnet ignored the count when he made remarks about bankers and merchants being the *nouveaux riches* in the city. 'At least they've been building like mad,' he said, 'which keeps people like Seryozha occupied.' Garnet had never been able to find out where the Burnovs got their money to live on. The count sat on a few boards but he was vague about their function and he usually returned from their meetings tipsy. According to Leo, the family estate near Orenburg in East Russia was dreadfully run down and had been mis-managed for years. The count had not paid it sufficient attention. Seryozha said when the war was over he was going to start taking an interest in it; perhaps it was time.

Garnet found she was tiring more quickly in this pregnancy and took refuge whenever possible in her sitting room, which she'd recently had refurbished. The heavy furniture had been replaced by a *chaise-longue* and easy chairs covered with apricot coloured velvet and she now had a desk of bamboo and mahogany, with shelves to match, on which she had arranged books and oriental vases and fans bought on the Nevsky. On the walls she had hung portraits of her Scottish family, her wedding photograph, the painting her father had given her of a woman in a red dress reflected in a mirror, some drawings of the Seine which she and Seryozha had purchased at the *bouquinistes*, and two ikons. The latter were *de rigueur* in any Russian room, and Garnet liked them, for their artistic rather than their religious value. She went reluctantly to worship at the Orthodox Church every week with the Burnovs. She had what she considered a natural aversion to kissing the crucifix after Mass; her Protestant blood rebelled against it. She barely brushed her lips against the cold cross, hating the idea of all the other mouths that had touched it, as she did with the communion cup. She was only twenty-two years old, so could not claim a lifetime of habit behind her, but firmly at her back were those serried ranks of Presbyterian forebears who would have gone to the stake rather than succumb. Her father's father had been a minister. She remembered his close-closeted Sabbath parlour where no book other than the Good Book might be opened and frivolity of any kind was frowned upon. Her father had rejected all that, would take a dram on Sunday as on any other day and read what he chose. She wouldn't even have minded going to the English Episcopal church of St Mary, only a few steps along the road, but that would upset the Burnovs. Religion permeated their lives every day, not just on Sundays, though not in a particularly pious way. It was simply part of their ritual. They crossed themselves in front of the ikons

127

when they came into a room, held prayers if someone was going on a journey, however short. Since the commencement of the war the crossing and praying had multiplied.

Leo had told her, in confidence, that he was an atheist, and she wondered if she might be moving that way herself. When she'd tried to discuss it with Seryozha he had laughed and said it was best to let sleeping wolves lie.

'We need our God, our Russian God. "Our God of potholes", as you like to refer to him! We need him now, especially. But remember there is another God, too, the God of singing and dancing and laughter.'

Garnet smiled to herself. That would always be Seryozha's deity: the God of pleasure. Pleasure here was not frowned upon, regarded as sinful, but accepted as *joie de vivre*.

She looked up as the door opened. Dolly poked her head in and asked if Garnet needed anything.

'Nothing, thanks, Dolly. I'll ring if I do.'

Dolly, instead of accepting that as a dismissal, crossed the threshold and hovered in a way that infuriated Garnet. She eyed the photographs on the wall and pointed to one of Andrew taken on the rugby field.

'Is that your brother? He's handsome. And looks strong. Is he a soldier?'

'He may soon be one, I fear.'

'Why should you fear it? It is noble to go and fight. Have you heard the latest news? We don't seem to be doing so well.'

'How do you mean?'

'On the front, in East Prussia.'

'You listen to too many rumours, Dolly.'

'If you say so, Madame,' said Dolly, and withdrew.

She had not long gone when Sergei came in looking gloomy. The Germans had counterattacked against General Samsonov's army and trapped it in a region of marshes and lakes. Seventy thousand Russian soldiers were reported killed or wounded, and a further hundred thousand had been taken prisoner.

Garnet again thought how glad she was that Seryozha hadn't had to go, and at the same time felt guilty that he should be standing here unscathed while others died.

'Samsonov has shot himself.' Sergei flung himself down on the *chaise-longue*. 'Play something for me, Garnet my love. I need soothing.'

She sat down at the piano. Seryozha had bought her a Bechstein, a baby grand. She'd been told not to mention the make of the piano outside the house – German pianos were being broken up with axes whenever pillagers could get their hands on them. She enjoyed the instrument. She played with competence, though fell a little short when it came to artistic interpretation, according to her old music teacher, Mr Phipps, who had not believed in mincing his words; whereas he'd said that Lily played less competently but with more feeling. Which was preferable? Sometimes Lily would get so carried away that she'd have to bring her fingers down on the keys and let them lie, her head bowed, admitting that she had lost her way. Garnet always made it through to the end.

Sergei had his hands linked behind his head and his eyes closed. What was he thinking about? Not General Samsonov or the poor soldiers going down under a hail of German bullets. A little smile was flirting around his mouth. Did he like her Chopin so much? How difficult it was to tell what was happening inside the mind of another person, even when one lived close to him, lay at night with one's thigh touching his, wakened in the morning to feel his breath on one's face.

When she'd finished he sat up, cried, '*Brava*!' and came to stand behind her. He massaged her shoulders and she let them arch into the rhythm of the movement. His hands slid below the neckline of her gown.

There came a swift tap on the door. It was Dolly again! The girl couldn't seem to stay away. Or else she didn't have enough to do. She stood in the doorway with her pert little head cocked to one side.

'Your mother is looking for you,' she said to Sergei. 'She heard you come in.'

129

'Tell her we're just coming down.' Sergei removed his hands and Garnet thought Dolly looked almost triumphant. She herself felt irritated, by the whole lot of them!

'So there you are!' The countess was petulant.

She was not alone. The count and Leo were in the salon drinking tea with another friend and discussing the news from the front. Father Paul was sitting beside the countess, watching her play patience. The game calmed her nerves, she said. Garnet had brought this set of cards from Aberdeen; their backs were patterned with the McKenzie tartan of dark green, with red and white overchecks. The countess liked the colours. She stroked the backs of the cards when she turned them over. The count and his friend, whose chest was larded with medals, were talking about Samsonov and agreeing he'd had to take his life. A matter of honour. And as for the casualties? Well, what else could you expect in war? Men fought and died. That was what it was all about. Father Paul crossed himself and his lips moved silently. It was fortunate Russia did have so many men to call on, said the count.

To be offered up as fodder for German cannons, thought Garnet, who could not put aside all the ideas of her parents. But she dared not voice her thought aloud.

'We're still doing well against the Austrians, though, aren't we?' said Sergei.

'Yes, we've broken through their front in Galicia,' said the count's friend.

'So all is not black,' said Sergei, visibly cheered.

'He always looks on the bright side, Garnet Alexandrovna,' said the countess. 'He never stays in doom and gloom. I hope the child in your womb will have as sunny a nature.'

'The Austrians should be easier to crush than the Germans,' said the friend.

'You know, I never did care for the Germans,' said the countess. 'Though I am sure, Father Paul, you are going to tell me they are all God's children! I can see that holy gleam in your eye. And I have to admit that we have had some *bonnes vacances* in the Black Forest in times past. I am rather fond of Heidelberg, too.' She turned over a red queen and laid it on top of a black king. The Queen of Hearts on the King of Clubs. What a perfect combination! She called upon Father Paul to admire it. 'They should have priests in these packs of cards. *Pourquoi pas*? You are part of society. What would you like to be, Father? The Priest of Clubs – *oui, c'est parfait*! It suits your shape, *n'est-ce pas*? I have cards for all of the members of the family. Garnet has the dark countenance of the Queen of Spades.' Then quickly she added, 'It is all right, Seryozha, I make only a joke!' Sergei had spun round, and was frowning at his mother. She said in a conciliatory voice, 'You can be the Queen of Clubs, Garnet Alexandrovna. It matters not that your shape is not right.'

Garnet knew her mother-in-law loved the red cards best.

'And what am I, Mother?' asked Sergei.

'Why, the Knave of Hearts! What else could you be?'

'And Leo?'

They looked over at Leo, who was standing by the window. He had his back to the room and was looking out into the street.

'Leo is the secretive one, aren't you, Leo Konstantinovich? I can see you only as the Knave of Spades.'

Later, Garnet asked Sergei why he'd been so annoyed at his mother comparing her to the Queen of Spades. 'I realised, of course, it wasn't meant as a compliment.'

'It was nothing,' he said offhandedly. 'Mother can be a little silly at times, but she doesn't mean any harm. You mustn't let it bother you.'

Next day, Garnet was shopping in Wilkins Bookshop, buying novels by Arnold Bennett and H. G. Wells, when she saw a volume of Pushkin's stories in English. Flipping through it she saw that one was entitled 'The Queen of Spades'. The quote prefacing it ran: 'The Queen of Spades means secret hostility.' She bought the book.

She sat down to read the story as soon as she returned.

131

'They were playing cards at the house of Narumov, an officer in the Horse Guards . . .' Had the lives of Russian men not changed *at all*? Garnet read on, wanting to know more about these men. A tale of male greed and treachery unfolded, and female gullibility. But the bounder got his comeuppance in the end, when he played the Queen of Spades, and the rather insipid heroine married someone suitable.

Garnet took one of Sergei's packs of cards from the drawer, an old pack, bought in Italy. The backs were decorated with the arms of the Duke of Modena. She riffled through the cards until she found the Queen of Spades. She laid it face upward on the table in front of her.

Dolly arrived just then to draw the curtains and see to the stove. She stopped when she saw the card lying on the table and her eyes fluttered from it to Garnet. Then she simulated spitting very rapidly three times over her left shoulder.

'And what's all that for, Dolly?'

'To ward off the devil.'

'Is *she* the devil? I know the Queen of Spades is not supposed to be lucky, but that doesn't bother me.' Garnet felt protected by her rational upbringing.

'But she's the *death* card, Madame!'

Riga

July 1993

'My father was pleased he was born in St Petersburg,' said Lydia. 'Or Petrograd, as it was then. His mother had wanted him to be born in Scotland. But it was not to be.'

They were on their way to Elisabeth Street, where Tom and Lily had lived as newlyweds, in four ground-floor rooms. Curtains were drawn at all the windows, looking as if they had been snatched hastily across. No amount of knocking raised any response. It was possible that all the inhabitants were at work, or didn't open their door to strangers.

They proceeded then to Albert Street, a few minutes' walk away, where Tomas had rented a larger, first-floor flat in an Art Nouveau building (with overtones of Classical Romanticism, as he'd explained to Lily), on his return from Aberdeen in 1914. The front door, of ornately carved oak, was set in carved stone surrounds, and had brass curvilinear handles and prominent brass hinges. The wood was scuffed and the brass in need of polishing. The door gave at a touch.

The hallway and staircase would once have been splendid. Not a sound was to be heard but the steady tap of their feet as they went up.

Several postcards were affixed to the door on the first landing. Each card bore a name.

Katrina knocked.

Nothing happened for a few moments, then a muffled voice behind the door asked, 'Who is that?'

'My name is Katrina Zale.' Katrina spoke loudly and her voice echoed in the stairwell. 'I am from Scotland. My grandmother used to live here, a long time ago.'

'Put your visiting card through the letter box,' urged Lydia.

Katrina fumbled in her wallet and found one, bent and dog-eared. She pushed it through the slot.

They waited.

The door opened part way to reveal an old woman with a face as wrinkled as a winter walnut. Her knobbly fingers kept a grip on the door's edge.

'This is my cousin Lydia Burnova,' said Katrina. 'Do you think it would be possible for us to have a look at the flat? We would be most grateful.' She wondered about offering a financial inducement, but decided not to.

The woman looked uncertain; she studied them, then she nodded and opened the door fully. They entered into a spacious hallway that someone had painted clay-red a long time ago. Strands of paper hung from the ceiling.

'I have only one room. That is all I can show you.'

They followed her to a door at the end of the hall. 'Go in, go in, please! I will fetch some refreshments from the kitchen.'

Katrina began to protest that really it was not necessary, they had come only to look, but the woman was already going, shuffling in loose slippers.

They crossed the threshold of the room and stopped, their eye arrested by a painting on the side wall.

'Surely that's a Cadell!' said Lydia.

It was unmistakable. They didn't have to go up close to read the signature, though they did, since they could scarcely believe what they saw. The painting was of a woman in a pale-lilac dress and black hat leaning against a mantelpiece, with a mirror behind.

Then Lydia said, 'Look!'

On the adjacent wall a framed photograph of a very familiar

134

looking building stared back at them.

'Our house in Queen's Road!' said Katrina.

'I feel spooked,' said Lydia.

The photograph was faded, and the trees in front of the house, which they knew to be bushy and full, were mere saplings.

They heard the rattling of glasses and Katrina went to help their hostess with her tray. Set upon it was an elegant decanter and three small matching glasses.

'This photograph?' said Katrina.

'It has been there a long time,' said the woman, busying herself laying glasses on a small bentwood table. Was it not of a Thonet design? There was also a larger bentwood table with four chairs. The rest of the furniture looked cheap and chipped. The bed in the corner was roped off by a line of washing.

The room was large and well-proportioned, and light, served by two casement windows and a glazed door set between them opening on to a small balcony. The floriated plasterwork on the ceiling was almost indiscernible under its thick covering of grime.

The woman poured the wine, handling the decanter clumsily but tenderly, and using both hands.

They raised their glasses. '*Prosit*!'

Lydia flicked her finger lightly against her glass. It pinged delicately. 'Crystal,' she murmured. 'Edinburgh, I could swear.' She smiled at the woman.

Katrina conversed with the old woman, who was willing to tell a little about her life. She was vague about time and details – no, she couldn't remember when she had come to live here – and she went off into spells of mumbling, when she appeared to be talking to herself. She had once had a husband and two sons. One son was good, the other not so. She inferred that he might be up to no good at all. He might be involved in car theft. 'The Mafia!' She looked up at Katrina with rheumy eyes, surprised to see her there. She said no more about the sons. And no, she had never met the Zales, had never heard of them. She kept herself to herself, inasmuch as she could, sharing the flat with four other families. Some of them were dirty. So her life had been a struggle, like everybody else's in this country, but she was happy now that Latvia was free. Not that it did much for her pocket, she added. And the streets were no longer safe.

They gave her presents from their bag – soap, English tea, tights – and then, thanking her, they rose to go.

On the way out, Katrina stopped in front of the painting of the woman in the lilac dress.

'That is a very beautiful picture,' she said.

It was an heirloom, said the woman, looking away.

Riga

April 1915

In the post that morning there were two letters, one with a British stamp, bearing the head of King George V, the other Russian, displaying Tsar Nikolai. Morag had brought them in and laid them on the desk in front of Lily and was standing to the side, her hands clasped in front of her, watching her mistress, who seemed to be a long way away. She sometimes was like this, had been more so since the birth of the last baby. It was the sight of the envelopes that had affected her. She'd be missing her own folk, Morag supposed. Especially her twin. Her other half. Once the mistress had turned and called *her* Garnet! And then had become confused. Morag herself spent little time missing anything; it was not in her nature. This was fortunate, since Riga was a long way from Orkney, and the seas between were patrolled by German submarines and men-at-war. The war did not disturb her much, either. Wars were the concern of men, she told Mara, who was more anxious about it, having two brothers at the front. Morag was not certain where her brothers would be, so did not worry about them. In her family they communicated by letter only at New Year, when cards were sent saying, 'Hope you are keeping well. We are not too bad, except that the catch has been not so good/poor/very poor.' All her siblings had been to school, could read and write, though it

137

was always the women who wrote.

So Morag, instead of pining for what could not be, got on with the job on hand, which for the most part was controlling the two boys. In the evenings she and Mara sat in the room they shared and drank tea and conversed in snatches of Latvian and Scots, each teaching the other words and phrases in her native tongue. They knitted white cotton socks for wounded soldiers. They were both expert knitters, having learned at their mothers' elbows. Mara kept her needles tucked underneath her arms; Morag held hers above. Such customs in countries vary for even the simplest task. (Though some might say that knitting is not that simple.) The girls argued about which manner was correct, which produced the better tension; neither would give way. It was never a serious dispute.

Now that the evenings were beginning to lengthen they would sometimes abandon their knitting, stick feathers in their hats and take a turn, strolling, arm in arm, along the dusky boulevards. Eyeing soldiers, said Veronika, who had seen them. And why should they not? She was not censoring them.

Morag cleared her throat to get her mistress's attention. She couldn't hang about all day. Dithering around like this would never get clean peenies on the weenies! (It was a phrase she'd taught Mara.) 'I'm off to the mairket, Mam, with Mara. To see what's going. The queues are getting to be gey long. We'll buy meat if we can get hold of it, will we?'

'Meat? Oh yes. Do your best, Morag.'

'We'll be taking the boys with us so ye'll nae need to fash yersel' wi' them.'

Morag went through to the kitchen to tell Mara that their mistress was away with the fairies this morning, which somewhat alarmed Mara.

Lily was distracted, had been since leaving her bed at seven to attend to the baby, and felt too nervous to open the letters, in case they should contain bad news. Letters often did these days. Tomas had risen with her and talked to her while he dressed and the baby fed. She liked this little time in the day they had together, with the baby at peace, and the house quiet. As soon as they went into the dining room the twins would be on top of them.

'I wish I'd sent you and the children to Aberdeen when we entered the war.' Tomas had his back to her but she could see his face in the mirror as he fastened his tie, grimacing slightly, not pleased with the lie of the knot. He liked things to be right.

'It looks fine,' she said, adding, 'I wouldn't have gone – to Aberdeen!'

'But the Germans are pressing us, love.' He turned. 'Hard! You know that! Or haven't you been listening? Sorry, I didn't mean to scold! But can't you understand why I feel anxious? They're only twenty-five miles to the south! There's a big battle raging for Jelgava.'

'You don't think they could take Riga, do you?' Lily could not quite conceive of living in a place that might be overrun and occupied by enemy soldiers.

'They could. They could be here in a day.'

'A *day*?'

'They could if our lines collapsed. We're running short of artillery. The Germans are better equipped. I keep thinking I should join up, Lily.'

She was silent then. She didn't want Tom to go to war – what woman would want her man to put himself in the line of enemy bullets? – yet she knew that if it came to defending them and the city of Riga he would have to put on a uniform and do what he could.

'But you're in the War Ministry.' Building, of course, had ceased. Tomas had laid down his drafting pens and covered up his drawing board.

'Doing a paper job. Lily, I want you and the children to go and stay with Mother and Father at Cesis. Don't argue, please! Half the population of Riga has left already. The boys will love being in the country.'

'They'll probably fall in the duck pond,' said Lily, trying to make a joke, though she felt little like laughing.

'Tell Mara and Morag to start packing.' Tomas kissed Lily and left the house without eating breakfast.

When she finished feeding the baby she took out a map. Jelgava did look terribly close. It had been the old ducal capital, had once rivalled Riga in importance. Tom had taken her there on a sunny day not long after she'd arrived in Riga. They'd looked at the castle, at other buildings (naturally), and walked around the town, and it had seemed to Lily like a sleepy backwater. It would not be sleeping now; its peace would be shattered by the boom of heavy artillery, the chatter of rifle fire and the screams of men. It was in the front line.

She went to the window to look out at the day and was in time to see a white funeral passing. Four white horses were pulling the hearse, and out in front walked four postilions garbed in long white coats, with white hats buckled at one side like highwaymen's. The sight set her shaking. Quickly she turned her back to the window. Afterwards, she wondered if she'd imagined the ghostly funeral. But there was no reason why she should have done. Funerals were regular occurrences in the city these days.

It had been a while since there had been mail from abroad. The last letter from Garnet had told of the safe arrival of her son Nikolai Sergeevich.

Lily opened the envelope with the Russian stamp first.

Garnet seemed cheerful, but then one tended to put on a good face when writing letters. Garnet didn't have much to say about the war; she'd have been concerned that her letter might be opened. She mentioned food shortages and said it was good that the weather at least was improving, so that people didn't have to stand in bread queues in the bitter cold or waken in the mornings with their eyelashes frozen to their cheeks. Fuel was terribly short. Lily presumed Garnet wouldn't have to queue for bread. The count's family must still be privileged, surely; they would be able to acquire extra food by some means or other, and the servants, though reduced in number, would do the shopping.

Sergei had joined the Tsar's entourage and was spending much of his time out at Tsarskoye Selo. Since the start of the war the royal family had been residing full-time at the Summer Palace. Garnet must be happy to know that Seryozha was there rather than at the front. The losses to the Russian army (which included soldiers from the Baltic provinces) had been appalling over the last few months. Well over a million men had been put out of commission, killed, wounded or taken prisoner. Fresh recruits were being called up weekly. 'To be ground up in the killing machine', as Veronika put it. Her friend Nils – he whom she'd talked about on a midsummer day whilst making floral headdresses – had gone to the eastern front.

Yesterday I went with my Irish friend Eithne at the British-Colony Hospital and we worked in the bandaging room. The Ambassador's daughter, Meriel, was there, too – we'd met before at one or two functions, though our paths do not cross too often. Petersburg society does not mix much with outsiders! We walked through the wards afterwards and saw some appalling sights. The stench was enough to turn your stomach over – the stench of sickness and of gangrene. Yet the soldiers seemed patient and accepting. I hope victory comes soon!

We've been entertaining soldiers in the house as another part of our war effort. They come to dinner or to tea. I don't know how much they enjoy it. I'm sure they must find the countess pretty overwhelming! They sit bolt upright on the brocade chairs with their cups rattling on their saucers and say hardly a word. She says it for them. She doesn't overwhelm me now as much as she used to. She's not a bad woman. Not evil.

But the pride and joy of my life is my little Nikolai! Or

141

Kolya, as we call him – his diminutive. He's a great consolation. And I have *not* given him to a wet nurse. I
couldn't bear to once I had him in my arms.

He is growing to look very like Seryozha, even has the
same bent pinkie! He reminds me of your Luke. How I
would love to see your boys again, and your new daughter. As soon as this war is over we must go home to
Aberdeen so that our children can get to know one
another.

Lily could hear her boys passing outside in the street with
Morag and Mara. They had lusty, carrying voices. Morag was
chivvying them, telling them to keep hold of her hand and
Mara's. She didn't want any of their nonsense! Alex was
quieter by disposition than his brother, would sit happily
with a book spread over his knees and look at the pictures, or
hold a pencil clumsily and scribble on paper – Tomas predicted he would be an architect.

Lily took up her mother's letter.

We wonder daily how everything is with you in Riga
and scan the newspapers for mention of the war in the
Baltic. You are so close to it all! It makes one realise
what a blessing it is to live surrounded by water.

I am keeping myself busy doing what I can to help
with the war effort, knitting mufflers and balaclavas in
khaki and Flying Corps blue. Women are being encouraged to leave their homes and go out to work! Lloyd
George has promised Mrs Pankhurst that they will be
paid like men for war work. Let us hope the policy will
be continued once the war is ended. The King is doing
his bit, too; he is setting an example to the workers by
giving up alcohol.

Lily smiled. Now came family news.

Andrew is being posted to France. Hamish has already

gone. Effie is in quite a state but I've told her she must try to be brave and not imagine the worst. I worry about her as well as you and Garnet! I have been trying to get her more involved with the Red Cross. She needs another interest apart from Hamish. Once you are a mother, worry becomes an integral part of your life. If marriage changes a woman, then motherhood most certainly effects an even bigger change. A conclusion you have no doubt come to yourself by this stage. I doubt if you appreciated beforehand how thoroughly you would be giving yourself up as a hostage to fortune.

Lily brushed her eyes with the back of her hand. She had not felt like this since the birth of Paula. As the baby had been placed in her arms she'd burst into tears and said, 'I want my mother,' and Tom, who a moment before had been smiling, delighted at the new addition to the family, had looked crestfallen, for he'd known that this was something he could not give her.

Veronika came in after school.

'What's going on?' she asked.

'We're packing,' said Lily. 'We're going to Cesis for a while.'

'Probably sensible. Though the news today is better, thank God. We appear to have won the battle for Jelgava!'

Mara, who was gathering up the children's clothes, cheered, then blushed.

'You're right, Mara, it is a cheering matter,' said Veronika. 'And we've had little to cheer about of late.'

Next week, they will hear that Mara's eighteen-year-old brother has been killed at Jelgava. She is fond of this brother; he is closest to her in age in the family, for she is seventeen. The other brother, aged twenty, will die the following month in the battle for Courland. But none of this does she know at present, and so she is cheering. Victory stirs the blood, brings a flush even to the faces of those who find war distasteful. All in the room are smiling, and the twins are bringing their pudgy hands together in a semblance of clapping. It is a moment of happiness in the house and the baby, waking to the excited sounds, gives a toothless grin, and crows.

Now that Jelgava had been saved, thought Lily, perhaps the tide had turned for their army.

A little hope raised the spirit immediately. Perhaps it wouldn't be necessary to leave Riga after all?

Veronika did not agree. 'One battle doesn't make a victory. Come on, let's go out for a while. Let's go and sit in a café and drink coffee!'

When they reached the main road they stopped to watch a military convoy pass. Some of the vehicles looked as if they'd been mired in mud up to their axles; others appeared to be on the verge of flying apart. Now came a line of open lorries packed with soldiers, their rifles bristling and glinting where the sun touched them. Raw recruits, judging from the freshness of their uniforms and the uneasiness in their eyes.

At least they all seemed to have rifles, commented Veronika. 'It might give them a chance, if not a particularly sporting one.' Some troops were reported to be fighting with their bare hands and had been told that, in the event of gas being used on the battlefield, they should protect themselves by urinating into their handkerchiefs. 'What does a man do if he doesn't own a handkerchief?' said Veronika.

They went to Reiner's Café on Sünder-Strasse in the old town. At a corner table sat Veronika's sister, Agita, with another woman. They waved to her and she gave them a nod in return.

'Do you want to go and speak to her?' asked Lily.

'No, let her come to us. If she wants to.'

They settled themselves, then ordered coffee and cake. The coffee, when it came, was dark and bitter, and tasted mostly of chicory, but they drank it nevertheless.

'Whose side is she on, anyway?' asked Lily. 'Isn't it odd for her? We're at war with Germany. She can't be pro German,

144

can she?'

Veronika shrugged. 'Why not?'

'But she'd have to keep quiet, wouldn't she?'

'Well, yes. Quite a few Balts have had bricks through their windows.'

At the beginning of the war Agita's husband, Herman, had taken off for Berlin, though many of the Balts had stayed. To guard their property, said Veronika. 'I dare say that's why Agita has remained behind. Herman has several houses and a lot of land, after all. That's what people fight for, Lily, not ideals.'

They ordered another pot of coffee. ('Let's be reckless!' said Veronika.)

When Agita was leaving she made a detour to come by their table. She inclined her head and stood, smiling faintly, looking down on them. She was a very beautiful woman, even Veronika had to admit that; she possessed classical features and wore her flaxen hair coiled into a smooth chignon. She dressed impeccably. Today she wore a grey-blue silk suit that matched her eyes and a wide-brimmed silk hat to match the suit. Her soft suede shoes must have been bought in Berlin or Milan. The war did not appear to have touched her.

'It's good news from Jelgava, isn't it?' said Veronika. 'Or perhaps you know it better under its German name of Mitau?'

'I haven't heard the news today.'

'We've routed the Germans.'

The smile did not fade. It looked as if it were pasted on, thought Lily. Agita asked after her children and Lily asked after Agita's.

'Lily's taking the children to Cesis,' said Veronika. 'What about you, Agita, are you staying put?'

'I see no reason why not.'

Agita sent her regards to Tom and their parents and excused herself.

'There are times when I can't believe she's my sister,' said Veronika. 'Most times. We've never been close. I feel closer to you, Lily, and you come from a country across the sea!'

145

Cesis, May 31

Dear Mother,

   I am writing to reassure you that we, the children and I, in spite of what news you might be hearing, are well.

Lily had no idea what they would be reading in the British press about the war in the Baltic. Would they know that there were German troops close to Riga? Fighting for possession of the Courland peninsula and control of the Baltic coast?

   We are living with Tom's parents here in the country, and you know how peaceful that is. Sitting in the garden under the elm tree, it is hard to imagine a war raging. Yet we know full well that it is. Mara has sadly lost two of her brothers, and Veronika's young man, Nils, has also been killed in battle. We heard only last week. Veronika has joined us, and we can only hope the country air and the peace and quiet will help mend both her grief and Mara's. Morag is wonderful, the tower of strength that you thought she would be. Tom has remained in Riga but comes to see us most weekends. I miss him.

At this point Lily sighed and put down her pen. It was difficult writing letters when there were so many restraints on what one could say and one didn't even know if the missive would reach its destination. It would have to traverse the treacherous waters of the Baltic before heading for the North Sea. And if the Germans did succeed in occupying the coast, then it might not be able to go at all, unless it travelled north by train to Reval or Petrograd. Would anyone in times like these bother to see that it was delivered?
   She could not tell her mother how afraid she felt when she lay in bed at night, alone, listening to the moan of the wind and the soft finger-like tap of a branch against her bedroom window. (Each night she'd resolve to tie it back in the morn-

ing.) The tap made her think of the Finger of Death. Could it be tapping for her? She'd think about Tom in Riga, with the German armies pushing steadily northward, towards him. (The victory at Jelgava had been short-lived.) She dared not open an atlas any more. If she did she might see little grey ants in hard helmets creeping up the page, swarming, over-running everything in sight, villages, towns, rivers, canals. Not a dot or line would be left uncovered. Her father-in-law feared the Germans looked set to take the Courland penin-sula. Refugees from Courland had been streaming through Cesis, in carts, a few in motorised vehicles, more on foot, on their way north. Some had stayed in the town; others camped in the fields. The townsfolk had taken as many as they could into their houses and barns. The Zale house was full, with Veronika and Lily and the children and Morag and Mara. It would be a case of trying to hold Riga next, said Markus Zale. No one expected the Russians to send more troops. They were having a tough enough time on the east-ern front.

Markus kept his rifle oiled and had shown Veronika and Lily how to handle his Mauser pistol. Veronika could shoot tin cans off a tree stump.

Lily had trembled when she'd felt the cold steel lying in her hands. She had not been able to hold the gun straight.

'No, no, Lily,' said her father-in-law, a patient man. 'Don't point it at the ground. You'll shoot yourself in the foot! Here, let me show you.' His steady hands guided hers. 'All right, we're going to fire it now. Only a blank, though.'

The vibration travelled up her arm, shocking her. Then it was her turn to do it alone. She braced herself, half closed her eyes, and fired.

'This time keep your eyes open,' said Markus.

He made her do it again, and again, until he was satisfied.

'I hope you'll never have to use it, Lily, but if you have to you'll know how.'

Lily wondered if her mother-in-law knew how to fire a gun. Gertrude remained serene, working in her garden, producing food and flowers. In the early mornings she took her little cylindrically shaped basket and went mushrooming, a favourite Latvian pastime, which had a tranquillising effect upon the nerves, Lily found. Gertrude said she might as well spend her time feeding the family, since she could do nothing about the war, other than pray. Everyone was praying. The churches in Cesis were packed on Sundays. People stood at the back, in the aisles. The wounded were propped up amongst them. Sobs could be heard in amongst the prayers. Lily wondered if God would listen to pleas to intercede for men who were stained with the blood of other men. The women on the other side must be praying also. Whom would He know to listen to? To deem right?

Nils had been killed on the eastern front, somewhere in Poland. It sounded so vague, yet was so definite. The Russian divisions had been short of ammunition, even of shoes. Tom had seen returning troops trudging through Riga in boots that were disintegrating as they walked, and some had been barefoot. Those who had lost a leg hirpled with the aid of rough-hewn staves.

Veronika had taken the news of Nils's death hard but calmly, as if she had always known it was going to be this way. She said her only regret was that she had not conceived his child; it would have been a fitting memorial for him.

Lily has been reflecting how sex seems often to result from heightened moods of all kinds (she knows this, after all, from personal experience), and not necessarily sensual. War isn't sensual. Or is it? She has heard of invading armies raping women. Everyone has. And the thought, of course, makes her shudder. When she was younger it puzzled her, this alliance of sexual and military plunder. She had thought the men would have more to do, for one thing, than pursue women, that they might even in their triumph feel protective of them.

She has discussed this with Veronika, who speaks openly of sex, using the plain unvarnished word. Lily and Garnet

148

always referred to the 'physical side of marriage'; all of their friends did. Or else 'making love', which is how Lily still prefers to think of it. For that is what it is, after all, when she and Tom are joined together. And when she was with Seryozha for those brief moments in the garden in Aberdeen? What was that? She prefers not to think of that, cannot afford to, and does not, except in odd moments when it comes upon her in a flash and she remembers the heady smell of the phlox and the night grass and the shape of Seryozha's head against the indigo-black sky. Of the *act* itself, she remembers nothing.

Veronika says in their discussions on men and sex in times of war – the German army *is* only a few days' march away – that victory in one area seems to arouse a need to be victorious in another. Though retreating armies also commit rape. Is it a form of release after the strain of battle? But it is more than that, for contained within it is the desire to inflict pain. After these discussions Lily dreams horribly and wakes in a sweat and has to get up and rinse her face and look out into the garden to make sure that no one – no enemy soldier – is lurking there, waiting to come and take the house and the women within. Veronika says if it comes to that she will use the Mauser.

On 28 July, the Baltischer Vertrauensrat, a body of Baltic nobles, sent a memorandum to the German Chancellor, requesting that when a peace settlement be drawn up the Baltic should be made a province of Germany. The nobles outlined their proposal: to bring a million and a half immigrants from small German colonies near the Volga, the Caucasus, and southern Russia, and settle them in the Baltic lands, and thus overwhelm the Russian and Latvian inhabitants.

Petrograd

August 1915

The war was going badly for Russia. The Tsar had to do something. He dismissed his uncle, the Grand Duke Nikolai Nikolaevich, and took command of the armed forces himself.

'That'll be about as much use as writing with a pitchfork on water!' said Leo. 'He lacks insight, our Little Father. He hasn't got what it takes.'

'What would it take?' asked the countess, who was still playing patience, though not the same game. *Her* patience did not extend that far.

'More arms! More transport! Shrewdness on his part. Experience. Ability to lead.'

'I know it's said he's unlucky because he was born on Job's name day, poor soul. But that should not necessarily be held against him.' The countess's tone was not convincing. No one was more superstitious than she. 'So he makes a mistake *de temps en temps*. We can all do that. I seem to have made one in this silly game!'

'Trouble is the Emperor's mistakes are costly.'

'The Grand Duke didn't know that much about strategy either, if all those reports from the front are to be believed. Are they, do you think? It is said we Russians rather like to exaggerate.'

'Not when it comes to casualties.'

'I do believe this game is not going to work out again!' The countess tossed the cards down on the table in disgust. Some slid to the floor, and she kicked one with her satin toe.

'There must be odds against the number of times it can work out. It's a game of chance, after all, not skill.'

'Odds, odds! I am fed up with odds. Where is Garnet Alexandrovna? She spends far too much time with that child. What does she have a nursemaid for?'

As she spoke, the door was pushed open and in came Garnet carrying young Kolya astride her hip. Like a peasant woman, her mother-in-law was thinking, and Garnet knew that, but did not care. She would carry her child as she pleased.

The baby was wriggling and arching his back towards the floor; he did not want to be carried and he could see much in the room that glinted and shone and tempted. Garnet set him down on the carpet.

'*Mon dieu*!' said his grandmother. 'I have never seen a child crawl like that – like a maniac! Not since Seryozha. He was just the same! I could never let him out of the nursery. He would have placed my salon upside down.' Her daughter-in-law was not going to take the hint; she was watching the child (which was just as well) as he flailed his way round the obstacle course of furniture like a high-speed crab.

Kolya had come to rest by the legs of the samovar table. He stared upward, his bottom lip jutting out. His eyes narrowed. Then he pushed himself off his rounded bottom, grasped the table legs, and began to try to haul himself on to his feet.

'He's after the samovar,' said his grandmother.

'It must seem to him like a great looming copper castle,' said Leo.

'As long as it looms. I do not want it toppled to the ground. I tell you, Garnet Alexandrovna, this is an *enfant terrible* that you have here, and soon nothing is to be safe, unless you chain him.'

Leo swept up the baby into his arms. Kolya squawked in protest.

'He has a strong back,' observed his grandmother. 'And a powerful temper.'

The next caller was Elena, in her Sister of Mercy uniform.

'You look like a nun,' said her mother. 'That wimple is not becoming, with all your pretty hair scraped underneath.'

'My work in the hospital is not becoming either! I've been learning to dress wounds. Some of them are quite appalling, especially when they turn septic, which most do, or gangrene sets in.'

'Should we have some tea? The pot is empty and the samovar needs topping up. Garnet Alexandrovna, ring for Dolly, would you?'

'Some of the men have lost legs stepping on mines, others have had their faces peppered with shrapne—'

'I don't think we need every detail, Lena.'

'You're not interested, are you, Mother?'

'*Ce n'est pas vrai!* But the details do not sit well with my stomach. I am proud of you, Lena. But you are very coiled-up today, like a spring. I know you must be worried about Dmitri. But can you not sit down? And be careful not to step on the child's fingers. He can make much noise.' Leo had been unable to contain the baby for long and had had to release him.

'Have a cigarette, Lena.' Leo held out his cigarette case.

'It will calm your nerves,' said the countess, who declined the offer herself. She would sometimes allow herself to be tempted, but she tended to choke and splutter on the smoke. She reached for another piece of Turkish delight instead.

Garnet took a cigarette. She enjoyed an occasional one and found that it did seem to calm her. The sight of Elena in her white nun's headgear puffing intently on a black cigarette made her want to laugh, which she dared not do. Elena was clearly not in a laughing frame of mind. And who could blame her? Who was, these days, with the shops half empty and queues clogging the pavements and people fainting in the heat and war-wounded pouring into the city, bandaged and crutched? And looking spiritless. It was the look on their faces that was the most frightening aspect of it all. Old women crossed themselves in the street when a line of soldiers filed by.

Sergei arrived soon afterwards, in his Chevalier Guards uniform. His entry brought a charge into the room.

'How handsome you look in your uniform, Seryozha!' said his mother. 'We don't often have the pleasure of seeing you at this time of day.'

'I thought I'd find you all at tea.'

He had to turn his attention straight away to Kolya, who was trying to scale his legs. He hoisted up the child and held him against his chest. 'So what mischief have you been getting into today, Kolya?'

'Plenty mischief,' said his grandmother. 'Plenty badness. You can see his face is covered with coal dust, and he has been chewing my playing card.' She held up a gnawed Jack of Diamonds. 'A red picture card too. He was a lucky card. He always found a black queen.'

'A passionate knave,' said Sergei, whirling his son around in a circle and making him laugh.

'Garnet Alexandrovna, pour some tea for your husband. Give him a *pâtisserie*. He has been working hard.'

'Hard!' sniffed Elena. 'Out at Tsarskoye Selo? Running after the royal family. Bowing and scraping to the Grand Duchesses! Yes, Marie! No, Tatiana! Oh, never *no*!'

Garnet began to protest.

Elena ignored her, kept her eye fixed on her brother. 'Look at him all dressed up in his uniform and going nowhere near the fighting!' Elena's husband, Dmitri, was at the front.

'You don't know what you're talking about!' Sergei set his son back down on the floor. He faced his sister. 'Just because you're flouncing about in that outfit pretending to be an Angel of Mercy! Some angel! Some mercy!'

'Seryozha!' cried Garnet.

Sergei ignored her, kept his eye on his sister. 'It reminds

153

me of when you and Natalya used to play at nurses when we were children. I'd have to lie on the bed and pretend to be injured so that you could bandage me. I was very long suffering.'

'We should have made you suffer more. We should have tied the bandages round your neck and pulled tight until we'd throttled you and your eyes bulged!' Elena was on her feet and shouting at her brother now.

'Lena!' protested her mother, but mildly.

'This is not a case of pretending any longer!' cried Elena, thumping the red cross on her chest with the middle fingers of her right hand.

'You mean you're dealing with real red blood? It must make you feel good.'

'Seryozha!' said his mother, even more mildly.

'It's more than you're doing! You've always been spoiled. The spoiled darling! The male child! Who thinks he can have anything he wants. Gets anything he wants.' Elena glanced accusingly at their mother, who was no longer paying any attention. She was counting her cards. Some seemed to be missing, apart from the recently ill-fated Jack of Diamonds. The countess found it difficult to bend over and search around her feet and Leo and Garnet were too absorbed by the drama taking place in the middle of the floor to be of any help. Leo stood, leaning on the top of the piano with his elbow. Garnet looked frozen, as if she were a player in the game of statues, but one who might at any moment erupt into life and spring to the defence of her husband.

'And you have always been stupid, Lena,' said Sergei, 'with no sense of perspective! That has been your problem.'

'Would you like to hear about *your* problems? Perhaps Garnet would like to hear about them?'

The countess banged suddenly on her card table with a spoon. 'Enough!, she cried.

Elena burst into tears, and Sergei came to console her.

Garnet sat down on the nearest chair. What had Elena meant? Nothing serious, surely. Of course not! She'd have thrown up some more childhood grievances. Garnet leaned back. She felt washed out, as if she'd been embroiled herself; and she was left bemused by the whole row, and astonished by the speed with which the protagonists had made up. When they'd had rows at home – and every family did have rows, every family could become heated, couldn't it? – they'd left their mark for hours, even days, and forgiveness had been hard bought. Their mother had sometimes had to intervene. (The McKenzies all had a stubborn streak in their characters, and all would have freely acknowledged it, even taken a little pride in it.)

Garnet, since marrying, had been doing her best to control her own lively temper and now, as a mother, she felt it necessary to try to set an example for her son. She feared this row might have upset him. To have heard his father and aunt shouting at each other, confronting each other . . . Where was he, anyway?

She found the child sitting behind his grandmother's sofa pushing the remains of her gâteau into his mouth with both hands. Much of the chocolate fudge filling appeared to have ended up on his clothes. Several playing cards were wedged between his fat knees and he was bending them backwards to see if they would break. Garnet, on hands and knees, peered round the side of the sofa and saw that the skirt of her mother-in-law's green satin gown was decorated with brown marks like the potato prints she and Lily used to do at kindergarten.

'Well, anyway, Lena,' said Sergei, when the room had settled down and fresh tea had been made, 'you will be pleased to hear that I am to go to Command Headquarters at Mogilev with His Excellency. I shall be nearer the front lines, and no longer at Tsarskoye Selo.'

Sergei was granted leave to attend the funeral of Elena's husband, Dmitri Andreevich, in St Isaac's Cathedral. Dmitri had been killed in the evacuation of Warsaw.

Gospodi pomilui.
God have mercy on us.

Standing in the rich interior of the cathedral amongst the black-clothed mourners, with the smell of incense hovering and candles flickering, and the purple-and-gold priest intoning, and Dmitri lying on his back in the open coffin, guarded by four of his fellow scarlet-clad Hussars, Garnet thought of Effie's fiancé, Hamish. He had been killed in a road accident in France. The armoured car he'd been travelling in had skidded on a heap of manure left by a farm cart, and had toppled down an embankment. He'd been thrown through the windscreen, and died on the way to hospital.

The letter from Aberdeen had come only that morning. Garnet had been dressing for the funeral when Dolly had brought up the post.

If he'd even died in battle it might have been easier for Effie to bear. At least she could have thought of him as some kind of hero. But happening this way it just seems senseless. Though I have to say that I think the loss of all this young male life is senseless. The funeral was a real trial for poor Effie.

In front of Garnet stood Dmitri's widow, her white wimple replaced by a black crêpe veil. To her bosom she clutched a wreath of white roses. Her shoulders were shaking. No one would tell her to be brave. She was entitled to weep. To beat her breast. In Queen's Cross church in Aberdeen the mourners would have been sternly dry-eyed, except for Effie, who would have pressed a white handkerchief against her eyes and cried silently behind it.

The church was packed, even though so many of the young men are away at the war. The young women were all there, looking red-eyed and startled, and the older generation, who remembered Hamish from when

156

he was a laddie. Andrew couldn't get leave. We are not sure where he is at present. Somewhere at sea.

For those in peril on the sea. And for those who had perished and were being led by the Good Shepherd to pastures green. The good folk of Aberdeen would have sung their hymns with stout voices, to show that the Hun would not easily defeat them. The organ music would have swelled around them, buoying them up, helping to carry them through.

Here, in this vast Russian cathedral, there was no music other than that made by the human voice.

Gospodi pomilui.

The voices were low and melancholy. Elena seemed to sway for a moment, and the count, at her side, slid his arm around her shoulders. The countess, on her other side, took her daughter's hand in hers.

Elena had been apprehensive for the last few weeks, claiming to have foreseen Dmitri's death. She'd gone to a fortune-teller in a back street, a well-known one, frequented by many of her friends. He'd prophesied a troubled time ahead, a change in her life, a removal. (Elena was to move into the Burnov house with her children after her husband's death.) Garnet had scorned his prediction. The *times* were troubled, and everyone's life was changing. It was a safe foretelling. She would not go to the fortune teller herself and offended her sisters-in-law when she said it was all a lot of nonsense. Her mother-in-law also set store by the words of fortune-tellers, but she was not offended by Garnet's scorn. The countess took offence at nothing, apart from aspersions cast at her only son.

We have been missing you and Lily and Andrew during these difficult times. The house is so quiet, and Effie is in need of distraction. To have her sisters around would have been a great boon, but we know it cannot be.

Tom has joined one of the newly formed Latvian Rifle regiments. Lily wrote to say that men from all walks of life have been rushing to volunteer. It is the first time, apparently, that there have been specifically Latvian regiments with their own inscriptions on their battle flags and badges, alongside the Russian. She says it is the first time in seven hundred years that the Latvian language has been officially accepted. She seems to think that has some significance. A step towards independence for them?

The Requiem Mass seemed interminably long. Especially when one had to stand. The service had lasted two hours already. Garnet hunched her shoulders deeper inside her fur coat. The chill in the church had crept into her bones, in spite of the envelopment of fur that contained her from head to foot. There was no heating, and outside the winter snows had commenced. A bitter wind had been whipping up the surface of the Neva when they'd left the house.

The moment had come for the congregation to say goodbye to Dmitri Andreevich, aged thirty-one, father of two sons, aged five years and three years respectively, husband of Elena Nikolaevna, widowed at the age of twenty-eight. Garnet rose with the others.

I cannot let Effie sink deep into dejection. I have to tell her that time will heal, and although she does not believe me I know it to be true. Within reason. She will carry the scar always, I am sure of that. I have to tell her she is young, and that she has her whole life in front of her. I cannot but wonder how many mothers are saying the same thing at this very moment throughout the land.

We have to hope that in due time Effie will find some other worthy young man. We would not like to think that her emotional life has been ended at the age of twenty. She is young to know such sadness. But who can say if she will have another chance? So many young men are being lost.

Gospodi pomilui.

Garnet followed Sergei up the aisle. Behind her came Leo. She knew what she had to do. On reaching the coffin each member of the congregation was expected to bend over and kiss the hand of Dmitri. He would be holding against his chest a small ikon, one that he'd had as a boy, portraying Christ crucified. He had prayed to it before setting out for the front.

Elena, as widow, went first. Candles flared at each corner of the bier. As she moved into the arc of light she appeared, in her voluminous black *vêtements*, like someone who has come from the Other Side. She laid her white wreath on the coffin and made the sign of the cross; then, in an instant, she had prostrated herself over the body of her husband. She clung to the sides of the coffin. She was allowed to stay there for a few seconds, then she was eased away by her father and brother.

When it was Garnet's turn she felt herself begin to shake. She had never been so close before to a dead person. When their grandmother in Orkney had died, she and Lily, aged ten, had been brought up to the bedroom to see her, but their mother had said it would do to look from the door. 'Remember Granny as she was in life,' she'd said. 'Remember her smiling and telling you the old tales.' Granny, though, had looked peaceful, had had a long life, and had died with her family gathered round. Now here was a man, still young, whom Garnet had known only superficially, related to her through marriage, resplendent in a clean scarlet uniform, hands waxy-white, eyes pressed shut, cheeks powdered to obscure his wounds. They showed still, though, the jagged scars; and the jaw had been partly blasted away. Nothing could conceal that.

'Garnet.' Leo touched her arm.

'Yes.'

She was holding up the queue. She raised her veil and, bending over, touched her lips very lightly to the cold hand. Then she let the veil drop. As she turned away her tears cascaded like a waterfall down inside the black crêpe. She wept not only for Dmitri Andreevich; and she wept in rage as well as sorrow.

Cesis

June 1916

Sergei had to go on a mission to Riga for the Tsar. He would travel by overnight train. Garnet begged him to take her with him.

'Please, Seryozha! Don't say it wouldn't be safe! You're going. Where you can go I can go. I won't go into Riga with you, I'll go to Cesis and stay with Lily. And when you've finished your business you can come and collect us. *Please*, Seryozha! I want to see Lily again. I want to see the twins. I want to see her new daughter. I want to show her our son. Why shouldn't Kolya go? Where I can go he can go. We can all go together. I want him to meet his cousins. I know he has cousins here. But these are cousins on *my* side.'

'She is very determined, that wife of yours, Seryozha,' said the countess. 'Her will is strong when she has made up her mind. She winds you round her finger. I never thought I should live to see it.'

'Only in certain areas,' murmured Sergei. 'But I like to please her. A man should please his wife.'

'I cannot disagree with that,' sighed his mother.

'I wouldn't take my children into danger,' said Elena.

'My sister is living there, every day. With three children.'

'That doesn't mean you have to take yours there. As mothers, we must put our children before ourselves.'

'You don't have to tell *me* what to do!' Garnet controlled herself. 'Anyway, the Germans are well to the south of Riga, and Cesis is north of Riga. Sergei says the Latvian regiments are doing an excellent job holding them at bay.'

'Kolya could stay with me. It's only for a few days. I could manage him for that length of time.'

Manage him! You'd think Kolya was a monster fit to be tied!

'He would miss me too much,' said Garnet, and left the room.

'Really,' she said to Sergei, 'your sister tries me at times.'

'You must remember—'

'I do remember. I *do*!'

Lily found Veronika in the garden, weeding the vegetable patch. She waved the telegram. 'Garnet's coming from Petersburg. Petrograd, rather!' She laughed. She was a little breathless. 'I keep forgetting it's changed its name. She's coming by train, with Seryozha.'

'That's wonderful,' said Veronika, rising up from her knees. 'I've always wanted to meet your sister. And it'll be good to see Seryozha again.'

'Oh, he won't be staying,' said Lily, folding up the telegram.

The train seemed like something out of *Anna Karenina*, thought Garnet. Not much had changed. A man in leather leggings and sleeveless leather jerkin pushed their luggage up the platform on a barrow. Kolya demanded to ride on top, and his father indulged him. Passengers and well-wishers crowded the platform and parted unwillingly to make way for the barrow. Most of the passengers were soldiers and most of the well-wishers were women. The engine hissed and gushed steam around them.

The Burnovs had a two-berth, first-class compartment,

161

with a little washroom off that would be shared with the compartment on the other side. The attendant (after receiving a sizeable tip) brought vodka for Sergei and tea for Garnet.

'You,' said Garnet to her son, who was reaching for her hot glass, 'shall have some jam and water. And when you're with your Latvian cousins you must learn not to grab. We don't want them to think you're a little Russian barbarian.'

Sergei, lying back on his bunk, laughed.

Her father-in-law drove Lily to the station in the trap. She had hardly slept the night before, had heard the birds begin their morning song, which they did early in June. She had got up and gone down into the garden to pick a huge bunch of flowers for Garnet's room.

The train was late. Only to be expected in wartime, said Markus Zale, who sat on a seat and puffed his pipe. Lily peered up the track, which remained empty. The air was still and quiet. She paced up and down and twice consulted the station master, who could offer no information.

By the time the train came chugging in two hours late Lily's nerves felt pulled like a piece of old knicker elastic, and she was almost wishing that Garnet had not decided to come.

Sergei was hanging out of the window, with his hand on the outside handle of the door, and had leapt down on to the platform before the train quite came to its juddering halt. Lily made to move back, but before she could take a step he had swept her right up off her feet and was giving her a tight hug. For a brief second he engaged her eyes with his vivid blue ones. She had forgotten how blue they were.

Then came Garnet, looking amazingly fresh and pretty in a pale-pink muslin dress sprigged with darker pink flowers, and a smart Petersburg hat to match, making Lily realise how countryish she must look, standing there hatless, sunburned feet bare inside her sandals, in her striped cotton skirt and white peasant-style blouse.

Garnet turned and lifted her son down from the high step,

162

and Lily saw how much he looked like her son Luke.

The likeness was remarked upon by everyone.

'They'd be like two peas in one of these pods if one weren't bigger than the other,' said Lily's mother-in-law, as she split the fresh green pods open with her thumbs and shot peas into the bowl in front of her. 'Though when you look at them you see the peas aren't all the same size anyway.'

Luke's hand came sneaking into the bowl, and he pulled out a handful. 'You're a rascal,' she told him. He grinned and ran, spilling peas in a trail behind him.

Alex waited with hand outstretched.

'You're better mannered than your brother.' His grand-mother rewarded him with a larger handful.

This left Kolya, who came charging full tilt at the bowl, and managed to toss the peas in a green funnel up into the air.

'You're a naughty boy, Kolya!' His mother scolded him and went down on her knees in the grass to try to rescue the peas.

But Gertrude Zale was not perturbed. There were plenty more peas on the stalks waiting to be picked and children liked their fun. 'And he's only eighteen months old, goodness me! You'd never think it. He's the size of Alex.' Alex was still much smaller than Luke.

From their first meeting Luke and Kolya seemed to feel competitive towards each other. They fought over toys and treats, and had to be separated by Morag, who'd tell them, 'That's enough, you two laddies! Stop, or I'll scud your bums!' It was as if the boys had taken a look at each other and both wondered what the other was doing masquerading in his image.

'Funny, isn't it?' said Garnet. 'To see them together?'

'Yes,' agreed Lily uneasily.

Sergei was to spend the last night with them before taking Garnet and Kolya back to Petrograd. The sisters had five clear midsummer days together. They left the children with Morag and Mara and went for long walks into the countryside.

Garnet had forgotten how slowly Lily could move; she hovered, like a butterfly, stopped to peer into hedgerows, pluck a flower or a long grass. Garnet had to moderate her pace to keep in step. She preferred to stride out, to feel the stretch and rhythm in the movement of her limbs. She remembered, as a child, having to turn, time and time again, to say, 'Hurry up, slowcoach! We'll be late.' There was nothing to be late for here; the long, light days seemed endless, and no times were set for meals. They happened when they happened.

'I can't get over how peaceful it is after Peter. Do you know, I've hardly ever left the city, except to go out to Tsarskoye Selo. It's like living on an island. I stay in the house a lot more than I used to. The streets are so depressing. There are army vehicles and soldiers everywhere and walking wounded who can scarcely drag themselves along and huge long queues clog the pavements from early morning. You can't get away from the thought of war.'

'It's the same in Riga, maybe worse. There, they can hear the sound of the German cannon.' Lily shivered.

'If only Russia could have stayed out of the war! It can't afford it, for one thing.'

'Can any country afford war?'

'The Germans can, more than us, anyway. Leo says Russia is bankrupting itself and the people are going to be very dissatisfied afterwards. They are already, what with inflation, and shortages, and losing so many of their men in battle.'

Sergei was driven out from Riga in an army car and, as a surprise, brought Tomas with him.

There was a party that night in the Zale house, one that they would always remember, for it was the last time that the two couples – Lily and Tom, and Garnet and Seryozha – would be together. The cook, aided by Mara, prepared a feast of roasted suckling pig (produced by a neighbour) served on a bed of buckwheat with spiced apples and fresh vegetables from the garden and, to follow, cheesecake and pancakes and home-made ice cream coloured violet and shaped like little obelisks in individual bowls. Markus Zale brought up from the cellar bottle after bottle of wine that he'd been saving for special occasions.

'None could be more special than this,' said Veronika. 'To have Tom back with us – and Seryozha. It's been a while since we saw you here.' She looked at Sergei.

'Only war would keep me away! You know how attached I am to all you Zales. I have many fond memories of Riga and Cesis.'

'We'll have an even bigger celebration when the war's over,' said Tomas.

His voice was ragged and he seemed excessively weary. There were moments when he seemed not to be with them, as if he were seeing something else beyond the candlelit circle at the table. He had the look of soldiers Lily had seen coming through Riga on their way back from the front. When she asked him if he was all right he flicked his head sharply and refocused his gaze. Sorry, he said. She repeated her question. He was fine, he said. He would never admit to being otherwise. She could not imagine him coming in and flinging himself down and declaring he was 'done for', as Garnet said Seryozha did when he was tired. That was usually when Seryozha had been out all night, said Garnet. *Out all night*? Garnet had backed off and said it didn't happen that often, but Petersburgers were notorious for their late nights and late mornings. 'They hate going to bed, but once they get into it they don't like getting out.'

'We need a victory first, though,' Sergei was saying. 'We must have that – a resounding one, with the enemy running scared.' He raised his glass. 'Here's to an Allied victory!'

They drank.

'An Allied victory!'

'And an end to all war,' put in Gertrude.

'Men will never allow that,' said Veronika.

'*Men*, Nika?' Sergei raised an eyebrow.

'You don't think we women want it, do you? We have too

much else we wish to do with our lives.'

'You want to be protected, though, don't you?'

'I am perfectly capable of protecting myself, thank you.'

'I know you are!' said Sergei, and laughed, and both Garnet and Lily wondered what he'd meant by that. Veronika's response had been rather crisp.

'It's time for pudding,' said Gertrude, passing out the ice cream.

The evening was mild, and the french window stood wide open on to the garden, letting in scents of warm grass and jasmine. What a pity, said Markus, that Garnet and Seryozha couldn't stay for John's Day; they would enjoy the celebrations. Garnet said it was a pity they couldn't stay for the whole summer.

'Isn't it, Seryozha?'

'Wouldn't it be wonderful! We could play tennis and have picnics and go swimming in the Daugava. What do you say, Tom? How does that sound to you?'

Tom merely smiled.

'Garnet could stay with young Kolya,' said Gertrude. 'Well, I don't see why not. The little one loves it here. It'd be better for him than going back to the city.'

For a few brief minutes it seemed possible. Lily said please do stay, she would love it if they did, think of all the things they could do together, and Garnet was taken by the idea, of being with Lily again and her son having the freedom of the countryside and his cousins to play with, and then she remembered that Seryozha would not be able to stay with her. He might not be stationed in Petrograd but he did come back from time to time. Also, if the Germans were to continue with their advance, they would be more likely to occupy Cesis than Petrograd.

'Some other summer,' she said. 'We'll come back.'

Veronika had wandered over to the gramophone and was winding it up. She placed the needle on the record. There was a crackle and then the strains of the Viennese Waltz drifted into the room.

'Shall we dance?' Sergei rose to his feet and put out a hand to his wife.

'Would you like to dance, Lily?' asked Tomas.

'Aren't you too tired?'

'I think I can stay upright. You can support me!'

Lily moved into his arms. They drifted in and out of the light, passing the other couple at intervals and exchanging a few words.

'Doesn't it take you back, Lily?' said Garnet over her shoulder. 'You remember how we used to enjoy going to balls?'

'Without us?' said Sergei mock-mournfully, and then Tomas swept Lily on, and the exchange was broken.

'You seem thinner, Tom.' Lily touched his face. 'Are you eating properly?'

'Meals in the mess are not like tonight's!'

'Are you sure you don't want to go to bed? Don't you think you need sleep?'

'I need a few hours of normality, too.'

'Is it very bad?'

'I don't know how long we can hang on, we're losing so many men. Lily, why don't you take the children and go with Garnet to Petrograd? It's further away from the enemy lines.'

But Lily could not contemplate leaving the tranquillity of her parents-in-law's house to go and live amongst all those noisy people in Seryozha's family home.

'There's trouble everywhere,' she said. 'Nowhere is safe.'

Except Aberdeen, perhaps, but to cross the seas at present was unthinkable. And, like Garnet, she did not want to go too far from her husband.

The music ended, and Sergei called for more.

'Dance with Veronika, Tom,' said Lily. 'She looks sad.'

Tomas went to his sister, and Sergei crossed the room to claim Lily, who thought she must plead a headache and go upstairs.

Sergei bowed. 'May I have a dance with my sister-in-law?' Without waiting for an answer, he took her hands in his.

He danced well, leading commandingly. Lily felt the energy in his body being transmitted to hers.

'I'm so happy to see you again, Lily.'

She murmured.

'It's good that my two children have had the chance to become acquainted. I was watching Kolya and Luke play together this afternoon. It was amusing to see them—'

'It's warm . . . I feel a little faint. And my head—'

With a laugh Sergei whirled her, protesting, through the french window and out on to the soft lawn.

'It's a glorious night.' He threw back his head. 'Look at all the stars! Yet it's scarcely dark. And there's a faint sickle moon. It's as if God has nicked a bit out of the sky with his fingernail. I love northern summer nights. You must come to Petersburg once the war is over, Lily, and experience our White Nights, when the sky is never dark.'

They danced round the apple trees and their shadows moved with them over the grass.

'This is crazy,' said Lily, letting herself go with him.

'A little craziness is necessary at times. Especially these times. Don't you agree?'

'You have always been crazy, Seryozha.'

'About you, yes. Can you blame me?'

'Yes!'

Lily glanced over at the french window. A dark figure stood in the opening, framed against the light. It was Garnet.

'Enough!' Lily said to Sergei, and forced him to return her to the room.

The parting next morning was difficult. All partings in wartime were, especially those made on station platforms. All over Europe they were being acted out. There was something about the hoot of the engine and the huffing of the steam and the track that would be left empty afterwards which created a mood of melancholy. Lily and Garnet were doing their best to hold back their tears; they did not want to upset the children.

In the end young Nikolai Burnov lightened the mood. As

the Russian family was about to board the train, he turned and shouted at Morag, 'Mo-ag, bad, yah, yah, yah!' and she turned and shouted, 'I'll give you what for, you wee tyke!' and pretended to chase him along the platform. The twins danced up and down with glee and cried, 'Give him what for, Morag! Give him what for!'

Riga

July 1993

The three women were talking about their fathers.

'Mine seemed to be a real tearaway,' said Lydia, daughter of Nikolai. 'I think he must have been called after the devil himself!' Katrina had always thought her cousin took rather a pride in that.

When Lydia had arrived in Aberdeen in 1953 the first thing she'd done was to pin up a photograph of Nikolai Burnov in Soviet Army uniform. She could see him when she lay in bed, as could Katrina, who responded by pinning up a picture of Luke Zale, her father, in his Latvian Army uniform.

'Nikolai was a hero,' said Lydia. 'He died in battle against your lot.'

It was not a way to ingratiate herself with her hosts, but then Lydia was not one for 'sooking up', as Katrina called it. Sooks were generally derided at school; on the other hand, you couldn't help being pleased when someone tried to please you. Lydia at fourteen didn't know much about pleasing. She was all sharp edges and angles. Her tongue, her elbows. Her body language, it might be called today.

'What did he do that was so brave?' asked Katrina, who was intent on hanging on to as much of her space as she could in her bedroom. She had placed an embroidered fire-screen in the centre of the room – well, perhaps not *dead* centre; it might be standing a fraction more into Lydia's half than her own. But it was *her* room, wasn't it? And had been for the past nine years. She had prior territorial rights.

'He didn't know the meaning of fear,' said Lydia loftily.

'In that case he wasn't really brave. To be brave you've got to know fear and overcome it.' Katrina had had to write an essay the week before on 'Courage and Glory', and so had been forced to think about it. She'd consulted her grandmother, Lily, who'd had to be brave in her life even though she said it hadn't come naturally.

'I felt the most terrible coward at times, Kate! I just wanted to hide under the bed. I suppose if you asked me to define what courage is, I'd say it was doing something you could never have imagined yourself doing.'

'Like what, Granny?'

'Firing a gun.'

'A *gun*? Have *you* ever fired a gun?'

'No, no, of course, not.'

But Katrina had been left unsure. She had not put any of that into her essay; well, not directly. She had not mentioned her grandmother by name.

On the concept of glory, Lily had been sceptical. 'It's ephemeral, like a brightly coloured soap bubble.' She'd given Katrina a poem by Pushkin to quote, about dreams of love and modest glory. 'Your grandfather used to quote it sometimes.' *Delusive hopes now quickly sped* . . . Katrina copied it into her essay . . . *yoked beneath a fateful power our country calls to us, heart-stricken*. Why did poets have to be so gloomy? She preferred poems about daffodils tossing their heads in a sprightly breeze, or something jolly like that.

Lydia had not agreed with her cousin. She maintained that the most fearless *must* be the bravest.

They did not settle that dispute. Many of their disagreements over the years had been left to hang in the air.

Helga's father, Alex, was still alive.

171

'The quiet one of the trio!' said Helga with a smile. She herself was on the quiet side, content to listen rather than talk, unless drawn out.

'Perhaps the quiet survive longer,' said Lydia. 'They don't burn themselves out. Which doesn't bode well for me, does it, Kate?'

Alex, at seventy-nine, was fit and well, said his daughter. Since retiring he'd lived exclusively in Cesis; he worked the garden, the one laid out by his grandmother, Gertrude, and he loved to go fishing. A real countryman. Lydia would meet him when they went down for the family reunion at the house in Cesis.

They were sitting round the table at Helga's flat, having eaten a good meal of cabbage rolls, pork escalope, tomato and cucumber salad with sour cream, and a shop-bought coffee and almond cake to follow. The visitors from outside knew that the food would have put a strain on their hostess's purse. They'd brought two bunches of flowers and carrier bags sagging with wine, ground coffee, chocolates and bananas. They were all drinking wine, and Helga was eating a banana. She loved bananas! They were her favourite fruit. For years they had never seen a banana here in Riga, but now they were freely available, sold from boxes in house doorways and barrows in the street, at a price. She allowed herself one a week as a treat.

The two rooms of the flat were small, but Helga and her friend, who had gone out, had made them as attractive as possible with books and posters and arrangements of dried flowers in earthenware jugs. The window was open on to the shallow balcony, from which one could look out over the housing scheme. It was state-owned, and looked similar to council estates on the fringes of large cities anywhere, with its shoddy buildings and areas of wasteland where bored youths roamed.

Helga's flat was on the fifth floor, and there was no lift. They'd had to grope their way, laden with their floral bouquets and clanking bags, up the dark, cat-and-cabbage-

172

smelling stairway. No lighting was permitted on stairs, because of the energy shortage. Sections of the handrail were missing. Helga had warned them beforehand to walk as close to the wall as possible, for fear of slipping on the greasy steps.

But the flat, inside, was unexpectedly light. Helga had made them welcome and been grateful for their gifts, more than they would have wished. She'd apologised for the clothes and bedding cluttering the room, though they were neatly folded, and for the bathroom. For some unaccountable reason they had no running water at present. But there was water in a bucket to flush the lavatory. They'd cut short her apologies by starting to admire the flat.

'You like it?'

'It's very nice!'

'But you are used to better places than this?'

'Different.'

'This was where I grew up, you know? Yes, with my mother and father and my grandfather, on my mother's side. Alex lived here until he got the house at Cesis back.'

Lydia had seen many similar flats in St Petersburg, had lived in one herself when it was Leningrad, sharing with three other families, arguing over space, hot water and light bulbs. As soon as she'd put her foot on the stair here she'd felt the echoes of recognition come flooding back, and had wanted to run.

The women spoke of the summer of 1916, when their three fathers had been together as small children at Cesis. They had all been told about it.

'I have photographs of the visit.' Helga jumped up to take an album from the shelf. She lifted it carefully; the binding was split and several of the pages were loose. 'It was Lily's album, brought from Aberdeen. Look – it's got "Made in Scotland" stamped in gold on the back. The letters are faint now but you can still make them out.'

She laid the book on the table and they crowded round it, their heads close together, their arms touching. The cover would have been a bright tartan originally, but was now faded.

'It's the McKenzie tartan!' said Katrina.

Helga eased the pages apart. The photographs had grown stiff and brown. She found the page headed SUMMER 1916.

There was the Zale family, gathered on the front steps of the house designed by Tomas, with their guests from Petrograd amongst them. Lily, grandmother of Katrina and Helga, and Garnet, grandmother of Lydia, were seated in the middle. But they were still young then, in 1916, a long way from being grandmothers, only twenty-four years old.

'They looked so alike, didn't they, Lily and Garnet?' said Helga.

Katrina peered closer. 'It's possible to see the difference, though, even in a photograph. Something to do with their expressions, the way they're sitting. Lily looks more dreamy – she seems to be thinking of something else. Garnet is more alert, gazing straight into the camera.'

'My grandfather is smiling,' said Lydia, smiling back at him. 'Look at Sergei!' His grin, even though two-dimensional and black-and-white – or, rather, brown-and-white – was infectious. 'It's not so usual to see people smiling in old photographs. You know the way they usually look solemn? As if they're afraid to blink. None of them here look solemn, which is amazing when you think that they were in the middle of the most God-awful war imaginable.'

Petrograd

Garnet took refuge in her room to finish writing a letter she'd started to Lily the day before.

> Had to break off in the middle of writing this yesterday as we were in the middle of a great drama! A real Petersburg-type one! With all the necessary elements of conspiracy, intrigue, treachery, and assignations on a midnight clear. It has provided a welcome diversion from thoughts of war.
>
> Rasputin has been found bound and gagged in a canal. His body had been pushed through a hole in the ice. The Empress is distraught. But due to the whole stramash and the ripples it's sending out, the Tsar has had to return to Tsarskoye Selo – and that means Seryozha is back too. Which is wonderful.

Garnet was interrupted again, by the arrival of Seryozha. This time she was happy to lay aside her pen.

He pulled off his greatcoat but did not sit down. 'Who are you writing to?'

'Lily.'

'Ah, sweet Lily-of-the-valley! Give her my love.'

'I shall.'

175

'There's no saying your letter will get through, of course.'

'I know that. But I have to keep writing to her. And to Mother. It's a way of talking to them.'

'Where is Kolya?' Sergei looked round as if his son might be lurking under a piece of furniture.

'In the kitchen with Dolly. He likes it down there.'

'Would you like to go out?' Sergei clearly was restless; he had lifted a fan from her desk and was opening and shutting it, and now he put it down and picked up a ruler.

'It's bitter outside, so Dolly says.'

'We could go to the Europe and have some tea. We could take a *drozhky*.' They would normally have gone to the Astoria, it being nearer, but the hotel had been taken over for high-ranking Russian and Allied officers.

'Won't your mother be expecting you downstairs?'

'We'll ring for Dolly and get her to tell Mama we've had to go out. By royal command!'

Before they went Garnet added another short paragraph to her letter to finish it.

So it will soon be 1917. A new year. Let's hope it will be a better one for all of us. We must try to take that holiday to Amalfi we spoke about. Just think of sitting on a terrace in the sunshine and swimming in warm, blue water!

Much love, Garnet

Sergei touched her shoulder. 'Don't forget to send her my love!'

Garnet wrote a postscript:

Seryozha sends his love to you and Tom both, and to all the rest of the family

The winter sun, which had broken through its lowering blanket of grey for a while earlier in the day, had sunk long since over the islands. The blue-mauve air seemed to tremble with cold. Garnet felt her eyelashes beginning to freeze. Her breath went ahead of her in small white puffs. She let her neck sink deeper inside her fur collar. What a weight all this fur was, pressing on the top of her head, on her shoulders, weighing against her thighs, slowing their movement. How heavy her feet felt, encased in felt and fur, plodding through the thick, crusty snow. How wonderful it would be to walk freely again, with a light gauzy skirt grazing her legs, billowing a little around the foot as a warm, lazy breeze lifted it, her arms and head bare to the sky. She thought of that summer week in the Latvian countryside with Lily, and remembered the children playing and laughing in the green-gold garden. On such a cold afternoon it was difficult to believe that summer would come again, impossible to remember what heat felt like.

Sergei hailed a *drozhky* waiting on the corner of the Embankment. When they turned on to the Nevsky and Garnet saw the beggars huddling in doorways she felt ashamed that she'd just been bemoaning the weight of her fur coat. How uneven life was. She said so to Sergei, and he made a noncommittal remark.

As the *drozhky* drew up at the front of the Europe the tattered men came scurrying. Sergei gave the supplicants a few kopeks apiece, and they touched their frozen forelocks.

It was warm in the hotel, and the atmosphere lazy. A man playing the piano provided suitable afternoon music, to accompany the light chatter and tinkle of teacups and glasses. Most of the men present wore uniform.

Garnet and Sergei settled themselves in a corner and were served tea and small almond cakes.

'Those poor men,' said Garnet, 'out there in the cold.'

'We could hardly bring them in.'

'I wasn't suggesting that.'

'There is a peasant saying: "In the forest the trees are unequal, and in the world so are men."'

'That only shows how fatalistic the peasants are. And how

177

bred into them it is. *Sayings* can be changed. They're not written in stone. Or does that sound too *radical* to your ears?'

'Do you actually think life could be equal for all men, Garnet?'

'And women,' she added. 'Don't forget my mother supports the suffragette movement.'

'How could I!'

'Well, naturally, I don't think there could be total equality. I'm not a fool!'

'Your colour is up! You know how I like it when you become heated. Your eyes have coals of fire in them.'

'We could move a little along the path of equality,' she said, ignoring his pleasantry. In disputes he always thought to disarm her in this way, whereas she liked to see an argument through.

'So, what would you propose? A redistribution of wealth?' He was looking amused. 'Do you want me to go out into the street and invite the beggars to come and share our house? It's not practical.'

'There are ways of leavening the lump without bringing the poor into your own home!'

'You're beginning to sound like your socialist father.'

'I knew that would come into it sooner or later!'

'Well, he should come over here and listen to our Bolsheviks. That would soon turn him against Socialism!'

'You're being ridiculous. Trying to belittle my father because he champions the causes of the poor! He is not a Bolshevik! He is the most gentle man imaginable.'

'Hey, hey! Calm down! You're rocking the table. Garnet, my love, I care about the poor too. What do you think I am – a totally selfish monster? Do you think I enjoy seeing the poor devils suffering? I want everyone to be happy! And I agree we'll have to do more, once this war is over. We've got to address the problem. The Tsar is aware of it.'

'He'll have to be, to save his neck.'

'Whom have you been talking to?'

'No one. I can think for myself!'

'I'm aware of that! But the Tsar really does care about his people. He sees them as his children.'

'Better if he saw them as grown-ups.'

'The trouble with you liberals is you see a beggar and your conscience is smitten, and then you come into a plush hotel and enjoy fine food and drink.'

Garnet put her almond cake down on her plate and left it uneaten.

'As if that will do any good,' said Sergei.

She made a poke with her napkin and slid the rest of the cakes into its hollow.

'What are you going to do with that, feed the five thousand?'

'You can be absolutely horrible at times!' she cried, flinging down the napkin. Cakes rolled and bounced, some of them hitting the floor, and a waiter came running with his arms outstretched, his eyebrows raised. People were looking, but Garnet did not care. 'I don't know why I ever married you, Sergei Nikolaevich!'

'Yes, you do.' He spoke soothingly, and he stroked her forearm, letting his fingers run down on to the back of her hand. 'I love you, Garnet. And you love me, don't you?'

She weakened when she felt his touch and was a little annoyed with herself. Her shoulders slumped. She sighed. It was seldom they had such a sharp row.

He lifted her hand, turned it over and implanted a kiss on the palm.

'Are we friends again?'

'I suppose!'

'And I will talk to the Tsar about the plight of the poor and press their case.'

His words were too easy, of course, and she recognised that, but she could only accept them.

They had more tea. The other had gone cold. The waiter brought it on his silver tray. It was no trouble! Sergei lay back in his chair and studied the room. He smiled, raised his hand to one or two people. There was their neighbour, the Duke of

Leuchtenberg, who surely, thought Garnet, must be having trouble with his name. Though he was in fact Russian. Sergei waved again. He couldn't go anywhere without recognising someone; in his own milieu, that was. Garnet saw her Irish friend Eithne at the far side of the room and they exchanged smiles. They called on each other regularly, met still to sew nightshirts for soldiers.

'Seen Leo recently?' asked Sergei.

'Not for a day or two.' The question had seemed casual, but Garnet felt that it was not quite, and was surprised. Did Sergei think she might be involved with Leo? The idea caused her some amusement but she did not give voice to it.

'You sometimes come in here with him, don't you?'

'Yes. Or the Writers' Café.'

'Does he introduce you to his friends?'

'Sometimes.'

'Other poets? Intellectuals?'

'Yes, mostly.'

'Gorky?'

'I believe Leo knows him.'

'I've often wondered how Leo occupies his time, when he's not with you or my mother.'

'I'm not sure. He writes, I think. I don't really know where he goes. I think he likes to keep his little mysteries.'

'Perhaps he has a mistress?'

Garnet did not believe that. Leo would have told her if there was a woman in his life. There was no reason why he should not.

'I've not heard a rumour of one certainly,' agreed Sergei. 'He guards himself well, I think.'

'Leo has been a very good friend to me. A good *platonic* friend,' Garnet stressed.

'Oh yes, yes, I know *that*.'

Any trace of daylight had gone by the time they left the hotel and fat flakes of snow were billowing out of an unseen sky. Lights glowed dimly in a few shop windows. The rest were dark. Shopkeepers had less and less to display. Everything had been reduced by the war, everything was scarce. There was no sign of a *drozhky* on the boulevard.

'Let's walk,' said Garnet.

Hearing muffled bells approaching, they waited till the ghostly sleigh had passed, then they crossed the wide Prospekt. Garnet held on to Sergei's arm, and with blind eyes and bent heads they made for the Moika Canal.

A woman, appearing from nowhere, stepped into their path, making them halt. They saw that her hand was extended.

'*Pazhalsta.*' Please. She was not a native Russian speaker.

Sergei fished in the bottom of his long pockets for some coins. He kept a few kopeks on him for beggars when he went out with Garnet; he knew he would get no peace otherwise.

A child was crying close by. Turning, Garnet saw, pressed into a shallow doorway, a man with two small children. The woman's family. The man was speaking to the children, trying to console them. Garnet caught a word or two and the lilt of the language.

'They're *Latvian*, Seryozha! They must be refugees. Ask them! You speak some Latvian.'

Sergei addressed the woman and she responded.

'They're from Courland. Refugees, as you said. Fleeing from the Germans.'

'Ask them if they came through Cesis!'

He asked them. 'They passed quite close.'

'Give them some roubles, Seryozha! Not just kopeks. Give them all the cash you've got.'

'All right! If you say so! But we can't do this for every refugee family.'

'That is no excuse not to give it to this one! And they are compatriots of Tom's.'

'*Spaseebo, spaseebo*!' The woman looked delirious as the rouble notes tumbled into her hands. She bowed and thanked them, over and over again.

Garnet took off her muff and hat and presented them to the woman. Then she unwound the soft cashmere scarf from her throat. '*Pazhalsta*!' she insisted.

The woman tried to kiss Garnet's hand, though Garnet pulled it away. '*Nyet*,' she said, shaking her head. 'It is nothing,' she added in English, the only language that would come to her at this moment. 'Nothing. You do not have to kiss my hand.' She would have taken off her fur coat and given that too but Seryozha stopped her.

'Shall we go home now, Garnet?' He took a firm hold of her arm.

The family continued to call thanks after them, their voices after a few moments beginning to fade and become as disembodied as the snowflakes. Sergei tried to give Garnet his hat but she would not take it.

She got a chill and suffered severe neuralgia in the head that kept her awake at night and she had to hold socks filled with salt pressed against her ears. She was confined to her room, but that did not seem too harsh a punishment, for, outside, blizzards raged and temperatures dropped to thirty-five below. Even by Petrograd standards, the frost was treacherous.

When she had recovered and was able to go out again, she kept a watchful eye for the Latvian refugee family. She scanned their doorway every time she passed. She never saw them again.

Riga

January 1917

Veronika accompanied Lily on the train up to Riga. She said straight away that she would, as soon as the telegram came. Markus Zale would have gone had he not been in bed with a bad bout of influenza. He was distraught and tried to struggle up, saying he must go, he must see Tom, when he was not fit enough to walk down the stairs. His wife, anxious on two fronts, persuaded him back to bed.

'Morag and Mara can take care of the children,' said Veronika. 'They're more than capable. You can't go on your own, Lily. You might give birth any moment!'

Lily was eight months pregnant and feeling exceedingly tired, more than she had on the two previous occasions. She kept saying that as if it was surprising. This was her third pregnancy in three years. Who wouldn't be tired? demanded Veronika. The winter was proving harsh. Heavy snow made it difficult to get about and the children's exuberance indoors was exhausting. Fierce blizzards had raged over Christmas. They had done their best to make it a happy time for the children, and indeed it had been, for the little ones were too young to be aware of what was happening beyond their home circle. It was one of the mercies of childhood, the adults were agreed.

There had been no word of Tomas for some weeks. They

knew only that his battalion was deployed against the German army somewhere to the south of Riga, and casualties were heavy. There was a stretch of land some three miles long, bounded by the Daugava river, which the Latvians were intent on holding, and paying dearly for. Later, it was to be called the Island of Death: washed on one side by the Daugava, and on the other by a river of Latvian blood.

As soon as Lily saw the telegram, she feared the worst, as all wives of soldiers would, faced by the official envelope. Lily called for Veronika before she opened it.

> . . . regret to inform you that Captain Tomas Zale has been seriously wounded in battle.

Lily was still rereading the telegram on the train.

'*Seriously* wounded. It doesn't say how seriously.'

'It cannot. Language is not precise enough when it comes to matters like this. Lily, put it away, dear. We'll know in a few hours.'

'I'm sorry.' Lily pushed the flimsy piece of paper into her bag. 'It seems all I have of him, all I have to hang on to. Do you know, Veronika, I'd actually been pleased that the weather had been so bad? I'd been thinking they couldn't possibly go on fighting in such appalling conditions. The cold was so terrible I'd thought no one could hold a rifle. You couldn't see half way down the garden. I'd thought they wouldn't be able to make out who was the enemy.' She gave a cracked little laugh. 'But it seems that they have.'

Tomas was in a military hospital in the city. Lily and Veronika sat on a bench, with all the other relatives, waiting to be called. It was nauseatingly warm. The corridors smelt of death and disinfectant. Lily removed her hat and eased her fur coat off her shoulders. Nurses and doctors scurried past. Stretcher-bearers moved along, carrying the wounded. The activity was constant.

At last, when they were beginning to think they'd been

forgotten, a nurse signalled to them, and led the way into a long ward that was lined with beds set close together. Lily was relieved to find that Tom was in a ward; if he was very serious he would have been put in a side room. Then she realised that the injuries of all the men were serious.

They stood at the foot of Tomas's bed. He was not conscious, and little of him was visible. They had to take the nurse's word that this was Tomas. He looked like a mummy, wrapped in bandages, stained with blood the colour of rust.

'How serious is he?' whispered Lily, turning to the nurse.

'He's lost an eye. And he's got internal bleeding and major wounds to several parts of the body.'

'Will he . . . ?' Lily could not get the word out.

'It's too early yet to say, I'm afraid. I'm really sorry, Mrs Zale.' They could see from the look on the nurse's face that she thought his survival unlikely. She brought a chair for Lily.

While Lily was sitting beside Tomas, her hands resting on the mound his body made under the sheet, and Veronika stood, tall and straight, by the foot, keeping guard, the soldier in the next bed, after suffering a convulsion, died. Lily watched, mesmerised, as the nurse, who had been holding him and speaking softly to him, as one might to a lover, closed his eyes and pulled the sheet up over his face with calm, matter-of-fact movements.

The flat was cold, from having been left unoccupied. They lit the big white corner stove in the living room – there was not enough fuel to heat the other rooms – and made up beds on the sofas. They lay awake in the dark, talking about Tom. Veronika recalled the little boy he'd been. 'He was always so good-natured. He wasn't the kind of boy who pulled wings off butterflies.' (As Luke had done – to see if they could still fly without. His grandfather, whilst not condoning the activity, had defended him, saying it showed scientific curiosity.) 'He was the ideal brother. He'd always share, look after the weaker and the underdog.' They talked as if Tom had all the virtues, and none of the vices; it was the way when someone was perched on the brink of death.

Veronika dropped off to sleep first. Lily stared up at the shadows on the ceiling, wanting to pray, yet unable to. She thought God might not want to listen, that he was punishing her for her sin, exacting penance for it. She'd been on the point of making a confession to Veronika, had sat up, and been about to speak, having compiled in her head her opening sentence. *Veronika, there's something I want to tell you.* And then Veronika had yawned and her voice had tailed off, and in the next instant Lily had heard her slow, even breathing. Perhaps it was as well. Veronika had a stern, highly honourable code of conduct, and she loved her brother fiercely. When Lily finally managed to drop over into sleep she tossed and turned, insofar as her bulk and the width of the sofa would allow.

In the morning, they went back to the hospital. No change. Lily sat by the bed and silently asked Tomas to forgive her since she felt she could not ask God. She sat until prised from the seat by Veronika, who took her off to a café, where they ate a meagre lunch.

'You look exhausted. Why don't you go to the flat and lie down? I'll go back to the hospital and do the next watch. After all,' said Veronika gently, 'Tomas won't know if you're there or not. And if there is any change I'll come for you at once.'

When they parted Lily did not go to the flat. She went into the nearest church. It was Lutheran. This was the faith in which Tomas had been reared. There was no service in progress, no music playing. A stillness hung in the cold air. Everywhere was cold, except for the hospital, which was hot, much too hot, and made one sweat and gasp for air. People were scattered about the pews, where they sat motionless, praying. Everyone seemed to be praying but her. They knew the words. Their heads were bowed, their lips moved. She slid into a pew, leaned forward against the one in front and closed her eyes. *Please God. Please God.* That was as far as she could get. She did not think she could please God. And why should He wish to please her? She needed to talk to someone, some lesser person than God.

She got up and looked around. A man in a black cassock was standing at the back. She went towards him.

'Could I talk to you, please? I'm desperate.'

'Many people are at present, my child. Come into the porch for a moment. We don't want to disturb the others. I can give you only a few minutes, I'm afraid. I have to take a funeral service. A soldier. Yet another.'

Lily was shivering. The porch stood open to the wind like a yawning mouth.

'Is it someone in your family? Your husband? You're young for such trouble. But you're not alone in that. You must put your trust in God, child, and have confidence that He will see you through this terrible time.'

'It's not *exactly* that. Well, it is . . . I mean, he's in a very bad way and he might well die and I do want to ask God about that but—'

'You must pray to God for his recovery.'

'I can't pray! That's the trouble. It's as if something has stuck in my throat. I can't pray!'

'Hush now, child. Go and sit in God's holy place and wait. And may He come to you!' The pastor touched her shoulder and then he disappeared, back through the door into the church.

Lily went down the icy steps into the street. The snow had started again, but in a way she welcomed it, for it obscured her from the world and the world from her. It was like walking in a swirling, white, cocooning bubble. She passed a few people, dim outlines, trudging with lowered heads, uninterested in her passing. She meandered through the streets. Dom Square was deserted, the cathedral spire invisible. She took a narrow side street, and another. She came down by the river, gazed across its grey frozen expanse, broken by the frenzied dancing of the eternal white dots. Somewhere over there, on the other side, not far away, soldiers bayoneted the guts out of one another, blasted their heads off, gouged out their eyes. When she listened she thought she heard the sound of shelling. Or was it the wail of the wind? Or ghosts? Her feet felt wet, her coat heavy. She carried on, came to the market. It, too, was deserted.

Down another white street she went, and another, each looking like the next. She slipped, struggled to save herself, and fell, flipping on to her back; and there she lay, with the snow descending on her face. She closed her eyes.

She was found by a woman, a market trader, who had been clearing up her stall after the morning's business. She lived nearby. She helped Lily to her feet, and took her home with her.

She peeled Lily's gloves from her hands, removed her hat and coat, knelt to ease the sodden boots from her feet.

'You're in quite a state! Had you been wandering long?'

For ever, thought Lily.

'You're a foreigner, aren't you?'

'Yes. But not German!'

'That's all right, then!' The woman smiled. 'Though I wouldn't have left you lying even if you had been.'

'I'm from Scotland.'

The woman, whose name was Vera, gave Lily tea and made her comfortable on the divan in the corner. She lived in this one room, had a little kitchenette behind a screen. She was a widow, and her two sons were away at the war.

'Whose sons are not?' she said.

'You're not Latvian, either?'

'I was married to one.'

'Like me.'

'I'm Russian. From Petersburg, originally.'

'My sister lives there!' They had things in common, then.

'I stayed after my husband died. Well, my sons were here, weren't they? That ties one to a place.'

'My husband might be dying.'

'Ah. You love him?'

188

'Yes, I do! He's my best friend. Can I tell you something, Vera? Something I've never told anyone else?'

Vera held Lily's hand while she talked. And when Lily had finished Vera said, 'We're all human, we can all behave in ways that God would not like. He knows that and doesn't expect us to be as good as He is. There are greater sins than this, Lily.'

Lily received the words gratefully. Vera was a Jew, and her religious faith was firm. It lapped against Lily like a warm tide. The little room with its few pieces of cheap furniture and religious pictures appeared to her like a sanctuary.

'Now don't think of confessing this to your husband if he lives,' said Vera. 'It would be only for yourself that you'd do it. And you must think of him.'

Lily felt amazingly at peace in spite of the pains that had been gnawing at the lower recesses of her abdomen ever since she'd fallen.

'Vera, I think my baby may be coming!'

And so it was that Lily's fourth child, a girl, whom she was to christen Vera (meaning faith), came to be born in the humble room of a Russian market trader.

Tomas remained suspended between life and death for more than a week. And then one morning, when Veronika arrived in the ward, his undamaged eyelid flickered and went back. He ran his tongue over his fissured, distended lips. She gave him water from a cup and he gulped and flinched as the first few droplets trickled down.

'Lily?' he asked, twisting his head from side to side.

'She's had a little daughter. Both are well. Lily should be strong enough to come out tomorrow. She'll come and see you.'

Tomas stayed in the hospital for another five weeks, and then he was allowed home. His father and Veronika took him between them on the train, helping him to move his legs up and down the high steps, and to find a comfortable way to sit. Some of his wounds were still suppurating. His left shoulder sat crookedly, and his arm was pinned to his body in a sling. His ears ached from frostbite.

He joked about his black patch. 'The children will think I'm Long John Silver.' *Treasure Island* had been a favourite book when he was a boy, along with *Kidnapped*, and he planned to read both to his children, when they were older. They're part of your heritage, he would tell them; they were written by a Scotsman.

The family could take one comforting thought from Tomas's wounding: he would not fight again. But he was a long time healing and he continued to have nightmares from that terrible Christmas battle, which the novelist Grins dubbed 'The Blizzard of Souls'.

Petrograd

February 1917

21st. We are all on edge, except for the countess, who does not appear to have any edges. She plays patience, and eats. She is fortunate that she can. Many out there cannot. Shortages are severe. The weather is severe. Temperatures are staying almost permanently below zero. Unseasonably so, people keep saying, and for Peter, that is something. The blizzards have been so fierce that snow is piled on the railway tracks. Locomotives cannot move. The peasants are refusing to bring their produce into the city. There is talk of bread rationing. People have been panic-buying, according to Dolly, who brings me much of my information. The family is doing its best to continue as if all is well even though it knows that it is not. The countess says, 'Let's have some champagne while there's some left in the cellar. We might as well drink while we can.' My father-in-law appears to be drinking heavily. He comes home late in the evening with bloodshot eyes. Sergei is in Mogilev, alas.

22nd. Shortages of fuel have forced several factories to close, among them the huge Putilov steelworks, which employs some 20,000 men. They are all very angry, which is understandable. No money, no food. Starvation. This city is like a tinderbox, in spite of the cold. Dolly's brother is one of the laid-off workers. They are out on the streets. Dolly says not to go out. There is much trouble afoot. Workers from other factories are coming out in support of the Putilov men. I feel like a prisoner in this big house, peering out of the windows, watching from behind the curtains. No sign even of Leo. I suppose he, too, may be staying at home, though I cannot imagine it.

23rd. I'd had enough of staying inside, so decided to go out. With Dolly! My mother-in-law would have had a fit but she was incarcerated in her sitting room with the samovar. And Elena. They had put on the electric light and drawn the curtains so that they wouldn't be able to see what was going on outside. I told them I had a migraine and was going to lie down.

It was International Women's Day. We put peasant shawls over our heads, Dolly and I, and slipped out by the tradesmen's entrance into Galernaya Street. There were thousands of women out in the streets demonstrating and carrying placards. One said: 'If woman is a slave there will be no freedom. Long live equal rights for women.' I could not but support that in my heart! I had my mother in my mind.

Temperatures rose well above zero as the day went on, which encouraged more and more people to come out. The sun shone. The sky was a brilliant winter blue and the air clear. It was like an unexpected holiday. The crowds were even quite gay. We heard that fifty factories have now closed. Their workers swelled the crowds. It was an amazing scene. Such a press of bodies! As Dolly said, there was no room for even an apple to fall. It was stirring, and, at the same time, frightening. The Cossacks were much in evidence, though leaving people more or less alone. The dreaded Cossacks, Dolly calls them. They were riding around with their rifles strapped to their backs and trusses of hay tied to their saddlebags so that they could stay on duty longer. I stuck close by Dolly. She seemed to have an instinct for how to survive in the crowd. The police tried to disperse people from time to time, and one took hold of my shoulder and handled me roughly. I almost shouted at him, 'What do you think you're doing?' and then I saw Dolly making a face at me, and I desisted. If I hadn't he'd probably have hit me with his baton.

We came upon Leo in Palace Square. He was standing on a step, watching. 'I haven't seen *you* for several days, Leo Konstantinovich,' I said, tapping him on the shoulder. 'What are *you* doing here?' he said, astonished to see me wrapped in a shawl, with Dolly! He insisted on staying with us and bringing us home afterwards. I said, 'Do you want to be seen by your friends escorting two peasant women?' He said he'd be happy to be seen so. I wanted to talk to him, to ask what he felt about the revolution – for surely that is what is happening, even though my father-in-law insists on referring to it as 'a little disturbance' and says scornfully that people are trying to make an elephant out of a fly – but we had no opportunity.

We slipped in by the back door again, Dolly and I, and when I came down into the countess's sitting room later there was Leo taking tea with his usual sang-froid! He'd come in by the front. We pretended to greet one another for the first time that day. I said, 'I haven't seen you for ages, Leo.' He'd been telling them about the demonstrations. Elena said, 'I hope we'll be able to get back to normal soon.' Silly fool. She really can try my patience at times. If she'd come out with Dolly and me she wouldn't have made that remark. The count, when he came back later (much later), said the streets were quietening down and most people seemed to be going home peacefully. 'They've let off their steam,' he said. 'Now they can go back to work.'

24th. The situation is getting worse, or better, depending from which side you're looking. Dolly's brother Vladimir was in the kitchen warming himself by the stove when I went down to see about lunch for Kolya. Dolly tried to hurry him out but I said he should stay to get thawed out. He looked frozen stiff, and unwell. He told us even more workers have gone on strike – 200,000, he estimates – and are out on the streets demonstrating and holding meetings. The police have been setting up barriers on the bridges that connect the residential areas to the city centre. But the workers have outfoxed them by walking over the frozen river.

25th. No newspapers today. No public transport running. Virtually all factories shut. There are 300,000 workers on the streets, according to Vladimir, who was here again today. Getting food for his family, I suspect. Well, he has to get it somewhere. In exchange, we get the news. Red banners are out. Some demand 'Down with the German woman!' There have been skirmishes between workers and police.

P.M. The count says two proclamations have been posted, one outlawing street gatherings and warning that troops will fire on the crowds, the other ordering strikers back to work. 'The Tsar has decided to be tough at last,' he said. 'Will the workers go back, do you think?' I asked him. 'They will if they know what's good for them,' he said. Dolly, when she came up later to bring me a hot drink, said that half the posters had been torn down the instant they were put up.

26th. Sunday. We shall not be going to church this morning. The military is out on the streets in combat gear, after a night of rioting and arson. Police stations were sacked and fired. The bridges over the Neva have been raised and a curfew imposed. But none of this is stopping the people from going out. From our windows we

194

can see them crossing the river and moving in on the city. Dolly said the troops fired on the crowd in Znamenskaya Square and a number of people have been killed. Elena said the servants were concocting rumours, trying to raise a mood of hysteria. I lost my temper, I'm afraid, and told her to open her eyes and ears and stop living in Cloud-cuckoo land. She burst into tears, and then I had to apologise, for I know her life has not been easy since being widowed.

For the first time I feel really frightened. It's being inside, and all of them outside. I didn't feel frightened when I was in among the crowd on Women's Day. I was part of it: that was the difference. And it wasn't aggressive. But the aggression is building on the streets; one can sense it, hear it. What if they were to fire our house? I am keeping Kolya by me all the time and last night had him sleep in my bedroom. Someone in the kitchen has given him a toy gun and he is running around jabbing both family and servants in the back of the leg and shouting, 'Bang, bang, you're dead!' As all small boys do at some stage. Mother used to ask Andrew how he'd like to be shot dead, and he'd lie on the floor with his eyes screwed tight shut and say, 'I like being deaded, I like it.' Such memories make my throat swell. In odd moments when the revolution has not been dominating my mind I've been thinking of Lily and wondering how her new baby is faring. And Tom, with his awful injuries. Though I feel sure he will fight them, and not give in. He is of a stalwart nature; reminds me of some Scotsmen I knew back home. I don't know how Seryozha would cope in similar circumstances. I shudder to think of it, and pray that it will never happen. I cannot imagine him without an *eye*.

Kolya lifts my spirits and keeps me from becoming too melancholy. He burst into his grandmother's room this morning brandishing his gun and screaming, "Putin, bang, bang!" I suppose he meant Rasputin! No doubt they've been teaching him that in the kitchen and finding it amusing. Elena says I should stop him from going down there. She keeps her children in the nursery and schoolroom, but they are more biddable. Kolya made the countess slop tea on her yellow satin dress, and was banished immediately! 'I can see him as a Cossack,' she said, 'when he's older.' (Over my dead body!)

By nightfall, the city was quiet. And Princess Radziwill held her soirée, as planned! During the day Elena and her mother had been talking about it, wondering what they would wear. I kept saying, 'There'll be no soirées tonight,' but they wouldn't believe me. And they were proved right! They know their Peter better than I do. The count had ordered up the carriage. I was in a mind not to go (I was reluctant to leave Kolya, apart from anything else), but they made me feel I'd be letting the side down if I didn't. So we rode through the almost deserted streets, which were littered with discarded placards and all the sorts of rubbish that crowds leave behind them, and when we got to the Fontanka Canal there ahead of us was the princess's palace lit up like a liner at sea and the aristocracy of Petersburg arriving in their carriages, decked out in their silks and satins and furs and jewels as if nothing had changed or ever would! The sight made me deeply uneasy. I felt distracted for much of the evening, found conversation difficult, and was relieved when we returned home to find our house still standing and Kolya sleeping peacefully in his cot at the side of my bed.

27th. There has been a mutiny in the army. The troops involved have come out in favour of the workers, and are now in Peter. We're not clear what happened exactly. But it seems it began when a sergeant in the Volinsky regiment shot his commanding officer dead. 'This is serious,' said the count for the first time! He is blaming it all on 'those damned intellectuals, those radicals'. He says they're behind the happenings, orchestrating them, that the workers don't have enough acumen to organise themselves.

28th. Half of our servants appear to have absconded, taking with them food and various household items. (Not Dolly.) 'Call the police!' said the countess. 'The police have other matters to attend to,' said the count. He heard from one of the Ministers at the Duma that the royal train left Mogilev early this morning with an escort, but it has taken a detour and so is not expected to arrive today. I am anxious, of course, about Seryozha.

1st March. The royal train has been diverted. What is happening?

2nd. Everything in a state of chaos. Tsar's train stuck at Pskov, so the count heard from one of his various sources. Rioters blocking the line. Royal family in bad way, so Dolly heard. Their guards have gone, and most of the servants, and they have no electricity or piped water. It is widely rumoured that the Tsar is about to abdicate.

Garnet closed her journal. She stared at the wall, then she let her elbows drop down on to the desk and her face fall forward into her cupped hands. The house around her seemed still. She could hear no sounds, except for the delicate tick of the French clock. Turning slightly sideways, she saw reflected in the gilt oval mirror a dark-haired woman in an olive green and grey striped dress. A frown was puckering the well-defined eyebrows, bringing them closer together. For a moment she was puzzled. Then she lifted her head and straightened her shoulders, and recognised herself. But she was changing, she was conscious of that, perceptibly, almost before her own eyes.

Cesis

April 1917

News of the revolution in Russia had trickled through slowly to Cesis, the wireless giving out only the bare details. The one hard fact they possessed was that the Tsar had abdicated.

'The Tsar of all the Russias!' said Veronika, who was mending socks, a job for which she had little aptitude. She preferred chopping wood. But socks had to be mended – children wore them out quickly – and Morag and Mara were too busy to do every chore in the house. Their handyman had gone off to the war, and his wife had removed herself to Latgale to stay with her sister. Veronika said it was probably just as well; there were too many of them to feed as it was.

'That includes us, doesn't it, amongst the Russias?' said Lily, who was nursing the new baby. 'We're part of the Russian Empire.'

'Which exists no more! Well, how can it when there's no longer an emperor!'

'I suppose they could call it something else. A republic?'

'At present, though, we are in something of a political vacuum.' Veronika looked thoughtful. 'And vacuums are there for the filling. If only we weren't embroiled in this bloody war!'

There had been no abatement in the battle for Riga, or in the loss of life. They had two families of refugees from

Courland in the little house at the back now, where the handyman had lived, and another in their basement.

Lily winced as she eased the baby off her nipple. She'd had an abscess, which was slowly healing. She had not complained. How could she when she saw the pain Tom suffered? For more than three years her breasts had been either tender in pregnancy or swollen with milk. She had almost forgotten the shape she'd had as a girl. Veronika said she must stop this flood of children. Four was enough for any woman, especially when the world – Europe – was in such a precarious state. And who knew if Tom would ever work again? Someone would have to earn a living and support the family. Veronika presumed it would have to be her, once the war was resolved and they could return to Riga. But when would that come? And even then a teacher's salary would not go far round a household of seven adults and four children.

Lily envied her sister-in-law her certainty. Veronika could make the statement 'Four children are enough'. Lily found it difficult to say what was enough, in any field. She felt her life was so *unplanned*; events happened, and she responded, or let them wash over her. This sat ill with the credo under which they had been raised, she and her sisters and brother. They had been taught by their parents to regard life as something which one strives to have under one's control. Life is what you make of it. No one will help you if you don't help yourself. You get what you deserve.

'Is that Tom?' said Veronika.

Lily cocked her head. Footsteps could be heard on the stair. They were dragging, bumping footsteps.

'Give Vera to me.' Veronika held out her arms. 'I'll de-wind her.'

Lily went out into the hall to see if she could help Tom. He hated to be helped. 'I can manage!' he'd say irritably. She stood by, watching, trying to pretend that she was not, telling him about something Luke had said at breakfast. Tom had fallen down the stairs twice and badly damaged his knees, which were in poor shape anyway.

He made it down the last step. 'There!'

'You're improving.'

'You think so?'

His face was very thin and drawn. But he was alive. And he could smile when he made it down the stairs. An achievement, he called it, one he'd had to work for.

When the twins came rushing in they flung themselves at their father.

'Steady,' cautioned Lily.

'You don't have to *keep* telling them that,' said Tomas.

'Sorry.' She turned away. Tom was understandably much more touchy than he used to be. It was a strain, though, trying to be understanding. Sometimes she wanted to scream. One night, after she'd fed Vera, she'd gone downstairs, pulled on her boots, and picked her way over the snow-crusted garden under icicles hanging like slender crystal daggers from the branches. It was dead of night, yet it was light, with the intensity of the snow, and the gleam of a full moon. She'd crept into the sauna cabin, and smelled its lingering woodsmoke smell, and thought of summer. What was she doing here, she'd wondered, the mother of four young children, the wife of a disabled man, in a foreign land, with an enemy army threatening at any time to overrun them? She'd bashed her fist into the wall and for the next few days bore a set of angry bruises on her knuckles to remind her of this moment of despair.

'There's a letter for you, mam.' Morag held it out. 'From Aberdeen.'

The letter had been written a month before.

> *Queen's Road, Aberdeen*
> *3 March 1917*

My dear Lily,

I am giving this to Andrew so that he can try to get it through to you by some means or other. He has been posted to the Admiralty, where he is employed as a press officer. A great relief to us, needless to say. To think he is no longer Somewhere at Sea. And he is enjoying the job. He's still holding to the idea of becoming a foreign correspondent. He says Europe should be interesting post-war, especially with the developments in Russia.

The situation in Petrograd has been alarming us greatly. How I wish we could get Garnet and little Kolya out of there. I have asked Andrew if anything could be done but he thinks not – at present, anyway. Perhaps later, when it all settles down, which surely it must.

Effie is in better spirits, you will be glad to hear. She helps me with my Red Cross activities, has managed to overcome her squeamishness, and has become quite religious. I am naturally pleased that she can find consolation in the Church, as long as she keeps it in perspective. By that I mean that she should not become too pious. I have warned her of that danger, but I am not certain that my words did not fall on deaf ears. Piety can be tedious. I have respect for the Lord, but I don't want to have His words quoted to me at table, for breakfast, lunch and dinner.

We trust Tom is progressing, and that you and all the children are well. I would send cod-liver oil and molasses, but I doubt if parcels would make it through.

Please give our warmest regards to the Zales. And tell Morag that her sister Florrie has had another baby boy.

Your loving mother,
Jemima McKenzie

Lily finished reading the letter aloud and looked up.

'So you've got another nephew, Morag.'

'More fool, Florrie!' Morag shook her head.

'That makes six boys she's got.'

'I think six would make a nice number for a family.' Tomas smiled. 'Three of each. What do you say, Lily?'

Veronika answered for her. 'I'd say more fool Lily if she

were to say yes.'

Lily noticed then that there was another flimsy sheet of paper in the envelope. She took it out. It was a letter from Effie.

Dearest sister,

I want you to know that I am praying for you in these troubled times. Man is full of Sin and has brought these Afflictions upon himself. But do not despair for Redemption is at hand. Only repent thy Sins and open thine heart to the great Goodness of the Almighty.

I urge you, Lily, to put your Trust in the Lord at all times. He is a Loving God and shall not fail thee, nor shall He let any ill come nigh thy dwelling.

Your loving sister in Christ,
Euphemia

'The *loving* God is the problem,' said Veronika, 'if one has to accept that He is powerful also. How is it that if He is so good and loving He can watch so much suffering going on under His nose? Mother no doubt would tell me He is working a purpose out – she is very trusting. *What* purpose, one cannot imagine!'

'There was I thinking I was a victim!' said Lily. 'While really I have brought the wrath of the German armies down on my own head!'

'I never thought Effie would go in for religion in such a big way,' said Tomas.

'War takes each of us differently,' said Veronika.

Petrograd

July 1917

Garnet took Nikolai down to the kitchen. It felt like the inside of a kettle. She could never understand why they wouldn't open the windows. It might help the stink if they did! The smell was one compounded of boiled cabbage, frying sunflower oil and wet sheepskin. One smelt it to a greater or lesser degree in everybody's house. An undercook, who had not gone with the others, was stirring a cauldron of cabbage soup (they had been virtually living on a diet of cabbage soup). The other two servants – apart from Dolly – were sprawled over the table, smoking. (Had they been drinking?) Before, they might have sprung up and set about some work. But not now.

Dolly was washing dishes. They were stacked in a rickety pile on the draining board. The floor needed scrubbing. Chewed sunflower seeds were stuck to the stone. Insects of some kind were scurrying round an overflowing refuse bucket.

'Can you look after Kolya, Dolly?' asked Garnet. 'Would you mind?'

'No trouble. Least, I'll see he's not.' Dolly dried the backs of her hands on her apron. Then she put one to her forehead and the other on the edge of the draining board.

'Are you feeling unwell, Dolly? You look pale. Do you

want to sit down?'

'No, I'm fine, Madame.'

'I'd take Kolya with me if I could. But the crowds—'

'No, no, it's all right.'

Dolly and a sulking Kolya (he would, of course, have preferred to go with his mother) saw Garnet off at the back door. Garnet had taken to leaving by the tradesmen's entrance, for two reasons: one, that she didn't wish to be seen by the family, and the other that the entrance (or exit, depending on which way one was approaching it) was less ostentatious, from the point of view of those who lived outside. And emerging from it one might even be taken for a tradeswoman or a servant. She was wearing a grey and white cotton striped dress, and no jewellery, and she had done her hair simply. Dolly refrained from telling her that she'd still be easily recognisable as one of *them*. Leo had come to the house after the Tsar's abdication and warned the family about standing out in the crowd. 'Keep a low profile,' he'd advised. He had not been well received. The count had thought it had been an effrontery on Leo's part to come and had taken him to the door himself and ushered him out.

The streets were awash with people. They always were these days; had been since before the revolution. People did not sit at home mulling over their grievances (of which they still had many); they came out to air them, to demonstrate, to listen to speeches (particularly Lenin's). Demonstrating had become a way of life. That, and the quest for food. Leo said their homes were so poor and lacking in comfort they might as well come out on the street, especially now that it was summer.

As Garnet wove her way through the crowd she took care not to look at anyone directly, not to catch their eye. Amongst the workers, who were either on strike or had been laid off, were soldiers. Deserters. In squalid uniforms. With a look of hunger in their eyes. They carried banners and shouted slogans. *All power to the Soviets*! The Russian armies had suffered a humiliating defeat on the Austrian front the previous month, and afterwards huge numbers of men had simply walked away from the battlefield. Some said a hundred thousand had deserted. They all seemed to be on the streets of Petrograd.

The day was close even though it was still early. Garnet dried her forehead on the back of her arm. Sweat was leaking from her armpits, gluing her dress to the upper half of her body. The crowd ballooned with every minute that passed. Someone trod full square on her foot and made her cry out. She wondered if a bone might have been broken. She seemed to have found herself in an impasse, unable to take a step either forward or back. It was like trying to move through a barrelful of herring. 'Who do you think you're shoving?' demanded a man with a frizzled beard and sour breath. The look he gave her was ugly, or so she interpreted it, as was the growing mood of the crowd. Their chanting was building. *Power to the Soviets! Power! Power! Power!* Arms were upraised, hands punched the air. She shoved again, with as much might as she could muster, and used the sharp points of her elbows.

She made it at last to the edge of the mass and rested against a wall. She was out of breath, felt pummelled and bruised. Her hair had fallen down. The hem of her dress was torn. Hems could be mended. Everything must now be mended, nothing could be thrown away, and of that she approved, in principle, having come from a home that had discouraged extravagance.

But the count had been right in what he'd been saying last night: the country was in dire straits.

'Russia is falling apart,' he'd said. 'The whole structure is collapsing, and there is nothing to take its place. The economy is bankrupt. The peasantry is burning manor houses and seizing land that it doesn't know what to do with. The workers are on strike. Nothing is being produced. We are short of food. We cannot afford to import. We have nothing to export. We are all going down, the aristocracy, the peasants, and the bloody, naïve, radical intellectuals – the *liberals*! God protect us from the liberal! He's like a man with a box of matches – when he lights one he's surprised to find he's got a fire on his hands; and when it gets out of hand he doesn't know what to do, so he crawls back to his books and sits muttering theories about the rights of man!'

Garnet had wanted to argue with him, to demand, 'And what are *you* producing, what have you ever produced?' But nothing would have come of such a question – nothing could – and Seryozha would have been annoyed with her. He had been there. Often he was not in the evening. He had business to attend to, he said vaguely. He needed to make contacts, now that the centres of power had shifted. He had to make money. Nothing would come in any more from their estates. She knew that, didn't she? Why, then, did she question him? She wasn't going to turn into one of those awful nagging wives, was she? He'd said to his father, 'We've got to make the best of this, Papa. It's happened, and there's no going back. We must support the Provisional Government, give it a chance. Kerensky seems a reasonable man. I heard at Yegorov's today that he's tipped to leave the War Ministry and become Prime Minister. I have a lot of time for him myself. He's doing his best.'

The count had capped that: 'His best may not be good enough.'

Garnet turned down a side street, away from the crowds. Coming towards her was a tall, familiar-looking figure. For a moment she could not place him, as is often the way when one sees someone out of context. Then as he came closer she recognised him.

'Why, Mr Gibbes!'

He stopped and bowed. 'Countess Burnova.'

'You're not out at Tsarskoye Selo? Well, obviously not!'

'I wasn't allowed entrance, sadly. I went and asked to be admitted, but the guards wouldn't let me pass. It was my day off the day they sealed the royal palace. I was here in Peter.'

How lucky, Garnet was thinking. So much seemed to depend on luck: where one happened to be at a given moment. When Seryozha had returned on the royal train with the Tsar's entourage he'd been given the choice of whether to enter the palace or not. His instinct for self-preservation was too strong for him to submit himself voluntarily to any form of confinement. And he'd had his family to consider, as he'd said.

Mr Gibbes was living in Petrograd, waiting to be reunited with the royal family. 'I'm still hopeful the British Government might relent and take in the imperial family. Then I would return to England with them. I was shocked when our government took the decision not to give them asylum.'

'Aren't all decisions political? Do you think the politicians actually care about *people*?' How cynical I've become, thought Garnet, and in such a short time. She asked Mr Gibbes if he still received news of the Tsar and his family.

'Some, from the few servants left. The Tsarevich has been having a dreadful time. His attendant appears to enjoy humiliating him. And the boy's health is so precarious.'

'And the Tsar?'

'He's been doing menial jobs – gardening, chopping wood.'

'That's what we're all going to have to do,' said Garnet.

Leo was waiting for her in the café. It was empty but for him and the waiter, and the blinds were half down. Leo had been talking to the waiter when she arrived. She met Leo now in run-down cafés in out-of-the way areas. Out of the way of the Burnovs and their friends. Not that the Burnovs frequented the cafés on the Nevsky much themselves any more; they stayed closeted in their palace with the doors and windows locked and strict instructions given to Dolly to admit no one unknown to them. But it was best not to make assumptions, Garnet had found, and there was always the chance she might run into Natalya or one of her friends coming out of the Medved or the Europe. The count had forbidden anyone in his family to have anything further to do with Leo. He wanted no further dealings with radicals. Traitors!

'*Kvas*?' suggested Leo. 'It's a warm day.'

'Is there some? A cool drink would be good.'

Leo signalled to the waiter. He was known in this café. The beer was brought, and they lit cigarettes.

'You look worried,' she said. More worried than usual, she meant.

He shrugged. 'The situation's not getting any better. Lenin's wily. I heard him speak again last night. He's blaming everything as usual on the Provisional Government – the war, shortages, inflation.'

'And they believed him?'

'Who else would they believe? How can they make any judgments of their own? They're not used to making judgments or taking decisions. And if you hear something often enough, you come to accept it as fact.'

'He's getting them out on the streets anyway.'

'He thinks he can bring down the government by demonstrations.'

'That's what brought the Tsar down in the end, wasn't it?'

'Exactly! Trouble is, Kerensky's coming under more and more pressure to deploy troops to contain the situation.'

'The count says liberalism doesn't work.'

'I know what he thinks. Keep the people screwed down, don't give them a chance to think for themselves. People like to be told what to do, to think, even to dream! For dreams can be dangerous.'

There was a sudden noise in the street and the waiter moved to the door. Leo stubbed out his cigarette and went to join him. Garnet followed.

'They're shooting,' said the waiter.

Garnet had never been so frightened in her life. When she came in by the back door she had to stand in the dark passageway and let her heart wind down. The kitchen door opened, sending a shaft of light on to her, and Dolly said,

'Who's there?'

'It's me, Dolly.'

'Are you all right? What's happened to you? You're shaking. Come into the kitchen. Come on now, and sit down. Young Kolya's asleep for once. He wore himself out running round the park like a whirligig.'

'The troops opened fire on the crowd, Dolly. The soldiers were firing at *people*.'

'That is what soldiers do.'

'But not ordinary men and women. Unarmed. Helpless. It was terrible, Dolly! You didn't know which way to go. Where to run. And Leo couldn't run, on account of his leg, and I had to help him. People were screaming and a man went down in front of us and there was blood all over . . .' Garnet put out her hands, expecting to see blood on them.

'Have some of this tea.'

Garnet took a sip. Tea was a great panacea. At home, too. During any crisis her mother would ring down to the kitchen and order up a fresh pot. The kettle steamed on the hob of the black range all day long. Drinking tea provided a lull before one decided what to do next or else submitted to fate.

'Thank God the man's had enough nerve to stamp on this rioting once and for all,' said the count.

'Once and for all times?' said the countess.

'And arrest the ringleaders,' added the count. 'Pity he didn't have Lenin shot rather than letting him go into exile.'

'Dolly says he's gone to Finland,' said the countess.

'The oracle! Where does she get her information from, that girl?' The count poured himself a glass of claret and held it to the light. He admired the colour, swirled it a little, stuck his nose in, drank, declared it excellent, a good vintage. He had finished all the champagne in the cellar (though he had been helped by others, unbeknownst to him) and was now working his way through his French table wines. His wife suggested he might save some for Christmas. 'Christmas?' he said. 'We'll replenish our stocks before then.'

He now addressed his daughter and his daughter-in-law. They were the audience for his evening dissertations. Not ideal, but less irritating than his wife. 'What Russia needs is a really strong man at the helm. Kornilov could be the answer.'

'*General* Kornilov?' said Elena, who could be relied on to give the prompts.

'He could send in the Cossacks. Get rid of this bloody government *and* the revolutionaries in one fell swoop!'

'Will he do it, do you think?'

'Matter of time,' said the count.

Garnet recorded it in her journal.

Kornilov has sent in his troops and Kerensky has allowed the Bolsheviks to set up a force to help defend the city. They're calling themselves the Red Guards.

Riga

July 1917

He was not a back-street abortionist, said Veronika, in the sense that he was not operating with knitting needles or plying women with vodka and advising immersion in hot baths. (Lily had already tried that, had drunk cheap, very cheap, vodka, which had made her so sick she'd retched all night, and Tomas, not knowing what was going on, had summoned the doctor from Cesis.)

'His clinic is not in a main street, admittedly,' said Veronika. 'But he's a professional doctor, and he'll give you some form of anaesthetic. I suppose some might say he's not acting very professionally.'

She herself would not say it. She thought he was being very professional in putting the needs of women before received ethics.

Lily, who was understandably nervous, and turning all sorts of matters over in her mind, especially at night, could not help wondering if the doctor might not be putting his own need for money before the good of women. Veronika did not like her voicing such thoughts; she perceived them as negativism. If one was going to undertake a certain course, then one must get on with it and not swither. A good Scots word that: swither. Lily had taught it to Veronika, whose English was gradually taking on a Scottish hue. She had learned to roll her 'r's admirably.

Raising the money to pay for the abortion presented some difficulty, as it always had for women. Lily would have to sell some jewellery. She decided on the emerald-and-diamond brooch which her parents had given her for her twenty-first birthday. (Garnet had been given rubies and diamonds.) She was upset at the idea of parting with it, but she had nothing else of value except her engagement ring (out of the question) or some of the antique amber jewellery presented to her by Tom on the occasion of her marriage (again, out of the question). He would not miss the brooch. She rarely wore it; jewellery did not sit well with this wartime, country life.

The next problem was where to sell it. Not Cesis, said Veronika. The town was too small, no one would give enough, and if a buyer could be found, news of the transaction might well find its way up to the Zales' house. 'We'll have to sell it in Riga.' No one other than themselves – and the abortionist – must know what they were up to. And they had to go to Riga, anyway, for the abortion. Making an excuse to go to the city at this stage in the war was not easy, and Lily left it to Veronika.

'The Germans are not actually in Riga.'

'Yet,' said Tomas.

'Our men are holding their positions.'

'They're bound to be weakening. It's gone on for so long.'

'For the Germans, too. And, all right, they're a bigger – and, yes, a stronger nation – but they're fighting on several fronts.'

'The Russian one has pretty well collapsed.'

'We'll stay only a couple of days – less, if there's any trouble.'

'What in God's name do you want to go to the city for anyway?'

'I want to see how Nils's sister Marga is getting on. She's a semi-invalid. I know Nils would have wanted me to keep an eye on her.'

'I don't see that Lily needs to go.'

'She wants to look up Vera, the Russian woman who took her in, and give her some small present. She feels she never thanked her properly. She saved her life, after all.'

'That could wait, surely.'

'We also thought we should take a look at your flat. In case vandals have broken in.'

Tomas wearied before Veronika did.

'There *used* to be a jeweller here,' said Veronika, rattling the rusted padlock on the door. 'I remember coming with Mother. She was getting some of her amber necklaces restrung. The jeweller was a little man. Jewish. With a white, wispy beard.'

'He might have died,' said Lily.

A notice pasted to the inside of the glass said in bleached letters: 'Closed temporarily due to circumstances beyond control. Apologies for any inconvenience caused.'

'Quite a bit of inconvenience, as it happens,' said Veronika. 'There must be others, however.'

Most shops round about were closed.

'Perhaps jewellers aren't much in demand these days,' said Lily, who was feeling hot and tired. The journey had been trying, had taken four hours instead of two. The train had been packed, and they'd stopped twice, for half an hour each time, and during these lulls rumours that they were being ambushed by a posse of German soldiers had run through the carriages like little licks of fire.

'I would have thought they were always in demand.' Veronika peered through the dusty window, to see nothing but a bare counter and pieces of paper lying on the floor. 'In times like these, jewels must be used as barter. Nothing much else has any value.'

They picked up their overnight bags and continued along the street. Veronika was also carrying a bunch of red and white carnations that she'd purchased from a woman in front of the station and planned to lay on Nils's grave. They jumped in closer to the wall as an army lorry rounded the

213

corner. It swerved past them at speed, coming dangerously near. Its back wheel mounted the narrow pavement. The street had not been designed for heavy vehicles. Then came another lorry, sounding its horn, and another. And another. The army seemed to be on the move. There was a feeling of urgency in the air. Of war. Which was not so very surprising. In Cesis one could almost forget it was happening. Lily began to wonder if they shouldn't just go back to the station and catch the next train home. She said so.

'If there is one,' she added, and felt panicked that there might not be, that they had come in on the last train before the Germans took Riga.

'You mean *forget* about the abortion?'

'Shush, Veronika, someone might hear!'

'They've got more to worry about than abortions.'

'That's what worries *me*.'

'Lily, we've come all this way. We talked about it. *You* decided.'

'I know, I know! For goodness' sake don't go on at me!'

'I am not going *on*.'

'You are. You don't know when you are, Veronika. You do *tend* to go on.'

'Look, why don't we go and have a cup of tea and talk about this calmly?'

'And where do you think we could get a cup of tea?'

'In one of the hotels. Let's go to the Rome.'

The lounge of the Hotel de Rome was full of army officers, a number of whom had women hanging on their arms. Prostitutes, mostly. Veronika and Lily found a free table in a corner and ordered tea, which would be a long time coming. The soldiers at the next table were sitting in a tight circle, shoulders hunched forward, cigarettes clenched between their fingers. Their eyes behind the smoke looked seared. They were talking feverishly. About a battle recently fought. *Horrific. Bloody. Nightmarish.* The adjectives rattled on, peppering Lily's ears like small gunshots, although she was doing her best not to listen.

'Maybe there's enough killing going on, Veronika.'

'Do you mean the baby?'

'Yes.'

'It's not a proper baby yet.'

'But it would be if it were left.'

'Do you want to have this child, Lily?'

'No.'

'Four is enough.'

'Yes.'

Veronika had said it would be more fool Lily if she were to say yes to having six children. Lily, in fact, had not said anything at the time. Later, Tom had said he hadn't meant they should have six children right now, of course not, not while the war was on, he wasn't that irresponsible, and he was very well aware that a disabled man did not make a very able father. 'You are an exceedingly able father,' Lily had told him, gently kneading the back of his neck, trying to ease the tight muscles. 'Not much of an able husband, though!' he'd said. Since being wounded he had stayed away from her in bed, had seemed to have lost either the energy or the desire. She had not dared ask which, but she had not minded too much, since she was so tired most nights that all she wanted to do was sleep.

'Tom was only talking about what the *ideal* family might constitute,' said Lily.

'From his point of view. He doesn't have to bear them.'

'He's not a selfish man,' said Lily.

'Oh, I know that! My brother is the kindest of men. He just hasn't *thought*.'

'This baby wasn't planned.'

'I presume it was an accident.'

'That doesn't mean he'd want me to go through with . . . He wouldn't want me to get *rid* of it, you know that, Veronika.'

'But what do *you* want?'

'I don't know.'

'Lily, you're not going to turn into one of those women

who, when you ask them what they think about anything, say "I'll have to ask my husband". *Are* you?'

Lily did not reply.

'I'm sorry, Lily, I shouldn't have said that! I know you have a mind of your own.'

'Thank you,' said Lily coolly.

'Oh, honestly, my big mouth! You don't feel I influenced you unduly, do you? That I pushed you into this decision?'

Lily shook her head.

'If only you'd taken the decision to practise contraception!' said Veronika, letting her conciliatory approach slip.

Lily did practise contraception most of the time, when she had a need to do so, though she didn't know how much faith she could put in a rubber sponge soaked in vinegar. When taking it out, one might easily let other elements in. Her mother had told her that nothing but total abstinence was a hundred per cent reliable.

On the night she had conceived this baby – this foetus, for that was how she had set herself to think of it – she had been half asleep. She'd been drowsy and warm and when Tomas had slid his hand across her stomach and pulled her close to him she had not had the heart to say 'Wait a minute!' and leap out of bed. The moment was too important, too delicate, and by the time she'd have returned, equipped, from the bathroom Tom might have found himself incapable again. It was the first time he had approached her for months. She had sensed his anxiety in his breathing. She had had to re-assure him, and respond immediately.

'Here comes our tea,' said Veronika.

Two cups of pale yellowish liquid were set in front of them.

'It looks as if a leaf might have been trailed through the water, but not much more. Never mind, it's a warm drink and it might do you good. You're looking pretty peely-wally.' Veronika grinned. 'Did I get it right? Peely-wally?'

Lily nodded.

'Do you mind if I smoke? It won't make you feel sick?'

Lily shook her head.

'Are you all right?'

'I'm not sure. I feel a little odd, to tell the truth, as if someone was twisting my inside with a screwdriver.'

'Maybe you should go to the ladies' room? Do you want me to come with you?'

Lily stood up. 'Something's happening,' she said, looking down at her legs. She could feel warm liquid trickling down between her thighs.

'Blood!' said Veronika.

A soldier at the next table looked round.

Lily fled across the lounge, leaving a trail of red dots behind her. Like Hansel and Gretel going into the wood, Veronika said later. She gathered up their bags and went flying after Lily. She forgot her flowers, which were later picked up by one of the soldiers' women.

Lily had a miscarriage in the lavatory of the ladies' room at the Hotel de Rome.

'You know how to pick your places, don't you?' said Veronika, who was holding her hand.

'Thank goodness I hadn't sold my brooch,' was the first thing Lily said, once she'd recovered her breath. She wanted to laugh but she could not quite, and if she did she thought she might become hysterical.

They couldn't find a cab – most of the horses had been requisitioned by the army – so they had to walk to the apartment, with Veronika half carrying Lily and urging her on. After they'd got in and Lily had lain down, Veronika went out again to look for a doctor. A straightforward one, who practised in the normal, front-street way.

'Nothing to worry about now,' she said to Lily while the doctor was in the bathroom washing his hands. 'It's just a miscarriage.'

The doctor was elderly, and unknown to Lily. The one who had attended her during her first pregnancy had been called up. He had been killed ministering to the wounded in a field tent on the Island of Death.

This doctor was kind, and paternal. 'Lie still, child, and relax. Everything's going to be all right.' He had seen many miscarriages in his time. It was Mother Nature's way of righting itself. Getting rid of abnormalities. 'I always tell mothers they should be grateful to miscarriages. Saves a lot of trouble later.'

Veronika sent a telegram to Tomas. 'Lily suffered miscarriage. Nothing to be alarmed about. Home in three to four days.'

Veronika, while Lily was resting in bed on doctor's orders, went to visit Vera and found her in a pitiful state.

'She looked ill and undernourished,' Veronika reported when she returned to the apartment. 'She's had to give up her market stall. Her legs were swelling up like sandbags and she was finding it more and more difficult to get anything to sell. She's half starving. I've asked her to come back to Cesis with us. I'm sure you approve?'

'Oh yes. But what will your mother say?'

'Nothing. She doesn't notice what's going on in the house half the time. We can manage for food. We've got plenty of garden produce for everyone and the hens are laying well.'

'While it's summer.'

'The war might end by winter.'

'You don't believe that, do you?'

Veronika shrugged.

During the night they had heard the sound of shelling. It was in the distance, said Veronika. Lily thought it was growing nearer. Half of their neighbours in the block seemed to have vacated their apartments. An eerie emptiness hung over the street in the long light evening. But lovers still wandered in the park, their arms entwined, and vanished into the bushes. The men all wore uniform.

Next day, Lily and Veronika returned to the country, taking Vera with them.

The Russian woman settled down quickly and her health improved. She made herself useful round the house, helping Morag and Mara, and she became especially attached to her little namesake. Old Vera and Young Vera, they were called.

Queen's Road, Aberdeen

My dear sister,

I have been thinking about you constantly in recent weeks and have sensed that you might be in Trouble. You will be comforted to know that I have been remembering you in my prayers night and morning, Garnet also. Evil is stalking the land of Russia. I pray too for the Tsar and his Family. Remember that the Lord is truly thy shepherd and therefore *Thou Shall Not Want.*

Your loving sister in Christ,
Euphemia

My dear Lily,

Just to let you know that we have had a brief note from Garnet, which she managed to send out through the British Embassy. At least we now know that they are alive and well. We get some news from our newspapers, and additional information from Andrew, but he says it is no easy matter, communications being what they are, to know exactly what is going on in Petrograd. There appears to be much confusion.

Andrew was home recently on a few days' leave. He is still 'walking out', as Nessie calls it, with little Rose Sibbald.

A quick tip from cook. She has found it works very well to use liquid paraffin instead of fat when making a cake. Especially for chocolate cakes. If you can get cocoa. I am sure the boys would enjoy a nice home-made cake. All children do. When the war is over you must bring your little family home and we shall make sure that we feed you all up!

In the meantime, be of stout heart!

I remain, as always,
Your ever loving mother,
Jemima McKenzie

The letters had taken six weeks to make their precarious journey across the seas, and would be the last for some time. The war was closing in. Hard news was difficult to come by, but any that they did hear was bad.

Having shelled Riga half to pieces, the German troops entered the city on the third of September, and were soon sweeping north toward Cesis.

Petrograd

October 1917

'It's obvious that Dolly is *enceinte*,' said the countess.

'That's the least of our troubles,' said Garnet. She had been finding of late that she was resorting more and more to well-worn phrases. *Keep your spirits up. Don't let things get you down.* They seemed to be comforting, the very well-wornness of them, as they flowed from the tongue.

'You are very restless this afternoon,' said the countess.

'Half the city is.'

'Where is your little monster?'

'He's gone to play with my friend Eithne's child.'

'That is most kind of your friend Eithne.'

'He is perfectly well behaved most of the time. It's only when he's bored that he's naughty. When he has to sit in a salon and pretend to be grown-up. He's not three yet! Some people forget what a child is like. Some people have never known.' Garnet knew that using sarcasm on her mother-in-law was like throwing peas against a wall, yet at times she had to indulge in it, for her own good.

'We shall have to ask Dolly to go.'

'Where?'

The countess looked surprised. 'That is her *affaire*, is it not?'

'I think it might be ours just as much. This is her home.'

'She has a brother, does she not?' said the countess vaguely, her hand straying to the table where her sweetmeats no longer were.

The subject was dropped and Garnet got up.

'Where are you going?' asked her mother-in-law, who hated to be left alone.

'To the kitchen.'

'You're always going to the kitchen!'

Garnet left the room.

When she pushed open the kitchen door she gave a start. Leo was sitting at the table. A night's growth fuzzed his chin.

'I thought you'd been forbidden the door!'

'Not the back one, though. They forget about the back of the house. They leave themselves open there.'

'You look as if you haven't slept.'

'I haven't. I came to let you know that the city is in the hands of the Bolsheviks.'

They went out into the streets together. Garnet felt it was of little importance now if the family were to see her with Leo. Leo was not a Bolshevik. And the Bolsheviks were the new enemy.

She was surprised to see the city functioning as normal.

'Most people aren't aware of what's been happening,' said Leo. 'It's all been staged so quietly, and efficiently. Scarcely a shot has been fired.' Lenin was later to say that starting the revolution was as easy as picking up a feather.

During the night, using darkness as a shield, the Bolsheviks had managed to place pickets in all the strategic positions in the city: telephone centres, post offices, railway stations, banks, bridges. The Red Guards had armed themselves with rifles from the Peter and Paul Fortress.

'They haven't taken the Winter Palace yet, but it's only a matter of time. Lenin hasn't bothered to wait till he gets the cabinet into his hands; he's already issued a declaration telling us, the citizens of Russia, that the Provisional Government has been deposed and replaced by the Petrograd

Soviet of Workers' and Soldiers' Deputies!'

The shops were open and selling the few goods they had. People were going in and out of banks and office buildings.

'Business as usual,' said Leo. 'Little do they know!'

'But they soon will.'

'It won't sink in for a while. People aren't that interested in politics. Strange, isn't it, considering the effect it has on our lives? "A new government," they'll say. "The last lot weren't much good. This lot can't be any worse! All we can do is hope they put food in our bellies. That's the main thing! Meanwhile, let me get on with my life!"'

Two days later, the count was jubilant. The people had gone on strike! Civil servants, bank employees, telegraph and telephone engineers, water and transport workers. 'Even the schoolteachers are out!'

'I went to the bank this morning,' said Elena, 'and found it shut.'

'Told you they wouldn't put up with it, didn't I? I'll tell you something else. A nice little story, this.' The count chuckled. 'Our dear Commissar – *Commissar*! – of Finance went to the state bank with armed soldiers *and* a military band to demand ten million dollars. Can you imagine it!'

'He must have some style,' said the countess, 'if he went with a band.'

That was what Garnet had been thinking, but had thought it better not to say so. The count had little sense of humour.

'I wonder what they played,' said the countess, who never knew when to let something be.

The count was glaring at her. 'He was refused, you'll be glad to hear, military band or not. This is the stuff Russia is made of. Standing up to blithering idiots! We'll bring those bloody Bolsheviks to their knees yet. What do you say, Seryozha?'

Sergei had just come in, and had gone to kiss his wife. He was telling her how beautiful she looked in the soft shade of blue she was wearing. His breath was warm on her neck.

'What colour would you say it was? Delphinium? I remember delphiniums growing in your garden in Aberdeen that first summer. Do you remember me commenting on their blueness? Saying I had never seen flowers so *blue* before?'

Garnet could not remember that.

'Seryozha,' said his father, impatient for his son to stop mumbling into his wife's neck, 'you agree, don't you?'

'With what?' Sergei traced his forefinger along the line of his wife's collarbone and smiled when she trembled.

'We've got to keep up the fight! We're not going to lie down like lambs.'

At last Sergei straightened himself up from his wife's embrace.

'Lambs? What an idea! If we don't resist those bloody Leninists now we'll go under for good.'

'Are *you* planning to strike, Seryozha?' asked his mother.

'Striking is not the only weapon in our armoury.'

'Be careful what you say,' cautioned his father. 'You must reveal none of your tactics. Remember we have servants in the house.'

'Only a very few,' said the countess petulantly. 'I rang and rang for Dolly this morning but she didn't come.'

'Dolly?' Garnet put her head round the kitchen door.

'I'm here, Madame.' Dolly was just coming in from the back entrance, with a clump of people behind her, crowding close on her heels, almost propelling her. 'You know my brother Vladimir, don't you? This is his wife, Nina. And these are their children.'

There were four children, Garnet counted, her eyes bobbing up and down. They ranged in age from about four to fourteen, were miserably dressed, and carried ill-tied bundles. The mother looked like a rabbit scared by a sudden flash of light.

Dolly ushered them into the kitchen, whereupon they dropped their various bits and pieces and swarmed towards the stove with outstretched hands.

'Could I have a word with you, Dolly?' asked Garnet.

They withdrew to the passageway.

'What's going on? They're not moving *in*, are they?'

'There's lots of rooms free, Madame, now that all the servants have gone.'

'They've *all* gone?'

'Seems so. They don't want to be servants any longer.'

'They've gone to join the Bolsheviks, have they?'

'Well, I don't know about that. But they've gone anyway. Most are making for their villages. They can get more food in the country, grow their own stuff and chop up trees to keep warm. It's cold, with winter settling in and the snow on the ground already. My brother's family has been near freezing to death. They were living in one horrible little room – you should have seen it!'

'I don't know what the count will say.'

'I wouldn't bother telling him if I was you. What he doesn't know doesn't hurt him.'

'Perhaps your sister-in-law could give a hand in the house?'

'I'll ask her. But she's not very strong. She's a poor soul; you could probably see that for yourself. She's had terrible trouble since her last miscarriage. She has a weakness. Always having miscarriages, she is. She's pregnant again at the moment, but don't suppose she'll keep it. Best if she doesn't, really. Just one more mouth to feed.'

'Oh well, do what you can, Dolly. There's no likelihood of you leaving us, is there?'

'None at all, Madame.'

'I'm worried about Felix,' said Eithne.

'We're all worried about our men,' said Garnet, who was doing her ironing. She had set up a table in one of the day nurseries. She and Lily had fortunately been taught to iron when they were small. Their mother had seen to it that they had known how to cook, launder and sew. Garnet had taken the *Woman's Book* down from its shelf and blown off the dust.

Its tips were coming in useful. Sergei's sisters were inept at any domestic accomplishments. Garnet was trying to teach Elena to mend socks and put patches on trouser knees.

'The Finance Commissar came back to the bank last night.' Eithne kept her voice down. 'With armed guards. He found it deserted, except for a few watchmen and couriers. I don't understand why they didn't keep it better protected.'

'What are the banks to do? They can't start employing armies.'

'They took over the building and sent the guards to bring in some of the personnel.'

'They came for Felix?'

'I was near terrified out of my wits. A knock on the door in the middle of the night and armed men standing there! Holy Mother of God!' Eithne crossed herself. 'He had to go with them and open up the vaults. They took five million roubles.'

'The count said they must be getting desperately short of cash.'

'Oh God,' said Elena. 'Red Guards!'

'Where?' said Garnet.

'Coming towards us. On the pavement.'

'They won't bother us. They've no reason to.'

'It's all right for you. You're not even Russian. They won't have any quarrel with you. You're a British citizen. You could go home any time you wanted to.'

'Could I? Don't forget that they consider foreigners married to natives to be Russian.'

The Guards were almost upon them, four walking cockily abreast, with their five-pointed red stars on their cloth helmets and red rosettes on their coats, and rifles slung haphazardly over their shoulders. The pavement was wide and there would have been room for everyone to pass but when the men drew closer to the women they moved over so that they were going to meet head on. Elena tugged at Garnet's arm, but Garnet was not inclined to give way.

She came to a dead halt, face to face with one of the Guards.

'One of *them*,' he said, and spat in her face. Her head jerked back, as if she had been shot, and then she stepped aside, into the bank of snow in the gutter, and would have lost her balance had Elena not caught hold of her arm and steadied her. The Guards laughed and carried on.

'Bloody Bolsheviks!' said Garnet, furiously scrubbing her face with a handkerchief.

'Are you all right?' asked Elena nervously.

'I will be when I get home and decontaminate my face. God, I could have killed him!'

'You looked as if you could. I thought for a minute you were going to hit him.'

'So did I.'

They resumed walking. Elena looked back over her shoulder to make sure no one was behind them.

'Natalya and Oscar are talking about leaving. They say Russia is finished. The press is no longer free. Oscar's editor friend was arrested yesterday, his paper's been closed down. They want to take the children and start a new life somewhere.'

'But where? Most of Europe's at war. And the Baltics are overrun by the Germans, God help them. God help Lily and Tom and the children. It would help if one believed in God.'

'Surely you do, Garnet?'

'What could be *sure* about that? About anything?'

'No, you're right! That's why Natalya and Oscar want to leave. They think they could still get out through Bessarabia. What about Seryozha? Would he go? You could live in Scotland.'

'I doubt if he'd do it. He loves his country. And as long as he stays, I stay. He says he'd rather die than see Russia go down the drain.'

'Do you think he might go and join the Volunteers?'

'Yes, that's why I'm worried. But maybe he has to. Some of his friends have already gone to join General Alekseev in southern Russia. Oh, isn't it difficult, Lena? I want him to do the honourable thing in his own eyes but I want him to be safe at the same time.'

'I know.' Elena sighed.

'No one is safe, though, any more. Anywhere.'

'Natalya has asked me to go with them.'

'And will you?'

'I don't know. I wouldn't like to leave Mother and Father. But one must think of one's children first, mustn't one?'

As they rounded the corner into the Embankment they saw that a large grey van was standing outside their house. They quickened their steps. Both halves of the front door were wide open.

'What's going on?' said Garnet.

A Red Guard was coming out of the door carrying a picture. It was the Matisse that Sergei had bought in Paris.

'What are you doing with that?' demanded Garnet.

'Doesn't belong to you, lady! State property.'

He put the painting into the van. At least the other Matisse was in Aberdeen. Though that was cold comfort. For now came another Guard with another picture. It was the woman in the red dress.

'That's mine!' cried Garnet. 'You can't take that! My father gave it to me.'

She was pushed aside and turned back to see two Guards lugging an eighteenth-century French armoire. As they went through the doorway they scraped its gleaming mahogany side on the jamb. And now the brocade sofa on which the countess liked to sit drinking tea and playing patience went past.

'What are we to sit on?' Garnet asked one of the men, as she watched her own rather modest velvet chair going by, the one from her little sitting room that she'd taken such pleasure in arranging.

'Your arse!'

She had asked for that.

Everything of value, including jewellery, was stripped from the house. The van had to return several times to carry it all away.

They wandered through the cold, empty rooms. On the walls blank rectangular spaces, edged with dark, smudged lines stared reproachfully down at them.

'They haven't taken *absolutely* everything,' said Garnet, who after the initial shock was determined to be cheerful. They had been half prepared for this to happen. Guards were stripping houses all over the city. Garnet could hear her mother at her side exhorting her. *Lots worse off than you. You didn't actually need all that stuff.* They had not taken the beds or many of the carpets and they'd left the odd chair and small table lying about. And her mother-in-law still had her samovar.

'But no tea,' wailed the countess. 'What's the use of a samovar without tea? And no sofa.' She was sitting on a leather Afghan pouffe (and overflowing it) in the middle of her salon. 'If only the count had been here. Or Seryozha. They wouldn't have let those men get away with it.'

'It's fortunate that they weren't,' said Garnet. A number of aristocrats had already been arrested, and Seryozha slept at night with a pistol beside the bed. 'Come on, Elena and I will give you a hand up the stairs. You need to lie down.'

As soon as they opened the bedroom door the smell assailed them. Someone had defecated in the middle of the four-poster bed. The Guard must have been excited. His bowels had been loose. The ikon-stand had been kicked over and the ikons lay scattered and splintered. A boot had been taken to them.

The countess gasped, and sagged between Garnet and Elena. They had to let her down on to the floor.

They eased off the satin bed cover, but even so were not careful enough and some of the mustard-coloured slime dripped on to their feet and the hems of their dresses. Elena's throat glugged and then she vomited into the chamber pot.

Dolly had gone to find fresh bedding. When she'd returned and they'd made up the bed, Elena persuaded her mother to lie down and Dolly eased the shoes off the countess's swollen feet.

229

'Why do you wear such tight shoes, Mama?' said Elena.

'They are such nice shoes,' moaned her mother. 'Such pretty, elegant shoes.' She lay back. 'I want Father Paul! Where is Father Paul? He hasn't come to see me for days.'

No one had seen him. Like many other members of the priesthood, he had vanished. His church had been pillaged and burnt.

'Find me a priest!' cried the countess. 'I want to die.'

Garnet went down to the kitchen with Dolly to see what was to be done about an evening meal.

Dolly's brother's family was seated around the table, eating some kind of gruel.

Dolly reached into a flour tin (which was empty of flour), and took out a small canvas sack. She swung it across to Garnet.

'What's this?' It felt knobbly.

'Your jewellery. We might have need of it. When I heard them coming I ran up and got it.'

'What would I do without you, Dolly?'

Next day, coming in, Garnet found the house again in a state of disruption and for a moment she thought the Guards had come back.

'What's going on?' she demanded. She must stop asking that. It had become her constant cry. To Dolly and Leo; Dolly inside the house, Leo out. So much was going on outside that it was impossible for even Leo to keep track. Decrees were being issued almost daily by the *Sovnarkom* (the Council of People's Commissars). Some sounded reasonable. For example, the decrees on work, which established an eight-hour day and a forty-eight-hour week for all industrial workers, with rules about overtime and holidays and unemployment insurance. As Leo said, one couldn't argue with that. It was not before time. But the decree saying Russia wanted to make peace with its enemies was more problematical, for where would that leave the Allies in their fight against Germany? And as for the ban on all non-Bolshevik newspapers, well, of course, that had made Leo gloomy. He'd been even gloomier the day the Constitutional Democratic Party, the main liberal party, had been banned, and its leaders arrested. No one knew how many people had been arrested. Both the count and Sergei used the back entrance to the house now – though, as Sergei said, that would scarcely fox the Red Guards if they were to come in the night. They'd cover both entrances.

'Don't talk about them coming for you,' begged Garnet.

'I must. You know it's a real possibility, don't you?' he said. 'The Bolsheviks have brought a reign of terror to the city.'

Garnet faced Dolly. 'What is going on?' she asked again.

'I thought they could do with more space. The servants' quarters are dreadfully cramped and there isn't much light from the barred windows.'

They stood to one side in the corridor as Vladimir, Nina and their four children filed past carrying their belongings, which had swollen visibly since their arrival in the house. Garnet recognised the red wool, high-necked dress Nina was wearing; it was Elena's. Her mind came in quickly to correct the statement: it *used* to be Elena's. Then she recognised Vladimir's jacket, which was hanging on him in the way that jackets do when they're too large for their wearers. It was of Harris tweed, in soft heathery shades that made Garnet think of the Deeside hills. Seryozha had bought it in Banchory. They'd gone shopping, she and Seryozha, Lily and Tom. Tom had bought a jacket, too. A greeny-blue one, if she remembered rightly. They'd posed together, he and Seryozha, in front of the cheval mirror in the shop, and they'd larked about and asked if they looked like Scotsmen, and Seryozha had said, 'What we need now is a couple of kilts,' and she (Garnet) and Lily had thrown up their hands in horror at the very idea. Was Tom still wearing his jacket? What were he and Lily doing? What would their daily lives be like under enemy occupation? Perhaps not so very different from theirs here: living on their nerves, watching over their shoulders, starting at sudden knocks, short of food and fuel, queuing on cold pavements, children crying, not understanding why they should be cold and hungry. Her child, and Elena's children, at any rate, could not understand. Vladimir's and Nina's four were amazingly silent. Garnet had not heard them either cry or speak.

'I've given them the guest rooms at the end of the corridor,' said Dolly. 'You won't be having any guests to stay, will you?'

'I suppose not.' Garnet had hoped to have Lily as a guest in her home one day and show her Petersburg; they'd talked about it before they were married. 'You can come and see my city and I'll come and see yours. Won't it be fun? They're only a night-train ride from each other, the two cities. That's nothing!'

'I thought I'd have the music room for myself,' said Dolly.

'The *music* room?'

'I've always liked that room. I used to sit in it sometimes for a minute or two when I was dusting. It's peaceful, don't you think? I haven't heard anyone playing music in it for ages.'

'No, you're right. They probably haven't.'

'And you have a piano of your own in your room.'

'I'm lucky to have it, I know that.' Garnet's sarcasm was wasted on Dolly. 'I'm glad the Guards didn't take it.'

'I expect they found the pianos too heavy.'

The two older children of Vladimir and Nina came back, dragging a mattress behind them.

'Mind you don't scuff the walls,' warned their aunt. She looked at Garnet. 'It's all for the best, you know, having them here. I'm doing you a service.'

'Oh?'

'When they come requisitioning it'll look better for you. Think what it would be like if the family was to be found sitting in the middle of all these empty rooms.'

Before they came 'requisitioning', Eithne arrived in a state of great agitation with her children. They were each carrying a large carpet bag. Maria's arms being short, hers had trailed on the snowy ground, so that its bottom was soaking wet.

'They've arrested Felix!' said Eithne, and burst into tears, though she dried them quickly. Maria's bottom lip was wobbling. 'Don't worry, darling. I'm sure Papa will be home with us again very soon.' To Garnet she said in a quiet aside, 'Not that we have a home for him to come back to. They've ransacked it and taken it over. For the workers, they said. It was the Cheka who came for him. I've never heard of them before, have you? They seem to be some kind of new secret police. They were simply terrifying.'

Dolly assigned to them another of the guest bedrooms. 'It has a dressing room off. Useful for keeping your clothes in.'

'Not that we have much to keep,' said Eithne.

The one in charge had a clipboard. 'How many living in the house?'

'There's myself and my son,' said Garnet, adding hastily, 'He's only little,' in case the Guard would think he was old enough to be arrested. 'Then there's my mother-in-law and my sister-in-law and her two children, and a friend and her two children, and Dolly' (she forbore to say 'the maid') 'and her brother's family of six.' Fortunately neither Seryozha nor the count was in the house. It was seldom these days that Seryozha slept in his own bed at night, for it was during the hours of darkness that the Cheka tended to come and take people away.

'How many rooms?'

'I'm not sure.'

Dolly offered to take him round to count.

'What are they doing?' asked the countess. 'What does that man want? He has *une figure pas agréable.*'

'Don't worry about it,' said Garnet.

When Dolly and the Guard came back, he said, 'I'm putting your sister-in-law and her children into one room. They don't need a room apiece. Some people in the city are

233

living ten to a room. And your mother-in-law can have your sitting room and you can keep your bedroom for the time being. One room, one family. These are big rooms. This salon could take half a dozen.'

'Half a dozen what?' asked the countess, but he was already leaving the room.

Garnet heard the knock. She'd slept lightly since the coming of the revolution, woke often in the night thinking she could hear knocking. She'd lift her head from the pillow and listen and then realise the noise was in her head. But this was not; it was a tremendous hammering, and it was accompanied by raised voices demanding the door be opened up. It woke most of the household, which was considerable. Men and women wearing a variety of nightshirts and nightcaps – strangers, inhabitants of the house – tumbled into the corridors with their hair on end, palming their eyes. Pale faces peered over the banisters. One or two braver souls ventured a step or two down the stairs.

Garnet's first thought on waking had been to thank God (she still did, even though she doubted His presence) that Seryozha was not there. Then she'd remembered that the count was in the house. Seryozha had told his father over and over again that it was foolish to go on sleeping at home, but the count could not quite believe that he was touchable. 'Those buffoons!' he'd say. 'I've got my pistol. I can protect myself.'

It was Dolly who went down to open the door.

Cesis

July 1993

They went to Cesis by train. Beside them, taking up the
fourth seat, was a Latvian woman in her late sixties with
short white hair and tanned, muscled arms and legs that suggested a lifetime of hard physical work. A hospital cleaner
until her retirement, Erika was friendly and talkative and
showed interest in the two women from abroad. She wanted
to see photographs of where they came from, and exclaimed
over the beauties of Aberdeenshire.

Erika had a flat in Riga but would prefer to live in Cesis; it
was her parents' home town and the place of her birth. 'It's
so peaceful compared with Riga. There are fewer Russians
too!' (Helga and Katrina did not bother to translate that
remark for Lydia.) She was going to visit her daughter and to
take part in a ceremony of remembrance at the cemetery for
her parents and husband. 'We Latvians never forget our
dead.' On her knee reposed a large bunch of damp marigolds
wrapped in newspaper. She'd grown them on her allotment.
She would go more often to visit her daughter, she said, if the
journey were not so expensive. The return fare cost just
under one lat. Her pension was fifteen lats a month. That was
equivalent to fifteen pounds sterling.

'We shall be going to the cemetery, too,' said Katrina.

'Do you have someone buried in Cesis?'

'Our fathers,' said Katrina. 'Lydia's and mine, that is.'

Lydia, since she could not participate directly in the conversation, was looking out of the window. They were going through the outskirts of Riga, past shoddily built factories and seedy apartment blocks. Everything looked cheaply constructed. Pieces of rusted machinery lay scattered about, weeds sprouted jungle-like around them.

'The Communists had a penchant for the ugly,' said Helga.

'We have our own complement of ugliness in the West,' said Katrina. 'You don't have a monopoly.'

'The Russians ruined our country,' said Erika.

Now they were out in the country, running through forests and green spaces. The train trundled, making no effort to pick up speed; the track was not in good enough shape for fast travel. They stopped at halts that had no stations, where passengers disembarked with their bundles and headed up sandy white tracks into the midst of birch groves.

'The wild flowers are very pretty,' said Lydia, and Helga translated it for Erika's benefit. Lydia found it frustrating having to sit in a fog of non-comprehension, waiting for Katrina or Helga to supply potted translations.

'You see the pink one?' said Erika. 'The one that grows everywhere?'

'The rosebay willowherb?' said Katrina.

Erika nodded. 'When my husband was in Siberia he was fed soup made with rosebay willowherb and tiny little fishes that made their teeth go black. That was all they gave them to eat. They were so weak they could hardly stand. He came home with his mouth encrusted with sores and when he opened it the children in the block screamed at the sight of his teeth. They thought he was Count Dracula! Is it any wonder he died a comparatively young man? He was a prisoner for twenty-eight years. In 1949 he wrote a letter to his mother, and because of that *she* was sent to Siberia.'

'What did she say?' asked Lydia. 'That was a very passionate speech.'

'Her husband was in Siberia.'

'Tell her that was the fate of many Russians also.'

Aberdeen

August 1918

'She's joined the Army.'

Andrew looked at his mother. 'The *army*? What army?'

'You might well ask. There seem to be armies everywhere – our own, dear love them, those poor soldiers, it isn't right, making men go through all that horror in the mud, when their mothers gave birth to them it was wasn't what they imagined for them – and I have to say I'm greatly relieved that *you* are serving in the Admiralty, Andrew. And then there's the German Army – don't suppose their mothers would have wanted it either – and the Red Army, and the White Army. Do you think Seryozha might have joined the White Army? I can't say I'm particularly sympathetic to the *Whites* – well, they mainly want to hang on to their privileges, don't they? – though I don't care for what the Reds are getting up to, on the other hand, and Sergei *is* my son-in-law, which means we cannot be against him. I just hope he can stop fighting soon. It's so difficult to learn anything much from Garnet's letters when they do come, which isn't all that often. I dare say most fall by the wayside. And she'd be ill-advised to say much, anyway, I appreciate that. As she said in one letter, "I have to haud my wheesht." That should have bamboozled any censor! But what *about* the White Army, Andrew? How are they doing?'

237

'Holding on. They'll fight to the death.'

Jemima sighed.

'It's war, Mother.'

'Indeed.'

'So what army has Effie joined?' Andrew had not taken his mother's initial remark seriously.

'The Salvation.'

'Truly?'

'She's got a bonnet and a tambourine.'

'Oh well, if it makes her happy,' said Andrew doubtfully.

'She's out at a meeting – or gathering. I'm not sure what they call it. She's gone to sing and play in Union Grove. If you recall, they have a stance there.'

'They do marvellous work.'

'Marvellous.' Jemima McKenzie sighed. 'Why, then, am I not more pleased to see her as a soldier of Christ? I suppose it's not quite what I *expected* for her.'

Expectations! thinks Jemima McKenzie, as she settles herself at the oak roll-top desk in the morning room to write to her daughters after Andrew has gone (looking handsome in his naval uniform) to meet his sweetheart Rose. That romance is still flourishing in spite of the separations of war. Jemima wonders if Rose's very insipidness might not be an attraction for Andrew: a counterbalance to the aggression in the world. If that should be so what will happen once peace comes? Mothers (herself included) like to delude themselves that they don't have expectations for their children, that they leave them free and unencumbered to make up their own minds. What a fallacy!

So there is Andrew out now with his Rose, strolling hand in hand through Hazelhead Park for all the world to see. For Rose's mother to see. As far as Mrs Sibbald is concerned, to walk so publicly, so *intimately*, with flesh touching flesh, is tantamount to a declaration of intent. Jemima sighs. Andrew might at least have chosen a girl with some *brains*, some *character*, someone it would have been interesting to have as a daughter-in-law. There you are, though – she, Jemima, is thinking of herself! Which is quite wrong. As a mother she should try to consider herself as little as possible.

She dips her pen into the inkwell and has to blot her finger, for she has dipped too high and stained her knuckle blue-black. Again she sighs.

They like their sons-in-law, she and Alexander; they have nothing against them personally. Or not much. (Both she and Alexander have always felt a little uneasy about Seryozha.) But by marrying these men their twin daughters have become trapped in foreign countries, with their children. Her grandchildren. Is she allowed to think that? Consider her own interests? And then there's her Soldier of Christ singing in the street in that most unbecoming uniform. Now, that was a rather trivial thought! Unworthy of her, Effie would say, and Jemima can only agree. It just slipped out. Effie was unlucky with her Hamish, mind you. And yet it had looked as if her life was more prescribed than the others'. Engaged to a nice young man whose parents the family knew. Then came those bitter winds of fate. Is that what it comes down to? Chance? Only up to a point, for they made the choices in the first place, and are still making them, thinks Jemima, redipping her pen, which has dried, and once again having to blot her finger. (Does one never learn?) Effie didn't *have* to pick up a tambourine. No wind blew that into her hand.

Jemima, though, did not suffer overwhelming anxiety over her children, which it would have been easy to do, given their circumstances. She had found after a while it was as if her ability to worry had reached saturation point; the sponge was full and could soak up no more. And the anxieties attached to Lily and Garnet were so immense and so complex that she did not know where to focus them. It was not a case of 'out of sight, out of mind', for she thought of them daily and offered prayers for their safety every evening before sleeping, but if she could have *seen* Garnet under siege in the Petrograd house, or Lily with German soldiers at her gate, then her anxiety would have risen again like a cork bobbing up when more water is added to a glass.

My dearest Lily,

Goodness knows when – or if – you will ever receive this. Andrew tells me that Russia has renounced sovereignty of the Baltic provinces under the Treaty of Brest-Litovsk. He says they've done it to get the Germans off their backs, not out of altruism. States seldom do anything for other people's interests. I don't suppose this will be making a great deal of difference to your lives at present since you have other uninvited guests on your soil. But, Andrew says, fingers crossed, this could mark the beginning of the way towards independence for you.

Jemima paused, wondering if this would be censored – by the British? the Germans (the uninvited guests)? Would there be a censor in Riga reading all incoming mail? – and then she continued on safer territory.

Another tip from cook. Use mashed parsnips or neeps – can you get neeps? – as the basis for a cake. We had a parsnip one the other day and it was delicious. I had some of my women friends in for tea and they commented favourably. If it passes that test it should pass the scrutiny of your family!

At Easter we – Effie and I – had some deprived children in for tea. I boiled up eggs with onion skins, as Tom instructed me to do, and they came out beautifully. Such lovely marbled colours, mustard and tan and orange and yellow. The children were thrilled. They rolled them down the bank, the way you all used to do.

We trust Tom is well, and that you are, too, and are looking after yourself. Remember to do that. Mothers usually put themselves last on the list. Andrew is home on leave and sends love. As indeed we all do, and we look forward to the day when we are reunited.

Your ever loving mother,
Jemima McKenzie

PS Effie has become a Sally Ann.

She had just slipped her letter into the box, when she saw the postman coming along the street. He had a letter for her from Lily.

'Looks a bitty the worse for wear,' he said, handing the battered envelope over.

'She's occupied by the Germans. It's a mercy any mail gets through at all.'

Jemima opened it standing there in the street.

Cesis, 10 March 1918

My dearest Mother and Father,

I want you to know that we are well, all things considered. And there are many things to consider, of which I will not speak, though it is not as bad as you might imagine. They pay little attention to us. I think their energies are occupied elsewhere. What threat can we present here?

Tom is almost back to full health, but it has taken all this time – well over a year, after all, since he was wounded. His eye socket still gives trouble, but he seldom complains.

The winter has been hard, the cold intense and food very scarce. Morag, though, is a wonder at making a little go a long way. Last night I dreamt I was in the house in Aberdeen eating lentil soup and steak-and-kidney pudding and you, Mother, were saying, "Eat up, child, eat up!" As if I needed to be urged! I could TASTE the food and SMELL it – that is the unkind thing about dreams – and then I woke!

I hope it will not be too long before I shall be there 'in the flesh'.

Much love,
From your daughter Lily

241

*

Jemima looked up from the letter to see a Sally Ann approaching and for a moment did not know her daughter.

'Mother!' Effie waved the tambourine.

'Ah, Effie! Have you had a good morning?'

Effie's cheeks were glowing. 'Wonderful. Two women came to the Lord! Sinners.'

'They said so?'

'Oh yes, indeed. They freely confessed and were filled with repentance.'

'How nice.' Jemima waved to Mrs Sibbald, who was at her window. 'I am really glad to see you looking so happy, Effie.'

'You could be happy, too, Mother.'

'I think not, dear,' said Jemima McKenzie, feeling suddenly tired.

Cesis

July 1918

Lily, in a need to escape from the house, the children, the grown-ups, and all those who comprised her extended family, went for a walk in the fields. An army of occupation was encamped around them, but not noticeably so. German soldiers could be seen in the streets of Cesis, but seldom on the country lanes near their house. It was easy, if not to forget about them, then not to think about them. Lily was not thinking about Germans as she went out that warm July afternoon. She was too consumed by the idea of escape, of solitariness, of having a few minutes' peace in which to try to make contact with the person that she felt must still be there somewhere at the centre of her being. If she still had a centre, which at times she doubted. She was the children's mother, Tom's wife, Veronika's sister-in-law, Markus and Gertrude's daughter-in-law. She had too many roles to play. She had lost sight of Lily McKenzie.

The sun was dazzling, the field empty. She cut a swathe through the long grasses, letting her fingers trail along their feathery tops. She hitched her skirt up at the waist so that her legs could be bare below the knees. She liked the feel of the grass as it brushed against her skin. The sensation brought with it a little shiver of pleasure. She felt better already, out in the open, with the sight of wild flowers and the smell of warm earth rising up around her and the immensity of the sky overhead. It seemed a long time since she had had the chance to look up.

She sank down in the midst of a rash of scarlet poppies, her arms outspread, her eyes half closed against the weight of the summer sun. The light shimmered on her lashes in a confusion of colours, golden, red, violet, blue. Her ears hummed with the sound of insects. She felt conscious of being a small speck on the edge of a great landmass stretching right across to Vladivostok and the Pacific Ocean. There were times yet, even after five years of being married to Tomas, when she wondered how it was she had come to be here.

For a few minutes she lay in a near trance, suspended in time and space, thinking of nothing at all, a state of being she had been longing for. Simply to *be*.

And then she became aware of a shadow passing before the sun. She opened her eyes, to see a man looking down at her. A German soldier. Wearing coarse cloth and a long row of shiny buttons up the front of his jacket.

'*Guten Tag,*' he said, and dropped down on to the ground beside her. Like a sack of potatoes falling. His body bruised the grass. She lay rigid. He leant on one elbow and inclined his head towards her, so that he kept the light from her face. She struggled to get up, but seemed not to have the strength to rise. His eyes, a clear, pale blue, fringed by white-blond lashes, were fixed on her. He looked young, no more than seventeen or eighteen. A boy, sent by the Kaiser to fight like a man on foreign soil.

Without taking his eyes from her, he plucked a grass and put it between his teeth. Strong, white, even teeth. His bottom lip looked heavy and damp. She could see the pores in his skin, see sweat breaking in them, feel the warmth of his breath on her cheek. Her heart was beating fast and irregularly. Why couldn't she get up? She must get up. Now! *Now!* She struggled again and he put out his hand and pushed her gently back.

Then he chucked the grass stem to one side and in one

swift movement had rolled on top of her, pinning her to the ground. His uniform felt rough through her thin cotton dress.

'No,' she said weakly. '*Nein.*'

'*Ja*!' He sounded almost joyous. '*Ja*!'

His face came down, his lips were parted seeking hers, and then another shadow swooped overhead like a giant bird, and an arm encircled the neck of the German and wrenched it back, away from her body, and she heard – or later imagined that she had heard – a sharp crack.

'I think I've broken his neck,' said Tomas.

The soldier lay limply on the ground, his cheek resting on a patch of poppies.

'Is he dead?' she whispered.

'I hope so.'

'Why hope it?'

'It was him or you, wasn't it? Did you want him to—?'

'Of course not!' cried Lily and began to sob, and Tomas put his arm round her and held her against him.

When she had quietened she said, 'But, Tom, you've *killed* a man.'

'He's not the first. Lily, I've been in a war, for Christ's sake! What did you think I was doing? Playing games?'

She looked down at the dead German. 'I only wanted to be alone for ten minutes! That wasn't much to ask, was it? Ten minutes to myself!' She felt angry now, with the German, herself, everything. 'It's terrible the things that men do to women!'

'It's terrible the things that men have to do,' said Tomas.

'I'm sorry, Tom.'

'It's not your fault.'

But was it her fault? The question would inevitably haunt Lily afterwards, and she would fluctuate between feeling guilty and feeling victimised. Had she been foolish to go alone into a field when there was a war on? (Or even if there were not?) Veronika, shrugging aside cautions from her mother and father, often walked along the lanes after dusk, and no harm had ever befallen her. In the winter she would take a short cut from the town, along a little-frequented path that led through a wood. Lily seldom went beyond the garden on her own. Perhaps the mistake had been in lying down, and closing her eyes. (She did not tell them she had been lying down.) 'She has her head in the clouds too much,' she'd overheard Veronika say to Gertrude. But it wasn't true! How could she, with four children to care for? It was only in odd moments that she allowed herself to drift away, to cut out from the reality around her. But Veronika would show sympathy for her after the event and say, 'It must have been awful for you. And yes, for Tom also. If I'd come along I'd have probably killed the German, too.'

The German: that was how they were always to refer to him, never as a man, or even a soldier. It was more impersonal. Lily sometimes thought of him as a person, secretly, for she had seen him living, face to face, had felt his breath, and she would suffer agonies of guilt and blame herself for having inadvertently caused the death of a man.

When the shock had passed, which it did quickly, out of necessity, they faced the problem of having a dead German soldier on their hands. Or at least at their feet. Lying in the grass.

'He can't be left here,' said Tomas, who to Lily seemed amazingly cool. 'If he's found, there could be reprisals.'

Lily shuddered.

'We'll have to bury him somewhere and hope they don't find him. If they don't, they might think he's deserted. Soldiers are deserting all the time.'

Lily was sent to fetch Veronika and Markus, who came without panic, bringing the cart, and parked it in the hollow of a nearby lane under overhanging trees. It was broad daylight, and would be until almost midnight. They couldn't wait for cover of darkness, said Tomas. Lily was lookout; the other three carried the body, covered with sacks, through the long grass under the burning sun. Standing on a knoll, scanning the empty, dusty roads on which nothing was fortunately moving but the three bowed figures of her husband, sister-in-law and father-in-law, Lily had a deep feeling of unreality. She no longer felt nervous. She no longer felt anything.

Lying in bed that night, unable to sleep, with the German resting in a woodland grave a couple of miles away, the emotions of the afternoon came flooding back. Tomas slept, muttering from time to time, and tossed. He had been very matter-of-fact. It had had to be done, so he had done it. His father and Veronika had reacted in the same way. They couldn't afford to have hysterics, said Veronika; the need to survive superseded all others.

With Tomas's breath rising and falling beside her, Lily remembered lying on the ground, saw again the German's face as he'd rested on his elbow and stared down at her. She'd felt like a bird held in the hypnotic thrall of a cat who knows it can take its time. She had seen their cat eyeball to eyeball with a bird, not touching it, yet the bird had been unable to lift off and fly away. She remembered, too, the sick feeling in the pit of her stomach when she'd heard the crack as the man's neck was jerked back.

She got up and went to sit by the window and look down into the garden. There was enough light to make out the shapes of the bushes and trees. It looked peaceful out there, but then so it had in the field, in the mellow afternoon sun.

Thinking she saw something move, she rose up in alarm. But it was only a low hanging branch being lifted by the wind.

'A car!' shouted Luke, coming running up the drive with Alex at his heels. 'A car!'

The family was sitting under the elm tree finishing a Sunday lunch of fresh fried fish (caught by Tomas and his father), fresh vegetables from the garden, and strawberries, also home-grown. Vera and Paula were playing in a bath of water, watched over by Old Vera; the other adults were feeling lazy, and Markus was half asleep, with his hat tipped over his eyes. Bees buzzed, as did the odd mosquito, but Morag was on hand with a fly swat. She had a good eye for 'the little black de'ils', as she called them. They were easier to down than Scottish midges, which you couldn't even see individually; they arrived in clouds.

The boys were excited. It was not often a car came to visit. All private ones had been requisitioned early in the war.

Lily had leapt up, banging her knee on the edge of the table and sending the water jug skidding. Morag came to mop up the spillage.

'Stay calm,' said Tomas. He had not moved, nor had his sister or parents. His mother knew nothing about the German soldier. She went on eating her fish.

'It's an army car,' she said, on looking up.

The armoured car swept round the curve of the drive and braked in front of the house. Tom got up and went to meet the two soldiers, a sergeant and a private.

'We're looking for one of our men,' said the sergeant. 'He's gone missing.' He gave a description that sounded like that of any other German soldier: well-built, blond hair, blue eyes. No distinguishing marks, or none that they knew of. Had Tom seen anyone answering to that description?

'Not up here, no. In town, yes – we see quite a few around.'

The sergeant strolled over to the elm tree and repeated his question to each person round the table. They shook their heads in turn and Lily was certain his eyes stayed longer on her than on the others.

'He was last seen heading this way. He was walking over there, apparently, by the field.' The sergeant gestured.

Lily thought he must hear the banging of her heart. It seemed terribly quiet. Even the cicadas had ceased their chatter.

'What about her?' The sergeant indicated Morag, who was carrying on with clearing the dishes from the table.

'She doesn't understand German,' said Veronika.

'Ask her, then!'

248

Veronika put the question to Morag in English.

'Is she English?' The sergeant's eyes narrowed.

'Scottish,' said Veronika.

'Same thing.'

Lily said nothing.

He pursed his lips and glanced around the garden as if unable to decide what to do next, then said he would take a look at the house. Tomas escorted him inside, and the other soldier followed.

Lily's hands were shaking.

'There's nothing for them to find,' said Veronika quietly.

'I hope they're not going to billet any soldiers on us,' said Gertrude.

The men were still in the house when another car came up the drive. A black shiny car, reported Alex, who saw it first. It was a Mercedes. At the wheel was Herman Walther, husband of Agita, who sat beside him, with their two children, Dieter and Hanna, on the back seat. The car doors opened, all four at the same time, as if orchestrated, and the family stepped out.

'What's going on?' Herman nodded at the armoured car.

'They're looking for a soldier,' said Gertrude. 'He seems to be lost.'

She kissed her daughter, who looked cool and uncreased in pale green voile with floating cape sleeves. Herman, too, was immaculately dressed, in cream linen trousers and a blue, buttoned-to-the-neck shirt, with a darker blue tie.

Agita was noting the mess in the garden: dishes strewn on the grass and the children's clothes lying where they'd been shed.

'There seem to be quite a few of you in the house these days,' said Herman.

'Most houses are crowded,' said Veronika, 'thanks to the occupation.'

'You shouldn't think of it that way, in terms of *occupation*.'

'They're hardly *invited* guests, are they? Or perhaps they are! Invited here by some.'

249

'Veronika!' murmured her father.

'Come and sit down, Agita,' said Gertrude. 'It's pleasant under the tree.'

Morag was taking a last drink of tea. She laid the empty cup on the tray and carried it with the rest of the dishes into the house. Lily wished she could go herself, but feared to. Where was Tom? There was no sign of him at any of the windows. What were they *doing*? Were they cross-questioning him?

'Do you eat with your servants?' asked Herman.

'War is a great leveller.' Markus smiled.

'We are happy to eat with them,' said Veronika. 'They are our friends.'

'You're beginning to talk like a socialist.'

'Horror of horrors!'

'Who's that old woman? The one with the white kerchief?'

'Her name's Vera. She's a widow with two sons away fighting the Germans. Her husband was Latvian. *She*'s Russian.'

'She looks it. And a Jew, isn't she? I thought so. A Russian Jew! What do you want with her in your household?'

'She saved Lily's life.'

'I don't see that means you've got to have her living in your house.'

'You're not trying to tell us what to do, are you, Herman? You're not our commandant – yet!'

They turned as the two soldiers emerged from the front door and came down the steps with Tomas.

'Is this your father?' The sergeant pointed to Markus.

'I am Markus Zale.' He stood up.

'You are the owner of this house?'

'Is there anything the matter?' intercepted Herman.

'We are requisitioning this house. It could accommodate many men. Who are you?'

Herman walked over to the group. 'Baron Herman Walther.' He clicked his heels, and took the soldiers aside.

'I don't want him intervening on our behalf,' muttered Veronika.

'He is only trying to help,' said Agita.

A few minutes later the soldiers got into their armoured car and drove off.

'You shouldn't have any further trouble,' said Herman.

'Thank you,' said Gertrude.

Veronika turned away.

The older children went off to play further down the garden and the adults settled under the tree to drink freshly brewed, *real* coffee, a present from their visitors, who had brought it in a hamper along with cheese, sausages, sugar, a leg of pork, tinned ham and tinned herrings.

Herman offered his gold-plated cigarette case around and Veronika, though she would have liked to refuse, accepted. Tomas also took one. Lily shook her head. She had never smoked, she said, though she believed her sister did.

'That's your sister in Petrograd? She must be having a rough time with the Reds?'

'We hear very little. Though apparently her father-in-law is in prison – I know that through my brother.'

'Have you heard that the imperial family has been murdered, at Ekaterinburg? Yes, all of them! The Tsar, the Empress, the young heir, and the four princesses. No mercy shown to any of them. Mown down. God protect *us* from the Bolsheviks!'

'I thought you would have called upon Germany rather than God to protect us,' said Veronika. 'But perhaps it has the ear of the Almighty?'

'I've forgotten the milk, Veronika,' said her mother. 'Would you fetch it, please, dear?'

'You've got the wrong idea, you know, about Germany,' said Herman. 'It only wants to ensure a stable Europe.'

'Don't be ridiculous!' Veronika was on her feet but showing little sign of moving in the direction of the kitchen.

'The garden's looking lovely, Mother,' said Agita. 'The marigolds make a wonderful splash of colour.'

'Germany could be a good friend to us,' said Herman.

'Could it indeed?' demanded Tomas. 'And would you say it's been a good friend to me? Look what a German bullet did to me!' He tore off his eye patch to reveal the red gaping socket.

Herman looked down, muttering that he was sorry about that.

'I'm glad you're sorry!'

'*He* didn't do it, Tom,' said Agita.

Tomas told Lily later that he was ashamed of having made the gesture. 'It was pretty melodramatic, wasn't it? Even childish! Worthy of the twins.'

'I think you can be excused a little melodrama,' said Lily, kissing his forehead above the black patch. She knew he still felt pain in the socket. It was like neuralgia, he said, penetrating into the centre of his brain like thin, red-hot, electric wires. Some nights he found it impossible to sleep.

Whatever else, Tomas's gesture had the effect of terminating the visit. Herman and Agita rose shortly afterwards, saying they must go.

Petrograd

November 1918

'What's going on?' Garnet went racing down the backstairs to
the kitchen. Children were crying and screaming. For a
moment the thought that the Cheka had come for her son
tore through her mind. They'd come for almost everyone else
in the last two or three months, including the countess.
They'd taken her in for questioning. Her legs were bad;
they'd had virtually to carry her. She'd moaned and groaned
and railed at them, calling them murderers. They'd released
her at the end of the day.

'They were polite enough,' she said when she came back,
'but I had no secrets to reveal. What would I have to tell
them now that they've murdered my husband? I told them
his blood was on their hands. I'm an old woman, I'll say what
I like. They asked about Seryozha, but how would I know
where he is? I told them mothers were the last to know
where their sons were or what they were doing – unless it
was their wives! They had no sense of humour. I asked them
if their mothers knew what they were doing.'

The count had been shot. Executed, they'd called it, not
murdered. For crimes against the state. After the attempt in
August on Lenin's life by Fanya Kaplan there had begun a
reign of terror that had become a way of life. Reprisals.
Knocks on the door in the night, the sound of booted feet

sending alarm into the hearts of people cowering in their beds. On a night in the middle of September the count had been taken from the Peter and Paul Fortress with several others and shot. The family had been allowed to have his body back for burial and since then the countess had not put a foot across the threshold except when abducted by the Cheka.

Leo had also been arrested, and held for three days, and not so politely questioned, then released. But he wasn't taken in by that. He knew they could come back again at any time. They liked to play cat-and-mouse, retreat for a while, then advance again. They'd even taken Dolly in for half a day, but so far had not come for either Garnet or Eithne, both of whom held British as well as Russian citizenship. Would that be sufficient protection? They did not know.

Garnet flung open the kitchen door. Her own Kolya, as she might have known, was at the centre of the disturbance. He was facing Vladimir and Nina's youngest boy, Boris. Dolly stood between them holding aloft a blue wooden railway engine with red wheels; and encircling the trio was a squadron of yelling children of varying ages.

'That's Kolya's,' said Garnet before she could stop herself. Seryozha had given it to him the night before he'd gone off to join the Volunteers. He'd come slipping back into the house in the small, quiet hours, dressed as a peasant in baggy trousers and a rough smock, his hair tousled and long. He'd walked on stockinged feet past closed doors behind which strange families slept, and tapped on her door, hers and Kolya's. She kept it locked always at night. She had crept up behind it and whispered, 'Who is it?'

She let him in. He told her he was going and she wept and wished he would not go and they made love and she wished for another child and knew while she wished it that it was impractical at such a time and in the midst of so much uncertainty. And so the hours slid by and dawn began to threaten. 'You must go,' she kept telling him. 'In a moment,' he said. He would always dare, wait until the last moment, tempt providence. She knew that was how he was and nothing she could say would change him. Light was showing at the edge of the curtain. 'Go,' she begged. 'The house will waken soon. It will be swarming. It's like an ant hill in daytime.'

It was then that Seryozha woke Kolya and gave him his blue-and-red engine.

'A special present,' he told his sleepy son. 'I had it made for you by an old man at Tsarskoye Selo. He made me an engine when I was young, just like this one. He made your crib, too, the one you had when you were a baby.'

'Is he very old?'

'Very old.'

Seryozha lifted Kolya's crooked little finger with the crook of his own bigger one and held it.

'Go, Seryozha, go now!' Garnet pleaded again. In the house there must be many informers who would take delight in running to the Cheka with the news. *The young Count Burnov is in the house*!

Before Seryozha left he knelt in front of the ikon of the Madonna and Child on the stand. He made the sign of the cross, then he closed his eyes. Garnet watched his lips move, and a tremor of fear threw her heart off balance. She put her hand over it, and when Seryozha had finished praying he came and put his hand over hers and said, 'I love you, Garnet. I love your brightness.'

She stood for a while in the corridor after he went, watching and listening. She saw a thread of light at Dolly's door and, when she cocked her ear, heard it close very quietly, almost like a whisper. Had Dolly seen Seryozha go? At breakfast-time Dolly's face had told nothing, but she'd said, 'That's a nice blue and red railway engine you've got there, Kolya,' and the child had said, 'My daddy gave it to me.' Dolly had asked no further questions.

'It's mine!' cried Kolya, reaching for the engine. Dolly extended her arm backwards, keeping the toy well out of his grasp.

Garnet engaged Dolly's eyes and the children, sensing confrontation, quietened.

'He has to learn to share,' said Dolly. 'He has more than the other children.'

'Not any longer.'

'He has to share a room only with you. There are seven in Boris's room.' Contrary to Dolly's predictions, Nina's baby had survived, though she was a puny little blue-mouthed thing, unlike the bouncing, golden-haired Sophia, Dolly's own child.

Dolly had given birth without trouble and carried the baby along the next morning to show her off to the countess. 'I've decided to call her after you, countess. I've always liked the name Sophia.' The countess had asked Garnet if she knew who the father was, but Garnet had shrugged and said she wouldn't expect Dolly to confide in her, about anything.

Sophia lay in the wooden crib that had housed Kolya in his time, the one made by the carpenter at Tsarskoye Selo. She was gurgling, had her toes in the air and was trying to reach them. She was a pretty, happy child, and advanced for four months. Kolya loved her and was protective of her, which Garnet saw as a good omen and hoped he would feel the same towards her baby when it came. He'd shown so little sign of tenderness before. She had written to her mother about this and Jemima had written back to say he was probably just being a little boy and in time would change.

Andrew used to chase cats and cut worms in half when he was small, but, as you know, he is not at all like that now! He has become very thoughtful indeed. I do hope Miss Rose Sibbald knows how lucky she is getting him. If she gets him. I rather think she will. So I shouldn't worry too much about little Kolya. I do know that mothers worry about all sorts of matters, large and small! Effie (though I know she is in no mortal danger, unless someone should throw a clout at her in the street for annoying them) bothers me at present. She is talking a great deal about a man called Norrie who plays the trombone. When he is not being a soldier (of Christ), he is a fireman. He's very brave, she says. The Lord called him to fight fires. A worthy calling, one must admit. I dare say you will think it ludicrous that I find any of this cause for concern. These matters must seem so trivial compared with your own trials and tribs, but all is relative, Garnet dear. Anyway, take heart – from the sounds of it, Lily's Luke is very similar.

'Boris can have the engine to play with this morning,' said Dolly. 'And Kolya can have it back this afternoon.'

'All right,' agreed Garnet, who had had to learn the art of compromise, though it went against her nature. Her instinct was still to reach out and take the engine from Dolly's hand and say, 'That belongs to *my* son!'

Garnet found Leo with the countess. He had come with the news that an armistice had been declared between the Allies and Germany.

'It won't make much difference to us, though, will it?' said the countess, who was looking like a bivouacked tent under a scabby bearskin rug. A feeble fire was flickering in the stove. It seldom built to a glow and would periodically go out and have to be coaxed back by Garnet, who had grown proficient at making fire, amongst other tasks. 'We're not at war with Germany any more, are we?' said the countess. 'Or are we? Sometimes I think people forget to tell me what's going on.'

'No,' said Leo, 'our own wars are internal!'

They were well aware of the one raging for possession of the heartland of Russia, for hadn't the son of the house gone to fight in it? His mother was proud of him and felt confident that he would return. 'He has always led a charmed life, my Seryozha. He was born with a shirt on. He fell down the kitchen stairs when he was only one year old and got up at the bottom with not even a dent and staggered off.' She

257

remained optimistic about the outcome of the civil war, in spite of the gloomy reports that that reached them, and thought of their present way of life as being temporary, a trial to be borne, until better days came back again.

'We have the Allies helping us, *n'est-ce pas*? Britain, France, America, Japan! *Et le bon Dieu*. With all of them on our side, how can we lose?'

'Be careful!' said Leo.

'Oh yes, I know – keep your voice down, speak softly, watch what you say! There are spies in the house of Burnov! I am sick of spies, sick, sick, sick! Sick of all these people in my house. How can we be expected to *live* with spies?'

'You have no option,' said Leo.

The countess frowned at him. 'Where is Dolly?' she demanded. 'I can't get the samovar to boil.'

'I'll do it,' said Garnet.

'She's better at it than you. Can't you call her? What does she do all day? She used to be so good. I never had any complaints before.'

'She's no longer a maid.'

'What is she, then? Part of the family?'

Dolly arrived shortly with Sophia on her arm. She'd left Kolya playing downstairs. 'He seems to have recovered from his little tantrum. Can you take Sophia for me?' Dolly passed the baby across to Garnet. 'I'm going to the market. I heard there might be some meat.'

'You'd need to get a whole animal for it to go round all of us,' said the countess.

'It might be horse flesh.'

'*Horse*?'

'It's a delicacy, these days.'

'These days, these days!'

Garnet frowned warningly at her mother-in-law.

'Oh well, buy what you can, Dolly.' The countess threw up her hands. 'You always seem to know where to go.'

'We're running short of money.' Dolly looked at Garnet. 'Perhaps it might be necessary to raise some more.'

*

'I'm thinking of going home,' said Eithne, 'now that the war with Germany is over. The seas should be safer. Though I might have to wait till spring.'

They turned off the Nevsky into a side street. A thin curtain of snow was descending; the streets were slushy. Daylight was failing early. On the corner stood a woman holding out both arms, on which was laid a long tress of hair. For sale. Everything was for sale these days. Yes, these days.

'They'd have to let me go, wouldn't they?' said Eithne. 'But what about the children?'

'I'm not sure. They're Soviet citizens.'

'I wouldn't go without the children.'

'They're hostages to fortune,' said Garnet.

'What about you?'

'I'll stay as long as Seryozha is away fighting. He might come back any time. I must be here.'

'Will you think badly of me if I don't go to Oscar?'

Eithne's husband had been shipped out to Perm, and the authorities had said she was free to take the children and join him. 'A Siberian winter would be even worse than this.'

'I'm sure everyone would tell you it would be wisest to leave Russia altogether.'

Elena and Natalya had gone with their families. They'd been heading for Odessa, which was reported to be in White Army hands, and from there planned to make their way across the border to Romania. No word had been received from them.

'Do you know where the shop is?' asked Eithne, peering at a dark window.

'Dolly said it's along here.'

They passed a notice pinned to a drainpipe. 'For Sale,' it read, 'an English Sheraton Sideboard.' Then there was another: 'For Sale, Fur Coat Tailored in Berlin.' The pieces of paper were turning soggy, the script beginning to run.

They found the shop, which was half-lit, with a curtain drawn across its window. The owner, a Jew, wrapped in a beaver coat, examined their jewellery under a tiny spotlight. He made his offer.

'That's next to nothing!' said Garnet. 'This is valuable stuff.'

He waved his hands. They could take it or leave it. Jewellery wasn't fetching much. Who could buy? There were people, responded Garnet. They had heard of the *nouveau riche* class that was springing up, the men – and women – who were in the system.

They took his offer and trudged back through the now thickening snow, past the beggars standing with outstretched hands and the crippled ones who sat in doorways and the woman with the tress of white-speckled hair. She looked as if she had not moved.

'I want to go home,' said Eithne. 'To *Ireland*.'

When they came back to their house they saw that a notice had been stuck on one of their downpipes.

'"For Sale",' read Eithne aloud, '"Bechstein Baby Grand." That's yours, isn't it? But that's not your writing.'

'No,' agreed Garnet, 'it's not.'

Opening the door, they heard men's voices.

'So how do you feel about Soviet Russia?'

'Well, naturally I have mixed feelings.'

'You think everything was good before?'

'Of course not.'

'You accept the old regime had to fall?'

'Yes, probably.'

'It's difficult for you, we understand that. We want to help you to make adjustments.'

'Thank you.'

'You were used to a grand life. You were born to riches.'

'Oh no! I'm not an aristocrat.'

'But you're married to one?'

'Well, yes. But my father was an architect in Aberdeen. In Scotland.'

'I know where Aberdeen is. We are not ignorant people.'

'I didn't mean to suggest that.'

'You weren't poor, though?'

'No, not poor. But we lived fairly plainly.'

'Not as plainly as our peasants?'

'Of course not. You'd call us middle class.'

'You like all these classes, I think, you English?'

'I'm not English.'

'I beg your pardon.'

A lull now while he smokes, turned half away from her in his swivel chair in his grey room. Staged, she's sure. Each move thought out. Each shift of direction. He must be a past master. He speaks English very well. He studied at Manchester University, he told her: politics and history.

'You must accept that everything is bound to be chaotic for a while here. When there are big changes it is bound to be so. We have much to do. A country to rebuild. That is no small task. We want to create an equal society. You approve of that?'

'Yes. If it's possible.'

'All things are possible, if one wants them enough. One must operate on that creed. Would you like a cigarette?'

'Thank you.'

'Do you intend to stay in our country and help us build?'

'I think so.'

'You're not sure? You have a child? One of us. Your hand is not trembling, no?'

'No.'

'You do not have to be afraid of me.'

He smokes again for a while and she keeps her eyes fixed on him. When he stubs out his cigarette his yellow fingers grind the butt into the tin tray.

He swings round to face her once more. His voice now is clipped.

'You must be aware that we cannot tolerate dissidents in our state? People who would undermine our work?'

'I am.'

'Tell me, Madame Burnova, where is your husband?'

'I have no idea.'

'Come, come, you must have some idea! Has he gone to fight with the Whites? The Lily-Whites? They won't last, you know.'

'I don't know anything about them.'

'When did you last see him?'

'Some months.'

'He's not been in touch? He's sent no messages?'

'No.'

'Not a very attentive husband, is he? I cannot believe he would leave an attractive young woman like yourself without any word.'

'Times are not normal.'

His smile makes her shiver.

'Where are your sisters-in-law, Madame Burnova?'

'I don't know.'

'You seem to know very little.'

She shrugs.

'Your answers are getting boring. I dislike very much to be bored.'

He lights another cigarette, flicks the match into a tin wastepaper basket. It lands with a slight ping.

'You are very friendly, are you not, with Leo Konstantinovich Burnov?'

'He is my husband's cousin.'

'A "liberal" intellectual. Do you know any of his friends?'

She shakes her head.

'Do you know how he spends his time? When he's not with you?'

'He does some teaching, I believe. Writes.'

'He writes articles, does he not?'

'And poetry.'

'Poetry can be subversive, no?'

'I suppose.'

'You like Pushkin?'

'Is he subversive?'

He laughs. He speaks softly. *Our dreams of love and modest*

262

glory . . .'

She starts. It was a verse Seryozha often quoted. They couldn't be holding him, could they?

'Delusive hopes now quickly sped,' she finishes.

'Brava, Madame Burnova! You will become a Russian yet.'

He leans forward, his hands clasped on top of the grey desk.

'Where is your husband, Madame Burnova?'

Where is your husband where is your husband where is your husband . . .

Tell me tell me tell me . . .

'It would be in your interest to tell me.'

Garnet and Eithne shuffled up the queue without speaking. The upper halves of their bodies ached. They rotated their shoulders, massaged each other's necks with callused hands. The hacks fissuring their fingers, those small gaping wounds that refused to close, seeped minute amounts of blood and were disproportionately painful to their size. They nursed their fingers in the comforting warmth of their armpits when the supervisor turned his back and they could rest their broad, heavy wooden shovels. They would get used to the work in time, they'd been told. Their bodies would harden. Their lives had been too soft, that was the trouble. Anyone could learn to shovel snow.

They reached the head of the queue, were given a coupon, then went to stand in another long wavering line.

'Why wouldn't one queue do?' murmured Eithne. 'Is it part of the system, do you think – intended to wear you down?'

When they reached the counter they were each given a greasy tin plate afloat with watery soup, and a small slice of dark bread.

'Luncheon!' said Eithne. 'I could go a good plate of ham and eggs right now! And fried tattie bread wouldn't go amiss, either.'

They sat at long tables with the other diners. All ate

heartily. For most it would be their only meal of the day. The smell of human bodies herded together in the huge room was suffocating, but they were learning to adjust to that, too. They used to shop in here, when it had been the Army and Navy Stores.

'Do you remember your wedding breakfast?' asked Eithne. 'Did you have champagne? Smoked salmon? Myself, I've never cared much for smoked salmon. I prefer it ordinary, poached, and served with thin slices of cucumber and a little hollandaise sauce.'

'Honestly, Eithne! I could brain you with my plate.' But Garnet raised a smile. They had agreed that they must try to keep a sense of humour, and so as they shovelled they made jokes and said *Do you remember as a child dying to have really deep deep snow so that you could make a big big snowman, the biggest in the world*? And here they were surrounded by mountains of snow and expected to shift them!

Dolly met them at the door on their return from work. She was unusually agitated.

'The whole house is to be requisitioned!'

Garnet had got into the habit of thinking that Dolly was infallible, that she could get – by some means or other which Garnet preferred not to know about – anything she wanted, but, of course, that was not so.

'They want it for themselves,' said Dolly. 'It's too good for ordinary people like us!'

Next day, they were moved into a decaying building in the Narva quarter, near the harbour, next to a factory with a reeking chimney. Their apartment had four rooms. One was allocated to Eithne and her children, another to Dolly, Sophia and two of her nieces, the third to her brother's family, which left Garnet and Kolya to share with the countess.

Aberdeen

18 November 1918

Jemima put the receiver back on its hook and hastened up the stairs to the drawing room to tell her husband the news.

'That was Andrew on the telephone. Something called the Latvian People's Council has met in Riga and declared Latvia to be a sovereign, independent, democratic republic!' She had written it on the messages pad beside the telephone, had it in her hand now. 'Imagine, Alex, they've actually got independence!'

'I think a dram is needed to celebrate,' said Alexander, getting up and going to the corner cupboard.

'Andrew said he knew you'd say that. I'll have a port. Andrew says, though, that the country's troubles will not be over.'

'Could hardly expect them to be, with German troops still on their soil.'

'I thought they'd been beaten by the Allies and were meant to go home? After the Armistice?'

'They didn't, though. And then there are the Bolsheviks.' Alexander handed his wife her glass. 'Latvians as well as Russians. The country's got a bit of a civil war on its hands as well as having to fight off two foreign armies. Both Germany and Russia are going to do their damnedest to hang on to the Baltic.'

'Sounds like a right mess, if you ask me! And there are poor Lily and Tom and the children caught in the middle of it.'

'Well, here's to a free Latvia!' Alexander raised his glass.

'*And* a free Russia!'

'However that might come about. And whatever it might comprise.'

They were discussing the situations of their two elder daughters, something they chewed over endlessly, wondering what they could do to help them and coming to the conclusion each time that there was nothing, when they heard Effie arrive in the hall downstairs. She had been out with the Army.

'Mother!' she called up. 'Father!'

Jemima went out on to the landing. 'Up here, Effie.'

Effie was not alone. She was being followed up the stairs by her friend with the trombone which to Jemima looked exceedingly cumbersome to carry about. Effie banged on her tambourine as she came up, whilst loudly humming 'Onward, Christian Soldiers'. She was clearly in high spirits. Infected by the Spirit of the Lord, her mother did not doubt.

Effie's cheeks were flushed almost to the colour of the dark-red ribbon on her bonnet. 'Mother, Father, this is Norrie!'

'Pleased to meet you, Norrie,' said Alexander, rising to extend his free hand, keeping hold of his drink in the other. 'We've heard a great deal about you.'

'You see, Norrie,' said Effie, 'I told you I'd told them.'

'Won't you sit down, Norrie?' invited Jemima. 'Please? Would you like to leave your trombone over here in the corner? It'll be quite safe, I assure you. No one will bang into it. I'm sure it must be very precious to you. It seems heavy?'

'He's very strong, Mother,' said Effie. 'He moves with the power of the Lord.'

Norrie, who had been holding the trombone close to his chest, parked it where Effie's mother had suggested and removed his hat. He had sleek dark hair and a sleek dark moustache. Effie did not remove her bonnet.

'Would you like some tea?' asked Jemima. Seeing Effie's

266

glance at their glasses (she had become censorious about alcohol and had much to say on its evils), she said, 'Latvia has declared independence. We've been drinking its health.'

'I've long been praying for its salvation. Praise be the Lord!'

'Amen,' said Norrie, speaking for the first time.

'Did you have a good meeting?' asked Alexander. 'Plenty of people turn up?'

'It rained,' said Norrie. He had a deep, rich voice, surprisingly so for someone with a rather thin face, though the pitch tended to the lugubrious.

'That was a pity,' said Jemima. 'I suppose it does tend to put people off. I thought you both looked a little damp when you came up the stairs.'

'I admire the way you go out in all weathers,' said Alexander, refilling his glass.

'The Lord doesn't stop for rain or snow,' said Effie.

'Do you belong to Aberdeen, Norrie?' asked Jemima, wishing that Effie didn't have to mention the Lord in every sentence. It seemed to make Him too ordinary, somehow, as if He were walking about the streets of Aberdeen in a mackintosh with His collar turned up against the cold.

'No, the Mearns,' said Norrie.

'So you're a country boy?' said Alexander.

'Mother! Father!' said Effie, jumping up and down, unable to restrain her joy any longer. 'Norrie has something to ask you.'

Riga

June 1919

Andrew picked his way through a mass of broken glass and other debris. The city lay half in ruins. Testimony to the massive German shelling. There were machine guns at every crossroad and much in evidence was the Landeswehr, the elite corps of German Baltic barons and their retainers, renowned, as Andrew had written in a dispatch to his paper, for their courage and physical and intellectual prowess. They also had a reputation for recklessness. They roamed the streets looking for Bolshevik sympathisers. At night the town was like a ghost city. Much of the populace had fled into the surrounding countryside. Andrew thanked God that Lily and her family hadn't stayed. He was desperate to reach her but that was not possible yet. The Germans were firmly entrenched around Riga and showed little sign of withdrawing, in spite of Allied pressure. There were reports, though, that Latvians with the help of Estonians had liberated the area round Cesis.

He came to Dom Square and hesitated on the corner. Some young Landeswehr soldiers were hanging about in front of the cathedral. They'd noticed him. They'd hardly think he was a Bolshevik, would they? He shouldn't really be here, though. The Germans were refusing travel permits to the British; he'd only managed to get to Riga because of his

American friend Hank, who worked for Reuters. Hank had acquired a permit and hired a car in Liepája, the Baltic port, and had brought Andrew with him.

He turned into a side street, doing his best to appear unflustered. They seemed not to be following him. He resisted looking round. He walked a little faster, and leapt over a twist of rusted metal and a broken paving stone. The pavement was splattered with pieces of shrapnel. Coming towards him was a woman in a long, faded evening gown, carrying a saucepan. She would be on her way to the soup kitchen. Fear marked her face but hunger would have driven her out. He stepped into the gutter since the pavement was narrow. She passed him with unseeing eyes, her long grey hair hanging like rotting hemp over her shoulders.

He was relieved when he made it into his hotel. He sat down in front of his typewriter. Write it up while it's fresh, he'd been told.

At the main prison I saw girls and boys – some little more than children – crammed into cells. A fixed number are executed each day. Thirty-three men and seven women. The unfortunates have to file out in front of the other prisoners, and as soon as they've gone the following day's contingent is picked out and put into a special room to await their fate. They have to dig their own graves, then they're lined up alongside and shot. Britain has made formal protests—

He looked up as the door opened and Hank came in.
'Are you all right?' asked Hank. 'You don't look too hot.'
'What the hell use are protests?'
'This is a difficult assignment for you, isn't it? I know you asked for it but you're sure as heck getting thrown in at the deep end. All the god-damn ends are deep right now. Why didn't you opt for local reporting? You could be covering weddings in Aberdeen right now.'
'It's my sister. I keep thinking— '

269

'I know. Here, have a slug of this black-market hooch. Says "Cognac" on the label – don't believe a word.'

'What can you believe these days?'

'Not much. With reports coming in from all sides, everyone making their own claims. Words are easy to dish out. Hell, we should know, shouldn't we?'

'It's a case, too, of what you decide to tell, isn't it?'

'Yep! What *you* select. The burden beginning to weigh on you?'

Hank had just interviewed the Landeswehr commander, Major Fletcher. He was also Governor of Riga, a German appointee.

'Fletcher?' said Andrew.

'A Prussian, but his grandfather was a Scot. I didn't detect anything very Scottish in him! While I was there, though, I met one of his aides, whom you'll also be interested to meet. I've set it up for us to see him this evening at the Rome.'

'Baron Herman Walther,' he said, with a short bow. 'At your service.' He had an upright bearing and short, clipped brown hair, and he wore the uniform of a Landeswehr officer.

'How is my sister?' asked Andrew at once. 'And the rest of the family?'

Herman had not had news of them for some time but he feared they would have had a rough time. 'They're in the country. I've been busy here in the city.'

'We've seen,' said Hank drily.

'So what would you do if the Bolsheviks tried to take over your home? Ask yourselves that! Look what has happened in Russia! We are protecting Latvia from the bloody Bolsheviks. Would you like to see them swamping the rest of Europe? Scotland?'

'Probably not,' Andrew agreed.

'You feel safe there, isn't that so? Here, we are in the thick of it. The Bolsheviks have been ravaging our countryside, burning and looting and raping our women.' The baron told them how one night a group of local peasants, led by a Red agitator, had killed the guard at his manor house, broken down the door and come charging up stairs into his bedroom. 'I was in bed with my wife, who was naturally alarmed. They commanded me to come downstairs into the yard, where they proposed to shoot me. They said they intended to take back my land, which was rightfully theirs. But I had a pistol under my pillow! Well, I'm not a fool, you know. I shot the ringleader and one other through the head, and the rest fled for their lives. These peasants have no brains. They had even less after I'd finished with them!'

'Charming fellow!' said Andrew, as they made their way back to the hotel, keeping close to the walls. They'd already been stopped by two young Landeswehr officers who'd been belligerent until told that the two Westerners were friends of Baron Herman Walther. 'He's my friend's brother-in-law,' Hank had said, 'by one remove.'

A burst of firing erupted ahead. They dodged into an alleyway, cut through into the street behind and sprinted the last few yards to their hotel.

'Christ!' said Andrew. 'Is this part of your daily grind?'

Hank grinned. 'You get used to it.'

They found a drink at the bar. This was another part of the life, Andrew was discovering. You had to do something to unwind.

At the bar they met up with another American journalist, who told them that he'd heard the Germans had agreed to sign an armistice the next day and that all their troops and Landeswehr men would be required to vacate Riga immediately.

Andrew got drunk that night and had to be put to bed by Hank.

Cesis

Dear Mother and Father,

I am with Lily and her family at last! They've had a very hard time but are well, on the whole, though terri-

271

bly thin [he had almost written 'emaciated'], so perhaps you could try to send parcels as soon as possible? I brought some food from Riga. Got for me on the black market by my American pal Hank, who knows his way around. Don't think I could have survived my first assignment without him.

You've probably heard that an armistice has been signed, but don't be alarmed by reports you may read that the Germans have only withdrawn to a line some fourteen miles to the south of Riga. I'm sure the Allies will lean on them to evacuate the whole country. At least they are south of Riga and well away from Cesis. The Landeswehr were supposed to leave the city as well but in the end have remained – they're stubborn devils. They claim they're Latvian, you see. However, they are to be put under a British commander, an Irish Guards officer called Colonel Alexander, who will have to contain them. Baltic politics are not simple!

Tom's younger sister, Veronika, has been filling in gaps in my knowledge. She is a super girl. I guess you'll have met her, so you'll know what I mean. She was a tower of strength throughout the war, Lily says. She doesn't know the meaning of panic. It's good that Lily has such a stalwart friend.

We had a party last night, a victory celebration. It was tremendous fun. Lots of singing and dancing. Veronika has been trying to teach me some of their folk songs, with not much success! They all seem to know the words. Amazing. They asked me to sing 'Loch Lomond' and I couldn't get beyond 'By yon bonnie banks and yon bonnie braes'. Then I had to hum!

Everyone sends love and hopes to see you here soon. Morag wishes to be remembered. She speaks Latvian like a native. With a Scots accent! says Tom.

Happy 24th birthday, too, to Effie. Has she fixed a date for her wedding yet? Will it be an Army one? The music could be rather jolly! Lily says she should wait to get married until she and Tom can come to the wedding. Perhaps Garnet will be able to come too, and then we shall all be together again as a family.

I repeat – don't worry!

Love, Andrew

Dear Mother and Father,

I know Andrew has written to reassure you that we are in reasonable health. We are grateful to be alive. One of our neighbours lost two sons. Taken away at dead of night. We holed up in our house and garden most of the time, kept our heads down, and left the premises only to forage for food.

We are happy that old Vera's two sons, Paulis and Matis, have come to join us. Such nice young men, with gentle temperaments like their mother. They were wounded in battle, and discharged early. Their haunted faces remind me of Tom's after he was wounded in that awful Christmas battle of 1916. Fresh air, and some fresh food, should help to restore them.

I have a great yearning to see Garnet again. It's so long since I've seen her that sometimes I wonder if I would know her. 'Look in the mirror,' Tom says. But I wouldn't see her there, would I? Garnet won't be having much peace in Petrograd, from what we hear. Russian refugees have been passing through this way, with more shocking tales to tell. There is no shortage of horror to be related. The children have kept well, thank God.

Much love, Lily

The children were outside. Lily could hear them, fighting over something. Always skirmishing and fighting! Why couldn't they play peacefully! She and Garnet hadn't fought like that. But boys seemed to feel a physical need to defend their territory and their possessions. She got up and put her head out of the window. Luke and Alex were wrestling for possession of a small yellow motor car. It belonged to Alex.

'Give it back to him, Luke!'

'You always take his part!'

'I said *give it back*! Why do you always want other people's things?'

Luke threw the car at his brother's feet and ran off. Alex followed him. To gloat, no doubt.

The garden was an enticement, lit by morning sun. Lily went out. She saw the two dark heads of Old Vera's sons bent over the vegetable patch. They were weeding. They greeted her shyly. She chatted a little with them, not about the war but about the morning and the garden. They liked to work with the soil; they were going to try to find work on one of the farms in the area, neither them having any desire to go back to Riga. Who would with it blasted half to bits!

'Paul!' They heard Morag calling – almost singing. 'We need radishes for lunch.' Morag burst into view between the blackcurrant bushes. She stopped abruptly when she saw Lily and said again, less boisterously, 'We need some radishes.'

Paulis passed her the vegetables and as he did so their hands brushed and appeared to linger and a sweet smile lit up the young man's thin face. Lily herself was smiling when she returned to the house.

Dear Mother,

Andrew is in love! With Veronika. I simply had to tell you. It's been quite astonishing to watch, the flaring of attraction between them. Like instant combustion. Perhaps it's the aftermath of war: the need for love and tenderness. Andrew was pretty shell-shocked when he arrived. I saw such a difference in him. He was no longer my young brother. He's become a man of the world, one who has seen the dark side. He witnessed some of the executions in Riga. And now he's found the light! Veronika, too, has been starved for a long time. So all is wonderful for them as long as one doesn't think of the future. I can't imagine Veronika uprooted and I can't see how Andrew could earn a living in Latvia. But why run

274

ahead? Poor Rose Sibbald. Still, we never did care for her an awful lot, did we? And you always wanted Andrew to find a strong, independent-minded girl. So now he has!

Morag and Mara are in love too, with Vera's sons, Paulis and Matis. It's like an infection running through the house.

Love, Lily

Aberdeen

September 1919

Jemima McKenzie, in receipt of letters from her children, is thinking it's all very well for them to tell her not to worry, but they are there and she is here, unable to see them. She has the letters spread out on her desk, but it is Garnet's that is arresting her primarily.

> I write to tell you that I gave birth to a daughter yester-day! I had no trouble at all, was in labour for only two hours. She was two weeks premature but she has no wrinkling or redness, and is absolutely perfect. I'm sure you'll think so too when you see her.

But when will Jemima see this new grandchild? Garnet writes as if she might be over in Aberdeen next week. Jemima is worrying about the conditions Garnet might be living under – she says little about them – and the fact that Seryozha is not at home to give her his support.

> I am calling her Anna. She is totally different from Kolya, being as dark as he is fair, though she does have Seryozha's blue eyes, and I rather think they will stay blue. They have that look to them. Kolya adores her. He hangs over her crib and sings to her. I think it will be

good for him to have a little sister. Or two little sisters. He already has Dolly's Sophia, whom he regards as one.

Garnet's letter was posted only two weeks previously, Andrew's and Lily's well over a month ago. A month is a long time. Don't be alarmed, says Andrew, that the Germans are only fourteen miles from Riga. But fourteen miles is nothing, thinks Jemima. You could motor it in half an hour, never mind a month. Imagine if an enemy army were encamped half an hour's drive from Aberdeen! At Stonehaven, say. You could *walk* it in the course of an afternoon. March. Andrew used to bicycle along the coast road to Stonehaven with Rose Sibbald, a picnic in their saddlebags. And that's another thing. Rose Sibbald.

Rose is due to come for tea this afternoon at four o'clock, and, knowing Rose, she will come at precisely two minutes to. She will be prettily dressed in either pale pink or pale blue and her pale-gold hair will shine like spun silk and she will smile very sweetly and she will ask, 'Any news of Andrew, Mrs McKenzie?' And an anxious little light will come into her eye, for she will not have received a letter herself. Poor Rose Sibbald. And what is she, Andrew's mother, to say to her?

How is it, Jemima wonders, that all her children – *their* children, for Alexander is implicated, too – have made, in their different ways, such unsuitable, or at least awkward, choices in life? Is it congeninal? But it can hardly be, can it, for look at herself and Alexander: so *suited*. Their lives had gone smoothly until the children started to make these choices. She and Alexander have understood each other's background from the beginning (even if they don't totally understand each another, but that she has never expected; nor, she presumed, has he); they didn't have to uproot themselves – she doesn't count sailing from Orkney to Aberdeen much of a displacement, she'd done it often before she came to marry, and had relatives in the city, and at least it was still Scotland. And yet she likes to think she and Alexander haven't led insular lives, either. They have always looked

277

outwards, travelled on the continent looking at buildings, and other things, until the war obtruded, and they've always made a point of welcoming foreigners into their home. And of course it was the latter that led to their daughters becoming embroiled in foreign wars and uprisings. Who would have thought on that day when they received the two young architects from the Russian Empire that it would end with Lily and Garnet in such predicaments? Jemima remembers the moment when Nessie brought the two young men into the drawing room. How handsome they looked, how fresh, eager for life's adventures. Seryozha, majestically tall, clicking his heels and stooping to kiss her hand, Tom also very polite and nice-mannered, giving a little bow, but not indulging in hand-kissing. Afterwards, she said, 'What nice young men! And what a lively evening we had with them! They had much more of interest to offer than many of the young men we know.' She supposes, therefore, that the girls' choices were not entirely uninfluenced. But as for Effie and her Norrie! Well, that is different altogether, something which Jemima understands less. It has been *so* unexpected, and is still taking her by surprise. And then there's Andrew, who has turned his back on the eminently suitable (from some points of view) Rose Sibbald to fall in love with Tom's sister, who lives at far remove from his working base. And is a very determined young woman, from what Jemima has seen of her.

Why does Jemima bother to turn such matters over in her mind? Alexander does not. Is it a female occupation? Alexander, after his day's work is done, sits and puffs his pipe and reads his books on architecture and fishing, and if he's challenged he says if he can't do anything about something he won't waste time thinking about it. After she'd read Garnet's letter aloud to him, he'd said, 'Aye, it's worrying, I'll admit. I wish we could get her home. But she sounds happy with her new baby. At least that's something.' Is he wise man or ostrich?

He looks up from his book now and says, 'Thinking about

the baby?'

'I was just wondering if you were an ostrich.'

They laugh. Really, they are so comfortable with each other. It is seldom they have an argument.

The doorbell rings downstairs.

'Expecting someone?' asks Alexander, glancing at the clock. Its reliable hands stand at two minutes to four.

Petrograd

May 1920

Narishkin Palace, Petrograd

Dear Mother and Father,

Here I am in Petrograd, travelling with the British Delegation in Bolshevik Russia! Arrived on the 12th, after tiresome journey via Bergen, Oslo and Stockholm. We are to stay in Petrograd for five days in all. And I will certainly do everything I can to try to slip away to see Garnet, though it will not be easy, as our party is tightly controlled. In theory we are supposed to have complete freedom to go anywhere we want and speak to anyone we want. I went for a walk with Bertrand Russell, the philosopher, and we were followed. Having come full of enthusiasm for Communism, he is finding the utilitarianism of the regime stifling. He is becoming sadly disillusioned remarkably quickly. Others in the delegation are the suffragette Ethel Snowden (wife of Philip, the MP), and various trade unionists. Mrs S. has been riding about in the imperial motor car and expressing sympathy for the Tsar! She'd do better to keep her mouth shut.

Andrew lifted his head and, looking out of the window, saw the view that Garnet must often have gazed on: the Academy of Arts across the river, directly opposite, and to his right the slim gold spire of the grim Peter and Paul Fortress. The Narishkin Palace was on the English Embankment, only a few doors along from the Burnovs' old house. He had walked along to see it as soon as he'd unpacked his bag. The building had become some kind of government office and had an air of dejection about it. The city was full of abandoned palaces.

I'm sharing a room with a man called Gerald from Birmingham. In former times it would have been a salon – the Narishkins were an eminent aristocratic family. We don't have any curtains or blinds and it is light early in the morning, but apart from that I cannot complain. Should not complain about anything! We've even got linen sheets and silk hangings and gilded furniture that I think is Louis XV. (I'm not much good at antiques, but it's got the kind of curly legs Father doesn't like.) Shades of former glory! I can see ghosts flitting out from behind the pillars.

Gerald is all right, except that he is something of a bore in that he will keep saying, 'Look at these hangings! Look at these sheets! The peasants slept on sacking.' I mean, we do know all that, so there doesn't seem much point in going on. He talks about when the Revolution comes to Britain, which he thinks it must, in order to right our social injustices. One cannot pretend we have none, what with strikes and soaring prices and taxes and men who were asked to lay down their lives for the country now not able to get a job. I won't start! But our Welsh Wizard had better look to his laurels.

Gerald was with me yesterday when I interviewed a prominent Communist leader. I made the point that the average man and woman seemed to have little freedom and the Communist replied by saying that Russians were like children. 'They're not educated. What do they know? They need to be told what to do. They don't know how to think for themselves. How can we give a vote to all these ignorant peasants? It would be like giving a box of matches to a baby.' Gerald didn't much like that.

I shall send this letter out through the Consulate. And I promise I shall do my very best to see G.

Your loving son, Andrew

Andrew managed to escape from the group on a visit to a factory near the docks. He had laid his plan beforehand, and consulted a map, and had a reasonable idea of how to find the street. He'd told no one he was going and when Gerald asked what he had in the carpet bag he was lugging about, he said: 'Tins of food for needy citizens.'

Garnet's street was a shambles, he could think of no better word to describe it, with its broken pavements and pits in the road that would have broken the axle of any vehicle that ventured down it. It seemed unlikely any would. There was little traffic in the city at all, except for the occasional ramshackle army lorry and the trams which were packed inside and outside with workers clinging on like black beetles.

The stench of dirt and poverty hung over the street. The pavements were littered. A flock of grubby children played in the road. On seeing Andrew, they came swooping, uttering cries, arms stretched wide. They swarmed around, pinching his arms, plucking at his clothes, trying to seize the bag.

'Keep back!' he shouted in English, holding up his hand to keep them at bay. They understood his tone, but that was not enough to deter them. He groped in his pocket and flung a handful of kopeks up the road. They went scrambling after them.

One boy, with reddish-gold hair, stayed still, watching him. The son of Sergei Burnov, surely. The spitting image of his father.

'Are you Nikolai Burnov?' asked Andrew.

The boy's eyes flickered in recognition, then he turned and ran off after the others. At least Andrew knew he was in the right street.

He continued on down until he found Garnet's number.

The door had been broken off its hinges; burned for firewood, probably. He climbed the foul stairway, searching in the poor light for names on doors. On the third floor he found what he was looking for. BURNOV.

With his heart thudding, he raised his knuckles and knocked.

The silence had an eerie quality to it. And he was not one for imagining things. He looked over one shoulder, then the other. He listened, put his ear against the door. Were they listening at the back of it? He thought he heard soft scuffling sounds. Footfalls? His throat was drying. He knocked again, said, 'Garnet?'

'Who is it?' It was his sister's voice!

'Garnet, it's me – your bother Andrew!'

The door opened, and Garnet stared incredulously round it.

'Andrew! Is it really you? I can't believe it, I simply cannot believe it!' Then she burst into tears and he hugged her and he thought how light she felt and she said, and kept saying, 'But how did you *get* here?'

'I'm a foreign correspondent!' he said and they laughed and Garnet, whom he had never seen cry before, cried again and he brushed his eyes with the back of his hand.

Then he saw that someone else was standing in the shadows of the hallway, watching them.

'Andrew, this is Dolly.'

Dolly stepped forward to shake hands.

'I knew he would be handsome, your brother.'

Garnet translated, and Andrew blushed, for Dolly was eyeing him very directly.

'Who is it?' a voice called querulously from one of the rooms.

'Come and meet my mother-in-law,' said Garnet. 'My roommate!'

The room was so cramped there was scarcely a place to put one's feet. Four people lived within these four walls. Andrew ducked under a string of wet washing and found himself face

283

to face with the countess. Or would have done had she not been lounging on a divan which served as her recliner by day and her bed by night. She seemed to him to be rather vast, though Garnet told him later that she was greatly reduced from her former self. Her clothes hung on her like loose sacks.

'This is your *brother*, Garnet Alexandrovna? *Mon dieu! Quelle surprise!*'

The countess put down her pack of greasy playing cards to offer Andrew her hand. He thought she might mean him to kiss it since she held it at an angle and palm down, but he seized it and gave it a hearty shake.

'Pleased to meet you, Countess.'

'*Enchantée!*' she said. 'Ah, how welcome you are – a *divertissement* in our drab life! My son is away fighting the enemy and my two daughters are abroad.' A letter had come recently from Natalya and Elena; they had managed to reach Paris. Oscar was driving a cab. 'A *cab*?' The countess was astounded. 'What else has he been trained for,' said Garnet, 'other than killing?'

Andrew unpacked his carpet bag and distributed the tins of meat, fish, tea and coffee, giving some to Garnet for her friend Eithne. He noticed that Dolly took her share without being invited, and some for her brother and his wife and children as well. Oh, well, fair enough! In this regime the idea was share and share alike, unless you were a party official – that went without saying. He made a joke about that and Garnet smiled, but he saw how she glanced at Dolly. Warily, he thought. Or was he becoming oversensitive about looks and innuendoes? The atmosphere in the city had that effect on one. Before leaving that evening he took off his jersey and gave it to Garnet, along with what cash in roubles he had in his pocket, and when he came back next day he brought a couple of shirts from his luggage, two undervests, several pairs of socks, and his spare pair of shoes, which he gave to Sergei's cousin Leo, who was living in an apartment across the street.

For the countess, right at the bottom of his bag, he had something special. When he presented her with the rectangular tin bearing the picture of Edinburgh Castle on its tartan lid he thought she was going to cry.

'She adores Edinburgh rock,' said Garnet.

The countess had removed the lid and was gazing with awe at the soft, coloured sticks of sweetness. What would she choose? Her puffy fingers fluttered up and down the rows and came to rest on the sandy-pink. Her teeth sank into the rock, and she emitted a sound halfway between a sigh and a moan.

'You are a very lovely man,' she declared, licking her fingers, and Andrew blushed. 'Very lovely. To bring me such heavenly delights! I shall eat one more stick and then permit myself one a day. I have learnt the art of rationing. Garnet tells me it makes the treats more precious. Tea, Garnet Alexandrovna! It is time for tea.'

Dolly had departed with her booty clutched to her chest and Garnet was already at the samovar.

'There is no need to shout,' said Garnet, though Andrew did not think that the countess had shouted. But no doubt the old woman would get on anyone's nerves lying there all day expecting to be waited on. When he had bent over to shake her hand he had thought she had not smelt overly sweet, either. But there might well not be any hot water in the flat, or even cold. He was appalled by his sister's living conditions. The place was no better than a slum! At least Lily, though painfully thin when he'd found her, had been living in a house with decent rooms and fresh air and water that could be heated on the kitchen stove.

'Old bitch!' said Garnet under her breath to Andrew. 'I have to help dress and undress her – can you imagine?'

Garnet also had to help her mother-in-law to the stinking lavatory on the landing and wait outside while she moaned and groaned and strained her flagging innards, but she did not tell Andrew that. The countess had become hypochondriacal, and each morning had a different ailment of which to complain. Constipation always, but added to that might be bronchitis, appendicitis, peritonitis, colitis. 'Fetch the doctor!' she would demand. 'What doctor?' Garnet would retort. Once, when the temperature outside had dropped to ten below, she had threatened to put the old woman down in the street (thinking of Eskimos setting their old on ice floes and pushing them off into the wide, freezing yonder), and for the rest of the day the countess had wailed, '*Aïe, aïe,* my daughter-in-law wants to murder me. I'm an old woman who's never done any harm.' 'Or any good, either,' Garnet had muttered.

'It's her snoring at night that gets me down, especially when I can't sleep. It sounds like a train in the room – only it stays, it doesn't go on through.'

'Do you often not sleep?'

'Quite often. But I don't mind. It's the only time I have to myself. I think of Seryozha then.'

'Any news there?'

Garnet shook her head.

She must know that the White Army was more or less finished, mustn't she, that there was little hope of their cause being revived? Andrew was not sure what she would know. All her information would be censored. He would not tell her; he couldn't bear to be the bringer of bad news, the quencher of hope – he had enough of that in his job. One contingent of Whites was still hanging on in the Crimea under General Wrangel. He supposed it was a possibility Sergei might be with it and escape over the border at some point.

'I'm dying of thirst,' said the countess.

'Why not die, then?' said Garnet, as the boiling water hissed into the pot and clouded her words. 'It would be good riddance. Don't look so shocked, brother!'

'Come sit by me, Andrei Alexandrovich!' The countess inched over and patted the small space left on the sofa. 'You see, I know your patronymic! Come and tell me all about the women in your life.'

'That reminds me!' said Andrew, and brought a letter from his pocket. 'From Mother.' He gave it to Garnet, who opened it at once.

Queen's Road, Aberdeen

Dear Garnet,

I am so pleased Andrew has the chance to come to P. and see you and give us a report at first hand. I hope he might be able to persuade you to apply for a permit to come back to Scotland with the children. Please do consider it carefully.

He will give you our news, and his own, no doubt, concerning his friendship with Tom's sister. It seems a serious affair and he goes to see her whenever he can. Which is not that often. It's hardly a weekend visit. We are anxious as to its resolution and he doesn't tell us a great deal. You know what men are like – at least, the men in our family – reticent where the emotions are concerned! He has broken off his friendship with Rose Sibbald, who is very distressed, so her mother tells me, and I have no reason to doubt it. 'Andrew led her to believe,' Mrs S. said. 'Believe what?' I asked. 'I wasn't aware that he'd proposed.' 'Not quite,' she said, 'not in so many *words*, but it isn't always necessary to put everything in *words*, is it, and you know how it is when there is an understanding between two young people?' I put it to her that such understandings can frequently be misunderstood. I have sympathy for Rose but my allegiances must lie with Andrew. Now Mrs Sibbald passes me in the street with a tight little nod, as do Rose's two maiden aunts, who live along the street and with whom I always used to exchange the time of day. It seems I, too, must suffer for the sins of my son!

However, that is the least of my troubles.

Andrew will give you the other piece of family news – that Effie has married her Norrie. The trombone man. It has all been very sudden, and so we had only the

287

immediate available family, which amounted to your father and myself and Andrew, who came up on the overnight train from London, and Norrie's mother, a little woman with an unstoppable tongue, who over lunch regaled us with tales of Norrie when young. You know how awful that can be. How he prayed to Jesus as soon as he could utter a word and always ate up his fat. He appeared not to be embarrassed, or bored; on the contrary he rather enjoyed it, I thought. Andrew left immediately after the lunch and so I did not have time to enlighten him further about the speediness of the marriage. But I shall tell you straight out that Effie is with child. Yes, I'm sure you'll be as astonished as I was when the news was first broken to me. How difficult it is to judge what people are capable of doing, even when they are closely related to you! Effie said they had been moved by the Spirit of the Lord! So I suppose that makes it all right. Norrie has made no attempt to apologise either to your father or myself, and we have said nothing to reproach him. Recriminations are just tiresome. Your father has bought them a flat in Rosemount, in Wallfield Crescent. It will do for them to start with, though no doubt Effie would prefer to have a garden for the child.

We long to see you and young Kolya again and to make the acquaintance of our new grandchild.

Your loving mother,
Jemima McKenzie

'You might have shared the letter with us,' said the countess.

'It's private,' said Garnet, putting it into her overall pocket. 'Nothing much else is, round here.'

'I never get letters. Why don't Elena and Natalya write to me more often?'

The countess turned her attention back to Andrew, asking him again to come and sit with her. 'It's not often I have a nice young man to sit beside me these days.'

Andrew hovered uncertainly. He had little experience in being rude.

'Pay no attention,' said Garnet.

Andrew was saved by the arrival of Eithne, bringing his niece Anna home from her crèche. The child put her thumb into her mouth and gazed dubiously at this new uncle.

'It's good to meet you, Andrew,' said Eithne. 'You're like a breath of fresh air come in our midst! You must tell us everything that's going on back home, what fashions are in and all that. It's ages since we've seen a magazine.'

He was not too sure about fashion. Skirts might be getting shorter, he thought.

'Garnet,' bleated the countess. 'What are you doing? You're not making tea, you're gossiping! Wait till you're an old woman and need someone to bring you a cup.'

'For God's sake, shut up!' said Garnet, and took her the tea.

Shortly afterwards, Leo came in with a large loaf of bread and a small slice of cheese. He had queued for both on his way home from the secondary school where he taught. Andrew took to him straight away and was pleased to be able to reassure his parents that Garnet had someone nearby as a support.

Leo is very intense, very Russian. (But perhaps you met him?) He talked to me about the soul of Russia. (Does Scotland have a soul? I kept wondering. People don't talk about it in the same way, do they?) I agreed with him, though, that the soul of Russia is being trampled on. The regime wears hobnailed boots. By the way, perhaps you could send some new playing cards for the countess? Her pack is just about worn out. She still plays patience much of the time, and laments the passing of the 'old days' and is scolded by Dolly (the former maid), who tells her she shouldn't forget she was privileged then. I find Dolly a rather curious girl. Very pert sort of face. Very determined, I would imagine.

Garnet is teaching English a few hours a week and has

289

a morning job cleaning state offices. I know you will be upset by this, but she says you should not be as it won't kill her and she needs to earn money in whatever way she can. Her friend Eithne is similarly employed and they go out to work together at 5 a.m.

I plan to take the two of them to the opera at the Maryinsky Theatre, with our party from the delegation. We are to see Gluck's *Orpheus*, which I anticipate with mixed feelings. As you know, I'm not an opera-lover. I hope it won't last too long.

We are off to Moscow after this and then go on a trip down the Volga. And after that, I shall be going to Cesis to see Lily, and Veronika.

Your loving son, Andrew

When the children and the countess had gone to sleep, Garnet also wrote a letter home. Andrew had said he would send it out with his.

Dear Mother and Father,

You can imagine my joy when I saw Andrew standing outside my door! He brought you all back so clearly, and Aberdeen, and the house, and Queen's Road. Not that I'd forgotten any of it, but I've tried not to let myself dwell too much. I get on with life! One must. Children make one live in the present.

We talked for hours, Andrew and I, and he told me about himself and Veronika. He hopes to persuade her to marry him and come to London. He says it would be impossible for him to work in Riga; he could never be fluent enough in the language. And language is essential for his work. Whether he will succeed with Veronika or not, we must wait and see.

I know he has told you about our living conditions, so I shall say no more on the subject. One adjusts. We have adjusted. And there are compensations. The theatre and concert halls are still thriving and crowded – Lenin is promoting the idea of Art for All, with which one cannot take issue. Workers can get into performances free, so sometimes Eithne and I manage to get tickets. We saw recently a wonderfully staged performance of Bizet's *Carmen*. The Maryinsky is no longer quite as splendid as it used to be – they've ripped out the imperial arms and the big golden eagles that surmounted the boxes, and the elegant gowns and colourful uniforms have been replaced by shabby, dull jackets, and there do tend to be a lot of soldiers lounging around in dirty, stained uniforms, smoking and spitting sunflower seeds – but the chandeliers have been retained and the blue velvet curtains, and when the house goes dim, and the music strikes up, and the curtains lift, there is still the same thrill.

When life is difficult, and on the grey side, it is good to have something to nourish the soul. You see how Russian I'm becoming!

Dolly came pouting into the room the following afternoon.

'Knock before you enter!' cried the countess. 'How many times do I have to tell you? This is not a public place.'

Dolly ignored her and looked at Garnet. 'Eithne says your brother is taking the two of you to the opera?'

'Yes, tonight.'

'I should like to go too.'

'What do you want to go to the opera for, Dolly?' demanded the countess. 'You don't care for opera, do you? I heard you saying the stories were stupid.'

'Nina can keep an eye on the children,' said Dolly to Garnet.

'Nina couldn't keep her eye on a fly for five seconds.' The countess laid a creased Knave of Diamonds on a tarnished Queen of Spades. Her eyes were none too good, which was perhaps fortunate, for she could not detect the dirt ingrained in the cards. 'I'm glad I can cover *her* up quickly!' she said, obliterating the dark queen.

'I'm not sure if Andrew would have a spare ticket,' Garnet

said to Dolly.

'One can always get tickets. People sell them at the door. Your brother has enough money to buy me a ticket, doesn't he?'

They heard voices on the stair and the flimsy door burst open. Nikolai was at the back of it, with Andrew coming behind.

'You'll break that door down one of these days, Kolya,' said the countess. 'And then all the thieves of the neighbourhood will get in.'

'I will fight them off!' Nikolai drew his stave.

'Put that nasty piece of wood away before you harm someone.' His grandmother, although she reproved him, was fond of the boy. He reminded her of her own Seryozha when young. In the evenings, when the building had quietened around them and Kolya and Anna slept in the big bed by the back wall (which would later be shared by their mother also), she would talk about Seryozha, perhaps much as Norrie's mother had done, but not boring Garnet, the listener, who sat quietly sewing and mending in the weak light. It was the one time of day when she was reconciled to sharing a room with Seryozha's mother.

'I come,' said Dolly, looking at Andrew and pointing to herself. 'Dolly come. To Maryinsky. With you.' Now she jabbed him. 'Opera. Tonight.'

Andrew nodded.

On the way to the theatre, Dolly slipped her arm through his and led him on ahead of the others. She stepped out with pointed toe, somewhat in the manner of a ballerina. Her ambition for her daughter, Sophia, was that she should become one. Dolly held her head high. Garnet thought the back of Andrew's neck looked flushed.

'I think Dolly has taken a fancy to my brother.' Garnet was amused. 'Poor Andrew – all these girls he doesn't want who want him! He finds it difficult to handle.'

'Dolly fancies anyone in trousers,' said Eithne, linking arms with Garnet. 'But it's not often they're as clean and

292

well-pressed. I wonder if she'll manage to take them off him. She has the nimblest hands I've ever seen working.'

'Eithne!'

'She's good at drawing in the men. She had an army officer in last night. He gave me the eye when he went past on the stair. He wasn't a bad looker. Gingery hair, though. I prefer dark men. Gaels. Why didn't I have enough sense to marry an honest-to-God Irishman? I could be living in a villa in Rathmines now, with a maid to bring up my tea tray.'

'Do you ever look at other men?'

'Sometimes.' Eithne shrugged. 'I might just take a wee look at the odd man, in passing. No law against that. Felix has been away a long time, for dear sake. I'm not an ould woman yet! What about you? You don't look at anyone?'

'Oh, I might. But none match up to Seryozha.'

'I hope he appreciates the way you carry a candle for him, that's all I can say!'

They had discussed her fidelity and Sergei's infidelity before. Garnet, although she loved him, was not blind to his faults. How could she be? 'He can't help being restless. It's a part of his nature I've had to accept if I was to accept him. It's his weak string, as they might put it here! So, all right, I know he's gone to other women from time to time. I can cope with that, as long as he always comes back to me.'

At the theatre, Dolly contrived to sit beside Andrew.

'He's putty in her hands,' said Eithne, as she and Garnet settled themselves in seats four rows behind.

During the first interval, when they were promenading around the long salon in the midst of the press of opera-goers, Andrew succeeded in giving Dolly the slip and joined Garnet. Eithne had gone to stand in the queue for the women's lavatory.

'Gosh, quite a crush.' Andrew blew a lock of hair up from his forehead and lifted his elbow to allow a small girl wearing a flouncy dress and ribbons in her hair to pass underneath. 'They start coming young, don't they?'

'They all adore opera. And they enjoy a crush. They call it

sobornost. Getting together. They hate solitude. They don't have a word for privacy.'

'Certainly couldn't be private here.' Andrew ran a finger round the inside of his collar and tried to pull it away from his neck.

'Why don't you slacken it?'

'Do you think?'

'No point in choking. And most people don't have a collar on.'

He undid the stud and let it drop into the palm of his hand. The ends of his stiffened collar stood out like wings.

'I should take it off.'

His neck was red where the collar had bitten.

'*Pazhalsta*!' A man in a droopy grey jacket with torn reveres was holding out his hand.

'He wants your collar.'

'Shall I give it him?'

'Why not? He'll probably treasure it. And it seems to be only a source of annoyance to you.'

'As long as he doesn't start kissing me!'

'I'll protect you.'

The man retreated, bowing, with the collar, his shoulders squeezed by the crowd.

'You're still quite Scottish, aren't you, Andrew, in spite of all your travelling?'

'Well, I should hope so! It's who I am.'

'Quite right.'

'Are *you* all right? You looked troubled suddenly.'

'I was just wondering who I could say *I* am. But pay no attention!'

She knew that he would not want to. Any kind of *angst* would send him off and running. Not that anyone could run through a space so thick with bodies as this. She had become used to people around her, she was realising; it had become her normality.

'Back in Scotland, you'll soon feel Scots again,' he said, taking out his handkerchief to dry his forehead. 'Do you think that woman over there has designs on my hanky now? She's staring at it.'

'People stare at everything. And it *is* good quality linen.'

'I'm short of handkerchiefs.' He stuffed it back into his pocket. 'And I doubt if we're going to get any laundry done at our digs.'

The bell rang and a few people made a move.

'No hurry,' said Garnet. 'There'll be another bell, or two.'

'Russians don't like to be early, I've observed.'

'They're loath to give up their conversation. They might be discussing matters of life and death.'

Andrew cleared his throat. 'Talking of sources of annoyance—'

'Were we?'

'Back there.'

'You mean Dolly?'

'This is a little awkward . . .' He glanced round.

'Don't worry about being overheard. I doubt if many here understand English.'

'Well, she was kind of . . . I don't know how to say this. It's rather embarrassing.' He pulled out his handkerchief, passed it over his forehead again. 'Her hands . . .'

'Were wandering?'

'I couldn't get rid of them.'

Garnet involuntarily looked down, then up. Andrew's face shone as brightly as a turkey cock's. No wonder his neck had swollen.

'It was damned difficult sitting there right through that act. Well, I couldn't very well make a fuss, could I? I mean, she might have accused *me* of interfering with *her*.'

Riga

September 1920

'It was a great sight, Morag. You'd have enjoyed it! The peasants were dancing in the meadow, in their national costumes.
The girls had on those floral headdresses, and the women
wore white headscarves.'

'That must have looked bonny on the green grass,' said
Morag, who was more interested in the spoils Andrew had
brought back, rather than the agricultural show itself. She
was gathering up the apples and plums in huge handfuls and
transferring them to bowls. 'You get to see a lot in your job,
Mr Andrew.'

'Oh, I do! Would you like to travel, Morag? See something
of the world?'

'I've enough to be getting on with here. And I'm not ower
fond of the sea, even though I grew up with it sucking at my
doorstep. It's all right as long as you're only looking at it.'

'You're not planning to come back to Scotland, then?'

'What would I do that for? I've got my man here, haven't
I? Mr Tom's given him a job in his office. General handyman,
that kind of thing. Paul's right knackie at fixing and mending.
His limp doesn't hold him back, any more than Mr Tom's eye
does him. Paul sorted all the windows here in the flat. He
rummaged around the town till he found the glass. You've
got to rummage for everything these days. We're used to

296

that, though. There was scarce a pane that wasne crackit. Well, you can see for yourself what the city looks like. It's sad to see it all battered to bits. It was such a fine-looking place when first I came. I mind the day your sister took me round the town to show me the old bit. I couldn't get over the coloured houses – after the grey stone back home – and the funny sloping roofs. They looked like something out of a fairy tale. A witch could have popped out any minute. Still, Mr Tom says everything will pick up from now on. He's sure the city'll get rebuilt, given time. It'll be work for him, too, won't it? He's keen to get going again after all these years of living in the country. It's been like one of those fairy tales where everyone's sent to sleep – with a few nightmares thrown in! – and now we've been wakened up and we're getting on with life.'

'So you'd always feel you should go where Paul's work is, would you, Morag?' said Andrew, following her around as she sorted the fruit and other provisions that he'd brought.

'Och well, I'm settled here now.' She sniffed an apple and nodded approvingly. She was not so daft that she didn't know what way Andrew's mind was working. (She was not daft at all.) 'So, were there lots of folk at your show?' She did not think it was her place to be giving her opinion on his private life.

'Masses. And a band. And a choir. Well, naturally!'

'Get half a dozen of them together and you've got a choir. I'm learning some of the songs myself. My Paul's a braw singer.'

'Ulmanis, the Prime Minister, was there.'

'What's that about Ulmanis?' asked Veronika, coming into the kitchen with a bucket of greasy water and a mop. She'd been washing the outside stair.

'He was at the agricultural show. He got a rousing welcome.'

'Did he make a speech?'

'You're telling me! It lasted an hour and three quarters! And the peasants stood listening throughout, and then the

297

choir sang "God Bless Latvia", not once but *several* times.'

'We have to be sure God is listening. We need His attention.'

'What did he say?' asked Morag. 'Mr Ulmanis?'

'He talked about Latvia's long struggle for freedom.'

'Aye, it's been mighty long and gey wearying,' agreed Morag. 'Still, it's all ower now.'

'Let's hope,' said Veronika, tipping the water from the bucket into the sink.

'I thought they'd signed their treaties?'

'Oh, they have.' Veronika picked up a jar. 'Honey!'

'He's brought all sorts of stuff,' said Morag. 'Butter and cheese and even some cloth. It'd make good winter dresses for the girls from that Butterick pattern Mrs McKenzie sent.'

Veronika smiled. 'He's a bearer of gifts, aren't you, Andrew?'

'Come for a walk,' he said, catching hold of her hand. 'Can you? Or have you got ten thousand other household chores to do?'

'You run along,' said Morag to Veronika. 'Mara'll mind the bairns.'

Lily coming in crossed with Veronika and Andrew going out. Morag was in the sitting room, flicking a feather duster over the paintings. She was very fond of the one of the lady in the lilac dress with the mirror.

'Did you get anything?' she asked.

'Quite a nice table, not too scuffed. It'll do for the children. What a lot of stuff there is for sale! Half the houses in Riga must have been emptied. And, do you know, I saw a Sheraton sideboard in an antique shop that I'm pretty sure used to belong to Mr Tom's sister and her husband! I recognised a nick in one drawer. Too expensive for us, though. Not that I'd want anything that used to be theirs.'

Herman had been stripped of his estates and he and Agita had departed to Germany with their children.

Morag had stopped by the window and was looking down. Lily joined her. Tom and Veronika were walking along the opposite side of the street. They were talking and their hands were joined, though their arms were not quite together.

'He's gey fond of her,' said Morag with a sigh.

'He is, isn't he?' said Lily.

She watched until they turned the corner.

That evening was to be Andrew's last before he returned to London. He had been in Riga on and off for the last couple of months, covering various peace conferences and their signings, interviewing people such as Sir Stephen Tallants, the head of the British Mission, and refugees who'd fled from Poland and Russia. One family from Petrograd had known Garnet and Sergei when they'd lived on the English Embankment; they'd been near neighbours. They had danced at their wedding, and remembered doing the Dashing White Sergeant. 'It was such good fun!' the wife had said. 'We all took straight away to Seroysha's Scottish wife.' Andrew had brought them back for the evening and they'd sat up talking and drinking wine until daybreak, when the Russian visitors had picked up their bundles and continued on their journey. They were heading for Paris, where they had relatives. Lily had been sorry to part from them; they'd been a link to Garnet. Andrew also came across a White Army officer who claimed to have seen Sergei as late as June somewhere in the Crimea. Sergei had told him he'd fight to the last ditch. 'But it's a hopeless case,' said the officer. He was also making for Paris. 'Half of Petersburg is in Paris!' Sergei had told him to look out for his sisters, Elena and Natalya.

They decided to go out to a restaurant for a meal, the four of them, Andrew and Veronika, Lily and Tomas.

'My treat,' said Andrew. He would take them to the Otto Schwarz, the smartest restaurant in Riga.

'A treat would be nice,' said Lily, looking at her weathered hands. 'I'm going to get a nice little frock out of the trunk. Something in silk or chiffon. Imagine!'

Rummaging in the trunk, she came across a dress of Garnet's. She must have taken it by mistake. A misty blue chiffon. She would wear it tonight. It smelled of must and mothballs when she pressed it to her face, a smell that made her feel nostalgic, and a little tearful.

'What's wrong?' asked Tomas.

She shivered slightly. 'Nothing. Just ghosts.'

She had Garnet much in her mind. Andrew had told them about her life in Petrograd and had brought photographs that he'd taken there. Garnet looked so tired and drawn, it was almost painful to look at her. The salt cellars were prominent in her neck. And she seemed to be wearing a drab, sack-like dress with no collar. The children appeared bright enough. They were sitting on a park bench, one on either side of their mother, and they were smiling into the camera. But then it is easy to smile momentarily, for a photograph.

Lily laid the blue dress aside. Perhaps it would be a mistake. She shook out another, a sea-green cobweb, shot through with silver. Tomas said she looked like a mermaid in it. She slid a silk stocking over her foot and eased it up over her knee. The silk was pure. And silvery. Smooth to the touch. To Tomas's touch. He could not resist stroking it. She put a silver band round her dark hair, then twisted this way and that to see herself in the silver mirror. Standing behind her, Tomas smiled at her shimmering image. The lamp on the dresser was flooding the glass with soft light. He went to the door and slid the bolt into its socket.

He came back to Lily and led her to the bed.

A child cried somewhere in the recesses of the flat. 'Ignore it,' said Tomas. 'Some time must belong to us.' Lily was happy to ignore it. Someone was rattling the door handle now. 'Mama! Mama!' The parents breathed quietly and said not a word. The rattling and the low complaining went on outside the door while the two bodies on the bed moved feverishly, and then Lily cried out and the child, in a roar of outraged anger, screamed, '*Mama!*'

Lily and Tom collapsed in a heap of laughter.

'Why can't we come?' demanded Luke. 'We need treats too.'

'I've said no!' said Lily. (She knew she allowed him to argue too much with her and was trying to put a stop to it.) 'If you ask Morag nicely she might read you a story from that nice book of Russian stories Uncle Andrew brought you.'

Andrew had met the writer Arthur Ransome, who had been the *Times* correspondent in Petrograd during the Revolution and was now living in Estonia, and he had given him a copy of his book *Old Peter's Russian Tales*.

'I don't like Russkies,' said Luke. 'Russkies are bad.'

'Not all,' said Lily.

'Only Bolsheviks,' said Tomas.

'Your cousins aren't Bolsheviks!' said Lily. 'They're not bad.'

'I want the stories,' said Alex, taking up the book. 'I want the story about the silver saucer and the apple you can look into and see the world.'

'Morag reads too slowly,' said Luke. 'It takes hours to get to the bottom of the page.'

'Any more of your cheek,' said Morag, 'and I'll belt you one and put you to bed without any supper.'

The restaurant was busy. Riga was becoming quite lively again in the evenings, more like its pre-war self. Andrew waved to some men he recognised from the British Mission and he brought over his American friend Hank to introduce to them. Hank had a cocktail and sat down and chatted for a while. He was off to Warsaw next. The Poles were still trying to fight off the Bolsheviks. There was no lack of stories to be covered in Europe!

'What a life you lead,' said Veronika. 'All over the place. It must make you restless.'

'Some of us are just rovers at heart.' Hank grinned. 'We get uneasy if our feet touch the same piece of ground for too long.'

Lily would never have thought of Andrew as a rover; she had always envisaged him settled in Aberdeen. He appeared to have had roving thrust upon him, or else it had been lying dormant and, once roused, was difficult to quell. She could see it was going to be difficult between him and Veronika. Veronika had no roving instincts in her at all; she wanted to stay in her own country.

Hank rose and shook hands with each of them in turn. 'Nice meeting you all. I'd heard such a lot about you. See you around, Andy – here, there, or wherever.'

'Wherever,' said Andrew.

Hank returned to his table.

'I think you know more people in Riga than we do nowadays, Andrew,' said Lily.

'Only superficially. In war situations you tend to get to know them after ten minutes.'

'Your Latvian is improving, though,' said Veronika. 'You sounded quite fluent when you ordered.'

'You could soon settle in here,' said Lily teasingly.

'Anyone can learn to order a meal in a foreign language,' said Andrew.

The pianist, who'd been warming up, began to play 'If You Were the Only Girl in the World'. A couple took the floor, and Andrew held out his hand to Veronika.

'Shall we?' Tomas asked Lily, and she rose. 'It's been a long time since we danced.'

Lily half closes her eyes. The music, the feel of her dress swirling around her legs, the smell of Tom, takes her back to what she was before. A girl on a dance floor held in the arms of a man she loves and who loves her, existing as if seen in a spotlight, without other entanglements. An illusion, she knows, even as she is feeling it, but that does not trouble her. To have it even for a little while is enough. It is something war has taught her: to savour the moment. And she does not think there is anything wrong in dreaming.

The man holding her tells her she looks beautiful and she tells him he looks dashing and even more handsome with his black eye patch and they laugh and feel pleasure in being together. His legs feel familiar to Lily as they brush against hers, guiding her, swinging her now to the right, now to the left. She goes with him, trusts him. Familiarity is important, thinks Lily; and trust. They are what tether us.

Andrew and Veronika are not smiling, and scarcely moving. They are going round and round in a tight circle, oblivious of the other dancers revolving about them. Their talk looks serious. Andrew is doing the greater part of it; he appears to be making a case. Veronika has her head cocked to one side, as if she is considering it, and withholding judgment.

They walked home afterwards through the mild evening, with Veronika and Andrew going out in front of the other couple.

'I feel this is a new beginning.' said Lily, looking up, seeing not the jagged rooftops of burnt-out buildings but the brightness of the stars.

'It is,' promised Tomas. 'We're going to build a strong new country for our children.'

Veronika turned back to say she would not be coming home.

In the morning, Andrew was gone.

Two months later, Lily received a letter from her mother.

You'll never believe this, but Andrew has taken up with Rose Sibbald again! I hope he means what he's doing this time. He surely can't let her down a second time. Hardly anyone in Queen's Road will be left speaking to me if he does!

At Christmas, Andrew wrote:

I know it has worked for you and Tom, but I've come to the conclusion that on the whole it's better to stick with what one knows in such matters.

'Matters of the heart, I suppose he means,' Lily said to Tom, 'though he wouldn't spell it out. I think what Andrew wants is a woman who will provide him with a stable base from which he can come and go and do his foreign-corresponding.'

On New Year's Day, the engagement was announced between Andrew Alexander McKenzie, son of Mr & Mrs Alexander McKenzie, Queen's Road, Aberdeen, and Rose Margaret Sibbald, daughter of Mr & Mrs Alastair Sibbald, of Queen's Road, Aberdeen.

Cesis

July 1993

The three women descended from the train at Cesis.

Helga's father, Alex, was at the station to meet them. He was agile for his eighty years and walked without any sign of a stoop or stiff knees. White hair grew thickly from his high forehead, and his dark eyes – Lily's eyes – flashed with warmth and humour. His arms and face were a ruddy-brown. He had inherited a love of gardening from his grandmother Gertrude.

Helga hugged and kissed him and told him he was looking well, then he turned to embrace Katrina. 'It's good to see my Scottish niece again!' He spoke English with a soft Scottish burr.

'And this is Lydia!' said Helga.

'Welcome to Cesis, Lydia!' He embraced her warmly also.

'I'm delighted to be here,' she said. 'I've long wanted to come.'

They went through the station into the forecourt and put their luggage into the boot of his car.

'It's pretty ancient,' said Alex, 'and the windscreen wipers don't work properly, but it fetches me up and down the road. I don't want to go further than that.'

He had to get some shopping at the market first. Would they mind accompanying him? It was only two minutes' walk away.

It being a Saturday morning, the market was busy. The stalls were set up around the edge of the square and, as in any market, were selling a myriad of things. Alex bought some locally produced yellow butter, a wedge of hard white cheese and two loaves of rye bread. The cousins from Scotland insisted on contributing a chicken and bananas and other groceries.

Numerous stalls were selling fresh flowers. Katrina and Lydia bought two large bunches of sweet-smelling carnations apiece.

'We could go back by the cemetery, if you like,' said Alex. 'I think you're wanting to see your father's grave, Lydia?'

Flowers bloomed on the well-tended plots and the leaves of the birch trees shimmered green and gold. After the bustle of the market the quietness of the graveyard spread over them like a hush. There was no one else about, except for an old woman in black who was kneeling by a grave, weeding prodigiously. She looked up as they went by and she and Alex exchanged a greeting.

'I know most people here,' he said, 'alive and dead!'

They came to the stretch where the Zale family was buried. The names were inscribed on simple headstones.

'I'm glad they don't go in for heavy black marble,' said Lydia.

Flowers flourished in colourful profusion on these plots. There was not a weed in sight.

'You look after the graves well, Alex,' said Lydia.

'It's the least I can do. Since I am left as the guardian.' He pointed. 'There are Markus and Gertrude, my grandparents. And my aunt Veronika.' He took a few steps. 'And here is Luke.' Alex bowed his head in memory of his twin brother.

Lukas Markus Zale
10 January 1914–24 September 1944

'Thirty was young to die,' said Helga.

Katrina laid flowers on Luke's grave and brushed a tear from her eye. She remembered little of her father from those early years, knew him more through photographs and tales told by her grandmother, but the sight of his name in this simple country churchyard always affected her.

'War!' Alex took a handkerchief from his pocket and blew his nose. 'It decimated most families.'

The Russian – the odd one out – was buried at the end of the line, since he did not quite belong, yet in death he had become part of the extended family.

Nikolai Sergeevich Burnov
15 January 1915–24 September 1944

'They died on the same day!' exclaimed Lydia. 'I didn't know that! Did you know, Kate? You must have done. Why didn't you tell me?'

Katrina shrugged. 'I didn't think to.'

'But surely . . .' began Lydia, then stopped.

Alex had turned away and was looking out beyond the perimeter of the graveyard. His face looked set, and inscrutable. Had he hated her father? Lydia wondered. Yet he had welcomed her.

Alex kept his back to her while she knelt to put flowers on her father's grave. She closed her eyes. She asked only that Nikolai Burnov should be at peace. Then she stood up.

She looked along the row at the other headstones, and frowned. Her father's was much newer than the others. It had not been put there at the same time as Luke Zale's, even though they had died on the same day. She made no comment, sensing that if she did she would meet another blank wall.

'Ready, Father?' Helga touched Alex's arm. 'Are you OK?'

'Ah, Helga.' He smiled at her, as if he'd forgotten she was there. 'It will soon be lunchtime, you must all be hungry.' He led the way back along the path towards the gate, stopping

307

on the way to show them the graves of Morag and Mara. Both women had died in the 1960s. They had remained friends, and Morag had become a citizen of Soviet Latvia. She had never returned to Scotland.

'And their husbands?' asked Lydia.

'They were both taken away by the Germans in '42. They must have died in a camp – we never heard. They were half-Jewish, you see. On their mother's side. Fortunately, Old Vera was dead by then.'

But Lydia could think only of 24 September 1944. The date that marked the death of the two cousins, the Latvian Lukas and the Russian Nikolai.

Aberdeen

April 1921

After the funeral, the family returned to the house, accompanied only by close relatives and Rose Sibbald, the fiancée of Andrew, and Rose's parents.

Jemima put the black veil back from her face and drew out the long hat pin with the black bobble on the end, then she removed her hat and gave her head a little shake.

'Are you all right, Mother?' asked Lily.

Lily and Garnet came and put their arms around her, and for a few moments the three women, garbed in heavy black, stood fused into one solid group, their tears mingling, their hearts beating close to one another's. Together for death, thought Jemima, when it had been so difficult for them to be reunited for life. It was seven years since the girls had been home. Seven years since they had seen their father. And now he was gone. That they had not seen him before he died was adding to their anguish.

He'd had a massive heart attack and died a few minutes later in her arms. He'd shown no sign of being ill before that, had often boasted of never being off work with sickness, not even for a day.

'It's too sudden,' she'd cried aloud as she'd held him, and Nessie had come running from the next room.

The three women dried their eyes and broke apart.

'He enjoyed his life,' said Jemima. 'We must remember that.'

Lily and Garnet began to cry afresh.

'Come on, now,' said their mother, 'he wouldn't have wanted us to sit weeping. Let's go down and join the others. And I want the two of you to eat some food and get some meat on those bones! You felt like two sticks in my arms there!'

They had been enjoying the plump, comfortable feel of their mother's body pressed against theirs. It had taken them back to childhood, and as they had rested there in the warm embrace they had each yearned for a return to that state. They had come to give their mother support, yet it was she was who was still supporting them.

Nessie was serving tea in the drawing room.

'I think some of us need something stronger,' said Jemima. 'Andrew, perhaps you might get out the whisky and port.'

'I'll give you a hand,' said Tomas.

'Just tea for me, please,' said Norrie.

Effie was sitting with their baby, John, on her knee. He looked extraordinarily like Norrie: a miniature version of him.

'He seems bright for his age,' said Mrs Sibbald, glancing briefly at him, not remembering what his age was exactly (it was something best passed over, anyway) but wishing to make pleasant conversation. No one would ever say that Maud Sibbald did not know her social obligations. She sat perched forward on the settee with her cup and saucer held on her lap, watching the young engaged couple, her eye veering from one to the other as if it would be dangerous to let either of them out of her sight. Not that she imagined that they would *do* what Effie and Norrie did. She knew her Rose too well for that; they had brought her up with high principles and she was reasonably sure that Andrew was too much of a gentleman to take advantage of a young and innocent girl. But, then, he had travelled a lot on the continent, and so one never knew, did one?

'He's very advanced,' said Norrie, and for a moment Mrs Sibbald could not think to whom he was referring. 'He's got his first tooth coming through already,' added Norrie.

'How nice,' she said.

'Can I hold him?' asked Rose, putting out her arms.

She promenaded up and down the room, smiling, with the baby pressed against her shoulder, patting his back with her free hand in a steady rhythm. *Rum-ta-tum-ta-tum*. She even hummed, quite audibly. She stopped at the drinks cabinet to show the child to Andrew, who had been called upon to admire him many times before.

'She loves children,' sighed her mother.

'Suffer little children, sayeth the Lord,' said Effie.

'Indeed,' said Mrs Sibbald.

'We are to be blessed again,' said Norrie.

'Again!' said Mrs Sibbald, looking at Effie's stomach. 'You've hardly had time.' And then she looked hurriedly to her other side and said to Garnet, 'Your mother must be greatly comforted to have you home. But what a pity you weren't able to bring the children. I'm sure she would have loved to have seen them. It's hard for a grandparent to be deprived.'

'I could only get a visa for myself.'

'Pretty harsh regime you've got yourselves over there, isn't it?' said Mr Sibbald, coming in on the conversation. 'Though I can't see how it can last. People won't put up with that kind of thing for ever. At least it's a lesson to those here who like to indulge in talk about a socialist state.'

'Father always thought we needed to embrace some aspects of Socialism,' said Garnet. 'There are great inequalities here, as everywhere.'

'Always will be,' said Mr Sibbald cheerfully. 'Nature of the world. Your father, God rest his soul, was a bit of an idealist.'

Garnet hoped that God would rest her father's soul, if He existed. 'Do you think there is such a thing as the soul, Mr Sibbald?'

'Well, yes.' He sounded less comfortable now. 'Difficult

thing to define, though, eh?'

'Surely it's in the soul that one finds idealism?'

'Are you trying to say that the less of an idealist you are, the smaller your soul?' He gave a hearty laugh, which emerged more like a guffaw. 'Have socialists got a monopoly on big souls? Every man's in it for what he can get out of it, if you ask me.'

Not surprisingly, Mrs Sibbald disliked political or philosophical turns of conversation. Well, they could often turn into heated arguments, couldn't they? They were areas of dispute which often seemed to make perfectly reasonable people lose their heads. She said: 'It was nice that Lily was able to bring her little family with her.'

'Of course, Latvia's become a democratic republic, hasn't it?' said Mr Sibbald. 'She wouldn't have had to get a permit to leave.'

'Such charming children,' his wife went on. 'The boys seem pretty lively. I met them in the park yesterday when they were out with their nursemaid. It's so good that she is Scottish. I've heard from friends who've lived abroad that you can't do better than have a good Scots girl to look after your children. They're much better at keeping a firm hand and they've got such a lot of common sense.'

'I wouldn't say that was an attribute of all Scots,' said Garnet.

'The Russians, though, I hear, can be pretty unstable. Very emotional at times.'

Garnet was rescued by her Aunt Hetty, her mother's wandering sister, home from travels in Indo-China, who came over and said, 'Garnet and I have a great deal of catching up to do. I'm sure you won't mind I steal her from you?' She took Garnet to the other side of the room and gave her a Turkish cigarette.

'You won't have any news of Seryozha?'

'Not yet. Nothing concrete.'

'The White Army's finished, you must know that.' Hetty believed in being blunt. 'Has been since November. Wrangel

312

was lucky to get out of the Crimea with his men – or what remained of them. French gave them protection, took them to Tunisia; otherwise they probably wouldn't have made it. Andrew went to Tunis himself and checked the lists – Sergei's name was not among them.'

'We heard that some of the Whites had gone to fight in Serbia.'

'He could have sent word from there, I imagine. Somehow or other.'

'He wouldn't be able to contact me in Petrograd. He doesn't know where I am.'

'He could send a message here, though, to Aberdeen.'

'He might not think to do that.'

Garnet knew the family thought she was being stubborn in not accepting Sergei's death. But what evidence was there for it? Not all White Army soldiers had perished. (Though many had.) And if Sergei had been taken prisoner (or executed by the Communists – she faced the possibility in the cold dark hours of the night), wouldn't the authorities have notified her? They had taken her in for questioning again only three months ago and they had gone through the ritual of *Where is your husband? Have you heard from your husband? Your sister-in-law's husband?* and back again to *Where is your husband?* She had taken that as a sign that they thought he might still be alive.

She couldn't believe Seryozha no longer existed. When she slept he entered her dreams, and came alive. He seemed so real that in the morning, waking, she expected to see his red-gold head beside hers, his arms flung back on the pillow, a smile making his mouth twitch in sleep.

'I think I would *know*, Hetty, if he were dead. I'd feel it in my bones.'

Hetty did not scoff; she had travelled too much in places where it was considered valid to have such feelings and in-tuitions.

Andrew came to ask what they would like to drink.

'Whisky,' said Hetty. 'Large one.'

313

'And for me, please,' said Garnet.

They watched Andrew return to the drinks cabinet.

'He's developed a lot,' said Hetty. 'Fine-looking man. Pity he's compromised so heavily on the marriage stakes.'

Garnet inclined to the view that Rose must be what Andrew needed.

'Your father's death has been a big shock for your mother.' Hetty blew smoke and smiled across at Mrs Sibbald. 'Theirs was a happy marriage. We know she'll survive, though, don't we? It's easy to say, I'm aware of that. The words trip off the tongue. But she is a strong woman.'

'It gets tiring at times, being strong.'

'Is there a choice?' Hetty stubbed out her cigarette. 'I thought I might take Jemima travelling with me. It would do her good, don't you think? To get away from the Salvation Army and Rose Sibbald.'

At that moment Rose cried out violently and her mother jumped up from her seat in alarm. But nothing too serious had transpired; the baby had merely been sick down the back of Rose's lilac-grey moiré taffeta.

While Rose was away being sponged down by Nessie, Andrew came to talk to Lily.

'How's life in Riga?' He sat down on the window seat beside her.

'Improving all the time,' said Lily, knowing this was not the answer Andrew wanted. For that he would have to ask, declare his interest outright. 'Shops are reopening, buildings going up. Investment is coming in from abroad. Tom's been busy.'

'Thought the place was going to make it. The Letts seem a pretty determined lot. They seem more European than the Russians.'

'Latvians, please! Surely you know they don't like being called Letts – that's German. They want as little as possible to do with both Germany and Russia.'

Andrew was nodding his head absent-mindedly, in the manner of someone who is thinking of something else. He swirled the whisky in his glass. 'And how's—' He cleared his throat. 'How's Veronika?' His voice croaked on the word, and Lily's heart went out to him. She softened her voice.

'She's gone back to teaching. And she's renting a tiny flat a few minutes' walk from us. You know she likes to be independent.'

'Yes, I do know that.'

How can I *not* tell him? Lily wondered. That Veronika was expecting his child. But Veronika had sworn her to secrecy. 'It's over between us,' she'd said. 'Since we cannot find a way to be compatible, I must put him out of my life and he must put me out of his. He must marry his Rose.'

'So you'd say she was all right, would you?'

'Yes, I would say that, on the whole.'

'That's good then,' said Andrew heavily, and downed the rest of his whisky.

Rose came back wrinkling her nose. She plumped herself down between Andrew and Lily.

'I must smell *awful*,' she said.

'Not at all,' said Andrew dutifully.

That was what he was going to be, thought Lily: a dutiful husband. While his wife was around, at any rate. He would opt for a quiet life in the house and Rose would have no idea of what was going on in his head. Might not want to have. Lily suspected she was not as stupid as they were inclined to think and might be wise enough to know that some questions should stay unasked.

Rose sniffed her shoulder. 'I'm sure I must smell as sour as anything.'

'Mothers of babies smell of milk nearly all the time,' said Lily.

Rose blushed and looked at Andrew under lowered lids.

'We do hope you and Tom will be able to come to our wedding, Lily,' she said.

'Depends when it is.'

'We're thinking of September. Aren't we, Andrew?'

'I'm not sure about September. I may have to cover an

315

important conference in the Far East in the autumn.'

'You and your paper! I had wanted to get married in June originally, Lily. Well, it's the perfect month for weddings! Everyone knows that. But Andrew said he'd have to go to Vienna and now it seems he doesn't. But it's just as well we didn't fix it for June, with *this* happening now. Your mother probably wouldn't have been out of mourning.'

'I doubt if she'll wear black for long,' said Lily. 'She doesn't believe in being dreary. So that needn't hold you up.'

'We'll have to fix *some* date, Andrew! Mother says people will start to think it odd if we don't. It can't be November or December – those months are far too cold and damp for Venice. As are January, February or March.' Rose ticked them off on her fingers and her diamond engagement ring flashed. 'I want to go to Venice for my honeymoon, Lily, the way you and Garnet did. I thought that was terribly romantic. You loved Venice, didn't you?'

'It's a strange place,' said Lily slowly. 'It draws you in.'

The house felt depleted, with just one person gone from it. Their father's chair looked empty. No one liked to take his seat at the head of the table. Nor did anyone like to raise the question of whether Jemima would stay on in the house herself. It was clearly too large for her, had been even for two. It had been built as a family house.

'Perhaps Norrie and I should move in with Mother,' said Effie.

'The garden would be good for the children,' said Norrie.

'We shall pray to the Lord,' said Effie, 'and ask for His guidance.'

'I feel confident the Lord is going to tell them that they should move in posthaste,' said Garnet, when she and Lily went upstairs to join the children. But they could not see their mother accepting the Lord's instructions if they went against her will.

Morag, having bathed the four children, had seated them on the floor and given them malted milk. She was bent on 'building them up' during their stay in Scotland.

Garnet sat down between the twins. 'So what did you see today?'

'Soldiers,' said Alex. 'Kilties. Playing those big pipes.'

'We're going to be soldiers when we grow up.' Luke puffed out his chest.

Please God no, said Lily to herself.

'My Kolya likes to play at soldiers,' said Garnet.

'Why didn't you bring him?' demanded Luke.

'I wish I could have!' Garnet lifted Luke's left hand and examined his little finger. 'Still crooked! Just like Kolya's.'

The sisters went out walking every day, as had been their custom in the old days. They looked smart in rakish felt hats and new costumes of fine tweed, Lily's a lilac mixture, Garnet's rust-coloured. On their feet they wore shoes of the finest kid with slender straps fastening over the top of the instep. They were amazed by their shoes, kept looking down at them, and their silken ankles. Jemima had given them a purseful of money and sent them downtown to shop for new wardrobes. She'd insisted they spend it all, every pound. 'Your father left me well enough off. He wouldn't want to see the pair of you traipsing about the town like tramps!' They had arrived in Aberdeen in outmoded pre-war clothes that were shabby to the point of being almost threadbare and Garnet had been wearing men's boots! Since the war, fashions had become much less heavy and cumbersome and hemlines were going up and up, which was causing the Wee Frees and other guardians of the nation's morals to deliver invectives. The twins were delighted to find the rigid corset in decline and that a woman was no longer expected to contort herself into an S-bend.

On their promenades in the park they talked about their children, and were in agreement that rearing a family had not proved to be as easy as they'd expected from their own experience of growing up. Their childhood household had been well ordered, with their mother firmly in command.

317

There had been few disruptions. And they had always known where the parameters were drawn.

'Mind you, we've had to rear ours in the middle of wars and revolutions,' said Lily.

And they talked about Sergei. Garnet kept bringing the conversation back to him. She had a need to speak of him, which Lily understood; it was not so much a need for Garnet to keep him alive in her own mind as in that of others.

'If anything *should* happen to him I would never love another man.'

'You can't really know how you'd feel.'

'Oh, yes, I do know!' said Garnet vehemently.

And so their talk ran on and on and helped to compensate for the years of separation that lay behind them and those that might still be to come. The physical act of walking seemed to help them cope with their grief – their mother was turning out cupboards and packing up bags of household linen for the Salvation Army, something she'd meant to do for a long time. She had declined Effie's offer to move in. She wanted to take time to think about the next stage in her life, she said.

Before Andrew returned to London he had a talk with Garnet.

'I can't bear to think of you going back to that life, Garnet. You mustn't go!'

'How can I stay? I've left the children behind.'

'I could try to get them out.'

'And how would you propose to do that? Kidnap them? Smuggle them out in your luggage?'

'There are ways. I do have connections – Hank knows a lot of people.'

The night before Garnet is due to return to Petrograd, Lily has a dream in which she sees the body of a man lying on snowy ground, spread-eagled, with a stave driven through his heart. Bright scarlet blood, the colour of postboxes, is slowly seep-

318

ing from the wound and spilling down on to the bright ground. It looks like paint spattered from a child's paintbox. Above him hovers a woman with arms stretched wide, casting a shadow on the landscape, like a giant bird. From the position of her right hand it is evident that it is the woman who has driven the stave into the man's chest.

The man is Sergei and the woman, Garnet.

And now Garnet is being lifted upward, on a current of air, into the glutinous, grey sky.

She is receding.

Dwindling

into a

dot.

She has gone.

'*Garnet*!' Lily woke up screaming.

'It's all right, love.' Tom switched on the bedlight.

'Where's Garnet?' Lily looked frenziedly around the room. 'I can't see Garnet!'

'You've been dreaming. You had a nightmare.'

She calmed and told him her dream. It was a silly dream, he said. Many dreams were, when you examined them in the cold light of day. Garnet would never want to *kill* Seryozha. That was a ridiculous idea! But it was all understandable: Seryozha was missing, very possibly dead, and Lily was anxious about Garnet having to go back to Soviet Russia, where she would be unreachable.

Petrograd

May 1921

The children flung themselves on Garnet the moment she opened the door.

'Why did you go away?' demanded Nikolai, butting her in the chest with his head. 'I hated it when you weren't here. Dolly said you might not come back.'

How dare Dolly say that and deliberately worry the children! Garnet knew it would have been deliberate; Dolly did little that was not calculated.

She glanced up, to see the woman standing in the doorway.

'Why did you tell them I might not come back?'

'You might not have.' Dolly shrugged. 'You might have decided to stay. Once you'd got out there with your wealthy family rolling around like cheese in butter! Who'd want to come back and live in this pigsty? And look at you – all dressed up like a countess!'

'Don't worry – you'll get some of the clothes!'

'Eithne said you'd come back,' said Nikolai.

'Eithne was right.' Garnet kept her arms round her children. 'I would always come back to you, remember that!'

'Eithne's leaving,' said Dolly. 'She's going to live in Odessa.'

The news came as a shock to Garnet. Eithne's going would be a real loss.

'Her husband's being allowed to settle in Odessa and she's got permission to join him.' Dolly was clearly enjoying the telling. 'She'd be a fool not to go. Imagine getting away from the winters in Peter! They say it seldom snows down there. I've always wanted to see the Black Sea.'

'Of course, she must go,' put in the countess. 'A woman must always go to her husband.'

'Have you got presents for us?' asked Nikolai.

'Yes, presents for everybody!'

'Your mother wouldn't forget me?' said the countess.

'No, she wouldn't!'

Garnet had had to bribe the customs official well to get past. She'd tucked five pounds sterling inside a packet of Earl Grey tea.

She unpacked her bag, brought out toys, sweets and clothes for the children, Edinburgh rock and tablets of vanilla and chocolate fudge for the countess, tea and coffee for the rest of the household. She hadn't been able to carry any more.

The countess piled up her sweetmeats and sat gloating, her hands spread protectively over them. 'There are thieves everywhere these days. They'd take anything off you.'

Leo embraced Garnet warmly when he came in. He sounded sombre even while he was saying how glad he was to have her back. Then he added, 'There's someone here to see you, Garnet. He's downstairs, in the street. Can you leave the children with Eithne?'

Her heart lurched. 'Not—?'

'No, not Seryozha,' said Leo quietly.

'Do you remember the coachman Ivan?' he asked, as they went down the dark stairs.

'The big one, with the wild red beard? Seryozha used to say birds nested in it! He used to tease him. "Let them fly out, Ivan!" he'd say. "Let them soar!" *He's* our visitor? Didn't he go with Seryozha when he joined the Volunteers?'

'He's just made his way back from the Crimea. It was a

long walk. He was with Wrangel's army.'

They emerged from the darkness of the stair into the lightness of the street.

Ivan was leaning against the wall. Garnet did not recognise him immediately. Formerly a big man, he was shrunken now and bent, his eyes sunk into dark sockets, his glorious beard grown dingy and speckled with grey.

'Ivan.' She touched his arm.

'Madame!' He straightened up.

'Let's go round the corner.' Leo took his arm and helped guide him. Ivan shuffled in flapping shoes.

'You have news of my husband?' Garnet's throat was dry. What a beautiful day it was. She looked up at the sky spread overhead like a canopy of madonna-blue, with not a cloud to mar its perfection. It was one of those crisp, Petrograd spring days when the clarity of the air seems to enter one's blood and invigorate one's whole system.

'Garnet' said Leo, 'Ivan's news is bad, I'm afraid. You must prepare yourself.'

'I'm sorry,' muttered Ivan. 'Very sorry.'

Sergei was dead.

Ivan had seen him die, on the battlefield, had watched him fall and had dragged his body away and stayed with it under cover of darkness until dawn, when he had buried it with the help of another soldier, on the edge of a wood. They had whittled a piece of stick and the other man, who could read and write, had patiently hacked out the letters SERGEI BURNOV on its side while Ivan had kept watch for wandering Red Army men. When it was done they'd stuck the stave in the ground to mark the grave and Ivan had recited a prayer.

'It was a very peaceful spot,' he said.

'At least he's not buried in an unmarked grave,' said Leo.

'But anyone could pull out the stick,' cried Garnet. 'Then his grave *would* be unmarked. And I'd never be able to find it.' She could not bear the idea of Sergei lying in lonely ground, so far away from those who'd loved him.

'Seryozha is dead, Garnet,' said Leo gently. 'But his soul has been freed. Think of it that way. It's not imprisoned in some wood in the Crimea.'

'You told me you didn't believe in survival after death!'

'I don't think I was ever quite so definite.'

Ivan delved into the recesses of his tattered coat to produce a wallet. The mahogany-coloured leather was stained and ripped at the corner, but Garnet knew it at once. Seryozha's initials were embossed in gold on the front. She had been with him the day he had bought it on the Nevsky. They had stood by the shop counter and waited while the man took it into the back room to have the initials inscribed. The moment came back to her; she saw the man, his long thin hands handling the leather, pointing out the excellence of its quality. 'It's soft,' he had said, showing its suppleness, 'but durable. It could last a lifetime.'

'Thank you, Ivan,' said Garnet. 'You have been a true friend to him.'

Ivan left them. He had somewhere to go, he assured them; he was making for his sister's house on the outskirts of the city. Leo pressed some roubles into his hand and Garnet embraced him.

'Come back and see us if you can,' she said.

He touched his forelock and bowed to her. He didn't have to do that, she wanted to tell him, but might offend him if she did. Then he went shambling off down the street in his broken shoes.

Garnet and Leo walked down to the river and sat on a wall in the sun. Her hands shook as she took Sergei's identity card from his wallet, and a few faded rouble notes. There was a photograph tucked in the back too.

She eased it out. It was a small photograph, with uneven edges, and looked as if it had been cut from a larger one.

'He must have taken it from one of your wedding photographs,' said Leo, peering at it with her. 'You're wearing a white veil.'

It showed only the head and shoulders. The veil was flung back from the hair and held by a wreath of flowers. The photographs had been taken after the church ceremony, in the garden of the Queen's Road house. Garnet recalled them being taken, how they'd stood together, the two couples, she and Seryozha on the right, Lily and Tom on the left. The men had cracked jokes and kept them smiling while the photographer set up his camera.

Frowning, she looked more closely at the picture. 'This isn't me! It's Lily.'

'It can't be.'

'It is. That's her pearl necklace, with the little bit at the front hanging down. Do you see it?'

Leo peered. 'Well, yes,' he agreed dubiously. 'I see something hanging down. But *just*.'

'It *is* Lily, I know it is. Don't you think I can tell my own sister apart from myself?'

'But in a photograph? And you're obviously very alike. You're identical, after all.'

'No two people can be ever be completely identical.'

'Maybe not, but it would be easy for anyone to confuse you.'

'Seryozha wouldn't confuse us.'

'Not even in a photograph?'

'I'd know Lily's smile anywhere! There's something mysterious about it, and secretive. Can't you see what I mean, Leo? Look again!'

Leo looked, since Garnet was becoming even more distressed, and admitted that he could see a difference now that he was trying to see it.

'But, Garnet, Seryozha could easily have made a mistake. He was probably in a hurry when he was getting ready to leave. He'd have snipped it out quickly.'

'But I was standing beside *him* in the photograph and Lily was next to Tom.'

'He wouldn't have done it deliberately, though, would he? For what reason?'

324

Garnet did not answer. She put the photograph back in the wallet and put the wallet in her pocket.

Garnet had to break the news of Sergei's death to the children and the countess, which meant that everyone else in the building heard it too. Nikolai kicked the door and said it wasn't fair, he didn't want his father to die and he hated God for letting him die and the teacher at school said there was no God and she was right and if ever he did see God anywhere he'd spit in His big, bad, horrible, nasty face. He spat now. Hush now, said Garnet. Anna cried because she didn't know what was going on and had never seen this man who was called her father. The countess wept noisily and long and railed at fate and declared she wished to die herself now that her only son, her darling, the light of her life, was gone, and Dolly sobbed behind her white apron, which she held pressed against her face. It seemed to Garnet that everyone was crying but herself. She could not weep. She tried but her eyes felt as arid as a field burn at the end of a long hot summer.

The photograph. She kept coming back to the photograph. She stared at it until her eyes began to lose their focus and the print blurred.

She was sure it was Lily. But had Seryozha known it? This was the question that haunted her and could never be answered. Some mornings, wakening early with the summer light, hearing the birds sing, she would think: *Of course, he had made a mistake*. He had loved her, hadn't he? He had often said so.

But Lily.

Garnet thought of that night before their wedding, Lily coming in from the garden looking flushed and excited, her dress crumpled. She thought of Lily's son Luke with his crooked little finger.

Seryozha had fallen in love first with Lily. The attraction between them had been obvious, that first summer of their meeting. But Garnet had wanted him for herself, and been determined to have him, at all costs. And now the levy was being exacted.

The thoughts crossed and crisscrossed her mind day after day, becoming tangled like skeins, until she thought they would drive her mad. She could not clear them from her head and there was no one in whom she could confide. She was too proud to let even Eithne know that her husband might have preferred her sister to herself and had almost certainly seeded a child in Lily's womb.

One morning, coming on Dolly crying in the kitchen, Garnet felt intensely irritated.

'What are you sniffling about now, Dolly?'

'Just because you don't care that he's dead!'

Garnet seized Dolly by the shoulders. 'Don't you dare say that to me! He was my husband!' She shook Dolly hard. Dolly was small-boned and felt light between Garnet's hands. I could bash her head against the wall, thought Garnet. I could kill her.

She let Dolly go.

Dolly rearranged her blouse and twisted her apron straight. She lifted her chin.

'He might have been your husband, but before that he was my lover! *And* after.'

'I've had enough of your lies!'

'It's true.'

'You can say that now that he's dead and isn't here to deny it.'

'He couldn't deny it. He's the father of Sophia.'

Garnet stared at her.

Dolly smiled. 'Haven't you noticed her little finger? Oh, it's not as crooked as Kolya's, but now that she's getting bigger you can see quite clearly that it's got a bend in it. The countess commented on it just the other day. "Your Sophia's got our family's peculiarity, Dolly," she said. She *knows*, does the countess. And Sophia looks very like your Anna, don't you think? Not surprising, considering they're half-sisters. Anna's hair might be dark but she and Sophia have the same eyes.

Seryozha's cornflower-blue eyes.'

Garnet left the kitchen. She ran down the rickety, foul-smelling stairs and out of the house, into the street. She walked for miles. She left the mean streets behind, cut along the Fontanka Canal to the Nevsky, then turned off that again on to the Moika. The palaces gleamed in the evening sun. Red flags flew from rooftops. Most of the palace windows looked blank, revealing nothing of what was happening within; others had ratty pieces of curtain draped across them. No carriages waited in the street, no doors spilled open to reveal women in glittering gowns, no men in evening dress, medals flashing, stood to attention ready to attend them. There was scarcely a soul around: only two men in caps, who walked briskly with their heads down and passed Garnet without a glance.

She ended up on the English Embankment, outside the Burnovs' old house. It was flying the red flag.

Strangers lived there now. Party members, Bolshevik supporters. She remembered coming as a bride, looking out of her window, enchanted with the city, enchanted with Seryozha.

She crossed the street and leant on the parapet, looking at the river. She believed Dolly. She knew that Dolly would lead on any man who came near her and Seryozha must have found it difficult to refuse her. But Garnet knew, too, that she was making excuses for Seryozha. Did it matter which of them had made the overture to the other? He had made love to Dolly and fathered her child. He had made love to her under the same roof. *Dolly*, of all people! With her sly looks and suggestive smiles. Garnet had never liked her, and Seryozha had known that. 'Can't we get rid of Dolly?' she'd asked him once, and he'd said, 'Out of the question. She belongs to the house.' Dolly had belonged to him: perhaps that was what he had meant.

When Garnet returned to the flat she took the photograph of Lily and tore it into so many tiny pieces it looked like snow drifting down to the ground. It made only the tiniest of pools.

She then tossed the framed copy of their wedding photo-

327

graph into the rubbish bucket so that she heard the glass crack. She shovelled on top hot ashes from the stove.

In August, at a civil ceremony, with only her children and two adult witnesses present – strangers, produced by the registrar – Garnet Henrietta Burnova *née* McKenzie married Leo Konstantinovich Burnov. 'At least I haven't had to change my surname,' she wrote home. The countess refused to come to the wedding. She accused Garnet of betraying Sergei when he was scarcely cold in his grave and dismissed as irrelevant the reason Garnet gave in self-defence. (She did not speak of Lily.) Everyone had always known that Seryozha loved women. 'So he went to Dolly's bed! But that was unimportant. She was only a maid.' He had committed no crime in his mother's eyes, whereas her daughter-in-law, recently widowed, did by remarrying in indecent haste.

When eventually they were able to send news of Sergei's death through to his sisters in Paris, Elena wrote back saying he had had too large a spirit to be contained. 'He was in love with life, in love with love. He was a true romantic.'

'Romantic, bah!' said Garnet, flinging aside the letter. 'That is a great excuse.'

She wrote a long, bitter letter to Lily, but it was opened by the authorities and never reached Riga.

Garnet was taken in again for questioning.

'So your husband is dead? Killed in battle? How do you know that? Who told you?'

'A man. A stranger.' She would say no more, even though they kept her for three days in a cell with common criminals and gave her only hard black bread and water.

They brought her back to the grey room each morning.

What was his name, this man who came?

How did he know your husband?

Where is your husband buried?

Are you sure your husband is dead?

Garnet answered only the last question. Very sure, she said.

328

Riga

June 1925

Jemima and Hetty came the long way round to Riga, as they said when they arrived. They sailed by cargo boat from Leith to Bergen, where they purchased a car, a second-hand Model T-Ford, which was a little temperamental and had to be coaxed from time to time, and even, Hetty admitted, kicked, when all else failed. She was the driver. Jemima had never learnt to drive and was content to sit in the passenger seat and navigate. Navigating was far from being a passive role, she'd discovered. And she was a good pusher. They'd motored up to the north of Norway, where day and night merged imperceptibly into each other and played havoc with their sleep patterns, crossed the top of Sweden into Finland and come down to Helsinki. From there a ferry had brought them through the Gulf of Finland to Reval, and after that it had been easy motoring down the Estonian coast into Latvia.

'So here we are!' said Jemima, who was seated on the sofa with the two girls, Paula and Vera, one on either side of her. The boys were playing at pilots with the women's travelling goggles and helmets. The adults were exchanging family news.

'How's Effie?' asked Lily.

'Expecting.'

'Not again!'

'They're breeding like rabbits,' said Hetty. 'Norrie didn't like it when I told him that. He doesn't like it being suggested that the conceiving of children could have an animal, rather than a spiritual, side to it.'

'But four in four years!' said Lily.

'You had that yourself,' said her mother.

'But two were twins. And I haven't had any since.' Lily avoided Tomas's eye. He had been saying only recently that now that there was peace and life had improved perhaps they could think of having just one more child. He wondered if she might have needed treatment after the miscarriage she'd had during the war. She thought he might be right but rejected his suggestion that she go and see a gynaecologist.

'It's a pity men can't have some of the children,' said Hetty. 'I said so to Norrie and he ticked me off smartly. He told me that God had made us male and female for a purpose and the role of women was for the procreation of the race.'

Jemima had in the end agreed to Norrie and Effie moving into the ground floor of the house in Queen's Road and had retained a flat on the upper floor for herself. The arrangement suited her well enough and it meant she could keep the house Alexander had built.

And Andrew and Rose? Lily wanted to know. How were they settling down to married life?

Andrew had eventually married Rose, in Queen's Cross Church of Scotland. The Zales had gone over for the wedding and Paula and Vera had been flower girls, much admired for their pretty blondness. They both resembled their father.

'Andrew is away half the time.' Jemima shrugged. How her son conducted his marriage had to be his business; she could not expend any more nervous energy on it. Rose seemed happy enough; at least she was always smiling when she called.

And Garnet? Lily asked last after Garnet.

She had not heard personally from Garnet for four years, not since Seryozha's death. Yet they had parted warmly in Aberdeen, had shed tears at their separation. Garnet's silence pained and troubled her. She had written several times, asking straight out if there was anything wrong, but none of the letters had been answered. She was unhappy about the break between them, wondered if she knew the reason, hoped she did not, but after a while had thought it better not to write again.

'The countess died!' said Jemima. 'At the back end of the winter. Poor soul. It'd have been better if she'd gone at the time of the revolution. Garnet looked after her. Can't have been much fun in one wee room. She was gey difficult, from the sounds of it. Seryozha's death seemed to finally tip her over. Put me on an ice floe and send me off into the Gulf of Finland if I get like that! She'd accuse poor Garnet of all manner of things.'

'Such as?'

'Oh, stealing her Turkish delight – which she didn't have in the first place. Betraying Seryozha.'

'Betraying Seryozha?'

'She was off her rocker! She took that Dolly girl to her bosom instead – bit of a viper, she is, if you ask me – said she was her real daughter-in-law and she was going to leave her all her worldly goods. She didn't have any, apart from a packet of playing cards, so that scarcely mattered.'

Garnet and Leo were now in a flat of their own. They had only two rooms, but at least they didn't have to share them with Dolly and her numerous relatives. And Garnet was doing more teaching, so she'd been able to give up her cleaning job.

Coming down through the Gulf of Finland, the travellers had strained their eyes in the direction of Petrograd – now Leningrad, though they still thought of it most of the time as Petersburg – as if they might catch a glimpse of its golden spires and domes, and had lamented the fact that there had been no response to their application for a visa to visit Garnet.

'Those damned Bolshies!' said Hetty. 'But we're not ready to give up yet.'

331

'You wouldn't go in without a visa?' Lily was alarmed. On leaving Latvia her mother and aunt planned to drive through Lithuania and Poland to Bessarabia. 'They might never let you out. Garnet is virtually a prisoner, isn't she?'

'Will there be bandits in Bessarabia?' asked Luke.

'We shall deal with them if there are,' said Hetty. 'We almost ran into some in Mexico last year, but your granny fortunately sensed trouble ahead and so we took a different turning. We always said she was blessed with the second sight.'

'Common sense is all I lay claim to.'

'*All*?' said Hetty. 'In Bessarabia we shall be close to the Russian border,' she added thoughtfully.

'But still a long way from Petersburg, so don't be getting any ideas!' said Tomas, who had come home early from work for once. The family was off to its seaside house on the Bay of Riga for a few days.

'Mother,' said Lily, when she and Jemima were alone together on the beach, sitting side by side on deck chairs, 'does Garnet ever ask about me?' She had tried to ask the question several times before but had bitten it back always at the last moment. Now, with the soothing sound of the sea and the children laughing and calling as they pranced in and out of the waves, she had been able to force it out. She did not look at her mother.

'Well, now that you ask – no.'

'Catch!' cried Hetty, veering close to them, sending up a fine spray of sand. She and Tomas were playing handball with the boys, both of whom were quite naked. All the children were. Not a Scottish custom, as Jemima remarked. Mind you, one would probably get goose pimples going about in the altogether on the Aberdeenshire coast. She had stuck her feet into the sea at Cruden Bay last year and been almost frozen to the spot. Adults bathed in the nude too, said Lily; different times of day were allotted to men and women, with mixed bathing (mostly clothed) in the afternoons. Jemima said she would forgo the pleasure of nude bathing.

'The sauna is one thing, enclosed in a little hut, but an open beach would be quite another. And at my age I am diffident about displaying my body.'

They watched the children for a while. It was easy to sit idle at the seaside. Lily began to feel dreamy. The sand was warm under her feet and the slight breeze caressing.

'The boys are getting big,' commented their grandmother. 'It's children that make you aware of the passing years.'

'You're filling yours well, though! Traipsing around the world, helping Hetty to write her books.'

'Oh, she doesn't need much helping. I'm enjoying myself immensely! But I don't feel that I was released by your father's death, you know, as someone suggested to me, so that I could be myself! I was happy with Alexander. There's nothing better in life than having a close and good relationship with another human being.'

'Hetty hasn't had one, though, has she? Oh, with you now, but not before. And she's seemed content.'

Content was not the word that would come into her sister's mind for Hetty. 'She's too restless for that. And I don't even know if you'd say we're *close* now. We're like chalk and cheese. Well, look at us! Hetty's tall and skinny, I'm on the small side, and round. But we let each other be. Hetty was always a loner, even as a child.'

Lily thought she might take after Hetty in that way. She confessed to sometimes yearning for solitude. 'Perhaps it comes partly from being brought up as a twin? I know Garnet and I were very dependent on one another, inseparable, and all that, but I remember wanting to be alone and not being able to be.'

'Yet here you are in the bosom of a large family! I tend to think one chooses one's own fate.'

Lily laughed. 'Oh well, I dare say we are all full of conflicting desires.'

'You're happy, though, with Tom?' Jemima put the question a little anxiously. She felt she shouldn't go round asking her children if they were happy – it was a very invasive question – but at times she found it difficult to resist. (When she'd asked Effie, she'd predictably said she was happy as long as she was serving the Lord.)

'Oh yes! We're such good friends.'

'He's a very nice man. And it's important to be able to say that of a person. Now I wouldn't have said it of Seryozha.'

'Perhaps not. Yet he was charming!'

'Indeed.' Jemima glanced at her daughter and thought her colour had deepened. 'I just hope Garnet is happy enough with her Leo. She was so in love with Seryozha!'

The children's red-and-white ball struck Lily on the knee and bounced into her lap. She half rose to throw it back to Alex, then sank back down into her chair.

Jemima sighed. It was most agreeable to sit motionless after all that motoring over dusty, potholed roads. She rather liked this douce Baltic coast, with its white sand and pine trees. Not as dramatic as their Aberdeenshire cliffs certainly, with their sheer drops, and puffins and guillemots screeching in the gullies, and the North Sea lashing the rocks below, but it was peaceful. And there was a time for peace. She was pleased that Lily had this pretty green wooden house, with its big balcony running round three sides, to bring the children to for weekends and holidays.

Lily's life had settled down really very well. Tom seemed to have plenty of work and the country was beginning to look, if not prosperous, well-ordered and comfortable. She didn't suppose it would ever be rich exactly – it was a peasant society basically, after all, apart from Riga, where both business and the arts were flourishing (she was amazed by how many people went regularly to the opera and ballet, as in Petersburg) – but, as long as folk could get enough to eat and didn't have to live in fear, then life could be accounted good. She said so to Lily, and they both thought inevitably of Garnet.

Jemima said, 'You say you haven't heard from Garnet for a while?'

'You know what letters are like coming out of Russia these

days!'

'Hers to me do get through, or most of them, from what I can make out.'

'Perhaps mine don't because they're destined for Latvia – they've got a grudge against us. They didn't like us pulling out of their empire. No one here is overly fond of Russia or the Russians, either. Not Soviet Russia, anyway.'

'You still hear lots of Russian spoken in the streets of Riga, though.'

'Oh yes! And German. And Yiddish. Some films have commentaries in all four languages. It can make for a long evening!' Lily started to talk about a German film she'd seen the week before with Veronika, when her mother interrupted.

'Nothing happened between you and Garnet, did it, Lily?'

'What could happen? We haven't seen each other for four years, not since we said goodbye at the station in Aberdeen. I think I'll go and join in the ball game.' Lily pushed herself up out of the chair and ran down the beach.

In the evening, the adults dined at the Pavilion restaurant at Edinburg, leaving the children with Morag and Mara and their husbands. Tom told the visitors that no one was quite sure why the place had been named after the Scottish capital. Some said an Edinburgh merchant had built the first villa here, others that it had been named in honour of the Duke of Edinburgh on the occasion of his marriage to the daughter of Tsar Alexander II in 1874.

'Either explanation will do,' said Hetty, scribbling both into the notebook she carried about. 'Readers often like a choice.'

The evening was soft and windless. They sat out on the veranda and, while they ate, a band played sweet music. Afterwards, they lingered, watching the sky across the gulf turn to turquoise-blue and indigo shot through with flames of orange and rosy-red. They ceased talking. Gradually the great red ball sank down into the calm, pearl-grey sea, setting it alight for a few seconds, until with an unexpected sudden-

335

ness the colour was extinguished and the evening seemed suddenly to be a little cooler.

'It always goes so quickly at the end,' sighed Lily.

'Like life,' said Hetty.

They walked back along the beach. Jemima was feeling tired now; she took Hetty's arm. Tom and Lily went ahead, dark silhouettes against the grey cloth of the sky. They were holding hands and their feet were bare. They kept close to the sea's edge, letting the rippling water run over the tops of their pale ankles.

The two women following behind heard Lily's laugh as a wave splashed too high and she leapt up in the air. They saw Tom shift his arm to encircle her waist and their bodies merged and Lily let her head fall against his shoulder.

'At least that's one you don't have to worry about,' said Hetty, who naturally thought her sister worried too much about her children.

In Riga, Hetty spent most of her time exploring the old town, photographing its ancient guild houses and exchanges and seventeenth-century warehouses, after which she moved into the Art Nouveau sectors, where her camera clicked constantly. People were curious and stopped to talk to her – tourists were rare, the government didn't believe in encouraging them, since they'd take scarce food from the mouths of the natives. A short-sighted policy, Hetty informed those who stopped; they needed pounds sterling and dollars to boost their economy. 'You'll have to change your tune!' she said. 'You have an economic crisis on your hands the same as the rest of Europe. It's paralysing trade. And you have to subsist on the transit trade of Russia, which is always going to be a problem. But at least your currency has been stabilised and your farmers are being equipped with agricultural machinery.' Rigans told her she was very well informed. She said that was her job. They conversed together in snatches of German, after the preliminaries had been exchanged in

Latvian. They addressed her always in their own language first. Well, she would do the same at home in Aberdeen, wouldn't she? Some spoke to her in Russian, and that she could not cope with, apart from *Dobraye utra*. Good morning. And *Dobre dyen*. Good afternoon. Etc. She pleased them by telling them their city was one of Europe's great capitals, and much less expensive than Paris or Warsaw.

She refreshed herself in the gardens with cups of Viennese coffee, listened to the band playing on the big wooden bandstand and watched the passing parade. While she sipped, she wrote in her notebook.

This is a clean and tidy city. The natives are friendly and polite and seem contented with their lot. There appear to be no great class divisions, now that the German Balts have been deposed. Dress tends to be modest, few are stylishly dressed. (Lily is, when she's in the city. She and Veronika make clothes from Vogue patterns. When we went to the Otto Schwarz restaurant last night they were wearing very fashionable dresses in georgette: straight lines, dropped waists, hems just below the knee. Both have bobbed their hair, as have I! So much easier for travelling than the old styles used to be.) Tips are not given in restaurants – an excellent idea, one that should be emulated at home. Unemployment is low, and few beggars are to be seen, although there is a constant stream of refugees still coming from its Soviet neighbour, eight years after its revolution. What is to be done with all these homeless people?

They went to Cesis for John's Day. Gertrude Zale bustled about, pleased to have her house full of people again. She baked cakes, cut cauliflowers from the garden, dug up delicate new potatoes, shelled bowlfuls of sweet green peas, and filled the rooms with vases of freshly cut flowers. The sun beamed in through the open windows, warming the wooden floors.

337

Jemima had learned a little German from Hetty, so the women were able to communicate with Gertrude. Sitting with her in the garden, shuttling peas between their thumbs into earthenware bowls and helping to slice green beans, they told her about their travels. She was amazed at the daring of these two women venturing into often dangerous terrains. She herself had spent years on end here in this house without travelling more than the mile or so into Cesis.

'But danger came to you without you stirring,' said Hetty.

The boys especially loved being in Cesis. They were allowed to take off in the morning, carrying their lunch in knapsacks on their backs, and come home in time for the evening meal.

They came running home one day in the middle of the afternoon. They were excited. Their voices could be heard from the bottom of the drive. Jemima was asleep in the hammock, Hetty had gone for a walk, and Lily and Veronika were in the dining room, cutting out dresses for the girls. Jemima had brought a bale of pretty printed cotton and some new patterns.

'Mother! Father! We've found a man!'

'A man?' said Tomas, emerging from the fruit bushes with a basket of raspberries. 'What kind of man?'

'A dead man,' said Luke.

'What is it, Tom?' asked Lily, pushing the window further back and leaning out, the silver cutting-out scissors in her hand flashing in the sun.

'We found a dead man in the woods,' said Alex.

Lily dropped the scissors into the rose bush below the window.

'The woods near Skilters' farm,' said Luke. 'He's got a uniform on, with lots of buttons up the front.'

'He's a soldier,' said Alex.

'He hasn't got much face,' said Luke, screwing up his. 'I expect the worms have eaten it.'

'He had holes for eyes,' said Alex. 'We saw the holes.'

By the time Tomas and Veronika got to the wood (having

338

forbidden the furious twins to follow), three or four other people had gathered.

'Been there some time,' said Farmer Skilters, touching him lightly though not irreverently with his boot. 'Some animal must have dug him up. Poor sod.'

'Some woman's son,' said the farmer's wife.

The police were called and the body removed to the police station in Cesis. No identification was found on the dead man and nobody was going to waste money sending the body up to Riga for an autopsy. What else did they need to know? He'd died in the war, that was obvious. Thousands had.

They buried him in a corner of the local cemetery and placed at the foot of his grave a simple wooden marker which said:

HERE LIES AN UNKNOWN GERMAN SOLDIER
20 JUNE 1925

Leningrad

August 1925

Having motored through Poland and Bessarabia as far as the banks of the Dniester, and had many adventures, which would later be written up in Hetty's book *From the Baltic to Bessarabia*, the travellers returned to Warsaw, where they did a deal with a man in the lounge of the Hotel Bristol and sold him the Ford for more than they had paid for it. (They realised he was a black marketeer, but since they had no direct evidence they didn't worry unduly that they might be breaking some law. In most of the countries they'd been in, the law was at sixes and sevens anyway, which did affect their own attitude to it, even though they felt it probably should not. At home they would never have considered illicit dealings.)

When they'd been just about to leave Riga, an envelope had arrived from Aberdeen containing their Russian visas. Effie, in a covering note, said they'd come the day after they'd sailed from Leith. 'The Lord must mean you to go.'

'Typical bureaucracy,' said Hetty. 'I don't mean the Lord. Though I suppose He could be a bureaucrat, too.'

'May He go with you,' Effie had ended her letter.

'We might as well have Him with us as not,' said Jemima, not intending any irreverence.

They had not received permission to drive through Soviet

Russia – 'Perhaps they think we will stumble unwittingly on dark secrets,' said Hetty – so they would have to go by train. Hence their transaction in the Hotel Bristol. They had decided against letting Garnet know in advance, in case their letter would be opened and they might be stopped at the frontier. They had not declared a relative in Leningrad on their visa application. To have a blood connection might be to get one-self banned from entering. Especially when the connection was one who had been married to *two* former Petersburg aristocrats. Garnet and Leo must be distinctly *personae non gratae*. On the form the sisters had said they were journalists. Jemima had been dubious. 'Anyone can claim to be a jour-nalist,' Hetty had reassured her. 'As long as one can string a few sentences together.' 'Tell that to Andrew!' said Jemima. If questioned, she was to say she wrote for the *Press and Journal*, and Hetty would nail her colours to the *Scotsman*'s mast; and, indeed, it was their intention to write articles for these two journals on their return. And if questioned further, Hetty thought they should say they were interested in crèches, since they were noncontroversial, on the whole, and the Communists were exceedingly proud of their progress in this field. From what Hetty had heard, every foreign journal-ist was taken to inspect crèches and their happy occupants.

When they reached the Polish–Russian frontier, they passed through without any trouble. Their passports were resoundingly stamped. 'You have been to many places,' said the official.

In Leningrad, they took a *drozhky* from the Warsaw station to the Hotel Europe. It proved a perilous ride over ruts and potholes. They had to remove their hats and hold on to each other. The cab driver appeared to be taking them on a detour, which they were unable to query. (They were at his mercy, a situation Hetty found difficult to cope with.) They passed through dismal streets where whole blocks of houses stood abandoned and still bore the scars of war: pockmarked walls, cracked windows, blackened roof rafters naked to the sky. Grass grew in side streets. There was a general air of dejection about the city and its people. Even the Nevsky Prospekt, once they reached it, and which Jemima remembered as being lively and cheerful, looked drab. Many of the old shop signs were gone. Dress was shabby. Leningrad was taking longer to recover than Riga, observed Jemima.

Outside the Hotel Europe stood a tall man in a threadbare uniform. His bearing was erect, though his eyes were cast down. His thick greying hair and forked beard had been carefully brushed. He had his hand held out. *Pomogite*. Help. When Jemima pressed a rouble note into his hand he said, '*Merci, Madame*,' and lifted his eyes to look at her face. '*Vous êtes très gentille. Je vous remercie beaucoup.*'

Inside, the Hotel Europe was still comfortable. From their window they could look over towards the Mikhailovsky Gardens, and to their left stood the remarkable, multicoloured and multifaceted towers and cupolas of the Church of the Resurrection, where Garnet and Sergei had undergone a second marriage ceremony.

'Come and look, Jemima!' said Hetty. 'We could be in the Byzantine Empire.'

But they were in the Soviet one; and they should not forget that, said Hetty. There were bound to be spies. They would have to be careful what they said indoors. (She wrote that down on a piece of paper and put it under Jemima's nose.) Walls could very easily have ears.

'What a wonderful country the new Soviet Russia is,' said Hetty loudly and clearly into the room. She winked at Jemima. Then she opened the door abruptly. There was no one loitering in the corridor. Jemima thought her sister looked disappointed.

Half the street names had been changed. The Nevsky Prospekt was now the Street of the 25th of October, in honour of the Revolution, though everyone, they were to find, still referred to it as the Nevsky. The street where their hotel was located off the Nevsky had become Lassalle Street, after the German Socialist leader. And the Ekaterinsky Canal had had its name changed to Griboyedov. It was all most confusing for the two women as they went about the city with their map, one which Jemima had kept from her previous visit during the reign of the Tsars. A new map seemed impossible to come by.

The day after their arrival, they made their way to the district where Garnet lived, going by devious routes. Hetty suspected they were being followed. A man with a bald head and dark glasses and who looked as if he'd originated in some Asian province seemed often to be a few paces behind them. They would stop at a shop window; he would stop and study the rooftops or retie his shoelace. 'You can always tell,' said Hetty, 'if they start tying their shoelaces.' They went into the Gostiny Dvor, the oriental-style bazaar which had booths instead of shops, and mingled with the locals. They were laden down with heavy bags. They dodged here and there, as nimbly as the weight of the bags would allow, bought a set of Russian dolls to show they were genuine shoppers, lingered for a while in one booth draped with rugs from Pakistan, raising the expectations of the trader, and when they'd seen the bald head go past they nipped back out on to the Nevsky and jumped on the nearest tram.

They arrived quite breathless in Garnet's street.

Jemima recognised Dolly straight away, even though it had been eleven years since their last meeting; and then Dolly had been in an apron, serving tea. She came out on to the landing while the two women were banging on Garnet's door. There was neither knocker nor bell.

'Dolly!' exclaimed Jemima. 'It is, isn't it?'

Dolly could not understand English, but she recognised the Scotswoman. She nodded and said, 'Dolly, *da, ya*!'

'Garnet?' queried Jemima.

'*Pyat*.' Dolly pointed at the Roman five on her watch face. '*Pazhalsta*!' She pushed open the door of her own flat and indicated that they should come in. It was ten minutes to four.

They went through a tiny hall into a sparsely furnished living room. A smell of cheap frying oil clung to the air. Damp clothes drooped from a line overhead. A girl of about seven sat on the floor, drawing in a notebook.

'This is my daughter Sophia,' said Dolly.

'What a bonny lass!' said Jemima, presenting her with a bar of chocolate that she'd been carrying in her pocket. She and Hetty found it useful to have offerings to hand.

'*Spaseebo*!' Sophia smiled and sprang to her feet in one fluid movement. She was a graceful child.

'*Pazhalsta*!' Dolly lifted some clothes to reveal two chairs.

The women ducked underneath the laundry and sat down. The springs went with them.

'*Tchai*?' offered Dolly.

How difficult to start trying to say you must be short of tea, and we don't want to bother you, we'd rather not bother you, we'll just wait until Garnet returns. On the other hand, to say, outright, '*Nyet*!' might be rude. Even in adversity Russians appeared to have remained hospitable.

'*Spaseebo*,' said Jemima.

Dolly gave them tea in cracked cups with a spoonful of runny red jam stirred in. It tasted brackishly sweet and did not resemble tea, not as they knew it, but that was of no importance and they drank the strange brew and mimed pleasure, and whenever their eyes engaged with Dolly's they smiled. Jemima noticed Dolly eyeing their bags and wondered if they should give her something but decided they would leave it to Garnet to distribute gifts. Hetty's fingers itched to get out her notebook and pen. There were times when this desire – this *need* – irritated her. She couldn't *be* anywhere (except Aberdeen) without having to record it.

At five minutes past five, Jemima showed her watch to Dolly. Dolly nodded and went out, leaving the door ajar.

They heard voices on the landing, and then Garnet came bursting into the room crying, 'Mother! Aunt Hetty! Is it really true?'

*

Garnet's flat was identical to Dolly's, though tidier, and an effort had been made to decorate it by putting posters and photographs on walls, and books on roughly made shelves.

'I've still got your Matisse in Aberdeen,' said Jemima. 'I keep wondering what to do with it.'

'Keep it in the mean time, until things get better. At the moment we wouldn't be allowed to have it ourselves. The state has confiscated all privately owned art. You can see lots of it in the Hermitage. Including some that used to belong to the Burnovs.'

Both of the visitors noticed the phrase 'until things get better', but made no comment.

'The shelves are Leo's handiwork,' said Garnet.

When Leo arrived he was almost as emotional about their coming as Garnet herself. Anna jumped about with excitement. 'My *babushka*!' she kept saying, and landing on Jemima's lap. Her other grandmother was dead. Of her brother there was no sign. He'd be playing volley ball, said Garnet, or he might be at fencing class. He stayed at school every afternoon to do sports and gymnastics. He was exceedingly athletic.

'It helps to work off his energy!' said Leo with a smile.

'And now we must get you some tea,' said Garnet. 'You'll be ready for a cup.'

'Dolly kindly gave us some,' said Hetty.

'Kindly?' Garnet made a face.

'You think the red jam might have contained poison?' said Hetty.

'I didn't think you were still living beside her,' said Jemima.

'She moved into the building not long after us. Was moved in, we think.'

'How so?'

'She runs the House Committee! She keeps an eye on the inhabitants; reports back.'

'A spy, do you mean?' asked Hetty.

345

'There are spies everywhere. The woman above us used to be a secretary at the French Embassy. She lost her job because she wouldn't agree to be a spy for the Party.'

'Careful,' said Leo, his eye on Anna.

'Oh, Anna knows to keep her mouth shut when she's outside. Children have to learn that early here.' Garnet sounded bitter, but neither her mother nor aunt could blame her. They were horrified at this picture of her life. She looked thin and drawn, and several years older than Lily.

Jemima opened her bag. 'We've brought you some goodies – as much as we could carry.' She took out a bottle of vodka. 'What do you say we all have a drink?'

They had several drinks, and when Nikolai came in he said in disgust, 'Are you all getting drunk in here? You know you're not allowed to drink vodka. It's against the law.' He spoke in Russian until Leo intercepted to tell him to talk in English.

'He's going through a po-faced stage, being terribly moral, aren't you, Kolya?' said Garnet, getting up to put her arm round him, which the onlookers could see he didn't much like. 'Kolya, this is Grandma Jemima from Scotland and Great-Aunt Hetty!'

The surprise of their visit softened him, and he behaved more like the ten-year-old boy that he was. He was delighted with the Scout knife Hetty had brought and ate his share of the chocolate.

'You look just like your cousin Luke in Latvia,' Jemima told him.

'I don't like Latvians! They're our enemies.'

'That's not true, Kolya,' said Leo. 'They just want to be independent. To have their own country.'

'They should have stayed part of Russia.'

'He is very patriotic!' said Garnet.

'That is because he is being trained to be,' murmured Leo.

'I've got some photographs of your cousins from Latvia,' said Jemima. 'But perhaps you don't want to see them?'

'Oh well, if you have them with you.'

They all crowded round.

'I remember that house!' Nikolai pointed to the one in Cesis.

'You were very young when you were there, Kolya,' said his mother.

'I remember it.' He remembered Luke and Alex too, he swore that he did, and Morag – 'She was fierce!' – and his Aunt Lily and Uncle Tom. He was very taken by a picture of Luke standing on the bank of the Gauja river, poised to dive into the water. He kept looking at it. Seeing his mirror image? his grandmother wondered.

'You can keep that one if you like,' she said offhandedly.

'OK.' He shrugged, but he took the photograph and carried it through to the bedroom next door, which he shared with Anna. Garnet and Leo slept in the living room.

Jemima observed that Garnet stared for a long time at all the photographs in which Lily appeared, then she laid them aside without a word.

The visitors had also brought with them food – ham, cheese, tinned fish – which provided the basis of a meal for the company. They finished the bottle of vodka.

'Don't worry!' said Hetty. 'There's another in my bag. And we'll bring more provisions tomorrow. If you've got foreign currency it seems you can find more or less anything you want in this city.'

After the children had gone to bed Garnet and Leo were able to tell them more about their lives under the present regime. After the death of Lenin a new reign of terror had begun; former members of the bourgeoisie and aristocracy were being hounded and spied upon, and their children were to be denied secondary and university education. This was worrying Leo and Garnet. Kolya would be furious if he couldn't be educated because his father and grandfather had been counts. He detested the idea that he came from a family of aristocrats.

'But you can't change the circumstances of your birth,' said Leo. 'I keep telling him that. And that he's not responsible for the past. But he doesn't want to listen. He's very hot-

347

headed, as you could see.'

'A handful,' commented Hetty.

'But a lovable and loving boy underneath,' protested his mother.

It was late when Jemima and Hetty rose to go. Garnet and Leo were unsure whether cabs would run so late. 'It's not like the old days!' said Garnet. They never had any reason to take a *drozhky*, couldn't afford to, though they still did go out sometimes in the evenings, to the opera and ballet.

'They are our treats! They lift our spirits. The music stays with me for days afterwards. '

'You never liked opera as a girl,' said Hetty, 'or ballet much, either, if I remember rightly.'

'She's become quite Russian!' Leo smiled. They could see that he adored Garnet.

He said he would go with the women to look for a cab. Garnet kissed her mother and aunt, holding tightly on to each in turn. 'This has been the best evening I've had in a long, long time!'

'Till tomorrow!' they said.

Come about five, said Garnet. She was doing some summer tutoring at the university, in the Department of Philology, and would finish at four. She enjoyed these afternoon outings, the teaching itself, and walking back afterwards along the Embankment and over the Dvortsovy Bridge and up the Nevsky. 'They take me out of here!'

They noticed Dolly's door stood ajar. As they went down the stairs they heard it click shut.

They were fortunate to find a cab fairly quickly. They could see that the streets might be dangerous (though, being full of vodka, they did not feel personally endangered), and not least from roving members of the police and Red Army who were in evidence and who might wonder what two women from the West were doing abroad at such an hour, accompanied by someone whose name was on their blacklist.

In the morning, they planned to go to the Hermitage, and in

348

the afternoon to shop for their visit to Garnet.

They had had breakfast and had returned to their room to get ready for the day's outing, when there came a knock on their door.

Jemima opened it, to find two men in suits standing there.

'Madame Jemima McKenzie?' They spoke in English. But they were not English, Jemima knew, not only by the brokenness of their accents but from the shapes of their heads, and the cut of their suits.

'Yes, that is me.' 'I', she thought. Well, she knew it should be 'I', but 'me' sounded more friendly. Did she want to be friendly towards these two men? Probably not. But diplomatically polite, yes, most definitely. She felt chilled just to look at them.

'May we speak with you? In private.'

'On what matter?' She kept her hand on the edge of the door.

'Passports. Visas.'

'I see,' she said, though she didn't, quite, yet, though a glimmering of understanding was beginning to come. '*Spaseebo!*' She stood aside and allowed them to enter. 'This is my sister, Miss Henrietta Hamilton.'

'Pleased to meet with you.'

'What is the problem?' asked Hetty.

The leading man, a tall, thick-chested fellow with greased-back hair, was holding their passports, which they had left at the hotel reception. The follower was the same height, but even heftier. He stood with feet planted wide. As a typical policeman was supposed to stand, thought Jemima.

'Your visas.'

'What is the matter with our visas?'

'They are not in order.'

'Not in order? But they must be. They were issued by your representative in London.'

'Sorry. Not in order.'

'But can you not make them in order?'

'Sorry. You must leave.'

349

'Leave? Russia, you mean? Leningrad?'

'Soviet Russia. You must leave Soviet Russia. Tonight.'

'*Tonight*?'

'Night train.'

Jemima, who was not a woman given to crying, burst into tears, astonishing herself and her sister and disconcerting the men, though they must have seen plenty of people weep. Perhaps it was because they were foreign women.

'You came to see your daughter?'

'Is that a crime?' demanded Hetty. 'We also came to see your marvellous crèches. We have heard much about them. We wish to write about them for the Scottish people.'

'No visa for seeing daughter. You must leave tonight.'

'This is outrageous. Quite outrageous. We shall report it to the British Ambassador in Moscow and your representative. We shall not let this rest.'

'Tonight. Night train.' And with that, they left.

'I'm sorry about that outburst, Hetty,' said Jemima. 'It was the thought of having to leave Leningrad after seeing Garnet only *once*. And she won't even know why we don't come. She'll be waiting for us. But we can't go to her flat, can we? They'll be watching.'

'Somebody will certainly be watching,' said Hetty grimly. 'We shall have to think of something else.'

Around the middle of the afternoon they made their way along the Moika Canal to St Isaac's Square. Their familiar tail was with them, had been since they'd emerged from the hotel in the morning.

'One couldn't call them subtle,' said Hetty. 'Just as well. At least it means we can spot them a mile off. But I don't think we should underestimate them, even so. We'll walk at a comfortable pace and not bother to look back. Let him think he has us foxed. How fortunate that Garnet told us where she would be this afternoon.'

The day was hot and sultry. Jemima was perspiring heavily; there were damp patches under the arms of her blue moiré silk dress. Nerves as well as heat; she was aware of that.

'It'll be cool in the cathedral,' said Hetty, as they mounted the steps. With a quick backward glance she saw that the man was loitering in front of the Hotel Astoria, waiting to cross.

The church had been turned into a museum. People were touring the walls, gazing solemnly at the holy pictures and the elaborate décor of malachite and marble.

'He's come in,' whispered Hetty.

They attached themselves to the back of a small group. An earnest woman was lecturing the tourists, who were listening intently. Most seemed to be Russian.

'It's as well you're small and I'm tall,' said Hetty. 'He'll be able to keep his eye on me.' She was wearing a vivid orange bandanna tied around her head. Rather like flying a flag, as she'd said when tying it in the hotel room.

Jemima sidled round the edge of the group, keeping her head down, and took refuge behind a fat marble pillar. Her heart was thumping. And, really, all she was going to do was leave the cathedral by the back door. They had been in before, she and Hetty, so knew the layout.

She moved quickly, and reached the next pillar, then made decisively for the exit. And was out on the steps, into the bright sunshine again, in less than a minute. And was fleeing down them, though watching her feet, in case she should trip and go sprawling.

She continued to walk very fast, in spite of the heaviness of the air, going up Majorova Prospekt, passing gardens on her left-hand side where beggars lay stretched out sleeping. On the corner of Gogol Street she let herself look back. The pavement behind her was empty, thank the Lord! Yes, I'm thanking Him, Effie. He – their shadow, though perhaps the Lord also – must still be in the cathedral, with his eye fixed on Hetty.

Jemima turned right and went along until she hit the Nevsky, where she could be lost in the crowd. Reasonably so,

351

at any rate. She was aware she would not be taken for a Russian woman. Hetty had said it was a pity it was so hot, otherwise they could have draped her head and shoulders with one of the shawls they'd bought in Romania.

At the Nevsky, she turned left. The Admiralty spire was glinting up ahead in the sun. An excellent landmark. At least she knew she was heading in the right direction. At the top of the Prospekt she veered to the right, continuing on round to the Dvortsovy Bridge, and crossed the Neva. To her right, on the other bank, stood the Peter and Paul Fortress. She thought of the count being led out one dark morning and shot and a little *frisson* travelled up her spine. She hadn't taken to him greatly, but he hadn't been a bad man, merely limited, and a victim of his time and birth.

A clock began to strike four. Looking up, Jemima noticed that the sky had turned black.

'That was clever of you,' said Garnet.

They were sitting in a mean little café; outside, torrential rain was slashing the pavement and blurring the window. Their heads were wet – they'd had to run as the thunder was cracking and lightning forking over the river. They were delighted to have the rain: it made a splendid curtain. Wet hair was a small price to pay, said Jemima, even if water was running down one's neck.

'I dare say not even the Cheka will be out on the trail in the midst of this!' said Garnet.

The proprietor was smoking behind the counter and reading a newspaper. He'd seemed uninterested in them, once he'd served them their beverage of jam and water, which they left untouched. His hands, as they'd set the smeared glasses in front of them, had been filthy and the nails encrusted with black.

'It'll have been our House Committee leader who reported you.' Garnet sighed. 'You can't beat the system.'

'Why don't you try to leave, Garnet? With Leo and the children.'

'How could we? The borders are not exactly open, as you've found out yourself.'

'Hetty thought maybe you could find a way to go to Odessa to your friend Eithne? It might be easier to get over the Romanian border. Though the bridges are all down over the Dniester for a start!'

'There you are!'

'I suppose you wouldn't be able to get a visa to visit Seryozha's sisters in Paris?'

Garnet shook her head.

'This is terrible!' declared Jemima, slapping the table and making the proprietor lift his head. She lowered her voice. 'I have never heard of a country before that did everything it could to keep its people *in*. One can understand sealing borders to keep the enemy *out*.'

'I'm not sure if Leo would want to leave. And I wouldn't go without him. He's a Russian! I think he would want to stay and see things through. He cares about his country. He says if all the moderates leave the immoderates will have no opposition.'

'But they allow no opposition!' Jemima had to drop her voice again. 'What does he imagine he can do?'

'He thinks there's bound to be a period of adjusting – we're living through the reaction at present.'

'The reaction's been going for a long time. Eight years!'

'The reign of the Tsars lasted longer. We hope some form of democracy will be forged eventually.'

Jemima sighed, hoped Leo and Garnet were right, and gave up on the argument. Arguing with Garnet had never got her anywhere at the best of times. And this was not one of them. Anyway, she could not actually envisage the four of them managing to flee the country. Losing one rather dozy man in St Isaac's was hardly on the same plane.

'So you're taking the night train to Riga?' Garnet sounded sad.

'Yes, we'll have a few days with Lily again before we set sail back to Leith.' Jemima studied this daughter's face.

353

'Garnet, did anything happen between you and Lily? No, don't shrug! You're no longer close, are you?'

'How can we be? She is there and I am here.'

'I'm talking about in spirit.'

'Let's just say it was a question of betrayal,' said Garnet, 'and leave it at that.'

Jemima left it. She no longer wanted to hear the answer.

The rain slackened gradually, and stopped, and the pavements outside began to steam. They had spent an hour together in the café when they rose to say goodbye and go their separate ways.

The Asiatic-looking man with the bald head and dark glasses was standing on the corner of the Nevsky and Lassalle Street. His eyes bulged when he saw Jemima. She passed him with a little smile, the first she'd felt like making since leaving Garnet.

On coming into their room, she kicked off her shoes.

'My feet have been fair murdering me! And I have a lump in my chest. Here!' She put a hand over her heart. 'It's hard at times being a mother, Hetty.'

Although Hetty had no direct experience, she could only agree.

Aberdeen

July 1929

'How the children have grown!' said Rose.

'Children do,' said Lily. 'Fortunately.' She was wondering where on earth the boys were. She hadn't seen either of them since lunchtime, and it was now half-past eight. She'd told them to be back by six, thinking that would bring them by seven. It wasn't like them to miss their food; they had appetites like wolves.

'Luke must be even taller than Tom now?'

'Oh yes, by a good inch or two.'

'I was just saying to Mother that he looks like a man! Yet he's only . . . what? – fifteen or sixteen?'

'Fifteen and a half.'

Lily looked down into the summer evening stillness of Queen's Road. Trees planted when she was a child had grown high and formed a screen between the house and the street. She heard the soft swish of car tyres passing. Rose sighed and Lily wished she could find an excuse to move away.

Poor Rose Sibbald! (They still thought of her as a Sibbald.) Everyone found her boring. Even Andrew, they suspected, though he did not say. He was loyal to his wife, in that way, at least. He would never say a word against her. Rose had not managed to have a child. She was sterile. A terrible word, and one which no one voiced. Rose didn't have the appearance of one who would be sterile; she was softly pink and looked made to nurse a child at her breast. It was a great tragedy, really. She looked longingly into prams, her pale blue eyes misted with tears, and gazed enviously at Lily's tall sons and pretty daughters.

Paula, at fourteen, had a well-shaped bosom and neat waist, which she enhanced in the time-honoured way by sucking in her breath and pulling in her belt. (Lily had thought girls didn't need to do that any more.) She'd stop herself breathing if she pulled any tighter, her Great-Aunt Hetty told her, but that didn't influence her. Neither was she put off by her sister telling her she was turning blue in the face. Vera herself was small and muscular.

The girls were sitting side by side on the sofa. Vera was picking a scab from her knee. Paula was looking as if she might spring up at any moment and be gone from the room in a flash. Lily had told them that they must sit in the drawing room for a little while after dinner. It would be impolite to the visitors if they did not.

The door bell rang below and Lily half rose in her seat.

'That might be them now,' she said to Tomas, who looked blank. 'The *twins*.'

'Oh them! They'll come home when they're hungry.' Tomas turned back to continue his conversation with Hetty. Lily kept her ear cocked, trying to hear what was going on downstairs. Tom didn't worry about the boys nearly as much as she did, of course.

There was a tap on the door, and Nessie announced two visitors for Miss Paula. Paula blushed and leapt to her feet.

Two boys dressed in white stood in the doorway, shuffling their feet. They held tennis rackets like shields against their chests.

'Come in, boys!' said Jemima. She knew their mothers.

They had called to see if Paula would like to come and make up a set. And her sister, they added, with a sideways glance at the younger Vera.

'Please, Mother, can I go?' pleaded Paula.

'Oh, I suppose so,' said Lily. 'As long as Vera goes too.'

Vera pouted and said she didn't want to go. She put on a face that said nothing in the world would persuade her to go. (They had already been through all this two or three times before. She was better than any of them at tennis, had a blistering serve for a twelve-year-old, girl or boy. Her ambitions were to play for Latvia, and to become a surgeon.)

'Oh, all right!' she said.

'Be back before ten!' Lily called after them. It annoyed her to have to be so conscious of time, aware of every passing hour. She looked again at the grandmother clock in the corner.

'They'll be all right,' said Tom. 'They know Aberdeen well enough by this time.'

'And it's not exactly a sink of iniquity,' said Hetty. 'Unless you go down by the docks, perhaps.'

The docks! thought Lily. Luke had been seen hanging around the docks in Riga on a couple of occasions and Tom had had to give him a good talking-to. Luke didn't appreciate what he might be getting himself into! 'You might think you're tough just because you're big but you're soft compared with some of the men down there.' Luke didn't like being told he was soft. He liked the thought of danger. And where he went Alex frequently followed, if only to keep an eye on him. Lily worried that they might be tempted to jump a ship from Riga, lured by the promise of the Orient. Or even Copenhagen. If she didn't have something to worry about, said Tom, she'd invent it. *She* could understand the temptation, she said, even if *he* couldn't. There were times when she'd felt like setting sail for the Orient herself. 'Really?' He'd been amused.

The room resettled itself, and the clock struck nine. Lily was the only one to register it.

'What do the boys plan to do when they leave school?' asked Rose.

'Alex wants to be an architect,' said Lily. The boy had been passionately interested in buildings since he was old enough to observe that not all were alike. At the age of eight he would stop and study the decorated motif over a doorway, ask his father why some arches were rounded and some met at the top in a point, and at ten he could define the terms renaissance, classical, baroque, which Lily still could not.

'And Luke?'

Lily shrugged. A stevedore perhaps. Oh no, of course not! She was only joking. Luke excelled at school in every subject, but was physically restless. He wanted to fly aeroplanes, be a foreign correspondent like his Uncle Andrew, a world traveller like his grandmother and great-aunt, or even a soldier. His parents, who had had enough of war, had reminded him of what it had been like in Latvia when they'd been fighting the Germans on one hand and the Bolsheviks on the other.

'But we won!' He couldn't see beyond that. When he thought of war he heard trumpets in his ears and felt the blood drumming in his veins.

'It was not as glorious as you might imagine,' his father had said.

'I'm sure they'll all do terribly well,' said Rose.

Rose's mother, who was sitting on her other side, was looking disapproving. Of the family in general, Lily felt. The McKenzies were not considered to be the average Queen's Road family, with one daughter living like a prisoner in the Soviet Union, not even able to come home and visit her widowed mother, another in Latvia, a country that not many people had ever heard of, a third in the Salvation Army, married with seven children – the back garden was like a gypsy encampment, and if it weren't that Jemima McKenzie was so well regarded locally there would have been a regular trail of complaints coming to the door about lowering the tone of the neighbourhood, and the property values – and then there was the only son off stravaiging around the world, leaving his beautiful wife to sit alone in her beautifully kept house, with no child to comfort her.

No one (but Lily and Tomas) could be sure whose fault it was that Rose was childless. Rose's mother naturally thought it must be Andrew's. All the women in *their* family had more than one child, she told Lily, when Rose had gone to fetch the sugar bowl; she herself had been the only exception. She hinted that it was due to a delicacy of disposition on her part. 'We are a very fertile family.'

Lily suggested adoption. 'There are lots of babies from poor families needing to be adopted. Effie and Norrie come across them all the time. Say what you like about the Salvation Army, they do help people, and they don't mind getting their hands dirty. I take my hat off to them!'

'But an illegitimate baby!'

'Rose and Andrew could legitimise it.'

'I'm sure Rose could have a child of her own.' She had been to a specialist, that was true, but Mrs Sibbald didn't think doctors always knew what they were doing. Look what had happened to Mr Sibbald! He'd had an ulcer and the doctor had told him to change his diet and take things easy and play golf more often and think less about business. And the very next day he'd had peritonitis on the golf course and been rushed to hospital, too late.

'They can't be magicians,' said Lily, 'see into glass balls.'

'I'm not asking for magic.' Mrs Sibbald sniffed. It was a way she had of drawing herself up.

They were joined by Hetty, who had a glass of sherry in one hand and a Turkish cigarette in the other. Mrs Sibbald batted a hand in the direction of the smoke.

'So, where are you and Jemima off to next time?' she asked.

'We're thinking of Afghanistan.'

Mrs Sibbald had no comment to make on that. She had only a vague idea of where the place was located, but knew that it would be wild and dangerous. She had plenty to say in private to her daughter about the wanderings of Rose's mother-in-law. She couldn't help thinking there was something vaguely indecent about living such a life at Jemima's age. Although, when she heard Effie's raggle-taggle brood screaming and yelling and banging tambourines, she wasn't

359

surprised their grandmother wanted to travel to faraway places.

Lily left them and went to sit beside Andrew. She broached the subject of adoption.

'If Rose wants to adopt, I won't stand in her way,' he said.

'That's hardly the right attitude.'

'It's the only one I've got. All right, I'll talk to her about it!'

'And don't let her listen to her mother.'

'She listens to her mother all the time. She's got no mind of her own. We even have to take the damned woman on holiday with us. I can see the next move coming – Mrs Sibbald will take up residence with us! And then—!' He stopped.

'Then?' prompted Lily.

He shrugged. 'God knows.'

He had never said so much about his marriage. He had had a couple of sherries before dinner and a couple of ports after.

'Veronika sent her regards, by the way,' said Lily. (Veronika had not. She was careful not to raise Andrew's name in front of Lily.) 'She's a headmistress now.'

'I can imagine her running a school.'

'And young Ivars is growing up to be a fine boy. He'll be eight in the summer.'

Andrew said nothing. He must suspect, thought Lily, but perhaps he couldn't bear to *know*. And that she understood, so she did not push it further.

'You haven't been to visit us in Riga for a long time,' she said.

'My assignments have been taking me to other parts of the world. To different trouble spots. There's no lack of them. If one settles, another opens up.'

'I hope we won't ever come into that category again!'

'I'm going to try to get to Leningrad. I'll find some excuse. This new Five-Year Plan they've just put into action – I could do something on that. It's time someone went to see how Garnet's getting on.'

On the last stroke of ten Mrs Sibbald rose, saying she must

go. It was past her bedtime. Rose got up, too. And Andrew, also.

'It's *ten o'clock*,' Lily said to Tomas.

'I can see the time! Are you still worrying about those two big boys of yours? They're not infants.'

'But they're not full-grown men, either.'

'It's still light, for goodness' sake!'

'Something can happen in the light as well as in the dark.'

'It's been a most pleasant evening,' said Mrs Sibbald to Jemima.

Rose kissed her mother-in-law's cheek.

Lily went downstairs with Jemima to see the visitors off. She wanted to look up the road.

As they reached the gate a policeman on a bicycle braked at the kerb, right in front of them. Lily's heart went into a spin.

'Looking for us, constable?' asked Andrew light-heartedly. It was all right for him to be light-hearted, thought Lily; he didn't know what it was like to worry about children.

The constable took a piece of paper out of his tunic pocket. 'For a Mr Zale.' He pronounced it to rhyme with tale, instead of Zal-e.

'What's happened to them?' cried Lily.

The twins had gone down to the docks, as Lily had feared, and got into a brawl.

'A *brawl*?' she said. 'Do you mean they were *fighting*?'

'Aye, they're a bitty chipped-looking. They'd a skinful in them.'

'A *skinful*?'

'They'd been in a few howffs, madam.'

'You mean drinking? In *pubs*?'

'You can find some gey rough customers doon there by the waterfront. I wouldne let my ain laddies ging to they places.'

'But they can't have been in pubs, they're not old enough. They're only—'

361

'Leave it to me, Lily.' Andrew stepped between them. 'And go up and get Tom.'

Andrew and Tom went down to the police station, where the boys were being held.

Lily paced the drawing room floor, setting the ornaments on the sideboard jingling.

'Wait till I get my hands on Luke!'

'Och, he's just a wee titch on the wild side,' said his grandmother. 'He's young.'

'It'll have been him, make no mistake about that! He'll have led Alex into it!'

The two men came back after an hour.

'Where are they?' cried Lily. 'Are they badly hurt?'

The police were holding the two young offenders till morning, when they'd release them without charge since they were under age and not citizens of the United Kingdom.

'Otherwise they might have been had up for being drunk and disorderly or for breach of the peace,' said Andrew cheerfully.

Tomas was having to guarantee his son's good behaviour for the rest of their stay in Scotland.

'A night in the cells will sober them up,' said Andrew.

'They weren't a pretty sight coming home, I can tell you!' said Mrs Sibbald, who had seen them from her window.

'Poor Lily,' sighed Rose. 'The disgrace of it! They got into a fight with some Russian sailors. Luke apparently said something that upset them. I don't know what I should do if I had a son like Luke!'

'Children *can* bring pleasure, Rose – *you* have been a great comfort to me – but some bring only pain. Parenthood is not all joy. You should remember that, dear. I was thinking it might be rather nice for you to get a couple of Scottie pups. I'm rather fond of Scotties myself – we used to have one, remember? When you were little. We could walk them in the park together.'

Leningrad

September 1929

'We are leading the world towards Socialism and Freedom,' said Nikolai.

'You sound confident,' said his uncle.

'I know that people from the West are always sceptical. If you write about me and my life in your newspaper I hope you will write the truth.'

'I will try to. But the truth as you and I see it might be different.'

'There is only one truth.'

'The Marxist–Leninist truth?'

'You may sneer—'

'I am not sneering, I assure you, Kolya. I'm your uncle, your mother's brother, and I wish you well. I want only to try to understand you, a young Komsomol, committed to the Party, ready to do whatever it tells you. Young people in my country wouldn't be so ready to do what the government tells them. Or your cousins in Riga, either.'

'Latvia has taken the wrong path and will regret it one day. Its fate is linked to ours. We are less selfish as citizens. We see that we must subsume our own interests for the good of the country. For it, in turn, looks after us. It provides our medical care, rest homes in the Crimea for convalescents . . .'

Andrew doodled on the edge of his pad and let the boy –

for he was still that, in spite of his height of six feet two inches, with arms and legs that seemed to go in all directions – run on. He spoke as if he were delivering a speech and, in fact, he often did make speeches, at the factory school where he was a pupil-cum-worker, and was highly praised for his delivery and clarity of thought. He spent one day in the classroom learning technical theory and the next on the factory floor as a worker.

'You wouldn't have liked to go to secondary school and then on to university?' asked his uncle.

'No, it is good to be a worker. To be producing and helping to build a great country. There is much demand for skilled workers. I have just had my wage raised from thirty to sixty roubles a month. And so I am able to help Mother feed the family. You must think that is good? Do Luke and Alex help their parents? Or are they parasites? When I am a full-time worker I shall go to Worker's School at night and if I prove myself there my trade union might then send me to university to study engineering. Here, we have to win our privileges. For you, you have them because you were born to them. But if your father had been a beggar you, too, would now probably be one also. Is that not so?'

'Kolya!' called his mother from the other room. 'I think you should eat something before you go out.'

'Go and eat, Kolya,' said Andrew. 'We can talk again tomorrow. And perhaps you could ask if I might come and see your factory?'

For the first time Andrew read uncertainty in the boy's face. He might be embarrassed to have a capitalist uncle from the West. He'd been working hard to live down his father's background and the fact that neither his mother nor stepfather belonged to the Party.

'It doesn't matter,' said Andrew. 'I have lots lined up to see – schools, factories, crèches!'

'Our crèches are better than yours, no?'

'Yes, I think they probably are. We don't have as many.'

'There you are! You don't think about the needs of

the workers.'

'Kolya, you've to come and eat!' Anna put her head round the door. 'We're going to be late if you don't. And Sophia will be here in a minute.'

Andrew sat looking out of the window after Nikolai had gone off with Anna. It was raining; the weather had turned squally with a sharp wind coming off the river, a foretaste of the winter ahead. His nephew frightened him, with his down-the-line, parrot-like answers. Yet the boy spoke with conviction and even passion and seemed to enjoy his life. It was obviously full, and left no time to sit and agonise – not that one would wish that on a fourteen-year-old! He had many like-minded friends, attended meetings at the Young Communist League, played sports after hours at the factory, excelling in them, shared a love of theatre with the rest of his family, and read, if not widely, then keenly. At present he was in the middle of *Oliver Twist*, in English (Dickens was approved of), had been anxious to discuss it, from a literary and a social point of view, with his uncle, which his uncle had regrettably been unable to do, having read only an abridged version of the book many years ago and not given it a moment's thought afterwards.

Andrew got up and went through to the other room, where Nikolai and Anna were finishing their meal. Plentiful, wholesome food was still a scarcity, although young people were allowed more than their parents. Rationing had been introduced under the Five-Year Plan, which no doubt meant better distribution amongst the populace, though Andrew was sure Party members came off better than the rest. Kolya's commitment might yet be the salvation of the family.

The door opened to admit eleven-year-old Sophia, the daughter of Dolly, and Dolly herself. Andrew avoided the woman's eye.

'I've got a sore toe,' announced Sophia.

'You *haven't*?' Anna jumped up from the table.

'Not too bad, though. I expect I'll manage.'

'I thought I was going to have a sore throat this morning!'

'A sore throat wouldn't be as bad as a sore toe!'

The girls were dancing at a school concert that evening. Their long hair had been wound around their heads and was held, ballerina-style, with broad bands. They were both slim and had expressive arms and hands, but their colouring presented a contrast, Anna having dark hair, Sophia blonde, with hints of red when she bobbed under the light. Their eyes, though, were the same vivid blue.

The girls were highly excited. They chattered and jumped about and pirouetted on their toes. Dolly told them to calm down and sit down or they'd damage themselves before they ever got there. 'Look, Sophia, you've banged your elbow now! You'll be black-and-blue. Who wants ballerinas that are black-and-blue?' The girls paid no attention.

Garnet and Leo would take Andrew to the concert later. Nikolai was to accompany them now and help at front-of-house.

'Get your coats on,' said Garnet. 'And keep your hoods over your heads – you don't want to look like drowned rats on the stage.'

Nikolai shepherded them out. He had lost his sharp edge in the company of the girls, Andrew noticed; he was almost tender with them and asked if they had their shoes and everything they needed. Dolly gave no sign of leaving. She perched on the edge of a chair and eyed Andrew. She had not learned any English other than yes, no, and dollars, and his Russian had remained elementary.

He'd had a terrible time yesterday with Dolly when Garnet had gone out. He began to sweat all over again when he thought about it. She'd tried to rub up against him, like a cat on heat, and he'd had to push both of her hands away and tell her, '*Nyet*! *Nyet*!' And all the time he'd been thinking that maybe he shouldn't offend her, on account of Garnet. But there were limits for God's sake!

Dolly was grinning at him now and showing a large gap in her bottom teeth.

'Excuse me, Dolly!' Garnet had to dislodge her to get to

the cupboard.

Dolly left with another backward glance at Andrew.

'I wish we could get rehoused,' said Garnet. 'But we'd probably just find another one like her in the next place.'

'Surely no one could be quite so bad?'

'Does Sophia remind you of anyone?' asked Garnet.

'Sophia?' Andrew looked surprised. They were drinking coffee in the lounge of the Hotel Europe. Garnet had demurred at first about coming in, citing her dowdiness as an excuse, then she'd perked up and said, 'Why not?' She didn't care about being seen around with Andrew; the authorities knew all about her connections with the West, and by now would have heard of his visits to her home. As for him, he was a bona-fide journalist carrying an NUJ card and it wouldn't be as easy for them to turf him out as it had Jemima and Hetty. Of course, they could accuse anyone of spying.

'Sophia?' repeated Andrew. 'She's a pretty girl; going to be a real beauty when she grows up. Doesn't look at all like her mother.'

'Don't you think she looks like Seryozha? And Kolya?'

'Seryozha? Good God! You're not trying to say—!'

'I am. And she is. There's no doubt.'

Andrew sat slumped in thought for a moment, then he called for the waiter and ordered two large brandies.

'She's some woman, is Dolly,' he said.

'She certainly has quite a turnover in men. I don't know whether it's greed for sex that motivates her, or power. Perhaps it's both. She claims Seryozha was her constant lover – it didn't just happen once or twice. She says he loved her.'

'Easy to say now that he's dead and can't speak back.'

'She says he'd have married her if it had been post-revolution, not pre-.'

Andrew guffawed.

'She was a lot younger then, and she did have her own doll-like appeal. I can see how she does attract men.'

'Not Leo, though?'

'Oh, I've no doubt she's had a go!' Garnet laughed. 'That would amuse her. And a way to get at me. She carries a lot of resentment against me, because Seryozha married me. And I was a foreigner.'

'She wouldn't have got anywhere, though, would she? With Leo?'

'Oh no. Leo is steadfast, in everything. It would benefit him to try to join the Party, but he won't. It would go against his principles. Kolya hectors him about it – you know what the young are like!'

'Does Sophia know about her father?'

Garnet shook her head. 'Dolly wouldn't be too keen to claim a count as grandfather for her daughter these days. Sophia could easily find herself disadvantaged, sent to Factory School or some similar institution, like Kolya. Dolly wants glory for Sophia! She is to be a famous ballerina with bouquets thrown at her feet. Like Pavlova. Pavlova's mother was a laundress, Dolly told me, and her father an officer. Dolly will sit in the audience at the Maryinsky – in the front row of the dress circle – and lead the applause! And I shall sit beside her and compliment her afterwards on the success of her daughter. I can see the vision in her eye, shining, like a light.'

'Sophia's good, though. I don't know much about ballet, but even I could see that at the concert last night. Anna, too.'

'Anna's not in the same class. Sophia has real quality, and style. She's inherited that from her father.' Garnet looked wistful for a moment.

'You don't' – Andrew cleared his throat – 'still miss Seryozha, do you?' He had never really talked to his sister about Sergei, had hesitated to open up this area of pain.

Garnet shook her head. 'It's more the passing of such carefree days. And I suppose one always feels sad about the loss of one's first love.'

'Mm,' said Andrew. 'I know what you mean.'

'Especially if one doesn't replace that love,' said Garnet,

looking at her brother.

'Shall we have another brandy?'

'Do you still think about Veronika?'

'I'm married now, Garnet!'

'Come on, Andrew!'

'Well, yes, I do think about Veronika. Even after all these years. Matter of fact, I'm thinking of going down to Riga when I leave here. Take the night train.' He had just decided. Being here in Leningrad with Garnet had made him reflect how chancy life was, which had led him on to thinking that one should take one's chances when they came, or even create them.

'Sounds easy. Just to get on a train and go!'

'I'll smuggle you on board with me! What about it?'

'Maybe I wouldn't choose Riga. Now, if it were Vienna or Rome . . .'

'Why not Riga? Not because of Lily, surely? Mother says you two haven't been hitting it off so well in recent years. Mind you, it's not as if you've seen one another.'

'What is she like now – Lily?'

'She's got plumper, reminds me more of Mother. She looks contented, is still dreamy, moves rather slowly, you know the way she always did, as if she's never in a rush, and is surprised if someone says to hurry up. She's come to love nature – like all Latvians! – and she's started to paint. Watercolours. Not bad, I thought. Some nice flower compositions.'

'And she's happy with Tom?'

'Oh yes, I would say so.'

'How lucky she's been!'

Andrew glanced at his sister; there had been a bite in her response. Oh well, he could understand that. Garnet had been hell of an unlucky! Yet when they'd been growing up, Garnet had always been the one to take the prizes and get the best parts in the school plays.

'You must write to me from Riga,' said Garnet, 'and let me know how you get on with Veronika.'

Dolly brought in the letter. 'It's from your brother, I think. I see his name on the back – Andrei. Though it's got a Latvian stamp.'

'He's visiting my sister.' Garnet put out her hand, but Dolly was not ready yet to pass the letter over.

'Is he coming back again, here to Peter?'

'You should mind your own business!' Garnet's patience had snapped. 'Or is it your business, Dolly? Yes, I suppose it is! Spying. Gathering information. Betraying!'

'You should be careful what you say to me!'

'In case you might report me? For what? Insolence? Speaking the truth? You wouldn't know truth if it was shoved in front of your nose.'

'I said you should be careful.'

'I'm not deaf. Anyway, perhaps you should be careful what you say to me.'

'What do you mean?'

'I don't suppose the Party would look kindly on Sophia if it knew she was the granddaughter of Count Burnov who was executed by the Bolsheviks, would it?' As soon as she'd said it Garnet despised herself. They'd corrupted her too! But she had some power over Dolly now and that gave her a small thrill. The woman's face had changed. She'd asked for it! (Had Sophia? Garnet thrust that question aside.) In war one had to resort to whatever weapons were at hand.

Dolly handed over the letter.

Dearest sis,

I wish you could have come with me so that you could have met Veronika. She's such a wonderful woman. But perhaps you did meet her once, a long time ago? One summer in Cesis, I seem to recollect. So you'll know, then, what I mean. She's so intelligent and amusing and strong. She reminds me of a clear, sparkling river flowing over cool, grey stones. Rather like our lovely Dee! Though she's not cool! And yes, I'm in love with her, again, or still. Whichever. And she with me. But we know there can be no future for us, no continuous one anyway, in the sense of day to day. But we don't ask that. We shall have what we can, see one another when we can. I can't work in Latvia, and she feels this country is her base, where her roots are, and she is committed to it. And I don't feel I can abandon Rose, as it might tip her over into a nervous collapse. She's quite delicate. It's something of a muddle, is it not? And yet, here, with Veronika, it all seems simple.

There is something else I must tell you. Her son Ivars is my son! She has confessed it now. I always thought he must be. I am so pleased to have a son, especially since I'd thought I'd never have children. (Oh yes, I know – poor Rose.) So you see, Veronika and I shall be bonded together for life, even when apart.

Garnet looked over the top of the letter at Leo. His hair was greying at the edges. He looked tired but relaxed and the room was warm and cosy in the shaded light. They'd just eaten. The dishes lay still on the table. Kolya had gone to a Komsomol meeting; Anna was at dance practice with Sophia.

'I can't get over Andrew telling me so much about his feelings!'

'Perhaps our Russian ways have rubbed off on him a little!'

'Perhaps.'

Sitting here like this, in the lamplight, the curtains closed against the ugliness of the street, the winter windows keeping out the sounds of traffic and unwelcome voices, reading Andrew's letter aloud, discussing it with Leo, knowing the children are happily engaged in their own activities, Garnet feels contented in the way she presumes Lily must in the bosom of her family. There is no doubt about it: a family makes a bosom, a soft nest in which to shelter when times are hard.

Cesis

July 1993

'So there it is,' said Alex. 'The house that Tomas built!'

The red and white flag of Latvia was flying from the rooftop.

The house looked to be in not too bad order, considering its long years of neglect and lack of repair. The front needed repointing, the guttering renewing, the balustrade on the upper floor was crumbling in places, a number of window panes were cracked and held together with brown paper, but, as Alex (whose point of view was different from his Western visitors') said, all these were minor matters. The house still stood.

Over the past forty-nine years numerous families had lived in it, sometimes as many as six units at a time, with children, even grandparents, inhabiting amongst them the three floors, sharing facilities, and the garden, which had been broken up into allotments. Alex was trying to unify the vegetable area, the produce of which would be shared amongst all the current house-dwellers.

The basement was occupied by a descendant of Mara's and his wife, a couple in their thirties who rode a dirty and noisy motor bike, but apart from that were no bother. They were building a house of their own a few kilometres away, doing it bit by bit as and when they could afford the materials, as and when the materials could be found.

Alex lived on the ground floor, along with seventy-one year-old Calum, the son of Morag. Both men were widowers.

'We're known in the district as the two Scotsmen!' said Alex. 'We're thinking of buying kilts when we come to Aberdeen!' They were planning a visit. Neither had been in Scotland since the summer of 1939, just before the outbreak of the Second World War, when they'd accompanied their mothers on a visit home. Like Alex, Calum spoke English with a Scottish inflection, though he was not as fluent.

The upper floor of the house was taken up by the family of Calum's daughter, Sandra. She and her husband had three teenage children, all of whom liked American-brand jeans and Western pop music and hoped that when McDonald's came to Latvia – surely it would? – it would open a branch in Cesis. Sandra looked after the two widowers, did their cooking and cleaning and laundry.

'Though we're not quite useless,' said Alex.

'He's a dab hand at the shirt ironing,' said Calum. 'Is that right – *dab* hand? It was an expression my mother would use. Or sometimes she'd call me a useless tomshie!'

His brand of Scots-English had been passed down to his daughter also.

The moment Sandra came into the room Katrina and Lydia felt a shock of recognition. She looked so like the photographs of Morag that it was as if the years had been rolled back. She was well-built, with a high colour, and had swift, decisive movements which they'd always imagined Morag would have had. Morag would never have dithered about. 'She left the dithering to me,' Lily, Katrina's grandmother, had said of her. 'While I was making up my mind what we'd have to eat she'd be away at the market buying it.'

Sandra had set out lunch – herring and cold pork and salads – in the dining room. Trees crowded close against the windows, keeping the room cool. It had been hot outside.

'We'll have to cut down some trees,' said Alex. 'Or at least prune them. Everything's overgrown, like a jungle!' But he sounded happy. He looked round the room. 'It needs a lick of paint too. Lick?' He smiled at the visitors. 'It's good to be back in the house, and to have you both with us.'

After lunch, they took their coffee into the garden and sat on the bench under the elm tree. Sandra had removed her apron and joined them for the meal, but her husband was shy. He had only a word or two of English. On being introduced, he'd shaken hands and said, 'How're you doing?' in broad Scots. Then he'd looked abashed, as if he'd surprised himself, and scurried off.

And the children were away on their bicycles. 'Gone swimming, and picking berries!' said Sandra. 'They've taken a picnic. They're never inside in summer.'

'So they don't spend all their time thinking about McDonald's!' said Lydia.

'They're always after me to take them to Scotland. Maybe one day, when we can get the money together. I'd like fine to see the place my grandmither came from.'

'When you do,' said Katrina, 'you must be our guests in Aberdeen. We've kept on the house our great-grandfather built – I live in the top half, Lydia in the bottom.'

'Didn't Lily have another sister who lived in the house?' said Calum.

'Effie. Her children and grandchildren are spread all over the world. Some went to Canada and Australia after the war.'

Helga and Katrina went off to the kitchen with Sandra to do the dishes, refusing Lydia's offer of help.

'No, no, this is your first time here and you are our guest! You stay and talk to the men.'

The kitchen looked as if it hadn't had a lick of paint in fifty years. Paint was difficult to acquire; Katrina made a note to send some. She noticed an old Harris tweed jacket on the back of the door. She touched it. The cuffs were frayed and the pockets had been mended.

'That's my faither's,' said Sandra. 'Bought for him in Scotland.'

Katrina nodded.

As she reached up to put a dish on a shelf she saw, lying on its side, an old, battered book. She pulled it down. *The Woman's Book*: Contains Everything A Woman Needs to Know. Ah, if only *that* could be encapsulated so easily! She looked inside. Published 1912. On the flyleaf Lily had written in neat, copperplate script, 'Lily McKenzie Zale, 8 April 1913'. The pages were yellowed and stained here and there where the user had spilt bits and pieces.

'Do you use this?' Katrina asked Sandra.

'No, I can't read English well enough. My grandmither used it, though. Calum says Morag treated it like a holy book.'

Outside, led on by Lydia, Alex was talking about old times, the ones before the war, when the country and the family had been in their heyday, but after a while he began to fidget and his eyes wandered down the garden. He excused himself and got up, saying he wanted to take a look at his tomatoes.

'He can't keep away from it,' said Calum, who seemed more content to sit. He'd lit a pipe, a meerschaum with a curved stem made of deer horn. He took it from his mouth to show it to them. 'It was my faither's. My mither bought it for him when we were across in Aberdeen in '39. I mind the shop. It was in the main street – what do you call it, now?'

'Union Street.'

'Aye, that's the one. The name of the shop was Finlay's, or something like. We stayed in the house on Queen's Road. She was a great lady, your great-grandmother Jemima. Her sister, Hetty, too. Feart for nothing, the pair of them! I liked the idea of staying on the road your Queen Victoria would have ridden through on the way to her castle at Balmoral. I cycled there one day myself. Never saw the king and queen, though. And now you've got a queen again. We used to have a tsar here, but that was before my time.'

'We'll take you back to Balmoral, when you come over. And up to Orkney.'

'Aye, I'd like that.'

'Were you here in '44, Calum?' asked Lydia. She'd calculated he'd have been about twenty then.

'I'd have been away at the war, at the Russian front. We didn't like the Germans but we were even more feart of the Bolshies. I'm sorry to have to say that to you. I don't want to offend you.'

'You're not. I wasn't pro-Soviet. They mangled my relatives, too – my *Russian* relatives.' Lydia made an effort and controlled her exasperation.

'You were born there, isn't that right?'

'Yes, in Leningrad, as it was then. I lived there until I was fourteen.'

'Ah, the years that make us what we are.'

'I suppose I do feel quite Russian as a result!'

'You look like your faither, you know. Verra like.'

'You saw him, then?' asked Lydia quickly.

'Only in photographs,' answered Calum equally quickly.

'Does Alex still have any photographs?'

'I wouldn't think so. The Soviets destroyed so much. They didn't give a hoot – hoot? – what they did with folk's personal belongings. They trampled on the place and banged it to bits and when they'd done they moved in as many people as they could cram. They used a shoehorn, my mither said! At one time there was as many as thirty in it. She was the yin that kept the house in order.'

'So you weren't here when my father came in September '44?' Lydia pressed him again.

He shook his head. His pipe had gone out and he was preoccupying himself relighting it. She thought he was avoiding her eye.

'What happened to him, Calum? Do you know?'

'He got killed in the war, didn't he?'

'Did he? I don't know.'

'He came in with the invading army. Our conquerors! He was a captain, so they said. A big man, six feet three or that.'

'Like Luke?'

376

'Aye, something similar. Damn this pipe! It takes a wee tantrum to itself now and again.'

'What else did they say about Nikolai? There'd have been talk, wouldn't there, about the Zales' Russian cousin coming? How was it that he came *here*, to Cesis?'

'Coincidence?' Calum shrugged. 'They happen, all the time. When I got captured at the front who should I find beside me, sharing a hut in the camp, but a lad I hadn't seen—'

Lydia cut him off. 'I don't believe it was a coincidence, Calum,' she said quietly. 'That my father died here in Cesis. Why didn't they send his body back to Russia for burial? Or bury him in a cemetery of their own war dead? It's not as if they were retreating and had to abandon their dead.'

'He was a blood relative of the Zales. They mebbe thought they'd just put him in the family plot.'

'*Who* must have thought? Lily and Tom? Were they still here then? And Alex? Luke was dead – he died on the same day. That seems odd to me.'

Calum got to his feet. 'I'll need to get some other matches. These ones seem to have gone damp.'

He didn't return with the matches. Lydia sat on under the elm tree, gazing into the garden.

Leningrad

September 1933

'Is Sophia at home, Mother, do you know?' It was Nikolai's first question after he'd given her a hug. He glanced around. 'Have you seen her?'

'Not this morning, no. But I expect she'll be back later. You're looking fit and brown, Kolya. Country life must agree with you.' His face might be a little thinner but his body had filled out and his shoulders broadened. He must have turned the heads of the girls on the collective farm! Garnet did not say so. She would only irritate him if she did.

He'd spent the last two months on a collective on the edge of the Urals, helping to bring in the bumper harvest. He'd been happy to go. After years of poor harvests this year's crops had suddenly bloomed, in time to save the country from starvation.

'Did you get enough to eat?' asked Garnet.

'Not always. But that was of no importance. We didn't take any more than the peasants – most of them went all day in the fields without food. They work hard, men and women alike.'

'I'm sure.'

'Their lives are hard. We should remember that when we eat our bread in warm rooms. Their houses are poor affairs, no more than hovels. Their carts are primitive, the roads

378

terrible. Some of the peasants were wearing shoes made from plaited birch bark and the bottom half of their legs were wrapped in filthy homespun cloth and tied with strings of twisted bark.'

He genuinely cares, Garnet thought, looking at his face, and that must be good, even though Leo worried that he swallowed whole everything the Party and Stalin advocated. Those poor people did need help. And she cared, too, when she thought about it, but in a more abstract way than Kolya. Really, they shouldn't complain so much about their lives here in the city! In comparison, they were well off. She had food on the table for her homecoming son – even though she'd had to stand in a queue for it: dark rye bread, cured ham, cheese, tomatoes and cucumber in sour cream – and they had properly made leather shoes on their feet (not very good quality, but good enough), and a roof over their heads that kept out the winter weather. And the children were growing up strong and healthy and getting a decent education. Kolya was to be admitted to the university the following week to study engineering and Anna had been allowed to attend the same school as Sophia. She talked of being a singer now that she was growing too tall for ballet, though Garnet thought her voice would not prove good enough. Sophia had mercifully stopped growing at a certain point; in build she took after her mother's, rather than her father's, side, though she was taller than Dolly. She was a gifted and charming girl. Garnet was very fond of her and thought of her almost as a second daughter.

'I suppose the peasants will still be pretty backward in such places?' she said, unable to take her eyes off her handsome young son.

'Kept that way by their old landlords.'

'That goes back some time now, though, Kolya – sixteen years, after all.'

'It's the legacy they inherited. It takes a long time to redress the faults of generations, and to re-educate people.'

Garnet sat beside him at the table and watched him eat.

She hoped he would be able to enjoy his meal without thinking too much about the peasants. She had missed him, though in a way it had been good to have him out of the flat for two months; he took up so much space and he still had to share with Anna, who at fifteen should have been able to have a room of her own, and he quarrelled with Leo, over politics. Always politics!

Nikolai was starving. He grinned and admitted it. They'd had nothing to eat but a hunk of dry bread on the journey and a swallow of cold tea to get it down. He ate very fast. He had a grimy line round his wrists; she traced it with her finger.

'Bathing was a luxury,' he said.

'Better wash before the girls come down wind of you!' She knew that would have an effect.

'We were near the Burnovs' old estate. I went to look at the house. It was all tumbled down. It's scandalous to think that our family did so little for the peasants.'

'I know,' sighed Garnet. 'If only they'd had more foresight—'

'There'd still have been a revolution!'

When Leo came in from work Nikolai rose and the two men embraced, the younger topping the elder by a few inches. Garnet went to the samovar to make fresh tea. It was the same samovar that the countess had used in the old days, one of the few possessions they'd managed to hold on to, along with a couple of ikons and a few pieces of crockery.

'So, Kolya,' said Leo, 'how was life on the collective? All working according to plan?'

'I suppose you think it wouldn't be? Why are you so dead set against the idea of collectivisation?'

'I'm not altogether. I can see it makes sense in some ways, to pool resources, rather than have land cut up into small strips. But at the end of the day there must be the question of individual satisfaction. That's a factor that doesn't seem to be taken into account.'

'But new Russians don't think that way! We think only of

the good of the people as a whole. So we pull together.'

'Like a happy band of pilgrims? Is it in the nature of people to band together? What about greed? Ambition? Desire for power? Jealousy? Resentment? Can you legislate them out?'

And so it had started up again. Leo said it was good for Nikolai to hear the other side of the story; he was subjected to too much propaganda. 'His mind is becoming warped. He doesn't know how to think for himself. Let him learn to think. Let him answer me.' Garnet thought Leo sometimes indulged in argument for the sake of it, though he was never vituperative and he put his points gently; he believed in dialectical discussion. But that, she feared, had a place only in a democracy. Here, it might be accounted as treason.

A chatter of voices was heard outside, and the men broke off. Anna and Sophia came whirling in, exclaiming over the sight of Nikolai. He jumped up to kiss them. Garnet was pleased by their civilising influence over him; he was deeply attached to them both, would listen to them when he wouldn't listen to either her or Leo. My two sisters, he called them, not knowing how close he was to the truth.

The girls had some food and then they and Nikolai, who had gone in the meantime to wash, went out. The young ones liked to be out, and the evening was fine, good for promenading.

'I wish you wouldn't argue quite so much with Kolya, Leo,' said Garnet. 'Don't you think it might be better to keep quiet at times?'

'Safer, you mean? You think he might feel he had to denounce me at one of his meetings?' Leo smiled.

'Don't joke!' said Garnet.

Anna came back alone in the middle of the evening. Garnet was rereading *Bleak House* for the third time – English books were difficult to come by, and although Andrew sent some, not all arrived. Leo had gone to play chess with a neighbour.

'On your own?' said Garnet. 'Where are Kolya and

Sophia?'

'Out walking. I left them on the Moika. The sky is still very bright.'

'Didn't you want to stay out too?'

'They don't want me, Mother! I'm the third wheel!'

'Third wheel? What do you mean?' Garnet felt as if her brain had gone dull.

'For goodness' sake, Mother! They're sweet on each other, surely you've seen that! Everybody knows it. Kolya and Sophia are sweethearts.'

'Sweethearts!' cried Garnet. 'But they can't be!'

'Why not? Oh, I know Sophia's only fifteen, but she's mature for her age. You've said so yourself. And they're not talking about getting married yet.'

'They're *talking* about getting married?'

'When Sophia is seventeen. Kolya will then be twenty. Many young couples are getting married at that age. But don't tell Kolya that I told you, will you? He'll want to tell you himself.'

Garnet asked Nikolai to come shopping with her, and afterwards suggested a walk in the park. She hadn't slept all night, had tossed and turned, and kept Leo awake. They'd got up and sat in the poor light of dawn, with the samovar steaming, and drunk cup after cup of weak tea, and talked it over. Leo had said she had no option but to tell Nikolai everything.

'I have something to tell you, Kolya,' she said, 'something I *must* tell you. Shall we sit on this bench?'

They sat for a moment and she covered her face with her hands.

'What's wrong, Mother? Are you ill?' Nikolai touched her arm hesitantly.

She looked into his eyes and then she braced herself and told him and watched the shock register on his face. He stared across the park. He seemed to have lost the power of speech. They sat like two players in the game of statues waiting to be set into motion and Garnet remembered a sunny afternoon in the garden at Queen's Road. It had been their birthday, hers and Lily's. They must have been seven or eight. She was wearing a yellow organdie frock, Lily a blue one. They had been dancing, flitting like butterflies, when their mother, who was conducting the game, had called, 'Freeze!' Garnet remembered the trembling effort it had been to hold her outstretched arms still. Now it seemed easy not to move. She wondered if she would ever move her leaden limbs again.

Finally, Nikolai spoke, and his voice was hard and cold. 'My father was an absolute bastard.'

'He could be kind and generous too. He had a large appetite for life. He loved women. He made love to Dolly.'

'You're making excuses for him!'

'I've had to try to understand him.'

'But he betrayed *you*. With Dolly. How could you forgive him that? Under the same roof?'

'I can forgive him that more easily than some others.'

'Which? I want to know all about him. He was my father. You owe me that. Please, Mother, *talk* to me!' Nikolai took her hand. His voice had softened, and that in turn softened Garnet and made her want to confide in him, and thus draw closer to him, for she loved this son dearly, even though she saw how harsh and difficult he could be; and there were not many moments when he allowed her to come close.

'I want to know the truth about my father,' he said.

She sighed. 'He made love once to Lily,' she said.

'Your sister? Your *twin*? When?'

'On the night before our wedding. You know your cousin Luke? He looks like you, everyone has always commented on it. He has the same little finger.' Garnet turned Nikolai's hand over. 'I'm virtually certain he's your half-brother. He and Alex were conceived at different times, from different eggs.'

Now Nikolai's anger rose to the boil and gushed over. He hated his father, and his aunt, and his half-brother, and the world! But most of all he hated his father. And Garnet felt pleased that he did. She could not delude herself about that.

Sergei had deserved to be hated by his son. He had betrayed her with her own sister! Whom he had loved until the end. Ah yes, that was the grit in the sore. Garnet kept hold of Kolya's hand while he raged. And then he cried, and she did, too, sharing his anguish, but troubled also by stirrings of guilt, for whereas she had told Sergei's son the truth she had not told him the whole truth.

When they had dried their eyes, she said, 'I'm sorry, Kolya love, really I am!'

'It's not your fault! It's his. I wish I could avenge the wrong he did you. And me. I wish he were standing here in front of me now!'

'You'd kill him, wouldn't you?' she said quietly. 'But it wouldn't solve anything.'

'It might not. But it might help to burn something out of me.'

Nikolai asked to be transferred to an engineering plant in a country district well removed from Leningrad, and was sent to Plavsk, in the southern part of Moscow province. He gave as his reason that it would be good for him to experience different conditions of work and living and he was not ready yet for the privilege of university. He told Sophia it was his duty as a Bolshevik to serve his country first. He did not want her to know the real reason, in case it would blight her career.

It was two years before he came back to Leningrad. He returned with a wife of his own age called Olga, a native of Plavsk, a serious-minded girl, as addicted to the principles of Marxist-Leninism as her husband. They were both to rise high in the Party. By then Sophia was dancing in the *corps de ballet* at the Maryinsky; she was living in an apartment with other dancers and travelling around Russia and even going out occasionally to the West. When she and Nikolai met, which was seldom, they nodded and murmured a greeting but did not look directly at one another. After Nikolai had gone away Dolly had feared her daughter would die of heartbreak. Sophia lost weight, her beautiful bright eyes grew dull, and she did not dance for weeks on end. Garnet worried about her also. She told Dolly what she had told Kolya. Dolly said she had made a mistake, she should just have let them marry. Would it have mattered if a half-brother and half-sister had married? As long as no one else knew. Garnet could never come to a decision on that, but later she wondered if by not telling she might have diverted the tragedies that were to follow.

Riga

May 1934

Andrew flew to Riga on the 14th of May to cover the deteri-
orating political situation, arriving a couple of days ahead of
his mother and aunt, who were motoring up from Italy
through Austria, Czechoslovakia, Poland and Lithuania for
Paula's wedding on the 20th. They'd been exploring the wilds
of Calabria, where they'd had a potentially nasty experience
with a group of bandits and had managed to subvert it by
talking the bandits round, giving them a bottle of whisky, or
some such thing. Could have been a tin of shortbread!

Veronika met Andrew at the airport. She looked tense.

'Things are going from bad to worse,' she said, linking her
arm through his.

'I'm so pleased to see you,' he said, landing a kiss on the
side of her neck.

'The country is rapidly becoming ungovernable. And the
Soviet Union is rattling its sabres at us and then there's that
man Hitler in Germany! I'm worried about the possibility of
revolution.'

'From whom? The Socialists? Communists? Rightists?
Surely not the Farmers' Union! There are too many factions,
aren't there, for any kind of unified revolt?'

'That's our main trouble! How can you run a government
with *forty-four* political parties all grinding their own axes? It's

crazy. The electoral laws should have been changed. At least you've got a system in your country that works.'

'Sort of,' said Andrew.

'Ulmanis is going to have to do something,' said Veronika.

'Martial law?' said Jemima, when they'd been handed back their passports at the border. 'Whatever's going on? Don't tell me there's been a revolution. My daughters have been caught up in enough revolutions in their time.'

A *coup d'état* had taken place, they were told. The customs official, who spoke some German, was a chatty man. There was little movement over the border today and the arrival of a mud-spattered car containing two Englishwomen – *Scots*, they insisted – had made a welcome break from staring into the murk. It had been a dull day, weather-wise. He was happy to answer their questions. No, there'd been no fighting. No blood spilt. And only a few arrests – some right-wing extremists belonging to an organisation called *Perkonkrusts* (Thundercross, in English) who were against all other nationalities, including Jews, Germans and Russians. The man thought some of the Socialist groups should have been taken into custody, too. They had a paramilitary sports organisation which he said was a training ground for revolutionaries. 'I'd lock them all up, if I were in charge.'

'That might be rather drastic,' said Hetty.

'It makes our politics seem terribly tame,' said Jemima. Travelling had brought that home to them and made them appreciate anew the advantages of being surrounded by water. It wasn't so easy for Russian Communists or German Nazis to chap at their door. Not that they were totally free of those influences, and they did have the problem of ongoing economic depression like everyone else.

'So who is running the country now?' asked Hetty. 'I presume somebody is?'

'Ulmanis, our PM. He's taken over. He's a good man – people of all parties like him. He'll get us sorted out. The country's quiet now. Very quiet. Hardly anything's been moving on the road all day. He's dissolved parliament and banned all political parties.'

'Even his own?' asked Hetty.

'Yes – the Farmers' Union. The parties have all been squabbling something terrible, like a pack of kids! Politicians! I'd lock them up as well.'

'You might not have enough jail space,' said Jemima.

Well, they'd best get on their way. The sky was darkening ominously with heavy rain clouds, and the day advancing. They'd have to get to Riga before nightfall or they might get arrested!

'You must have many adventures,' said the man mournfully, gazing back over the border into Lithuania, and beyond. The countryside was looking even more dreich in the fading light.

'Quite a few,' agreed Jemima.

'Borders are funny places. You feel you're neither in nor out. It's like standing on a line.'

'The line is not always rigid, though, is it?' said Hetty, moving towards the driver's side of the car. 'It can be a moveable feast.'

'It's been nice talking to you,' said Jemima, moving to her side.

He stood in the middle of the road to wave them off and Jemima turned in her seat and waved back until she felt her shoulder beginning to twist.

A clap of thunder overhead heralded a vigorous rainstorm. The windscreen wipers flailed madly until they surrendered, at which point Hetty pulled into the side of the road to wait until the torrent reduced itself to a drizzle. By the time it had, it was too late to make Riga that night, since there was a curfew in force.

They took shelter in a primitive wayside inn, where foreign women travelling alone had never before been seen, ate a meagre supper, drank a glass or two of Balzams (a rather bitter local drink, tasting, as its name suggested, of balsam), entertained the landlord with some travellers' tales, and retired to bed.

'I hope this political trouble won't affect little Paula's wedding,' said Jemima, as she removed her dress and pulled up her shift to unlace her stays. She sighed with relief. Hetty said she should stop corseting herself, but it was all right for Hetty to give such advice, she had no extra flesh to keep under control. Jemima kept on her peachy-pink Interlock knickers and the shift and put a Fair Isle cardigan on top. It was chilly in the comb-ceilinged room and a draught was blowing in round the ill-fitting windows. (They had slept in much worse places, so did not even comment on the discomforts.) 'At nineteen one's marriage must seem the most important thing on earth, more important even than revolutions.'

The bride looked beautiful, everybody said so. What else would they say? Her skin was flawless, her eyes as bright as daisies. The bride's mother looked beautiful too, said Tomas, and scarcely a day older than on the day of their wedding.

Lily blushes at the compliment. She is happy! Happy that the sun is shining, that her mother is here to join in the celebrations and see her first grandchild married (Nikolai will be next, with his bride from Plavsk, where they will plight their troth in a register office, with two workmates as witnesses, and not even his mother or hers present); happy that the family has come through to this point, with two grown-up sons and daughters doing well, fingers-crossed, and Tomas recovered from his trauma of the war, with a high and growing reputation as an architect in the city, working much too long hours, that is true, but one has to accept that from architects, and she herself contented and healthy, enjoying her painting ever more as time goes on and even contemplating an exhibition, with Tom's encouragement; and happy for her daughter who looks radiant, as brides should, and who is marrying such an agreeable and clever young man. Armands is a physician, specialising in nervous diseases, and is tipped for a brilliant career. He hopes to work abroad, in Berlin or Vienna, which will mean them going away, but Lily feels she

cannot rightly grudge her daughter that. For hasn't she travelled far from her home town? And her mother has never
chided her for it.

She is happy also that the declaration of martial law seems
not to have kept anyone away. Amongst the two hundred
guests are several MPs of various parties (one or two from the
Farmers' Union, the rest from the Democratic Centre, which
is supported by white-collar workers and civil servants) – or,
rather, *former* MPs. She can't quite take it in that parliament
has been dismissed and they are no longer living in a democracy. Though no one thinks Ulmanis will be a harsh dictator.
Not like Stalin in the Soviet Union! He sounds absolutely
dreadful, with those gruesome labour camps and harsh laws.
Lily gives a moment's thought to Garnet and half wishes she
could be here, and would wholly wish it if she could be sure
that her twin would greet her warmly. But she cannot.
Whenever Garnet's name comes up, Lily thinks her mother
looks at her strangely. Or is it that pangs of conscience make
her think so? She gives her head a little shake. Such thoughts
are not for today. She wants to enjoy herself, be light-
hearted.

Over the past few days her head has ached from political
talk. It has gone on and on until late in the night, with people
calling in spite of the curfew, and then there's been Andrew
talking incessantly on the telephone, interviewing people,
writing dispatches. Usually when he comes to Riga he stays
with Veronika – they make no secret of their affair here – but
when his mother is in town he takes up residence with Lily
and Tom. Tom's parents, who are beginning to fail (both will
die in the following year, within a month of each other), are
with them for the few days spanning the wedding, as well as
a couple of other elderly cousins. The flat is creaking at the
seams. Morag says they'd need a shoehorn to get any more
in and cooking for that mob is like feeding the five thousand.
It's a pity they can't work the miracle of the loaves and the
fishes.

Now if Effie and Norrie were here they might manage it!

But they weren't able to leave the children (who now number ten). 'They'll have to stop soon surely,' Lily said to her mother. 'I shudder to think what her insides must be like. Can't you speak to her?' Jemima had, and given her Marie Stopes. 'It's Norrie you should speak to,' said Hetty. Jemima had tried that, too. 'But you know Norrie, he can only talk about the desires of the Lord.' Hetty was withering. 'Bloody hypocrite! It's the lusts of his too fleshy flesh that are the problem. One would need to tie him down.' Lily had a rather obscene vision of Norrie and had to leave the room to indulge her giggles.

That she is able to relax and enjoy the reception and move amongst the guests, chatting and receiving their compliments on the beauty of her daughter, is due to Morag. Resplendent in a petrol-blue dress with a feathered hat to match, Morag is orchestrating the event, bossing the caterers and chivvying the waiters and keeping an eye on the youngest guests, making sure they don't get out of hand or sneak a glass of wine. Earlier, she marched up and down the long, white-clothed tables inspecting the suckling pig with the apple in its mouth, the sturgeon-in-aspic, the *saumon-en-croûte*, the stuffed partridges and glazed chicken breasts, the bowls of salad and dessert, making a comment here, tweaking an arrangement to satisfy herself there.

The tables look magnificent, as does the room itself, bedecked with garlands of sweet-smelling blossoms. On the back wall hang the dark-red and white banded flag of Latvia and the blue and white St Andrew's Cross of Scotland. Andrew is wearing full Highland dress and has given Veronika a sprig of white heather to wear on her dress with a silver Orcadian brooch to hold it in place. He wondered about bringing a kilt for young Ivars, but Lily thought that would surely arouse their mother's suspicions. Though she must *see* what is going on. She's not blind. Or stupid. Far from. Age is not dulling her faculties, merely greying her hair and scribbling a few more lines on her face. Andrew and Veronika behave like a couple; they turn to look for each other in a room, exchange glances of intimacy across the table, get up to dance, and move smoothly into each other's arms. They are in tune. How much longer, Lily wonders, can Andrew get away with leading a double life?

Lily sat down at the side, next to Hetty.

'Aren't weddings wonderful for bringing people together?'

'Better than funerals, anyway,' said Hetty. 'What a fine-looking gathering. And so well dressed. I feel quite fuddy-duddy in comparison.' Lily smiled. Her aunt was wearing a Turkish kaftan in a range of red and orange hues. 'This must be the *crème de la crème* of Riga. Who's that man over there? The tall one with the steely-grey hair and the very straight back. German. I didn't expect to find any Germans here.'

'We do have a few German friends. Well, one or two. And some Russian.'

'Well, I should hope so! Your own twin sister's married to one, after all – a second one!'

'The man you were pointing out – that's Herman, Tom's brother-in-law. He's a Balt. We can't stand him.'

'What's he doing here, then?'

'You know what family weddings are like! You always have to have a few people you can't stand. We thought we'd better ask him and Agita, for Tom's parents' sake. Forgive and forget and all that.'

'I thought they'd skedaddled when the German army got the push?'

'They came back after a few years. He's in banking. Got interests in various capitals. He lost his estates but somehow he doesn't seem to have lost his money. They never do, do they? That's Agita there. She's very handsome, don't you think?'

'If you like icebergs. He was telling me what a wonderful man Hitler is, how someone like him is needed to pull Europe together. To pull Latvia together. He seemed to think it will be only a matter of time before Latvia becomes part of Germany.'

'Herman talks a lot of hot air. We try to make sure he and

Veronika don't come together.'

'Mm' said Hetty. 'Veronika!'

'What about her? Don't you like her?'

'Oh yes, indeed. She's a fine woman. Strong. Doesn't thole weakness much, but fair. Andrew likes her too, that's obvious.'

'Do you think it must also be obvious to Mother?'

'She has never mentioned it. Sometimes when people don't want to see something they manage not to. Only last night she was saying to me that it was nonsense to think there shouldn't be secrets within a family and that she had no wish to know everything her children were getting up to.'

'Oh well,' said Lily offhandedly.

'Mother!' Luke came weaving through the crowd. He had a girl by the hand, was tugging her after him, and she was laughing and pushing her long blonde hair back from her face. She was called Irena, and was the latest in a long line of Luke's girlfriends. He whisked through them like a whirlwind, not always treating them well. He had a low boredom threshold. Lily would chide him. 'Can I help it if they bore me?' he would demand. Alex had had the same girlfriend, Liza, for two years and appeared to be in love. She was a quiet girl, and pretty in her own way, but not flamboyantly so, as Luke's girlfriends tended to be. Lily was glad that Alex had such a nice girl, one who would look after him. She felt he needed looking after. He was inclined to be dreamy (like herself!), and he was not as worldly as Luke, who made no secret of wanting to make money so that he could buy fast cars, drink the best wines, and travel the world, in style, not in the way that his ageing female relatives did, roughing it under canvas or in flea-bitten hotels. Irena, Luke's chosen, was strikingly beautiful, and intelligent. She was studying English literature and language. She and Lily enjoyed long literary conversations together. Irena admired Virginia Woolf, which had shamed Lily, who had never been able to get on with her and was now patiently making her way through *The Years*. Lily liked Irena, thought beauty had not turned her

393

head and that she was good for Luke, though she wouldn't dream of saying so, to him. Whether Luke would be good for Irena was another matter. His wife would not be able to expect peace and quiet.

'Mother,' he said impatiently, 'you've to come and have your photograph taken! You, too, Aunt Hetty! It's to be the whole family.'

They were all in the photograph which Jemima would carry back to Aberdeen and hang on the wall of the drawing room in Queen's Road beside the other family pictures. Jemima also took several shots of the young ones in different poses: talking and laughing and dancing and popping champagne corks and throwing flowers at one another. Enjoying themselves with a wholeheartedness which only the confident and carefree young are able to do.

Aberdeen

January 1935

Andrew and Rose came for lunch on New Year's Day, bringing Mrs Sibbald with them. Rose's mother, fearful of draughts, insisted on keeping on her fur tippet. The little eyes gleamed in the foxy head, keeping a greedy watch on the diners round the table. Jemima felt she couldn't very well object to the beast's presence, since it was dead, but she did draw a firm line at having live dogs in either her dining or drawing room, even if they were prepared to sit in a corner and mind their own business. Rose had, therefore, been obliged to leave her two Scotch terriers at home and was worried that they would be pining for her.

Andrew had arrived with a bottle of Islay Mist in one hand and a lump of coal in the other. He was their First Foot.

'It would have been better if you were dark,' said Hetty. 'But never mind. At least you're a man!'

Before sitting down to eat, they drank a toast to Absent Friends.

'To those in Russia,' said Jemima. 'Garnet and Leo, Kolya and his new wife Olga, and Anna.'

'And those in Latvia,' said Andrew. 'Lily and Tom, Luke and Alex, Paula and her husband Armands, Vera, Markus and Gertrude.'

'And Veronika and Ivars,' said Hetty, to save him from

having to say it.

'And Morag,' added Jemima. 'Let's not forget Morag! Happy New Year to all of them!'

'Happy New Year!' The glasses were raised in a circle and clinked.

'What a lot of absentees!' said Mrs Sibbald, which made Jemima feel she'd been careless, mislaying so many of her family.

'It snowballs,' she said, by way of defence.

They took their places at the table and pulled their crackers. All was quiet downstairs.

'What's happened to them down there?' asked Mrs Sibbald, putting on a purple crenellated paper hat. 'They can't be sleeping still, surely?'

They'd gone to a meeting, said Jemima. Effie had trooped them all up in the morning to wish their elders season's greetings. 'Happy New Year, Grandma,' they'd chanted in unison. 'Happy New Year, Great-Aunt Hetty. And may the Good Lord go with you both on your travels amongst the heathen in foreign lands.' And then off they'd gone, banging their toy drums and shaking their tambourines. Hetty had hung over the banisters and sung them on their way. 'Onward, Christian soldiers, marching as to war, with the cross of Jesus going on before!' The tune made you want to go to war, she'd remarked.

For lunch they had pheasant stewed in red wine, followed by cloutie dumpling.

'You do like to be traditional, don't you?' said Mrs Sibbald, surveying the dumpling as Jemima unwrapped it from its steaming cloth. 'Just a little for me, if you don't mind. It's rather heavy for the figure, with all that suet. Not that it isn't delicious, I'm sure.' She put a hand over her glass. 'No, thank you, Andrew, no more wine for me – I won't be able to walk a straight line going home!'

Andrew refilled the glasses of his mother and aunt without asking and as he replaced the bottle on the sideboard he glanced at his watch.

396

'Going somewhere?' asked his mother.

'No, nowhere.'

'The dumpling is absolutely magnificent,' said Hetty. 'A veritable queen of dumplings! Jemima made it herself.'

'It's all right for you,' said Mrs Sibbald, 'you're as thin as a garden rake.'

'Have you ever seen my sharp teeth?' asked Hetty with a laugh, and Mrs Sibbald smiled uncertainly.

After oatcakes with Stilton and Orkney cheddar, accompanied by a glass or two of fine ruby-red port, they adjourned to the drawing room for coffee and shortbread.

'And there's Black Bun, if you'd like it?' said Jemima.

'My goodness!' exclaimed Mrs Sibbald, dropping into the settee and patting her diaphragm. She lay spread-eagled, looking, as Hetty could not help thinking, uncharitably, she knew, like a beached porpoise, and stared ahead, at the Matisse, which hung over the fireplace. 'I must be honest with you, Jemima, I can't say I care for that picture. It's rather vague. Could do with more definition, don't you think?' Mrs Sibbald had a Landseer over her drawing-room mantelpiece and a stag's head on the opposite wall that her late husband had shot up Glen Muick. She was always pleased when her antlers were admired. 'Garnet's first poor husband bought it for her in Paris, didn't he?' she went on. 'It was very sad for Garnet to be widowed so young. One never recovers.' Her eye travelled lazily along the side wall and came to rest on a photograph. 'That was Lily's daughter's wedding, wasn't it?'

'Yes,' said Jemima. 'Paula's.'

'Don't think I've noticed it before.'

'I've just recently had it framed, didn't have time before.'

'Well, yes, you've been away so much.' Mrs Sibbald heaved herself up to go and take a closer look. She felt sentimental about wedding photographs. Her daughter, who took after her in this respect, and in some others, tagged on behind. 'Now, do tell me who everyone is,' said Mrs Sibbald.

Jemima stood between the two to point out the people. 'There are Tom's parents, and you recognise Lily and Tom, of course, and their children – yes, time does fly, doesn't it? – and that's Morag and her husband, and this is Andrew!'

'What a shame Rose wasn't able to go. But her tummy isn't good on the sea. Who's that woman there, the tall one next to Andrew?'

'That's Veronika, Tom's sister.'

'Is she a widow too?'

'Well, yes,' said Jemima vaguely.

'There are always a lot of widows left after a war,' sighed Mrs Sibbald.

'I didn't think Tom's sister had ever been married?' piped up Rose.

'Her fiancé was killed in 1914,' said Andrew shortly. He remained seated, apparently contemplating the drink in his hand.

'But she's got a son, hasn't she?' said Rose.

'A son?' said Mrs Sibbald. 'And she's not married?' She closed her mouth.

Andrew got up and poured himself another glass of port, splashing some of the ruby-red liquid on to his wrist. He wiped it with his handkerchief, where it left a stain.

Rose pointed to Ivars. 'Is that the boy? *He* wasn't born before 1914! He must be about twelve?'

Jemima shrugged. 'I can never remember birthdays or ages.'

Mrs Sibbald put her head on one side. 'He reminds me of someone.'

'Yes, he does me too,' said Rose.

'Let's have our coffee before it gets cold,' said Jemima. 'And I think I may have another little drop of port too, Andrew, if there's any left. New Year comes but once a year, after all.'

'Just as well,' said Hetty.

Rose stayed where she was gazing at the photograph with drawn brows, looking like one on whom light is beginning to dawn.

'Coffee, Rose?' said her mother-in-law.

'No, no, thank you. *Andrew* . . . ' His wife was appealing to him.

'Yes?'

'Nothing.'

Rose went to the settee and sat down beside her mother. Jemima and Hetty eyed one another, and then Andrew. He had his back to the room and was looking out of the window.

He turned. 'Think I'd better call the office,' he said, already halfway to the door. 'See if there are any messages or cables in for me.'

'Do they work on New Year's Day?' asked Mrs Sibbald. 'Surely it's a holiday!'

'Not outside Scotland. Anyway, news doesn't stop coming in just because the year's changed.'

'Such a hard worker,' said his mother-in-law after he'd gone out. 'Just as well you're so understanding, isn't it, Rose dear?'

Andrew had a job getting through, had to wait forty minutes before the operator called him back, but he couldn't risk leaving the phone during that time. He sighed with relief when he heard Veronika's voice. The Zales, young and old, were all in Cesis, and having a good time. He heard the rise and fall of talk and laughter at the back of Veronika's voice. It had been snowing hard, she said, but had now stopped and the sun was shining and they'd been out cross-country skiing. The forests had looked like the ones in the old fairy tales, with their branches weighted down with snow and the air so sparkling and so still you could hear sounds from miles away. Ivars was an able skier and had declared an interest in trying downhill.

'Maybe we could go to the Swiss Alps for a week,' said Andrew.

'That would be fun.'

'What about the end of March, when your term finishes?'

'Sorry, I couldn't quite catch that.'

The line sounded as if it were awash with the North Sea,

and Andrew was trying not to speak too loudly. He had his mouth right up against the receiver, which was sprinkled with droplets of water. After taking a quick glance over his shoulder he repeated what he had just said in a louder voice.

'Sounds good to me,' said Veronika at the other end of the waves. 'Can you get away?'

The door opened abruptly behind Andrew and he swung round.

'We were just wondering what had happened to you,' said Rose. 'You've been ages.'

'It's taken a while to get through. Probably aren't so many lines open on New Year's Day.'

'I thought you said it wasn't a holiday, except in Scotland.'

'Some people are off. Look, I'll be through in a minute.'

'I want to talk to you, Andrew.'

'Not now, not this minute. Can't you see I'm on the phone?'

'Who are you speaking to?'

'The office.'

'I don't think you're telling the truth, Andrew. Let me speak to them!'

'Don't be silly! What would they think if you started to speak? Come on now, Rose, *please*! Be sensible! For God's sake, this is ridiculous!'

'Give me the phone!' She advanced into the room with unusual determination.

'Go back to the drawing room!'

In the wrestle for possession of the receiver it was dropped. Rose snatched it up and pressed it to her ear.

'Who is there?' she demanded, rattling the receiver rest. 'Who is there? It's gone dead.' She crashed it on to the rest and set the telephone base tingling.

'I hope you haven't broken it,' he said.

'Why do you keep going to Latvia?' she asked.

'It's my work. You know I specialise in the Baltic and Eastern Europe. Apart from the fact that I do have a sister there.'

400

'Is she the only attraction? Why do you never take me with you?'

'You get queasy on boats. You're seasick if you go as far as Orkney.'

'Why don't you take me for Easter? I'd like to meet Veronika.'

'Veronika?'

'Don't play the innocent! Don't ask, "Why Veronika?"!'

He didn't ask anything. Fortunately the phone rang at that moment. He snatched the receiver. 'It's the office,' he said, and it was.

'Give it to me,' demanded Rose. She held out her hand.

He gave it to her.

'Hello,' she said. 'Who is this?' She passed it back. 'How did they know where to reach you on New Year's Day?'

'I told them if I wasn't at home I'd be here.'

'You could have allowed us *one* day without interruption,' said Rose, and marched out.

'Sorry about that,' said Andrew. 'You know how it is at New Year – we've all had quite a bit to drink. So, what's new?'

His old friend Hank had called and left a message asking him to call back as soon as possible. As he was dialling Hank's number, Rose opened the door again.

'I'm phoning Hank – the American, remember? Who works for Reuters.'

Rose waited by the door.

Hank answered immediately and they exchanged Happy New Years, then Hank said, 'I managed to get to Leningrad.'

'Did you see Garnet?'

'Yep! Took her to tea at the Europe.'

'How is she?'

'News isn't good, I'm afraid, Andy.'

'What's happened?' asked Andrew, alarmed.

'What is it?' asked Rose.

'For Christ's sake! Do you have to keep getting your tuppence ha'penny in? It's bad news, that's what it bloody well is!'

Rose fled, sobbing.

'Sorry about that, Hank.'

'Domestic problems?' said Hank, who made sure he never had any but wasn't surprised Andrew did.

'What's up then, Hank? With Garnet?'

The door opened yet again and Andrew swung round angrily. His mother stood there.

'Perhaps you should come,' she said. 'Rose is having hysterics.'

Leningrad

February 1935

Garnet felt like an empty vessel as she went about her daily life, performing all the necessary tasks, cleaning her two rooms, cooking meals for herself and Anna, waiting in food queues, standing in front of students, opening her mouth, listening with one part of her mind, while the other was pre-occupied elsewhere. It was fixed on barbed wire, bleak build-ings, bleak figures moving against a bare, frozen landscape. Sometimes her head would jolt up and she would realise that one of the students had asked a question and she hadn't heard it. She worried that they might report her for ineffi-ciency and inattention to duty.

They'd come at dawn, the traditional time. At first she'd thought they were just taking Leo in for routine questioning, that he'd be back in a day or two, as before.

Leo could pack a small bag, said the men, but he'd better be quick about it. They leaned against the wall, looking bored. Leo packed night-clothes, toothbrush, toothpaste, slip-pers, and a volume of Pushkin's poetry.

'Should I take a spare shirt, I wonder?'

'Do you think you'll need it?'

'Might as well be on the safe side.' He put one in – it had belonged to Andrew, had a Savile Row label, and might be

403

useful to offer as a bribe to a guard – and a set of under-clothes. He closed the bag.

The men straightened up.

Leo came to Garnet and embraced her. 'Don't worry,' he said. 'I'm sure I'll be back soon.'

Then he was gone. It had taken only a few minutes from wakening to the thundering knock on the door to them driving away. Garnet watched from the window as Leo was bundled into a grey van. Before his head ducked inside and out of sight he looked up. Their eyes met. She raised her hand. The grey door slammed shut.

'I'm so sorry about Leo.' Sophia put her arms round Garnet and they held on tightly to one another. 'Mother's just told me. Do you know where he is?'

Garnet shook her head. Some camp, somewhere. The authorities had said they'd forward her letters on to him.

'How can I trust them to do it?'

'You can't,' said Sophia sadly. 'Shall I make us some tea?'

'Yes, let's have some tea! The samovar's been boiling.'

They were drinking the tea when a visitor arrived. Sophia went to answer the door.

It was Nikolai who stood on the landing.

'Sophia!' he said, looking hard at her.

'Kolya,' she said, lowering her eyes.

'How are you?'

'I am well. And you?'

'Yes, very well.'

'You'd better come in.'

Nikolai walked over to his mother and kissed her. He took a seat beside her. Sophia stood by the window.

'You've heard about Leo?' said Garnet.

'Yes, I'm sorry.' Nikolai was still looking at Sophia. It was as if there was an electric charge in the room. Garnet felt acutely aware of it, thought if she were to hold her hands between the two of them they would tingle. He asked a question or two about Leo, almost absent-mindedly. He was too preoccupied by the other presence in the room.

'What are you doing at present, Sophia?' he asked.

'Preparing for *Coppélia*.'

'Are you playing the lead role? I can imagine you in it! I saw you in *Swan Lake*.'

'You saw me!' She seemed startled by the idea that he had been watching her when she had not known it.

'You were excellent! I went twice.'

'I must go,' said Sophia quickly, and slipped from the room.

Nikolai sighed. Garnet could not bear to look at his face. She got up and went to pour two more cups of tea. She put one into his hand.

'Oh, thank you.' He had forgotten her.

'Kolya, is there anything you could do for Leo?' she asked.

'I don't know—'

'You know a lot of people.'

'It's difficult, though.'

'Oh, why have they taken him?' Garnet burst out. 'He's the kindest of men – you know that! He hasn't committed any crime.'

'He talks foolishly at times.'

'Is that a crime?'

'Loose talk undermines the state. Undoes the good we are doing.'

Could Kolya have betrayed Leo? Garnet had reasoned with herself in the night. Leo and Nikolai had disagreed on most matters fundamental, even quarrelled outright, quite bitterly at times, but that didn't mean Kolya would betray his step-father. He wouldn't betray the man she loved, would he, the man who'd cared for him as a child, had worked at any kind of menial job so that he and Anna might eat, who had read bedtime stories to him, bound his cuts, comforted him when he was unhappy? Surely he would not!

It had been either him or Dolly.

'Why should men like Leo be scorned?' she asked quietly. 'First by the count your grandfather, and now by you. For

405

being *liberal*, fair-minded?'

'They are ineffectual.'

'It seems you're right.' Garnet was wearied now. She only wanted Nikolai to go.

He had brought provisions. He laid them on the table.

'Your atonement?' she said.

'What do you mean?'

'Whatever you think I mean.'

He said stiffly that Olga was sorry she had not been able to come but she was busy with her work.

'You must both be busy. With the Party. The bloody Party!'

'*Mama*!'

'Are you going to tell *me* to be careful now? Give me my first warning?'

'Don't be ridiculous!'

'I wish it were ridiculous.'

'But you know you should watch whom you see.'

'What do you mean?'

'You had tea at the Europe with an American reporter recently?'

'I did. His name was Hank Cooper. He works for Reuters and he's a friend of your Uncle Andrew. But no doubt you know all that already.'

'Don't be angry with me! I'm telling you for your own good.'

'I'm sure!'

'Look, Mama, I've got to go. I'm sorry, but I have an important engagement.'

'I dare say it is very important.'

'I'll come back and see you in a few days. I realise you're under a strain. It's been a shock . . .'

'Yes,' she agreed, 'a shock.'

Dolly was making soup. The room smelt of boiled cabbage and the window was steamed up.

Garnet stopped in the doorway.

'Dolly,' she said, 'I want a straight answer.'

*

When Andrew turned up in the middle of a violent February snowstorm, his head and moustache frosted, his nose and cheeks blue with cold, Garnet was not unduly surprised.

'You're a good brother,' she said, reaching up to brush the snow from his head. 'Don't tell me you didn't have a hat on!'

'I just took it off outside.' He held up his trilby to show how sodden it was.

'You should have had a proper hat on – a Russian *fur* hat! We know how to protect ourselves.'

'I had to pick my way along the street holding on to whatever could be held on to. The wind is fierce! How do you stand it, Garnet? There are no trams running and I didn't see a single cab.'

'Sane people will be indoors.'

The blizzard was so bad he would be stormbound and have to hole up for the night in Garnet's room. Anna had gone to Moscow for the weekend. Andrew had brought with him a bottle of Scotch, bought at the airport, and cigarettes. He'd come in from Berlin.

'I didn't have time to get anything else. First excuse I had I was on my way out of London heading east!'

'You're the best gift!'

'I hope I'm not compromising you, with the authorities?'

'To hell with them! God, I wish I could send them to hell.'

'What about Dolly?'

'Give her a few dollars if she appears. That'll shut her mouth. And speak sweetly to her.' Garnet barred the door.

'Hell's teeth, I don't want to encourage her! I'm in enough trouble.'

Garnet raised an eyebrow.

'I'll tell you later. First, I want to hear about Leo. What did they take him in for?'

'Treason. Speaking against the regime. Questioning Communism. They said he was an Enemy of the People.'

Apart from that, there was not much to tell. It was as if Leo had disappeared into a black hole. And perhaps he had.

'I'm sorry,' said Garnet, when she'd dried her tears.

'Don't be sorry. God, it's awful! One feels so helpless.'

'That's just it!'

'Kolya and his wife don't live with you?'

'They've got a three-roomed flat up at the other end of the Moscow Prospekt.'

'On their own?'

'They are well thought of. Too well thought of. I fear Kolya might have been the one who betrayed Leo.'

'You don't mean it? My God, if he should come here tonight!'

But Nikolai would not come. The wind was howling outside like a pack of wolves prowling the steppe; hail and snow were assaulting the window. Even Dolly had not appeared. Garnet thought she must have missed Andrew's arrival.

'The snow masked you! Made you anonymous. I wish I could go anonymously around the city. But I know I'm listed. A marked woman.'

'Don't say that! You don't think they could come after you next?'

'Who can read their minds?'

The rest of the family, out there in the West, what could *they* do? asked Andrew. There must be something. Garnet did not know what. They could at least protest, said Andrew, appeal for Leo's release.

'You could write to Stalin!' Garnet laughed. 'Let's have another drink. Let's get drunk! And tell me about your life. And Effie's life. And Mother's life. I want to know what's going on outside the walls of this city. And how is my sister-in-law, Rose?'

Andrew made a face. 'I've left her. No, that's not quite true – she threw me out.'

'Little Rose Sibbald? Well, well! I never would have imagined it. You're quite large to throw anywhere. It wasn't physical, I take it? Did she merely point to the door? In a melodramatic way!'

'It was more than that. She didn't throw me *personally*, but almost. She flung out into the snowy night all my clothes, books, golf clubs, tennis rackets, tennis trophies, skis, my old rugby kit, my dirty laundry, even my toothpaste and tooth-brush – she didn't forget those!'

'Out on to Queen's Road!' Garnet began to laugh, and Andrew joined in. Garnet laughed until tears ran down her face and her side began to hurt. 'I presume she found out about Veronika?'

He nodded. 'It was quite a relief, actually. Though the whole thing is a bloody awful mess. She's trying to screw me for every penny I've got. She's keeping the house. It's in our joint names but I wouldn't dream of trying to get my half share from it.'

'What's Effie got to say about it?'

'Oh, urging repentance and all that and telling me the Lord is merciful to penitent sinners. She thinks I should give up Veronika for Rose. So does Rose.'

'But *you* don't? You won't?'

He shook his head. 'I feel as guilty as hell about Rose. Well, I've messed up her life, haven't I? I never should have married her.'

'Those kind of regrets are a waste of time.'

Getting up to replenish their whisky glasses, Andrew noticed a piece of paper pinned to the dresser.

'What's this? A poem? "The Russian God".' His eye ran down the lines.

> *God of potholes . . .*
> *God of frostbite . . .*
> *God of pickle-vendors . . .*
> *God of famine, cripples by the yard . . .*
> *God of breasts all sagging*
> *and swollen legs in bast shoes shod . . .*

'*God of everything contrary, that's him – that's your Russian God*!' Garnet finished up, and they laughed.

'I'm glad you've been able to keep your sense of humour,'

said Andrew, splashing whisky into her upheld glass.

Around three in the morning they were exhausted and needed to lie down and close their eyes. 'You can share the bed,' said Garnet. She pulled back the heavy quilt. They removed their outer clothes and lay down, side by side, their arms touching, conscious of each other's warmth, grateful for it, taking comfort, not drawing away even when they felt the touch of the other's leg. And so, lying close, totally at ease, brother and sister slept. They woke at dawn, which came late in the month of February, to silence. The storm had abated.

Lifting the edge of the curtain, Garnet saw that colour was nudging the darkness from the eastern sky. 'You'd better go,' she said.

Andrew nodded and began to dress. She watched him knotting his tie in front of the mirror, grimacing when in his hurry he could not get it to sit quite right. She remembered their father teaching him how to knot a tie, when he'd just started school, and how he'd wriggled and wouldn't stand still. She smiled at him in the mirror and he smiled back.

He put his hand into the pocket of his trench coat and pulled out a folded copy of the *New Yorker* and one of *Picture Post*, and a Penguin paperback copy of W. H. Hudson's *The Purple Land*.

'You might as well have these. Mother gave me the Hudson just before she left for Argentina.'

That, and the two magazines, would be Garnet's English reading material for the next three months. They would be read and reread.

They kissed and held on to each other for a moment, then she said, 'Thanks for coming, little brother; come again soon,' and took the bar off the door and let him out.

'May the Russian God watch over you!' he said, making her smile.

She watched while he groped his way down the unlit stair, a shadowy, familiar figure. And then the door at the bottom banged shut.

410

*

On the border with Latvia, Andrew was detained and taken into custody. What was the charge? he demanded. Spying, he was told. He was a regular visitor into the Soviet Union, was he not? Yes, he said, he was an accredited journalist with an interest in Soviet affairs. Too much interest, they said. He was taken back to Leningrad and held in detention, though of this Garnet remained unaware, and as she went about the city she passed at times the place where he was held. He was partly sorry that he had given away all his reading material – only partly, though, for Garnet's need was surely greater than his. Wasn't it? He was bound to be released soon. They couldn't hold him for ever. He hadn't done anything. But you didn't need to, did you? He of all people should know that. He was not naïve, or uninformed. He had his dark moments in the night. He was sure the British government would be protesting strongly, he had to keep telling himself that, and indeed it was, and his mother and aunt were protesting strongly to the government in their turn, and after four weeks he was released suddenly one morning and put on a plane to London. As they took off, in the midst of a violent snowstorm, with the aircraft bucking uncomfortably, he looked down through the crazy snow and thought of his sister marooned below. For ever, it would seem.

He would not be admitted again to the Soviet Union, he knew that. It was his main regret.

Aberdeen

July 1939

Luke and Alex brought Katrina and Helga, their respective baby daughters, born in the spring, only a few days apart, to show to their grandmother.

'I've got three great-granddaughters now!' said Jemima. Nikolai and his wife Olga had had a daughter, Lydia, in April. 'But goodness knows when I'll ever see the Russian one.'

Garnet had sent a photograph of herself with the baby on her knee. It was difficult to tell anything about the baby from the photograph, but they could see that Garnet was going grey and looking even thinner.

'Of course,' sighed Jemima, 'her life has been very difficult.'

Leo had died after four years in the labour camp. Garnet had been informed just after New Year. 'Died of pneumonia.' True or false? It was perfectly possible that it had been pneumonia; Leo's chest had not been strong. Andrew had heard many rumours about the camps, how the prisoners often worked up to sixteen hours a day in the bitter cold to earn a meagre ration of food, and if they fell ill and worked less they were given less and so their chances of recovery were minimal. They hoped Garnet didn't hear such rumours. They couldn't imagine what Garnet heard. She lived in a country ruled by terror, was cut off from them behind a curtain of iron, which even Andrew, who had access to most places, could no longer penetrate.

Leo was buried in Siberia. The graves of both Garnet's husbands lay far from Leningrad, beyond her reach.

'Thank goodness the Soviets didn't manage to take over Latvia in 1919!' Irena, Luke's wife, shivered. 'Just imagine what our lives would have been like if they had!'

Liza, Alex's wife, nodded. The sacrifices had been great, they all knew that, in keeping both Russian and German armies at bay. Once a year they went to the Brothers Cemetery in Riga to remember the fallen. Liza's father was one of Latvia's glorious heroes; he'd shown great courage and perished in the battle of the 'Blizzard of Souls', at which Tomas had been wounded.

'The young ones all look well,' said Jemima to Lily, as she watched them from her seat by the window. The two couples, with the wives pushing the high Silver Cross prams they'd hired (Effie's pram, which had been out of use for three years now, was much too battered to put a sweet-smelling baby girl in), were crossing the road, heading for the park. It reminded Jemima of when Lily and Tom, and Garnet and Sergei, had pushed their prams. 'Marriage seems to suit the boys.'

'I must say I never thought I'd see Luke walking beside a pram!' said Lily. 'In fact I haven't seen him walking beside one before.'

'He's just put his hand on the handle! He's helping push it up the kerb and look at that – Irena is letting him take it by himself!'

'It must be the Aberdeen air that's affected him. And he's not got much else to do here. At home he'd be away sailing or playing tennis if he wasn't working. He works like a maniac. The way he does everything. No half measures for Luke. He hates sitting in the house.'

'And one has to spend quite a lot of time in the house when one's married.'

'He's not the best of husbands, I fear. A difficult son and a difficult husband! But he and Irena seem to get on all right. I don't think she'd stand too much nonsense.'

'I hope not,' said Hetty, who was fixing photographs of Japan into an album to make a record of their latest – and, as it would turn out to be, their last – trip. 'Travel's like a drug,' she remarked idly.

Lily felt rather feeble where travel was concerned, in comparison with her mother and aunt, who were both approaching seventy. Well, anyone would! She and Tomas travelled a fair amount in Europe, looking at buildings mostly. To see the work of people like Le Corbusier. Tom's own work had become less decorative since the war, more functional, in keeping with the spirit of the times. In May they'd gone to Italy, but they hadn't slept in a tent and cooked in billycans, as her two elder relatives might have done. Nor had they strayed off the beaten path and run the risk of being confronted by brigands. They'd stayed in a very pleasant hotel looking over the Gulf of Salerno and had sat on their balcony in the evenings before dinner watching the sun set on the water. They had only passed through Rome, so hadn't seen much of the effects of Mussolini's Fascism except for a Blackshirt march, which had been rather disturbing and had made Tom gloomy.

And then in June they'd gone to Vienna for a few days to visit Paula and Armands. Tom had thought they should make a visit then, the way world affairs were shaping up. 'You don't mean *war*?' Lily had been doing her best not to let the word into her consciousness. 'You don't believe it's going to come to that? Not again. Not after last time. People can't forget, surely?'

They'd found Armands also deeply uneasy about the political situation. He talked about going to the United States, and was currently considering an offer from Boston. Tom thought he should take it. 'Maybe all the young ones should get out of Europe. Before they're called upon to shed their blood as well.' Lily was shocked. 'You can't mean that, can you, Tom?

414

That they should *leave*?' It wasn't like him to be so pessimistic. He said one could hardly fail to read the signs. People were deluding themselves if they thought Hitler could be appeased. Ask Andrew!

Andrew was no more encouraging. He'd been over in Riga the previous month to see Veronika and Ivars. He came as often as he could, though in the last year had not managed it as often as he would have liked. Pressure of news elsewhere kept him on the hop. He was spending a lot of time in Berlin. Lily thought the suitcase life suited him, and that he must have inherited this from their mother. Whereas she and Garnet and Effie stayed put for the most part, for one reason or another. She herself travelled more than either of her sisters; she and Tom went abroad every year at least once, to France and Italy (though not Venice – they had never been back there, which puzzled Tom somewhat, she knew), with regular visits home to Scotland. Garnet couldn't move much beyond the boundaries of Leningrad and Effie and Norrie had no money to go further than Deeside.

'There's Rose!' said Jemima, half rising from her seat to get a better view. 'And the dogs. She's got four now.'

Lily went to the window. Rose had each of the Scotties attached to her hands by a lead. Her back was braced and her arms at full stretch.

'Does she ever call these days?'

'Oh no! She gives me a nod when we pass in the street, a very cool little nod, and pulls the dogs in closer to her as if I might try to snatch them. Mrs Sibbald still says good morning, but it's meant as a reproach. I can understand their point of view. And I do feel sorry for Rose.'

'Poor Rose Sibbald. Though she has been pretty horrible to Andrew. I mean, what's the point in keeping it up? She might as well bow to fate. She's not going to get him back.'

Andrew had asked Rose for a divorce so that he could marry Veronika and become Ivars' legitimate father, though he had not said so in so many words. Rose would be able to deduce it herself. He'd said he would provide the evidence, which would not be difficult – he'd make it as easy for her as he could: he didn't want her to be cross-questioned in the witness box, or anything unpleasant like that – but she'd refused. Point blank. Would not even consider. Stood with her little rosy mouth pursed. It was stalemate for Andrew. There was no way he could divorce Rose. What grounds could he have? A model wife. A model housewife. Her house was always spick-and-span. She was always spick-and-span. She didn't drink, or disturb the peace, and she had no other lover, nor ever had had, nor ever was likely to have.

'You might want to marry again,' Andrew had said to her. 'You're young still. And attractive.' He'd covered the last remark with a cough.

Once was enough, she'd said.

Mrs Sibbald, when she was still speaking to Jemima, said that Andrew had put Rose off men for life. She dropped dark hints. About his sexual demands, though had not brought the word 'sex' into the conversation. 'It would take a lot to please *him*. No wonder he's taken up with a foreigner.'

His scandalous life sent a *frisson* of delight and disapproval along the street and, as in the game of Chinese whispers, by the time it had travelled a number of houses along, Veronika had turned into a scarlet-nailed *femme fatale* who haunted the beer *kellers* of Berlin, Vienna, and Riga. The gossip did not trouble Jemima and gave positive pleasure to Hetty. It was she who brought the titbits back.

Rose went on her way down Queen's Road.

Now they saw Morag emerging below, dressed in a hat and her best coat, her handbag dangling from her arm. Her back had broadened over the years. Seventeen-year-old Calum was following behind in his new Harris tweed jacket, bought for him by Jemima. He would still have it when he was seventy-one and show it proudly to Jemima's great-grand-daughters Katrina and Lydia.

'He must be boiling in that on a day like this,' said Lily. 'Morag says he's reluctant to take it off even to go to bed!'

'They're going shopping,' said Jemima. 'Morag wants to

get a pipe for Paulis.'

'Calum's a good son to her,' said Lily.

They had a happy visit to Aberdeen, with parties in the garden and on the beach. The young ones braved the chilly waters of the North Sea and their elders did their best not to think about the rumblings on mainland Europe.

Shortly after the Zales returned home, the Germans entered Poland and sent spasms of fear rippling up through Lithuania into Latvia and Estonia.

Riga

October 1939

Lily went shopping for winter boots for herself and woollen socks and underwear for Tomas and afterwards slipped into the Café Lonar on Theatre Boulevard. The café was crowded; students, with heads huddled close, talked intently, and older women like herself drank coffee and ate cakes. The afternoons were drawing in; there was a decided catch to the air and the trees in the park had a ragged look. It was good at a time such as this when everyone was talking about the only subject that could be talked about to have an ordinary task to do, and to think about simple things, like socks and boots. And then afterwards to sit relaxing in a buzz of voices and clink of crockery and sip hot, fragrant coffee. It was almost possible to delude oneself that all was normal.

She took out her mother's letter, which had arrived that morning. She'd had time only to skim through it to make sure it didn't contain bad news. She opened all letters apprehensively these days. Jemima was lamenting the fact that she and Hetty would not now be able to go on their long-planned trip to Malaysia and Thailand.

It's something we'd have liked to have done before we got too far over the hill. But I'm not really complaining, not for a second. Such a sacrifice is paltry compared with

418

what others are called upon to make in war. We went down to the ARP post to see if they would take us on as wardens but were told we were too old! No doubt we can roll bandages or knit mufflers. The Andersons' son three doors down has been called up.

Lily glanced up as a shadow fell over her table, and saw Agita. Her sister-in-law looked pale.

'Can I join you?'

'Please do.' Lily lifted a parcel from the seat. 'Would you like some coffee?' She signalled to the waitress.

'I was going to come round to say goodbye—'

'You're leaving?' Again! Lily wanted to say. They'd been here before, hadn't they? She stirred a heaped spoonful of sugar into her coffee. It was only occasionally that she took sugar.

They'd known the Walthers would be going. Hitler had summoned all Balts (not excluding prisoners and inmates of the lunatic asylum) back to the Fatherland. He had sent ships for them, ships which were now waiting in Riga harbour. Many of the Balts were going against their wishes; they knew no one in Germany, had no connections there. Some had already departed, amongst them eminent physicians and other professional men. There was a shortage of doctors in the city, chemists also. They'd piled their belongings into cars, roped heirlooms to the roofs. Lily couldn't understand why they didn't just stay. Tom said German propagandists were reinforcing Hitler's orders by putting the fear of God into them, telling them that secret pacts had been made between Russia and Germany and maps had been drawn up by the Soviet High Command showing the three Baltic states as Soviet Socialist Republics. Tom believed them.

'Why are you going, Agita?' asked Lily. 'Why not just *stay*? He can't make you, can he? I mean, he's not *here*?' She wondered if she should be thinking about the Führer in capital letters, like God.

'No, but he might soon be. And besides, Herman has

419

interests in Germany.'

Ah, yes, interests. Lily nodded. Money. Of course: it all came down to that.

'Herman is such a clever businessman. The only one in our family with a head for business is Luke. Would you like a cake? I feel like one myself today. Something rich, with chocolate and cream. And I've put sugar in my coffee. You can feel winter's on its way, can't you? I find I start to eat more. So where are you going?'

'Leipzig. It's rather a pleasant city. Didn't you and Tom stop off there one year on the way to Switzerland?'

'Yes, we liked it very much. We heard the "St Matthew Passion" in St Thomas's Church – Bach was organ master there. He wrote the "Passion" for St Thomas's.'

'Lily, Herman says you should leave. Do it while you've got the chance. You'd be fools not to. You could go to Scotland.'

'We couldn't leave the children.'

'Why shouldn't they go too?'

'They have to earn their livings, Agita. We don't have "interests" there and they wouldn't be professionally quali-fied. And my mother couldn't support all of us! She's only got enough for herself and she has to help my younger sister out. Effie's got eleven children. Think of the squad we ourselves would make arriving in Aberdeen!' And they couldn't leave Morag and her family behind. As a matter of fact Lily had thought about leaving, had imagined chartering a ship and all of them sailing across the Baltic and North Seas, to safety. She'd envisaged them on deck, in a grey light, watching the shore recede. 'It's out of the question,' she said.

'You must be glad Paula and Armands have gone to the United States?'

'Oh yes. And that Vera went with them. I had a letter from Paula this morning.' Paula had said that if either Germany or Russia looked like invading Latvia they were to get out at once and come over there. They reckoned the USA should be the safest place in a war, with the whole of the Atlantic Ocean between it and Europe. Lily did not bother to relay any of that to Agita. There was even less chance of them going to America than to Aberdeen.

She ordered another pot of coffee and helped herself to a second cake. Her waistline was expanding, and she supposed she ought to 'watch it', but it seemed rather petty, with everything else going on, even to think about it. Anyway, Tom said he rather liked her a little plump: it became her and made her face youthful. He said she looked more like thirty-seven than forty-seven.

'They seem to like Boston,' she said, biting into a concoction of apricot mousse and cream. Agita had left half of her chocolate gâteau on her plate and was smoking a cigarette with nervous intensity. 'And how about your two?' asked Lily.

'I'm afraid Dieter will be called up.' Agita meant for the German army. Her son Dieter had gone to university in Heidelberg, and had remained there and married a very nice German girl called Greta. He'd brought her over to Riga last summer and they'd all liked her. 'You must be worried about the twins too?'

'What a mess,' sighed Lily, and scraped up the last of her mousse on her fork.

'It is, isn't it?' said Agita, and the two women's eyes met, and for the first time in their many years of acquaintance they warmed to each other.

'The Walthers are going,' announced Lily, when she'd come in and dropped her bags. She'd bought much more than socks and boots.

'Only to be expected,' said Tomas.

'Agita asked me to say goodbye for her.'

'Afraid to face us herself,' said Veronika, who had arrived with Andrew just before Lily.

Lily kissed her brother and said he was looking tired.

'He was out carousing with his friend Hank last night,' said Veronika.

'Not carousing! Drinking maybe, but not in a riotous way.

Drowning sorrows, more.'

Lily looked at him sharply.

'Hank is just back from Moscow,' said Veronika.

Lily hated it when anyone was just back from Moscow. It was always with bad news.

'Your Foreign Minister was there too,' said Andrew.

'Munters?'

'He has signed a pact with the Soviets. "Of Mutual Assistance": or so they describe it.'

'What does mutual mean?'

'You might well ask!' said Veronika.

'It was pretty well dictated by Stalin,' said Andrew. 'Munters didn't have much choice.'

'Latvia never does,' said Tomas.

'So what does it mean?' asked Lily.

'The Soviets have promised not to interfere in Latvia's internal affairs,' said Andrew.

'Believe that if you can!' said Veronika.

'And in return?' asked Lily.

'Oh, yes, there's a price!' said Tomas. 'We've agreed to let them lease bases on our soil for *ten* years and to station *thirty thousand* men here for the duration of the war.'

'They'll control the Gulf of Riga,' said Andrew.

Nine months later, in June 1940, the Soviets took over full occupation of Latvia. Any promises that had been made were tossed to the winds. No one was surprised.

Lily decamped from the city with her two daughters-in-law and their daughters. Veronika and Ivars went with them, as did Morag and her family. Luke and Alex had already joined the Latvian army and gone off to fight the Russians. Tom, listed by the Soviets as an 'Enemy of the People' went into hiding. He moved around from one 'safehouse' to another in the city and various parts of the countryside. Lily did not know where he was most of the time, or if he was alive or dead.

There followed a year of appallingly bloody purges and

economic 'reforms'. The Soviets brought in 'agrarian reform', introducing their own system of collectivisation. The peasants were unhappy at losing their land and some of the bigger farmers were shipped to Siberia. Their neighbour Farmer Skilters was amongst them. His daughter went too; she was a medical student.

The Zales dug up the flower plots, grew vegetables, kept chickens and bought two cows. Morag became skilled in dairying and her 'Orkney' cheese acquired a reputation in the area. She traded it for other commodities. Bartering was part of their way of life.

It was Morag who answered the Bolshevik knock when it came to their door. 'Leave them to me,' she said.

Five red-starred soldiers stood crowded on the front steps. The June sun struck sparks on the steel of their rifles.

'This is a house of women and children,' Morag told them. 'We're ordinary folk that keep ourselves to ourselves. We are not on any of your lists. I myself am from Scotland.'

Scotland, they said. Wasn't that part of England?

'Great Britain.'

But the British were their allies?

'Aye, so I believe,' said Morag. 'That must mean we're on the same side.'

The men called her 'Comrade' and went away. 'They were only laddies,' said Morag.

That night, the Soviets pulled out of Latvia, slaughtering as they went. Corpses were left stacked high in the courtyard of the main prison in Riga. The Russians carried away with them thirty-four thousand people. Slaves to work in their mines and factories. Twenty-three thousand men. Seven thousand women. Four thousand children. The numbers, once known, became engraved on the inside of Latvian skulls. Many of the Zales' friends were taken. It was 13 June, another date of remembrance to be added to all the others. It became known as Latvia's 'St Bartholomew's Night', to be compared with the massacre of the Huguenots in Paris.

After their experiences under the Bolsheviks most Latvians were pleased to see the German army arrive and accepted its presence in their country as the lesser of two evils. The new-comers did not seem to be interested in reforming them or breaking up their economy. They left them more or less alone, unless they were gypsies, Jews, or foreign nationals at war with Germany.

Lily received a communication telling her to report to the *Sicherheizpolizei* – the Security Police – in Riga twice weekly. She felt panicked. What if they were to intern her?

Veronika went with her on the train and left her at the police station while she went off to hunt for food unobtainable in Cesis.

Lily stood in a weary queue for three hours.

She passed the time talking to an eighty-four-year-old Englishwoman who'd been in Latvia for sixty years and couldn't conceive of returning to England even if the Germans would allow her to go. This was her home. Her husband, who had been too frail to come, had owned and managed a timber business. He'd known Markus Zale. Before they reached the head of the queue the woman had fainted and had to be taken out.

When it was Lily's turn to go forward and be interviewed she found the official little interested in her.

'You're married to a citizen of Latvia? You should have written in to say so.'

'I thought you would know from my surname.'

'Please to write down here the names of all the people in your house, and their nationalities.'

When it came to Paulis and Matis, Lily hesitated. But she couldn't not list them. They lived openly with them. She comforted herself with the thought that they didn't look as if they had any Jewish blood in them. She wrote down their names, adding the tag 'Latvian' to both.

From there, Lily and Veronika went to the flat in Albert Street.

On the opposite side of the road they came to an abrupt halt. There was washing draped over the front balcony of the Zales' flat and the glazed door off it stood open. A child was making a funny flat face against one of the other windows.

An old man opened the door to them on a short chain, revealing one fiercely pouched eye and half a nose and mouth.

'I'm sorry to bother you,' said Lily, 'but this is actually my flat. My name is Zale.'

'You don't live here.' The door closed, and they heard the rattle of the chain as it was fastened into place.

'I think we'll have to leave it,' said Veronika, which was not like her. 'My flat's been requisitioned too. I went round to see.'

'But all our *things* are in there,' said Lily. And then sighed and consoled herself that at least she had taken her wedding photograph off the wall.

Coming out on to the main road, they saw a gang of bare-foot women working on the road. They were repairing the tramlines. Yellow stars lit up their foreheads.

Veronika spoke to one woman, even though it was strictly forbidden to talk to Jews or Russian prisoners. The supervisor seemed not to be in sight, had perhaps gone to relieve himself or drink a cup of tea and smoke a cigarette. He might even be dozing, his face turned to the sun. The woman was German, from Cologne. She'd taught the violin to school-children. She, along with the others, had been shipped in to Latvia as labour and they were living in the ghetto in the Moscow suburb, one of the poorest areas of the city. They'd been allowed to bring with them one suitcase containing their valuables and been told that their husbands and children would follow. They hadn't seen their families since leaving home and doubted if they ever would again. In Berlin, where they'd had to change trains, porters had seized their luggage. They'd never seen that again, either.

Shortly afterwards, news seeped through to Cesis of the massacre of Jews in Bickern Woods near Jügli. Most of them had been taken from the Moscow suburb.

Tomas was home again. They lived quietly, staying close to the house, going no further than the market. When German soldiers came round they gave them butter and cheese and they went away. For several months nobody bothered them.

And then they came for Paulis and Matis. Morag's only consolation was that Calum had left the previous week to join the army.

Tomas listened to the BBC whenever he managed to tune in to it on his wireless. The voice confidently proclaiming 'This is London calling!' gave Lily a quiet thrill. She kept watch from an upper window while Tomas twiddled knobs and sent the little marker spinning up and down the wavelengths – penalties for listening to the BBC were severe. There could be deportation, even death.

All their information on the outside world came from these broadcasts. Some were mere snippets, broken by crackles and tidal sounds, and sometimes silence.

They learned that the Germans had destroyed the Warsaw ghetto, killing some 50,000 Jews.

That the IRA had murdered two policemen in Belfast.

That the RAF had carried out its hundredth bombing on Bremen.

That Field Marshal Montgomery had Rommel on the run in North Africa.

In January 1943, they heard that the Soviets had broken the sixteen-month siege of the city of Leningrad and were greatly relieved. They had been anxious about Garnet. How confusing it was, thought Lily; they hated the Soviets, yet were glad when they won this battle. They wanted both the Germans and the Soviets to lose, but knew that could not be.

The Red Army was driving the Germans inch by inch out of Russia. A commentator spoke of Stalin's 'military genius'. Lily wondered which front Andrew would be reporting from. They had lost touch with everyone outside their own tight little world.

Hamburg was blitzed and seven square miles of the city centre eliminated.

The Archbishop of Canterbury warned about moral laxity in Britain and deplored the rise in the rates of venereal disease.

Kiev fell to the Russians.

On Hitler's birthday, 20 April 1944, the RAF set a new record by dropping 4,500 bombs in a single raid.

The BBC announced that its first post-war aim was television for all.

The Allies landed in Normandy.

On 13 July, the Soviets captured Vilnius, the capital of Lithuania.

On 22 September, they entered Tallinn, the capital of Estonia.

'We are going to have to take a decision,' said Tomas.

Cesis

September 1944

Katrina didn't want to ride in the cart.

'I can walk,' she said. 'I'm a big girl.' But after a while her legs lagged and Tomas had to hoist her up on to the cart beside old Mrs Stamguts from the village. Irena walked alongside, holding her hand, and when Katrina asked, 'Why is Daddy not coming?' Irena said he might come later.

Lily walked part of the time and then, tiring, bowed to Tom's suggestion that she ride for a while. She was not a girl any longer, not like Irena, who was fit and strong and moved smoothly on long legs. Lily's mind and heart were numb; she thought of little as they lurched along, knew only that behind them lay a deep pit of misery. She listened to the rumble of the cartwheels and the soft moaning of old Mrs Stamguts swaying beside her and the lowing of cows that were heavy with milk. Lily thought they sounded in pain. Her own breasts felt tight and sore.

People would be astonished to hear they'd brought *cows* with them. No wonder it was to take six weeks to walk to the coast! The farmers wouldn't leave their animals behind. Their livelihood. And the milk would be needed for the children: so the reasoning went, although Tom had tried to talk them out of it.

Progress was slow over the rutted roads, especially in the

428

pitch-dark of the night, without the flicker of a torch to guide them. When the moon slid momentarily from behind heavy clouds the road showed up ahead as a pale, uninviting ribbon. The line of carts stretched back, broken at intervals by gaggles of lumbering cows.

They travelled all night and at the hint of first light looked for somewhere to sleep, in woods, barns, abandoned houses. There was no shortage of abandoned houses. It was as if someone had taken a giant yard brush and was sweeping the whole lot downward and westward, towards the sea, the only means of escape. The Soviets already occupied Estonia to the north, Latgale to the east, and Lithuania in the south, and were closing in on Riga. The only strip left open was a narrow one running down the edge of the Courland peninsula.

September faded into October and the gold fell from the trees to carpet the paths through the woods and the days grew shorter and colder and their stomachs groaned with emptiness. And then the rains started. They trudged stoutly on. They did not dare to look back. Nor in the day to look up, for above them flew planes shattering their snatches of sleep. Planes sporting iron crosses, and others, red stars, fighting one another to the death in their desire to take possession of the skies. And they made life miserable for those who inhabited the earth by bombing the roads, carving out craters that later the refugee carts would have to circumnavigate. The young cried; the elderly began to fail, visibly, from day to day. Old Mrs Stamguts fell ill of a chest complaint and, after a convulsive night, died. They buried her on the edge of a wood, and laid leaves on her shallow grave. 'She's resting now,' Irena told Katrina.

'Where's Daddy?' Katrina asked again. 'Why hasn't he come?'

Irena could hold off no longer. 'Daddy's gone to heaven, darling,' she said, gathering the child to her.

At last they came to Liepája, the port on the Baltic. People clung to the quays like flies and when a boat docked they swarmed towards it. The Zales had to wait in the rain for a day and a night before managing to board a German vessel.

After twenty-four hours of dodging bombs from above and torpedoes from below, they came to Gdynia, in Poland. There were even more refugees there.

And that was where the trains began.

In the first camp, they were deloused.

Lily was indignant. 'I have never had any kind of lice on my body in my life,' she told the white-coated woman carrying the bucket and brush. When she and Garnet used to go with their mother to visit the poor in Aberdeen, Jemima would comb out their hair afterwards with a fine comb and get them to shake out their clothes. 'Remember that poor people can't *help* having lice,' she'd said.

Lily's protestations were ignored. She was herded into the room with the rest. They had become displaced people. Without a home. Without a voice. Without rights.

They were told to strip.

'Take off our clothes?' said Lily. '*Here*?'

'Here,' said another woman in white. 'Men first. Women and children second.'

The women and children crowded against the walls, clutching one another. Katrina's lip trembled.

'It's nothing to worry about, Kate,' said Irena. 'It's like having a bath. To make sure you're clean.'

The men, having shed their clothes, stood naked amongst the pathetic heaps. Most of the men were old. The younger ones had gone to the front to fight the Russians, or had been taken prisoner, or were dead. The old men's bodies looked as pathetic as their clothes; dejected, ill-cared for, spent.

The attendants lined up the men so that they faced a box at the other end of the room. One by one they were told to stand up on the box, with their legs apart and arms raised. The woman with the bucket then dipped her brush into the disinfectant and slashed it in broad strokes under the man's

430

arms and between his legs.

'Next!'

The men having been dealt with, the women were called. Irena kept a tight hold of Katrina's hand. Lily went in front of them.

When she stepped up on to the box she closed her eyes. She braced herself. She heard the swoosh of the brush in the powder and smelt the acrid stench of the disinfectant. She felt the harsh bristles graze her armpits and then the delicate parts between her legs. The disinfectant stung. She bit her lip sharply, tasted salt blood, which helped her to bear the other pain.

In Hanover, their lives were made even more difficult by Allied bombing. Night after night sirens went, planes flew over. Tom was still listening to the BBC. He'd brought the wireless with him, had managed to conceal it on their journeys. He kept it underneath his blanket and lowered the sound to a whisper.

'The Germans seem to be in real trouble now,' he said. The Americans had crossed the German frontier in several places and were fighting in the valleys of the Ruhr and Saar. The faces of two emaciated Belgian priests lit up when he told them. They'd been interned here since the outbreak of the war.

The Zales had a room to themselves, whereas in some camps they'd slept in long dormitories where each family had hung a blanket between itself and the next, in order to have a measure of privacy.

One night, Irena had gone to the washroom across the compound when the bombers came over. A stray bomb fell on the camp.

Lily and Tomas heard the explosion, and the screams, and ran out to see orange flame and black smoke rising from the washroom. The bomb had scored a direct hit.

Whilst in the camp in Hanover, Tomas managed to secure a

pass and train vouchers for them to travel to Leipzig, on the grounds that they had relatives there. The name Baron Walther impressed, and the authorities were glad to get rid of any refugees. They had more on their hands than they could cope with. As long as they had somewhere to go, said the commandant, stamping their pass.

They arrived in Leipzig early in March, 1945. Snow lay on the ground and a bitter wind blew. Their journey had been another long and slow one, and they were weary. Lily worried that Agita and Herman might not take them in. But Tom said of course they would! Agita was his sister, wasn't she?

'Blood must count for something in times of need.' He flinched, put his hand up to his eye patch. The socket had become infected on the journey and was giving him trouble.

'We'll have to get you to a doctor as soon as possible,' said Lily.

They set off from the train station, the three of them, to walk to the Walthers' house. The city had been heavily bombed. Many of its buildings lay in total ruin. Some still smoked. People scrabbled in amongst them. Salvaging. Looting. A terrible smell hung in the air, one that Lily and Tom recognised. Of burnt timber and charred flesh. Men went by with sheeted bodies on makeshift stretchers. There must have been a raid the night before. No ambulances were in evidence, few vehicles of any kind. German soldiers hobbled on crutches, with arms in slings, their uniforms in shreds, their boots held together with string.

Tomas had a map, one that they'd used when they were here before the war, but, even so, finding their way was difficult. A number of streets had disappeared altogether. They climbed over piles of rubble, disturbed rats that ran and made Katrina cry out in alarm. They saw houses sliced in half, their rooms standing exposed to the air, some with pictures and mirrors hanging askew on tilted walls. Sofas and beds and burst armchairs threatened to slip and slide and topple outward in slow motion. In one half-room a man and woman camped, suspended above the street, a rope ladder dangling to the ground. They were eating something out of a paper bag.

The sight of them worried Katrina. 'Won't they fall out?' she asked.

At last, as twilight was gathering around the ruined city, blurring its wounds, they came to Herman and Agita's street. It was still there, even its name was intact on the wall. Lily allowed herself to thank God.

It was a suburban road of big, heavy houses, with over-hanging eaves and long gardens. In houses as large as these there would surely be room for them.

The Walthers lived in number ten. A weak light shone from an upper room in number eight. They went on by, and then they stopped.

Where number ten should have been there yawned a huge crater.

Aberdeen

August 1945

Andrew arrived with Lily and the child late in the evening off the London train. They were exhausted, having crossed from France that morning and made the long journey overland from Esslingen in southern Germany the day before. Transportation was chaotic in Europe, especially in Germany, which was milling with some ten million refugees. The Allies had been totally taken aback by the numbers and were finding it difficult to cope. All the systems in the country were under strain. Trains seldom ran to time; they started and stopped, often in the middle of nowhere, for hours at a time, and passengers grew hot and weary and hungry and the toilets overflowed and the stench built up. The refugees were patient; they had made many worse journeys.

Andrew brought his charges in a cab to Queen's Road. He'd told his mother not to come to the station. 'Better wait at home for us. Have some hot food ready.'

But they were too tired to eat much. The emotion of meeting after so many years and so many happenings had left them all feeling washed out. Lily, as they'd travelled northward from London, had felt as if she were being borne on the crest of a wave, unstoppable now; and here she was, deposited on the shore, where she lay limp, incapable of further movement or thought.

The little girl was almost asleep standing up; she could manage nothing more than a sip of Lucozade.

'I'll put her to bed,' said Hetty. 'Will you come with me, love?'

'Go with Aunt Hetty, Kate,' said Lily. 'She'll look after you. She'll put you in a nice soft bed with clean white linen sheets. Maybe they'll even smell of lavender.'

'And fresh Aberdeen air,' said Jemima, kissing the top of her great-granddaughter's dark head. The child reminded her of Lily at that age. And of Garnet. 'We always dry our linen on the line.'

'I'll come soon, Kate,' promised Lily. 'We'll be sleeping together, don't worry! I'm not going away.'

Katrina let Hetty take her hand and lead her away.

'She hasn't slept a night apart from me since we left Cesis.'

'She's a good child,' said Andrew. 'She didn't complain once on the whole journey.'

'If it weren't for her I don't think I'd be here,' said Lily. 'She gave me the will to keep going.'

'What about Tom?' asked her mother gently.

'He got an infection in his eye socket. We couldn't get a doctor soon enough.' Lily's voice wavered. 'In the end it was a merciful release – isn't that what they call it?'

She opened her bag and took out the wedding photograph that matched the one on the wall. 'Look, I brought it with me! I carried it all the way.'

'Why don't you go to bed yourself, dear?' Jemima came to help Lily to her feet. 'You can tell us everything later. We'll have plenty of time. You're not going anywhere else. You're home.'

This is the end of the line, thought Lily, as she allowed her mother to come to her assistance. I am back at the beginning.

'And Veronika?' Jemima asked Andrew, when she'd rejoined him in the drawing room.

'She stayed in Cesis. She wouldn't come, because of Ivars. He'd joined the Latvian Army and gone to fight the Russians.'

Jemima reached out and took her son's hand.

'I've a feeling she might not have left anyway. She's too stubborn,' said Andrew. He managed a smile.

Lily phoned Boston the next day. Vera and Paula were ecstatic to hear their mother's voice, but saddened to learn of the deaths of their father and brother Luke. And they were worried that Alex had got left behind, as was Lily.

'He was to follow on with Liza and Helga.' And, who knows, perhaps they'd turn up yet. 'They might have got on different trains from us. They could have been in any of the other dozens of refugee camps in Europe.' Lily had not given up hope.

'And Father?' asked Vera. 'Where is he buried?'

'In Leipzig.' He was buried in consecrated ground, and for that, at least, Lily was grateful. She would have hated the thought of him lying in a wood, like old Mrs Stamguts, or Seryozha.

'Leipzig! How can we go there to see his grave? The Russians have got that part of Germany now, haven't they?'

'That was why Kate and I had to leave,' said Lily.

They'd been living in a farmhouse outside the town. They'd been on the verge of starving. Even the stocks of potatoes had run out. The farmer and his wife had been good to them, had shared their food. They'd taken pity on Lily, left on her own with a small child, and let her have the room in exchange for help around the house. Lily had scrubbed stone-flagged floors, washed pots, helped with the laundry.

Look at her hands! Lily showed them to her mother, and smiled ruefully. They were walking in the park, having left Katrina with Hetty.

'It was hard work but a lot better than living in another camp behind barbed wire. And Kate enjoyed the farm.'

'Good grief,' said Jemima, 'here comes Mrs Sibbald!'

Their paths were going to meet. Jemima would have passed with a 'Good morning, nice morning,' but Rose's mother, on seeing Lily, stopped.

'It's not Lily, is it? Goodness gracious, I hardly would have known you!'

'It's been a long time,' said Lily. Mrs Sibbald was looking a little hunched herself and her hair was white.

'I thought you were still in Latvia?'

'No, I left last year. When the Russians invaded us.'

'The politics of that part of the world are quite beyond me, I'm afraid. What lives you've led, you McKenzies!'

'How is Rose?' asked Lily politely.

'As well as can be expected.'

'We must go,' said Jemima. 'Hetty is cooking lunch.'

'So where were we?' asked Jemima, as they left the park and Mrs Sibbald behind. 'On the farm.'

'The Americans reached us first. We were absolutely delighted. Kate went with the other children to meet the US tanks and came running back to tell me she'd seen a black man! Her first, ever. She couldn't get over how white his teeth were when he smiled.' Lily smiled now at the recollection.

'And then the Allies divided up Europe,' said Jemima, as they headed down Queen's Road.

'When we realised we were to be in the Russian zone there was nothing else for it but to take to the cattle trucks again and head west. That's how we came to Esslingen.'

They crossed the road. Hetty and Katrina were in the front garden. Hetty was trimming the side hedge and Katrina was picking up the clippings and putting them in a wheelbarrow, laying each armful very neatly, concentrating intently. Her legs looked like little brown twigs poking out below the yellow gingham dress that had once belonged to one of Effie's girls. But Jemima and Hetty had already embarked on a fattening-up process. For lunch they were having steak-and-kidney pudding – Hetty was in with the butcher, who usually gave her something extra on top of the ration – and, to follow, trifle well doused in sherry and covered with thick yellow custard.

Cesis

July 1993

'You were in Siberia, weren't you, Alex?' asked Lydia.

'Aye, for a while.'

Katrina frowned at Lydia, who was not looking at her.

Alex had got up to recharge their glasses. 'Good brandy.'
He held the bottle up to admire it against the failing light.

'French,' said Katrina. 'Duty-free.'

'My father always had a bottle of French brandy in the
cupboard.'

'I'm enjoying the tobacco, too,' said Calum, tapping the
bowl of his pipe.

'Should we put on the light?' said Lydia, making to rise.

'It'll just attract the bugs,' said Katrina.

Lydia sat down again, pushing a cushion in behind her
back. 'How long were you in Siberia, Alex?'

'Nine years.' He shrugged, as if the number did not matter.
And perhaps it had not. After the first year or two he might
have lost count.

'*Quite* a while.'

'Long enough.'

'He came home in 1953,' said Helga. 'There was an
amnesty for political prisoners, after the death of Stalin.'

'Oh yes, I know!' said Lydia.

'Oh course you were still in Leningrad then, weren't you?'

438

'We left that year. For a while it seemed that the regime was slackening a little. Garnet said it was now or never to make the break. Were you and your mother living here in Cesis at that time?'

'Yes, we stayed and waited for Father.' Helga reached out and squeezed his hand. 'We knew he'd come back. He has a quiet way of getting through when times are tough, isn't that right, Alex?'

He laughed. 'If you say so!'

'I don't think my father would have survived nine years of imprisonment!' said Lydia. 'From what I know of him, he was much too confrontational. Yours too, Kate!'

'Kate might look like her father,' said Alex, 'but she resembles her mother more in temperament.'

'Irena was bonny,' said Calum. 'I mind the day she and Luke were married. And yourself and Liza, Alex.'

They were silent for a moment. They heard the manic chirping of the cicadas beyond the window and then the roar of a motor bike as the tenants in the basement returned home. A door slammed. It was quiet again.

Liza had survived the war and been here when Alex returned from Siberia. She'd lived to a fair age, had died about five years back. So Alex and Liza had been luckier than Luke and Irena; they'd had a good long life together. Not that either of the two Western visitors would account them 'lucky'.

Calum had lived in the house after the war, first with Morag, and, later, with his wife and his mother. The two women had got on fine, he said. 'No bother at all.' His wife must have been douce, Katrina and Lydia presumed.

'We had this room here for living and sleeping, and we shared the kitchen and bathroom with everybody else, but my mither ran the place.' He grinned. 'Few wanted to fall foul of her.' He went to fetch a photograph.

There was Morag sitting on the bench beneath the elm tree, with her arms folded under her spreading bosom. She was wearing an apron and looked as if she hadn't wanted to sit down at all, and had had to be cajoled.

How reassuring to know that neither wars nor invasions nor the loss of her husband had intimidated or changed Morag! Katrina and Lydia smiled at each other and held on to the image of Morag as the rock, the salt of the earth. They would not have wanted to see her bowed over, speared with grief, listening to the booted feet of the men taking her husband away.

'She made old bones.' Calum seemed proud of that.

'Some of us are long-livers in the family.' Alex smiled. 'Jemima lived to a ripe old age, didn't she? Ripe?'

'Yes, ripe,' agreed Katrina. 'That described her. She was ninety-five when she died. And alert to the end. Hetty, too. Though she didn't make it past ninety! In their seventies and early eighties they still talked about another trip to India. I think they enjoyed poring over the maps as much as anything. They didn't have the money to go, anyway.'

'They had us to support,' said Lydia. 'Unforeseen expense in their old age!'

'And Lily – Mother –,' said Alex, 'she lived to be ninety as well.'

'It was sad that you never got saw her again,' said Katrina. 'She pined to see you. She applied for a visa year after year for you to come out and visit Aberdeen, but they always turned it down.'

'I pined to see her, too.' Alex shook his head.

'Why didn't you go with Lily and Tom, when they left, in 1944?' asked Lydia. 'And take Liza and Helga?'

'Oh, we intended to go. We left a little after them. A couple of hours – that made all the difference. The dividing line of destiny! We were cut off by the Soviets.'

He got up, saying he must get himself a drink of water. He had a terrible drouth on him. Lydia had been about to ask why the two-hour delay – what happened then? – but knew he was not going to answer, not yet.

Aberdeen

September 1953

It was Andrew who also brought Garnet and Lydia back to Aberdeen. He went to Paris to fetch them from the home of Tomas's sister Elena, who had been living there since 1920.

Fourteen-year-old Katrina was excited at the prospect of the arrival of her Russian cousin. They were the same age. They could be friends. They would have to share a room; there were not enough spare bedrooms for everyone to have one. Would Lydia speak English? Her grandmother was not sure. They knew so little about Garnet and Lydia's life in Russia.

They'd been astounded when one day the phone had rung and Lily had picked up the receiver and said hello and a faint voice at the other end had said, 'This is Garnet. I'm in Paris.' Lily had dropped the receiver and Garnet had had to ring again and this time it was Jemima who had answered.

'Garnet? This is wonderful! Incredible! But how did you get there? Where are you, exactly. *Paris*? The boulevard Voltaire? Can you speak up, dear? This doesn't seem to be a very clear line.'

Garnet had applied for a visa to visit her sister-in-law and, owing to the change of political climate, it had been granted. Or so it seemed.

'I find it incredible that I'm here too,' said Garnet, whose voice to Jemima still did not sound too strong. But then Garnet must be feeling weak after her journey, and her emotional return to the West. 'I think someone with influence must have spoken up for me. It might even have been Dolly. Took pity on me at last.' When Garnet would get to Aberdeen they would see why Dolly might have taken pity.

'Dolly?' said Jemima. 'Oh yes – your former maid?'

'She's quite high up in the Party. Her daughter Sophia is here in Paris – the ballerina. She came out to the West and defected. She's quite well known. Sophia Burnova.'

'Burnova? But that's your name.'

'Yes, she took it. She doesn't dance herself any longer, she teaches. She's coming to see me tomorrow. I was always fond of her when she was young.'

'And what about Anna?'

Anna was in Moscow, said Garnet, with her new husband, Mikhail. He was her third husband.

'She doesn't stick long at anything, I'm afraid. She has some of her father's restlessness. She was disappointed when she didn't make it as a dancer.'

Jemima did not ask after Nikolai. She knew his fate already: that he had died in Cesis. As had Luke. Lily, who became distressed when speaking of either of them, had told her that much, but little more. And then there was Alex. He was a pain Lily carried locked inside her, not even knowing whether he was alive. They'd had a couple of letters from his wife Liza in Cesis and she'd managed to let them know in a cryptic way that Alex had been taken by the Russians.

'When are you coming home?' asked Jemima.

'As soon as possible,' said Garnet.

'Andrew will be over to fetch you. He loves travelling. Doesn't get the chance much these days, since he went on to Home Affairs on the paper. And Rose hates him to go away. She's nervous on her own in the house at night. Her mother died last year. You remember Mrs Sibbald, I'm sure? How could you not! Yes, he came back to Rose in the end. They never were divorced. His son Ivars was killed on the Russian front, and then he had to face the fact that Veronika was cut off from him behind that terrible Iron Curtain, possibly for ever. Or until it was too late.

'I'd have come to Paris with Andrew, but I've got a touch of rheumatism in one knee and it tends to swell if I sit too long. I think I'd prefer, anyway, to wait for you here.'

Andrew phoned from Paris. 'Just want to warn you that Garnet is ill – very ill, from the looks of it. I got quite a shock. Of course, I expected her to look older – we're all getting on! And she is sixty-one, but she looks seventy-one, or even eighty-one. Actually, she looks older than you, Mother. But the girl is very perky and vivacious.'

'What about *her* mother? Olga?'

'She died in the siege of Leningrad.'

'I wonder what she'll be like,' said Katrina for the umpteenth time.

'We'll soon know,' said Lily, peering up the empty track. She felt so nervous, she thought she might be sick.

They stood back as the train came steaming in and waited for the doors to spill open. If it had not been for Andrew, Lily wondered if she would have recognised Garnet. The skin stretched over her cheekbones had given her the transparent look of one approaching death. Lily kissed her gingerly. The eyes were the same, though, and there was still a gleam in their depths that Lily recognised.

They put her to bed as soon as they arrived at Queen's Road and Jemima summoned a doctor.

'I've got TB,' said Garnet. 'It's far advanced. I know I haven't got long. But at least I'm home.'

'Don't cry, Granny,' said Katrina, putting her arms round Lily. 'Maybe Aunt Garnet will get better now that she's here in the fresh Aberdeen air and having proper medicine. And she'll have Aunt Hetty's good food to build her up. I was thin too, when I came here, wasn't I?'

Lily blew her nose. 'It'd take more than Aberdeen air and Hetty's steak-and-kidney pie to save her, Kate. We can't delude ourselves. You seem to be getting on well with Lydia, though?'

'She's nervy and quite bossy, but she's OK. Just as well she speaks English, isn't it? With a Russian accent! I'm going to take her to the tennis club this afternoon.'

'That's a good idea. Introduce her to some of your friends.' (This was to prove a minefield, as Lydia, being more extrovert, and more amusing, and also with the advantage of foreignness and strange tales to tell – her grandfather had been a *count*, after all, who'd once upon a time lived in a palace, albeit a minor one, and had perished fighting the wicked Bolsheviks – became more popular at school than Katrina, and stole her best friend.) 'It'll help take her mind off things.'

'She's worried about her gran. She tries to act as if she's not, but I heard her crying in bed last night.'

'You must be *very* nice to her now, Kate! No squabbling!'

'Of course not! What do you take me for?' Katrina flounced off.

'It's a trying time in a girl's life,' said Hetty, who had just come into the room. 'Being fourteen. Even leaving out being orphaned.'

Garnet lived for three months, longer than the doctor had anticipated. He'd given her a week or two. But after those two weeks had passed she'd seemed to strengthen and gain a new lease of energy, enough to enable her to come through to the dining room in the evenings and eat with the family and spend an hour or so afterwards in the drawing room; and on days when the sun shone and the north-east wind ceased to blow she walked a little in Hazelhead Park, on the arm of her twin sister. The neighbours who had known them all their lives (growing progressively fewer) commented on how close they were, when they observed them from their windows, strolling, their heads together, grey where they'd once been black, one a little stout, the other painfully thin, the pair of them no longer identical, talking.

So they were talking again.

Garnet talked about the siege of Leningrad. It had been a dreadful time. Lily must have heard? So many had died. Garnet had watched her daughter-in-law turn to skin and bone, and gradually fade away. She'd been worried about Lydia, had thought at one point the child was going the same way.

Garnet spoke about Nikolai on one occasion only. They'd grown apart in recent years, she said. He'd grown away from his wife, too, had been cold with her, and Garnet wondered if that might not have made Olga give up. 'She knew he didn't love her. Yet she loved him – he was handsome and full of energy. He looked very like Seryozha.'

'Yes, he did,' said Lily, and when Garnet looked at her, added quickly, 'One could see it in him as a child. Was he like Seryozha in temperament?'

'Not really. He was much more determined, didn't give up easily. Didn't forgive easily, either. More like me!' Garnet gave a smile.

She'd been notified that Nikolai had been killed in battle in Latvia, but she seemed not to want to know the circumstances, and Lily, who knew of them – another secret she had to bear – was relieved not to be questioned.

They met Rose out walking her Scotch terriers. Their tartan leads were twisted and they were yapping in a tight circle round Rose's legs.

'Garnet!' she said, flustered, birling about, trying to disentangle herself and getting into even more of a tangle. 'Now, stop that, Hector! Hamish, heel! They don't pay much attention, do they? Such naughty boys! But how are *you*, Garnet?' Rose's pale blue eyes began to fill with tears. 'I've been meaning to call . . .' Andrew said Rose found anything to do with sickness difficult.

'I'm quite well, thank you,' said Garnet, 'though I think

we might have to move on, Rose, if you don't mind. I find standing difficult.'

'Of course, of course! See you soon!'

Rose tugged her excited dogs off to further reaches of the park.

'Why on earth did Andrew go back to her?' asked Garnet.

'He was in need of consolation.'

During the last month, Garnet seldom left her bed. She slept, and listened to music on the wireless. She was particularly fond of opera and ballet music. And she played patience. It was a calming occupation, she said; one simply had to go with the cards.

'Don't you think she's rather handsome?' She held up the Queen of Spades. 'Her face is grave, but rather appealing. And here is the knave.' He seemed to make her smile. She held both cards together in her hand.

Lily was dusting the mantelpiece, lifting up all the photographs and ornaments. She handled with special care the old ikon of madonna and child. Garnet liked to have candles lit on either side of it. 'You see how Russian I've become! All I need is the smell of incense. And the countess's old samovar!' The ikon was one of the few things Garnet had brought from Russia.

The women of the house – Lily, Jemima and Hetty – took turns to tend the invalid, rejecting the doctor's suggestion of a nurse. 'We've got three good pairs of hands on us,' said Jemima. 'And they're none the worse for being a bit on in years.'

Lydia sat with her grandmother for spells during the day, the two of them staying often in companionable silence, with the fire sparking in the grate and the wind prowling about the window. They talked, too, and Lydia read aloud, poems by Pushkin, mostly, in Russian, from a book that Leo Burnov had given to Garnet shortly after her arrival in St Petersburg in 1913.

And sometimes Effie, when she could be spared from her

446

numerous family commitments and calamities, would come up and speak of the Lord and sing hymns to Garnet, who seemed not to mind. She would lie back against her pillows and a little smile would touch the corners of her mouth. 'Onward, Christian soldiers . . .' 'There is a Green Hill Far Away . . .' 'The Lord's My Shepherd . . .'

'All the old familiar tunes,' she murmured. 'Effie is really very soothing. There are no uncertainties about her. Not like you and me, eh, Lily?'

'Perhaps we have seen more.' Lily smoothed the top sheet. It was she who spent the longest hours with Garnet, doing usually the shift through the night, as she was now. She liked being with her sister when everyone else was sleeping. She felt then that Garnet belonged exclusively to her.

'Sit down,' said Garnet. 'I'm smooth enough.'

Lily pulled a chair up to the bed.

'We've still to talk about Seryozha,' said Garnet.

It was a relief for Lily to hear the words. She had feared that Garnet might go to her grave leaving this unspoken between them.

Lily looked Garnet in the face. 'I think Luke was Seryozha's son. In fact, I'm sure he was.'

'I, too,' said Garnet.

'I cannot excuse myself.' For a long time Lily had attributed her liaison with Sergei to a momentary loss of reason, a derangement of the brain that had allowed the senses to take over total control. If it had not been for Luke the memory of it might have taken on the nature of a dream barely recalled which ultimately would have faded. But Luke had belonged to no dream; he'd been sturdy and voluble, from the start, and she had not been able to doubt his reality. She had loved him (even though he could be difficult), had not once wished him unborn, and had mourned his death. 'I am responsible for what happened – along with Seryozha. I recognise that now. I've carried my guilt— '

'So have I!' interrupted Garnet. 'So have I! I knew before we married that it was you Seryozha wanted to marry. The

447

attraction between you was palpable. I can admit it now! But I was more outgoing when we were young and I knew how to capture a man. And I did. I wanted Seryozha so I put myself out to get him. He was easy prey for any woman who set her cap at him, I think we both knew that.

'We were so close people always thought there was never any aggression between us.' The little smile was lurking at the corners of Garnet's mouth again. 'But there was a certain rivalry, wasn't there?'

'Yes, there was,' admitted Lily. 'Perhaps inevitably so, when you have to look at someone *identical* to you day after day!' She took Garnet's cold, skeletal hand into her warm, plump one.

Lily kept one secret back from Garnet. It was one that she never could have revealed to her sister.

Garnet died in the early hours of the morning. Only Lily was with her.

'Did she die peacefully?' asked Jemima anxiously.

'Yes,' said Lily.

Before dying, Garnet had said something about potholes. Lily had thought she'd said, 'God of potholes.' But she might have been mistaken. She'd not quite been able to follow her.

Cesis

July 1993

'I'm going to ask him straight out,' said Lydia, when they were getting ready for bed.

There was a full moon and the curtains failed to meet, so they had left them open. They were too thin anyway to have much effect. The room was flooded with pale white light.

Katrina groaned. 'Do you have to start upsetting people?'

'I just want to know the truth.'

'If he knows it.'

'Oh, he knows it!'

They were due to leave next day and return to Riga.

In the morning, they paid another visit to the cemetery. Alex went with them while Helga stayed at the house to help Sandra prepare lunch.

Alex could not withstand Lydia's battery of questions. They watched him crumble. He sighed, and held up his hands. There seemed no point in his trying to conceal the truth any longer.

'This is not going to be easy for me to tell to you. To either of you.'

In the summer of 1944 Alex and Luke were both wounded on the Russian front and sent home to recuperate.

449

'It seems awful,' said Lily, 'to feel pleased that you're wounded! But I am.' For the time being her sons were here, under her eye, sleeping in their own beds at night, alongside their wives, with their children across the landing, and so she could sleep, too. Paula and Vera were safe in America, and Tomas was by her side. Fingers crossed, she said to herself, crossing them on both hands.

The Soviets, though, as they knew from listening to the BBC, were only a few miles away, and moving steadily southward and westward.

'We *must* make a stand,' said Luke, whose right arm was in a sling.

'No.' Tomas shook his head. 'We're going to have to go.'

'*Run?*' said Luke. 'For God's sake, Father, do you know what you're saying? That we should leave our home? Leave *Latvia*? After you helped fight for it? You nearly died. And Irena's father did die. We can't let all those sacrifices go in vain.'

'We don't stand a chance.'

'Father's right,' said Alex.

'You're going to go?' Luke turned on his brother. 'I don't believe it. We can't be like rats abandoning the ship.'

'What use is it to go down? I want to save Liza and Helga. If the Soviets overrun us, life will be hell.'

'*If* we're allowed to live,' said Tomas. 'We'll be on their list. We remember St Bartholomew's Night – your mother and Veronika and I – when they took away thousands of our people. They're not going to take *me* – I'd rather die first!'

To go or not to go. The issue was debated endlessly and, meanwhile, the noise of battle drew closer. On a still night they could hear the thud of the heavy guns. The streams of refugees flowing through Cesis thickened. Veronika said she would not leave. If Ivars were to return, how would he feel to find her and everyone else gone?

Irena finally talked Luke round. She said her father wouldn't have wanted her to die too. 'If you won't go, Luke, I'll go without you. For Kate's sake.'

The women packed bags and suitcases, filling every recep-
tacle they could find, and buried their more valuable objects
in tin boxes in the garden.

Morag said that since her son Calum was also away at the
front, she, like Veronika, would stay. 'Any road, the Russians
aren't going to bother their heads about the likes of me, are
they? I willne be on their list. So I'll stay here and look after
the place for you until the war's ower and you can come
back.'

The decision was taken: they would leave in two days'
time on what was expected to be the last train out of Cesis.
In the event, they were to miss it, due to an unexpected
caller.

'You can't take all that lot!' said Tomas, when the bags
were brought down and lined up in the hall. 'One small one
each is as much as we'll be able to manage.'

He took the pony and trap and went down to the village
for the last time. He wouldn't be long, he said. He had a few
errands to do, and a couple of old friends to whom he wanted
to say goodbye.

The women were unpacking the bags, trying to make up
their minds what to take, and what not, when they heard a
car draw up outside. They were immediately alarmed, for
none of their neighbours had petrol and most private cars
had been banned from the roads.

'Was it my father?' asked Lydia.

'You're a jump ahead of me!' said Alex. 'Aye, it was Nikolai
Burnov. He'd come in advance of his platoon. He'd driven on
a quiet country road through what was left of the German
lines – he was in an intelligence corps – and he'd come
alone.'

'Is this a social visit?' asked Luke, when Nikolai had
announced himself. He stood on their doorstep: a high-ranking Soviet Army officer, red stars on his epaulettes, the hat
which he carried under his left arm encircled with red and

encrusted with gold. His right hand rested lightly against the heavy pistol holstered in his belt.

Lily had known him straight away, had not had to wait for his introduction, for through the door had walked a mirror image of her own son Luke.

'In a way it might be described as social,' said Nikolai in stilted English, moving from the hall through into the sitting room, glancing around as he did so, as if he had come to requisition their home, and perhaps he had. 'I do remember the house, even though I was quite young when I was here before. I have a photographic memory.'

Luke and Alex followed him into the room.

'Perhaps you should go into the kitchen, Mother,' said Luke, turning and barring the way, 'and leave this to us.'

'He was a hard man,' said Alex. 'And vengeful. I'm sorry to have to speak this way about your father, Lydia. There was a bitterness in him, as if something had twisted him inside. A deep disappointment in life, maybe. We read it in his face the minute he put his foot over the step. We never should have let him come in. We should have killed him then and there, when he stood in the porch. We smelled danger. But he said, "I am your cousin Nikolai Burnov," and we felt we had no choice.

'He'd come with a purpose, we could tell that. He started by telling us how much he hated the Germans and was personally going to squeeze every last ounce of blood out of them that he could.'

'My wife Olga died in the siege of Leningrad. The mother of my child.'

They murmured commiserations. They stood side by side, Alex and Luke, facing their cousin. They held themselves very still, whereas Nikolai moved about, not watching them as closely as they were watching him. Alex was conscious of Luke, body braced, with legs apart, knees slightly bent, ready to spring if necessary. Luke was a natural soldier, a man of action, who would always be prepared to act. Alex feared his own responses might be too slow. Luke would normally have been a fair match for Nikolai Burnov, but his right arm was weakened. And he was unarmed.

'You probably don't share my hatred of the Germans?' said Nikolai.

'We have no great liking for them,' said Alex.

'*Liking*!' Nikolai laughed.

'Our father fought them in the last war,' said Luke. 'He lost an eye.'

'We'd like to be left alone,' said Alex. 'By everybody.'

'We'd like to keep our country for ourselves!' said Luke.

'You are a Latvian patriot?' Nikolai sounded amused.

'I am. And you?'

'Oh yes, my country is the only thing that matters to me now.' Nikolai swung round suddenly and looked straight at them. 'Shall I tell you about my father? He was an absolute bastard. He left me a legacy I didn't want. And as well as that, he betrayed my mother.' Then he said softly, 'With your mother.'

'*Grandmother*?' said Katrina. '*Lily*? I don't believe it! She had an *affair* with Sergei Burnov?'

'Well, not *exactly* an affair, but one night, it seems, in Aberdeen . . . The night before their wedding.'

They stared at the simple headstone on Nikolai's grave, then their eyes travelled along to Luke's.

'We didn't believe him at first, either,' said Alex. 'But only for a minute or two. You just had to look at the two of them – Luke and Nikolai.' His voice trailed off.

'What happened then?' asked Lydia.

'Nikolai said, "So what do you think of that, *brother*?" and Luke went for his jugular.'

Alex and Helga saw them off at the station. They made them promise to come back soon.

'Will ye no come back again?' said Alex, and grinned.

The train was not crowded; they found two seats with no one sitting opposite. They did not feel like getting into conversation with strangers today.

'Do you realise the Zales are not actually my *blood* relatives?' said Katrina. That had shocked her most of all. 'Tom wasn't my grandfather! And all these years I've thought he was.'

'But you're still *related* to the family, aren't you?' said Lydia. 'Emotionally? And perhaps in the end that's the strongest tie.'

'Think how Luke must have felt when he heard he had no Latvian blood in him! That he was half *Russian*. No wonder he went for Nikolai's jugular.'

Sergei Burnov had been *their* grandfather, thought Katrina: hers and Lydia's. It was a concept that would take time to assimilate, that and being part Russian herself. So she and Lydia were even more closely related than they had thought. That would be the easiest aspect of it all to accept, for in reality she and Lydia had lived as sisters, alternately hating and loving each other, falling out, falling in, but ready to stand by the other when it mattered most.

'I thought it was going to be Alex who killed Nikolai,' said Lydia. 'I thought he'd have jumped in to avenge his brother's death.'

Alex had hesitated before telling them the final part and had looked close to tears.

'Our mother heard the scuffle and came in. She saw that Nikolai had killed Luke. He'd throttled him with his bare hands. I'd tried to pull him off but he had the strength of a giant. Lily took the gun from his holster and shot him. Quite calmly. Through the temple. She said afterwards she'd been taught to shoot, should she ever find herself at the mercy of an enemy.

'But *I* should have done it! He was *my* brother. I should have saved my mother from having blood on her hands.'

*

The women fell silent. They gazed out at the quiet country-side, at the flickering birch trees and the green, undulating fields. They thought of the little group of mourners – Tomas, Lily, Veronika, Alex, and Luke's widow, Irena – moving through the dark night with their cart, taking the two dead men to the graveyard, to be buried in the Zale family plot.

Alex had broken down by the graveside and they had had to comfort him. Lily had remained remarkably cool. She was grieving for Luke, but did not regret taking the life of her sister's son. She'd had no option but to do what she did; she'd seen that Nikolai had been capable of taking her other son from her as well.

'It was better for Alex's sake that he told us everything,' said Lydia.

'Yes,' said Katrina, 'I think you're probably right. In this instance,' she added, and smiled.